The Half-Caste

A Novel

Jason Zeitler

Polyphony Press | Tucson, AZ 85719

The Half-Caste: A Novel

Polyphony Press
Tucson, AZ 85719

This book is a work of fiction. While some of the names, characters, places, and incidents portrayed here are based on actual historical accounts, they have been modified to suit the purposes of storytelling and are therefore solely the products of the author's imagination.

Manufactured in the United States of America

Cover Design by Damonza.com

US Copyright Office Registration Number: TXu 2-363-554

Library of Congress Control Number: 2023921057

ISBN: 979-8-9892692-2-8

For Dilan and for anyone else who sees the world in technicolour

'A man [or woman] of genius makes no mistakes. His [or her] errors are volitional and are the portals of discovery.'

— James Joyce, *Ulysses*

Part 1

London, England

Chapter 1

Jackboots

Over six thousand people had crowded into the auditorium to hear The Leader speak. They included fascists and fellow travellers and the simply curious. Mostly they were from the working class, but in the more expensive seats, there were also men in evening dress and ladies in long flowing gowns. On the stage behind the rostrum stood several Jackboot trumpeters and standard bearers. Stewards—whom The Leader endearingly referred to as his 'shock troops'—flanked the rostrum and hovered on gangways and in the foyers and corridors throughout the great hall.

Vernon Price was one of the stewards. He had been assigned to guard a stairwell off the arena, closest to the stage. Like the other stewards, he wore a peaked cap, a military jacket, leather gauntlets, jodhpurs, a Sam Browne belt, and jackboots. A red-and-white armband, with the fascist insignia of speed lines enclosed in a circle, graced his right arm.

He was nervous. His meagre training had not prepared him for any of this. Ever since he joined the Jackboots, two weeks ago, everything had been so rushed. And now he was at a Party rally, his first meaningful assignment. What if, when the pinch came, he mucked something up? He folded his hands for a moment and, as he did so, felt the reassuring firmness of the knuckledusters beneath his gauntlets.

Excited whispers passed through the stall seats near the south foyer. The Leader had arrived. A hush fell over the audience as he entered the auditorium house left, accompanied by his entourage of bodyguards.

Amid blaring trumpets and flashing spotlights, The Leader limped across the stage until he reached the rostrum. He looked formidable standing there in a pool of light, with the pipe organ rising up behind him and enormous Jackboot banners hanging down from the ceiling on either side. His black-leather trench coat added to his mystique, as did his brilliantined hair and closely clipped moustache. The Leader reminded Vernon of a photograph of Heinrich Himmler, the German SS commander, he had seen recently in *The Times*.

The sound of trumpets died away.

'We Britons,' The Leader began, his voice resonant, 'face today the greatest challenge in our nation's history.' He paused and looked out over the audience, swept a hand above the rostrum in a gesture of solidarity. 'We're in a battle against decadence. And who are our enemies in this battle? Complacency and inaction, of course. And also a moribund Parliament. But there's another, more dangerous enemy. By which I mean the Red menace. Under normal circumstances, we'd be equal to the task. The corporate state, as proposed by the Fascist Party, could easily defeat communism. But things aren't so simple. The communists have an advantage over us. They're in league with the Hidden Hand, a cabal of international financiers who have only their own mercenary interests at heart, not the interests of Great Britain. To serve their ends, these Shylocks are orchestrating an alien invasion, driving the sweepings of Continental ghettos onto our shores and into our cities. One has to look no farther than the East End to see what I mean. The same parasites are sweating our citizens in Whitechapel and putting others out of work by the million to maintain their system of usury. All this must end. We must wrest control of the sources of finance from our enemies, and we must strike now' — he slammed a fist onto the rostrum — 'before it's too late.'

'Fascism means war!' a voice suddenly broke out from the gallery.

Heads turned or tilted up. A man in a woollen pull-over and corduroy breeches was hanging over an upper balustrade with his fist raised in the air.

Other antifascists rose from their seats, one by one: in the arena, the gallery, the loggia boxes. 'Fascism means slavery!' they heckled. 'Down with fascism!'

The Leader motioned to a steward on the stage, then turned back to the audience. 'Pardon the interruption,' he said. 'We have undesirables in our midst.'

Vernon's heart skipped. That was the signal he had been waiting for.

In one swift movement the stewards sprang to attention, clicked their heels together, and fanned out across the auditorium.

Violence was in the air. Even before the scuffles began, the audience grew restless, some of them looking toward the exits as if at any moment police constables would arrive.

'I *say*,' a gentleman protested as Vernon and another steward grabbed an antifascist and dragged him from the arena kicking and screaming. On their way out, a youngish woman in a pale gold tunic put the back of her hand to her forehead, said 'Oh dear,' and fainted into the arms of the gentleman next to her.

'Let go of me, you fuckin' fascist scum,' the antifascist cursed in a thick Irish brogue, and lunged for Vernon's arm and sunk his teeth in, like a rabid dog.

'Bleeding hell.' Vernon pried the Irishman off his jacket and tightened his grip.

The Irishman whinged.

'You'll have something worse than that to whinge about soon enough,' Vernon said.

'You all right, mate?' the other steward asked.

Vernon laughed. 'Actually, he did me a good turn. The butterfly in my stomach's gone.'

They struggled with their captive all the way to the south foyer, where a phalanx of Jackboots surrounded a beleaguered-looking group of antifascists. There, they flung the Irishman to the floor.

'You had better join your mates,' Vernon taunted. 'Things are about to get hairy.'

'We ain't afraid of you,' one of the brawnier antifascists said, stepping forward. He drew up his fists in the attitude of a pugilist.

At that moment a short fat man with a pig-like face materialised from a corridor. 'We'll see about that,' he said. It was Aubrey Goodheart, a shock troop captain and Vernon's immediate superior. He held a large box of weapons: bicycle chains, brush staves with inch-long nails attached, chair legs wrapped in barbed wire, rubber hoses loaded with lead shot, various truncheons, and woollen stockings filled with broken glass. He made short work of distributing the weapons, and Vernon ended up with a chair leg. 'So far so good, boys,' Captain Goodheart said. 'Now let's see what you're made of.' He selected a rubber truncheon for himself and slapped it across the palm of his hand. 'Let it rip.'

The troops descended, moving as if in a choreographed dance. A welter of fascists and antifascists converged. Weapons and fists clashed.

In the melee, Vernon was only half-aware of his surroundings. Indiscriminately he swung the chair leg at anyone not in a Jackboot uniform. When he connected with flesh or clothing, the barbed wire cut or tore. At one point the Irishman struck him in the back of the head. His cap went flying and the chair leg dropped from his hands. He spun round. There was nothing for it but to fight with his fists. He threw down his gauntlets. The brass of the knuckledusters glinted in the pale light of the electric lanterns, distracting the Irishman just long enough for Vernon to land a powerful left jab.

The Irishman staggered. Then he touched his nose and stared at his bloodied fingers in disbelief. 'You fuckin' —' he started to say just as Vernon landed a right hook. The Irishman's knees buckled and he crumpled to the floor.

Vernon retrieved his cap and his gauntlets and knelt down

beside the Irishman, who was out for the count. 'Sorry, comrade,' he said under his breath, patting the man's face. 'That hurt me almost as much as it hurt you.'

'Jolly good show, Price,' Captain Goodheart said from across the foyer. 'Served the bugger damned well right.'

The fighting soon ended, and a truce was declared. Bodies, mostly of antifascists, lay writhing on the floor. Every so often someone let out a moan. The antifascists were allowed to minister to their injured before being escorted from the hall. After the last of them had gone, Captain Goodheart and Vernon and a few other Jackboots stood outside next to a police cordon on the mews, watching the vanquished antifascists melt into the shadows of Kensington Gore.

'You've done Prince Albert proud, boys,' Captain Goodheart said.

At the remark, a couple of nearby police constables grinned fatuously.

Vernon returned to the great hall to take up his position guarding the arena. He was badly bruised but otherwise none the worse for wear. In the auditorium, a deafening racket greeted him.

Most of the audience were on their feet, right arms raised in a Roman salute. 'Hail Leader!' they were shouting. Again and again they shouted it, the words echoing from one end of the auditorium to the other.

'Hail Leader! Hail Leader! Hail Leader!'

//

The Jackboot headquarters, Action House, was hidden from view off Kirkwall Place in Bethnal Green. It was more like an army barracks than a house, sitting as it did on a five-acre lot with its own parade ground, pitch, and horse stables. Every morning at the sound of reveille, the shock troops would jump from their bunks and hurriedly dress. Within minutes—as the sun crept up over the beech trees that lined the eastern edge of the acreage—a large platoon of uniformed men would fall in to marching-column formation on the parade ground. A sergeant at the head of the formation would give commands for drill or call out cadence for a run. Birdsong from the trees would be muffled by shouts of 'left, right, left, right, left, right, left' or by nationalistic lyrics from the Fascist Party anthem.

It became a recurring joke among area residents to say in the early hours of a morning, 'There go the jackboots again, tramping in the barrack yard.' Eventually the epithet stuck, and Fascist Party members thenceforth became known as Jackboots. The public originally used the term in a derogatory sense, but with time, its force was blunted, and the fascists themselves embraced it as a badge of honour, a symbol of power, and a subtle nod, even, to Mussolini's Italy, which on the map of Europe was shaped like a boot.

No longer, however, could the Jackboots be dismissed with a joke or a jeer. And the recent activities of their compatriots across the Channel—the Rhineland remilitarisation, the Abyssinian invasion, the Spanish coup—only served to embolden them. All over Great Britain now violence and anti-alien feeling were on the rise, and the fascists were helping stoke the fire. They held rallies almost weekly in London's boroughs. Battersea, Hyde Park, Trafalgar Square, Victoria Park—all these places and more were inundated with goose-stepping Jackboots praising The Leader and spouting slogans about the benefits of the corporate state. In the four years since its founding, the Fascist Party had become, as its leadership so often boasted, a force to be reckoned with. The latest rally at the great hall, the most prestigious venue the Party had yet secured, was thought to be a sign of things to come.

That same night after the rally, Vernon Price arrived at Action House to find his fellow Jackboots gathered in the bay on the ground floor, revelling in their victory over the antifascists.

'There's the young tough,' Arthur Fitch said as Vernon came in. Fitch was the oldest of the rank-and-file Jackboots, in his late forties and nearly twice Vernon's age. He was sitting on a stool polishing his boots. 'We were just talking about you, Price. Where'd you learn to fight like that?' Tonight was the first time anyone had seen Vernon in action.

'My pater,' Vernon said. 'He was a Royal Marine during the Great War.'

'He landed at Antwerp?' Fitch asked.

'No, Gallipoli.'

Fitch fell silent for a moment. 'I've heard some of the stories. The Gallipoli campaign was a bloody cock-up. I was in the 21st Division myself. Your pater's a brave man, Price, and you're a chip off the old block.'

'Awfully decent of you to say so, Arthur.' Vernon crossed the room to a back table where a game of three-card brag was in progress.

One of the card players, Stewart Morley—a burly, thirty-something former stevedore—was talking. 'You should have seen the look on the bloke's face when Price clocked him.' Morley gathered up the cards from the last game and placed them at the bottom of the deck. 'Like a young lad who has just been spanked. I thought for sure he was going to start blubbering.'

'Yeah,' Fitch said. 'It was priceless, wasn't it, Price?'

Everyone laughed.

The card players anted up a shilling.

'Care to join us, Price?' Morley asked.

'No, thanks. I'm not much of a cards man. Besides, I have to report for guard duty soon. I just came to say hello.'

Morley dealt the cards and then took a peek at his hand. 'Well, I'll be damned.'

'You still haven't learnt the subtleties of the game, have you, Morley?' Fitch said.

'He's bluffin',' one of the other players said in a Cockney accent. He was in his late teens and went by the nickname Jack.

'It's not in his nature to bluff,' Fitch said.

Jack was the only other player in the first round of betting not to fold. Instead, he added a florin to the pot.

Morley matched the florin and again doubled the bet. 'All right,' he said. 'Let's see what you've got.'

Jack turned over his cards: three kings. He leaned forward to collect his winnings.

Morley smirked. 'Not so fast, Jack the lad.' He revealed his own hand: a straight flush in spades, ace high. 'What were the odds of that?'

The question set off a spate of laughter.

'About one to twenty-two thousand, I should think,' Vernon hazarded, after doing a rough calculation of the odds in his head.

As quickly as the laughter started, it stopped.

Morley turned and looked at Vernon. 'I thought you said you weren't a cards man?'

'I told you he was clever,' Zoe Tilston said from a corner of the room. During the card game, she had been tending to men's wounds. She was the only woman to be allowed into Action House after dark. No one seemed to mind that she wore her hair in an Eton crop and dressed in men's clothing. She was just one of the 'boys'. She came up to Vernon now, with a roll of surgical gauze still in her hand, and stood on the tips of her brogues and kissed him full on the lips.

'Oi,' Fitch said. 'None of that in here.'

'Tough *and* clever,' she said, smiling coyly. 'A deadly combination.'

Vernon reddened. 'Hello, Zoe.' From the moment he first spoke to her the week before, he knew he liked her. There was something strangely alluring about her ambiguous sex.

'A-tten-tion!' Fitch suddenly called out. He dropped his boots and jumped to his feet.

Everyone else followed suit and snapped to attention.

'At ease, men,' Captain Goodheart said, entering the room. 'I've come to relay a communiqué from Director Walsh. Before I do, though, I want to congratulate you on a job well done. You routed those Bolshies tonight, and it was a sight to see.'

'Hear hear,' Fitch said.

Captain Goodheart's expression turned grave. 'And yet, while the battle was won, the war's far from over.' He held up a piece of paper. 'I have here information on a new tactic of our enemies. I won't bore you with all the details. You can read the communiqué for yourselves after I leave. Suffice it to say, the Hidden Hand have hired mercenaries to do their dirty work. This gang of ruffians are known as the Sicarii, and for several months now they've been terrorising our brethren in Manchester and Leeds. We've received intelligence that a Sicarii cell are also becoming active in London. You're to be on the lookout and report any suspicious behaviour directly to me. Is that understood?'

'Yes, sir!' the men shouted.

'Very good. That is all.' Captain Goodheart handed Fitch the piece of paper and left the room.

'Let me see that,' Morley said, going over and snatching the paper from Fitch. He read silently for a minute. 'It says here the Sicarii sneak up on their unsuspecting victims in crowds and cut them with razors.'

'I'd like to see 'em try,' said Jack.

'But that's guerrilla warfare,' Morley said and crumpled up the paper. 'What kind of a cowardly thing to do is that?'

The last-post bugle call sounded on the parade ground. It was time for the changing of the guard.

Vernon started for the door. 'See you all in the morning.'

'Good night,' Fitch said.

'You're a good bloke, Price,' Morley put in chummily. The common threat of the Sicarii, it seemed, had made him sentimental.

//

His post was on the eastern perimeter. He had been there for only an hour when he heard a twig snap among the trees. He crouched down — with his Lee-Enfield rifle in one hand and his unlit torch in the other — and squinted in the dark.

A human silhouette emerged from the trees.

'Who goes there?' Vernon said and switched on his torch.

'It's only me,' said Zoe. Her face glowed in the incandescent light.

He stood up. 'What are you doing out here?'

'I wanted to talk. The others' — she glanced back at Action House — 'aren't what you'd call conversationalists.'

'What makes you think *I* am?' He slung the rifle over his shoulder, then switched off the torch and pocketed it along with his gauntlets.

She moved closer. He could see the faint outlines of her breasts beneath her chunky-knit sweater. 'I can just tell,' she said.

He held up a packet of Player's. 'A cigarette?' She took one, and he cupped his hand and lit hers and then lit one for himself. The tips of their cigarettes pulsed in the darkness. He refrained from saying it, but he had been wanting to talk to her too — about politics, life, the world. Only, he was not sure he could trust her. What if she had some ulterior motive for coming to see him just now?

They remained silent for a while, smoking and enjoying the balmy night air and listening to the cicadas sing in the trees.

Finally she said, 'What do you think of this Hidden Hand business?'

He did not respond immediately. He had been wondering himself about the Party's claims of a 'cabal'. But he thought it best to be noncommittal with Zoe for now. 'I don't know,' he said.

'You must have some opinion,' she needled him. 'You don't seem like the obtuse, navvy type.' She took a drag of her cigarette. When he failed to respond, she said, 'I'll tell you what I think. I think it's nothing more than Jew-baiting. And it has fair put me against the Party.'

He choked on his cigarette. 'Quiet, someone will hear you.'

'So? What are you afraid of?'

'I'm not afraid, but—' He stopped and looked toward Action House. Lights were still on in some of the rooms, and a group of Jackboots were milling about on the verandah.

'But what?'

'Never mind.'

'I know you're not a coward,' she said and kissed him on the cheek.

She has to stop doing that, he thought. He flicked his cigarette to the ground and toed it out with a boot. 'Fancy a drink sometime?'

'You're not going to change the subject on me,' she said with a laugh. 'I won't allow it.' She looked him in the eyes. 'I don't like what's happening to the Party, and I have to talk to someone about it. Someone I can trust. I can trust you, can't I, Vernon?'

He felt ashamed for not having trusted *her*. But he had good reason for keeping his cards close to his chest. He said, 'Yes, you can trust me.'

'The Leader wasn't always this way,' she said, lowering her voice. 'He wasn't always so … bigoted. It's that Director Walsh's doing.' She took another drag of her cigarette. 'Director of Propaganda is right. The man gives me the creeps.'

'How's that?'

'Have you never seen him?'

'No.'

'He's a horrid-looking man. He has scars on his face from the corners of his mouth to his ears. A Glasgow smile, they call it. He claims a Jew did it to him during the Black and Tan War. He's an antisemite through and through. Why, if I didn't know any better, I'd say he was the devil incarnate.' She stared into the dark recesses of the trees, as if the devil himself might appear. 'I don't like it, Vernon. Not one bit. I have friends who are Jews.'

'So do I,' he said, thinking of his friend Saul. He was as uneasy about the Party's antisemitism as Zoe was. The Leader's remarks about the 'cabal of international financiers', the 'Shylocks' — it did not require cleverness to read between the lines and see the words for what they were: a deliberate provocation against the Jews. Vernon was afraid of where it all might lead. He had assumed that the desecration of the Bensham Synagogue in Gateshead two months ago was an isolated incident. But now he was unsure. He added soberly, 'None of it portends well.'

His thoughts returned to Saul. He had to see him again, to warn him and rekindle their friendship. They had been out of touch these past several months, ever since the death of Saul's wife — which Saul had not taken well. So far as Vernon knew, Saul had been in deep mourning all this time and had not left the house even once.

Chapter 2

Sackcloth and Ashes

Saul Maccabee *had* left his house, but it was true that since his wife's death, he had become a recluse of sorts. On occasion, he would visit her grave or play billiards at The Odd Fellows Club, a West End gentlemen's club of which he was a member. In public, however, he generally kept to himself, speaking only to the people he could not avoid. After months of living like this, he was a shadow of his former self. He had taken to sleeping in later and later.

The day after Vernon's conversation with Zoe, the noon hour came and went and Saul still lay in bed. Four hours earlier, Sidney, the manservant, had tiptoed into the room, set down a tray with tea and breakfast, drawn back the curtains, and departed. Saul had not so much as budged.

Now, finally, he awoke. He groaned and poked his head out from beneath a pillow. The sunlight coming through the windows hurt his eyes, so he covered his head with the duvet and just lay there, trying not to think about his damnable headache or about the acrid taste of absinthe and pipe tobacco in his mouth.

There was a knock at the door.

He drew back the duvet and lifted his head with an effort. 'Yes?'

'Someone is here to see you, sir,' Sidney said tentatively through the door.

'Whoever it is, tell them to come back later. I'm in no fit state to welcome visitors.'

'I have told him, sir, but he is most persistent. He says it is a matter of urgency.'

Saul sat up and clutched his head. 'What could possibly be — ?'

The door swung open and Vernon burst in.

'Sorry, sir,' said Sidney. 'He pushed right past me.'

'Vernon, old chap!' Saul said good-humouredly, in spite of his headache. 'It's quite all right, Sidney. If I had known it was Vernon, I dare say I wouldn't have made such a fuss.'

'Pardon the intrusion, Saul, but I wasn't expecting to find you in bed.' At a glance Vernon took in the room. Things were worse than he thought. Clothes were strewn about the floor. A stack of newspapers, three feet high, rested against a chaise longue that appeared to have tea stains on it. The pelmet box above one of the windows hung precariously from the wall. And as for Saul himself, with his facial hair, he was hardly recognisable. He looked like a bearded Jew from an East End ghetto.

'Where are my manners?' Saul said, getting up. He wore a pair of black silk pyjamas with strange Egyptian motifs on them. If he had been on the street, and not in his Belgravia home, he might have been mistaken for a vagrant wearing a rich man's clothes. He went about tidying the room, picking up articles from the floor and tossing them haphazardly behind a folding screen.

'Really, Saul, you needn't trouble yourself,' Vernon said.

'Shall I take away the tray, sir?' Sidney asked.

Saul stopped what he was doing. 'Ah, right.' He looked with embarrassment at the untouched breakfast tray. 'Let me have some water first. My head feels like it's in a vice.' He poured himself a glass of water from a carafe on the tray and drank it down in a single quaff.

'Mrs Grant is making asparagus sandwiches for you and the young gentleman, sir. When they are ready, I could bring them here, if you like.'

'That would be splendid, Sidney. And I dare say a new pot of tea wouldn't go amiss.'

'Very well, sir.' Sidney gathered up the tray and left.

Saul brought over a cantilevered chair from a corner of the room for his guest to sit on. 'What do you have there?' he asked, noticing the Selfridges bag in Vernon's hand.

'Something for you.' Vernon pulled out a gramophone record from the bag and handed it to Saul. As he sat on the chair, he added, 'I know how much you like American jazz. It has Benny Goodman on the clarinet.' The record was a Billie Holiday song, 'What a Little Moonlight Can Do'. Vernon had chosen it deliberately because of its up-tempo beat. He thought it might help rouse Saul from his doldrums.

'You shouldn't have,' Saul said. 'You don't mind if I forego the foxtrot, though, do you?'

Vernon laughed. 'Not at all.'

Saul went to the radiogram next to the bed, removed the shellac disc from its jacket and sleeve, and placed it onto the turntable. His hands were shaking. It took him a couple of tries to steady the tone arm and drop the needle. The record crackled during its first few revolutions.

Like horses out of the gate, a piano and a clarinet opened the song at a cracking pace, exuberantly responding to each other and to the rest of the rhythm section. Halfway into the instrumental interlude, the clarinet wailed and the tempo quickened, before abruptly slowing again. Then the voice came — that relaxed, slightly slurred, purr of a voice — with the piano comping in the background and filling in the gaps.

Saul sat on the edge of the bed. 'Listen to that phrasing,' he said, tapping a foot to the rhythm of the music. 'She's a female Satchmo.'

After a minute, Holiday's voice died away, and the song's lilting syncopation resumed. A saxophone solo followed, then a piano solo, then a trumpet solo, and then the entire orchestral ensemble climbed to a final crescendo.

The gramophone whished as the needle oscillated across the

lead-out groove.

'Just what the doctor ordered,' Saul said. He switched off the turntable. 'It's time I got dressed, don't you think? It wouldn't do to eat lunch in my pyjamas.' He selected some clothes from a wardrobe and disappeared behind the screen.

Vernon was pleased with himself. The music seemed to have brightened Saul's mood.

Just as Saul was stepping out from behind the screen, Sidney arrived with lunch. He served the sandwiches and tea. 'Will there be anything else, sir?'

'That'll do, Sidney.' After Sidney had left, Saul said to Vernon, 'How are you, old chap? It has been donkey's ears, what?'

'I'm well, thank you.' Before coming, Vernon decided to stick to generalities because he did not want to say anything that might seem insensitive. 'A lot has happened since last we met.'

'Has it? … Yes, I suppose it has.'

Vernon glanced at the pile of newspapers on the floor. 'Haven't you been following the news?'

'Oh, that. I'm well aware of *that*.' Saul grew pensive.

Vernon knew what Saul's silence meant, and he felt his bile rise. He had heard Saul's arguments before, about the unassailable tradition of British liberalism. Vernon once believed the same thing himself, but not now, not anymore. 'What's happening on the Continent is happening in Britain, too. The fascists are gaining ground. It's only a matter of time before —'

'Before what?' Saul interrupted. 'How do you know all this?'

'Just take a look at the latest headlines,' Vernon said, redirecting the question. He had to tread carefully to avoid arousing Saul's suspicions. He picked up the topmost newspaper from the pile on the floor. It was today's *London Morning Post*. The front-page headline read 'Hurrah for the Jackboots'. He thrust the paper into Saul's hands, which were shaking again.

Saul skimmed the article. 'The world has gone mad,' he said midway through. When he finished reading, he let the paper slip from his fingers. He had a distant look in his eyes. 'Lloyd George was right. We live in a lunatic asylum run by lunatics. …' Saul dropped to his knees in front of the pile of newspapers. 'Now, where did I see that? In *The Observer*, I think it was. Yes yes, *The Observer*.' Frantically he searched through the pile.

Vernon suddenly became alarmed. 'What are you doing?' he said, and jumped up from his chair and lifted Saul to his feet. As their eyes met, Saul looked away.

'All is vanity,' Saul said in a diminished voice. 'All is vanity.'

Vernon helped him to the bed. He was about to call for Sidney when he noticed the decanter of emerald-green liquid on a side table. All the mixing paraphernalia were there. He poured a shot of the spirit into the bottom of the reservoir glass, perched a sugar cube atop the slotted spoon, added water, and then watched the concoction turn milky green. 'Here,' he said finally, handing Saul the drink.

Saul sipped from the glass absently.

'You can't go on like this.'

'No,' Saul said, with his eyes on the radiogram. He raised the glass to his mouth, then lowered it again. 'What do you say we have some more of that music?'

'All right.' Vernon switched on the turntable and reset the needle.

At once the room swelled with imagery and meaning.

//

It had been Saul's idea, in the early days of their friendship, to meet regularly at a Lyons' Corner House for what he called tête-à-têtes. It did the soul good, he used to say, to have real, in-depth conversations—none of that damnable gossip and small-talk nonsense of drawing rooms and banquet halls. He would always say this—*It does the soul good*—a little tongue in cheek because of the resemblance between his name and the word 'soul', as though he were referring to himself in third person. Of course, he meant the word as a figure of speech. He did not believe in the Judeo-

Christian conception of a soul any more than he believed in God. Despite his upbringing in the Reformed Synagogue, he was a secular Jew. From the time he read economics and the natural sciences at Trinity College, Cambridge, right before the war years, the only god he worshipped was Common Sense.

He had chosen the Corner House on Coventry Street because of its atmosphere. It had an orchestra on each floor, and pretty young waitresses in maid-like uniforms went about briskly serving tea and cakes. The shop's location was also convenient, as it was halfway between Saul's home in Belgravia and Vernon's student lodgings in Covent Garden. A simple telephone call and in less than fifteen minutes the two friends could be sitting at a posh table in the teashop, listening to classical music and intently discussing world affairs.

Their first meeting happened late one morning after separately attending a public lecture at the London School of Economics, where Vernon was a doctoral student. In the university hall, as the guest speaker concluded his lecture and the attendees filed out, Saul made a passing remark about how splendid the speaker had been. Vernon overheard and said he agreed. They got talking. One thing led to another, and a half-hour later they were sitting at a table in the Corner House.

'I envy you,' Saul said, stirring milk and sugar into his tea. 'Learning the latest theories. Doing research. Exchanging ideas. It's all rather exciting, isn't it?'

Vernon had to admit that it was, although it was not all fun and games. 'I would find it much more exciting, for instance, if the professors left their politics at the door.'

A waitress came by with their order of Bakewell tarts.

They stopped talking for a minute to eat, during which time the orchestra began to play a Bach violin concerto.

Saul was still mulling over Vernon's comment about LSE. He was curious to know more. 'These professors of yours — could you give me an example of how they bring politics into the classroom?'

Vernon set down his fork. 'I won't name any names, but certain of them selectively teach theories and present data that suit their political leanings.' Intellectual integrity and fealty to the scientific method, Vernon added, fell by the wayside the moment politics became involved. If a professor was a conservative, he espoused capitalism and free markets; if a liberal, socialism and governmental controls.

Saul could not recall such dogmatism among the economics dons at Trinity College, but surely, he thought, the mingling of politics and science was nothing new? Copernicus, Galileo, Darwin — at times their scientific theories were accepted or rejected based solely on a person's religious convictions. 'It's an age-old story,' Saul responded. 'But science will win out in the end.'

'Will it?' Vernon said with a dubious expression.

Saul regarded him. *'You're* a dark horse.' He appreciated Vernon's zeal, even if he did not quite understand it. As he poured himself another cup of tea, he added, 'I can't figure you out. Somehow you're a cynic and an idealist at the same time.'

'I'm not a partisan, if that's what you mean.'

'Nor am I, I'm proud to say.' Saul, too, was sceptical of radicalism. Left-wingers, right-wingers — narrow-minded and myopic sods, the whole lot. Like most things in life, the truest path in politics lay somewhere between the extremes. 'Would you agree, at least, that economic efficiency and social justice are laudable political aims?'

'Without a doubt.'

'So the question is whether capitalism and socialism in their ideal forms are workable.'

'Right,' Vernon said. 'And I put it to you that they're not.' He caught the eye of the waitress and waved her over. 'When you have a moment,' he said to her, 'could I get some more of that clotted cream, please?'

'Yes, of course, sir.'

'They never provide enough of the good stuff, what?' Saul said after the waitress had gone.

Vernon took a sip of his tea, then said, 'What we need is an economic system that takes the best from both capitalism and socialism.' He went on to say that the British had been slowly moving in that direction since the turn of the century, but they had yet to get things right. He was certain that 'getting things right' was a matter of will. With every change in the political winds — as power shifted from the Conservative Party to the Labour Party and back again — Britain vacillated between laissez-faire and socialist policies, never really committing to either. But in the extreme, neither set of policies would work, anyway. Pure capitalism was efficient but gave preference to the privileged. Pure socialism gave preference to no one but was inefficient. In a hybrid system like the one Vernon envisaged — similar to the system the British themselves had been moving toward at a snail's pace, starting with the Liberal Party reforms instituted before the Great War — private businesses would control the means of production and governments would redistribute wealth and keep businesses in check. The result would be efficiency *and* fairness.

Saul agreed in principle, but he also understood the value of patience. Good things, it seemed to him, rarely came quickly or easily in the affairs of men. 'Bravo,' he said, lightly clapping. 'Except you're forgetting one thing: human behaviour. Like your LSE professors, members of Parliament are a pigheaded lot.'

The waitress delivered the clotted cream.

Vernon poured some of it onto the remainder of his tart and then sat there quietly, contemplating Saul's remark. 'Are you saying the MPs are incapable of compromise?'

'Don't get me wrong,' Saul said. He took off his spectacles, wiped them briefly with a handkerchief, and put them back on. 'There's no place I'd rather be than in good old England. God save the King and all that. But there are two impediments to human progress as far as I can discover: ideological fanaticism and greed. The socialist ideal of a classless society is a utopian fantasy, as is the capitalist ideal of perfect competition. And it's a short step from the idealist to the fanatic. As for greed, neither side — the Tories on the one hand, the Labour Party on the other — is immune. We saw in the last decade the world over the attitude of "every man for himself and the devil take the hindmost", and we'll see it again. Heaven knows I don't like it any more than you do, but there it is. Concentration in markets, like concentration in political power, leads to corruption, inefficiency, exploitation. It's the inexorable law of human nature. So what I'm saying is, I agree with you in every respect, just not in how progress is likely to be achieved. That may sound like hair-splitting, but it's the difference between night and day. I view progress in evolutionary, not in revolutionary, terms. Evolutionary progress is gradual, directional change that involves improvement. Revolutionary progress is an oxymoron: it is sudden, random change that may or may not lead to improvement. If in this country we're to progress at all, it's incumbent upon us to maintain our parliamentary democracy. Competition in ideas is as important as competition in industry. Even if MPs are sometimes inept and often reach a stalemate — better that than what would result from a one-party system: the loss of liberty and the quelling of dissent.' He pulled out his watch from his waistcoat pocket and flicked it open. 'My wife will be wondering where I am about now.'

'You have to go?' Vernon asked, sounding disappointed.

'A pity, I know, but yes, I must.'

'We should meet again.'

'Indeed,' Saul said, re-checking his watch, 'we should.'

//

That was in 1934, when the Fascist Party seemed destined to be a footnote in British history. It was before the creeping nationalism on the Continent infected Spain, before Mussolini rattled his sabre in Abyssinia, before Hitler ordered extrajudicial killings and consolidated power, before news of the horrors of Dachau reached the outside world.

Saul and his wife Esther were among the first Londoners to be personally affected by the persecution in Germany. One evening after playing billiards at The Odd Fellows Club, Saul came home for dinner to find Esther missing. She was not in the dining room or her bedroom. Sidney could not say where she was, either. Nor could Mrs Grant, the cook and housekeeper.

'It's not like her,' Mrs Grant said, her podgy fingers tucked into the pockets of her pinafore. 'Mrs Maccabee is always so punctual.' Doubtless Mrs Grant was distressed that the duck and potatoes and roasted vegetables she had cooked for dinner might grow cold.

'Have you tried the study, sir?' Sidney asked. The study served as a reading room for Saul and a studio for Esther. 'She was painting earlier.'

Saul had not checked the study because Esther rarely painted in the evening, but at Sidney's suggestion he went there. She sat at the desk in the semi-dark, reading something. The curtains were closed. The torchére lamp, which stood in a corner of the room, cast a conical beam of light onto the ceiling. She did not hear Saul come in. He walked over and stood next to the desk. 'Esther, darling? Dinner's ready.'

She looked up with a vacant stare. 'I've received a letter,' she said. 'From Mother.'

'What is it? What happened?'

She said nothing.

He picked up the letter. It was in German, from Esther's mother in Detmold. His German was barely passable, but he could read it well enough to understand the letter's drift. Esther's twin brother Ernst—a journalist and socialist, the tract-writing type who was not afraid to voice his antifascism—had been arrested. For exactly what, Saul could not discern, only that it was an offence against the Nazi government. 'What's "*Aufwiegelung*"?' he asked.

'Sedition. He was arrested for sedition. Oh, Saul. What are we to do?' Esther hugged him round the waist. 'I told him to be careful— he was making enemies. But he wouldn't listen.'

'A beastly business.' Saul was not sure what else to say, but then it occurred to him that he was not completely powerless. 'I'll make enquiries at the club in the morning. Sir Addington has connections at the Foreign Office.' Saul kissed her on the forehead. 'Why don't you come join me for dinner. It would do you good to eat.'

'I'd rather not, if it's all the same. I seem to have lost my appetite.'

'So have I, come to think of it.' He glanced toward the door. 'Mrs Grant will be none too pleased.'

Mrs Grant, indeed, was beside herself. Not eat? She had never heard of such a thing—and after the hours and hours she had slaved away in the kitchen. What was she going to do with all that leftover food, that was what she wanted to know?

Saul suggested she put it away in the refrigerator for dinner tomorrow and offered her a fully paid day off as recompense. That pacified her. She resumed scrubbing the pots in the kitchen sink, humming the folksong 'Early One Morning', and Saul, having averted one crisis, retired to the garden to consider the other.

Big Ben struck eight as he stepped through the French doors onto the terrace. He lit his pipe and watched the sunset. The flowers along the terrace were a riot of colour: dahlias and geraniums and hydrangeas and peonies. From across the garden he could smell the fragrant aroma of Matthiola, vanilla mingled with rose and spice. He wanted Esther to be here to enjoy it all with him. It was her favourite time of day, a time they would usually spend together in the garden, when her dark moods would retreat, in sync with the deepening twilight.

Damn Ernst. Why did he have to go and get himself into trouble? It was a selfish thought, Saul knew, but he had to think of Esther. Her symptoms were getting worse. The headaches, the insomnia, the racing thoughts. Neurasthenia, her doctors called it. A disorder of the mind. What did they know? She was a genius. He could see it in her paintings. The bright colours, the bold forms, the abstraction—and something else. What was it? The soul? Yes, the soul. There was no other word for it. Her painting was like a visual rendition of jazz. She allowed him to watch her work sometimes, on her good days. Her concentration would be so intense, he could almost feel it. She would have paint everywhere, on her clothes, her hair, her face. And yet the painting itself would be flawless, as if she had ordered the chaos of her mind onto the canvas. He would love her beyond description at such times. His *belle juive*, he would call her teasingly. His beautiful Jewess. That was reason enough, he thought, for him to protect her: to nurture her genius. But every day was a delicate balance, managing her moods, helping her avoid stress. The slightest thing could upset her. Now Ernst had gone and got himself into trouble.

The sun was sinking lower in the sky. Saul took a slow, contemplative puff on his pipe. He must be getting old, he thought. With greater and greater frequency he found himself longing for a simpler time. That was what old men did: they became wistful and looked back on their youth and saw only halcyon days and none of the hardship. Still, life *was* simpler thirty years ago. There were fewer miracles of modern electrical science then. No mass-produced motorcars crowding the thoroughfares of London. No Flying Scotsman locomotives tearing up the railway to Edinburgh. No aeroplanes hurtling through the sky overhead. Just broughams and hansom cabs moving at a leisurely two miles per hour, the soothing sound of their horses' hooves clop-clopping on the cobbled streets.

Chapter 3

Different Worlds

G et him over there!' Captain Goodheart shouted.

Between them, Vernon and Arthur Fitch carried Jack's lifeless body to the divan at the back of the bay. Stewart Morley followed closely behind.

Zoe rushed over with her medical bag. 'What happened?'

'No one knows,' Morley said.

The men looked at Jack with a mixture of horror and fellow feeling. His face was bloodied beyond recognition.

'"No one knows", my arse,' Fitch said.

'We know damn well what happened,' Captain Goodheart put in. 'And there'll be the devil to pay.'

'All I'm saying is, no one saw.' Morley doffed his cap and raked his gauntleted fingers through his hair, then glanced at Zoe. 'We were marching in Limehouse. Over there by Regent's Canal Dock. We turned off Horseferry Road, and before you could say "razor", Jack broke ranks and disappeared down an alleyway. He was like this'—Morley pointed to Jack lying unconscious on the divan— 'when we found him, cut to pieces. You can help the lad, can't you?'

Zoe held up Jack's arm and placed her index and middle fingers on his wrist. 'His pulse is regular.' She turned to Vernon. 'Get me a clean cloth and some water.'

Vernon hurried to the lavatory and came back with a cloth and a ewer.

Ever so gently Zoe wiped the blood from Jack's face. The four men stood by and watched. Gradually what had been done to Jack became clear. His face was ghastly. Raw symmetrical gashes ran from the corners of his mouth to his ears, like a demented smile.

'Blimey.' Fitch turned away at the sight.

'Those bastards,' Morley said viciously. 'Those pot-bellied, sneering, money-mad bastards. Whatever has been done to them in Germany is nothing to what I'm going to do to them here when I get my hands on them.'

Fitch put a hand on Morley's shoulder. 'Easy, old fellow.'

'Hadn't we better take him to a doctor?' Vernon asked.

'We can't risk getting the authorities involved,' Captain Goodheart said. 'Besides, Zoe can patch him up, can't you, Zoe?'

'I'll do my best.'

Jack came to his senses. 'What's goin' on?'

'It's all right,' Zoe said. 'You've been injured. But you're safe and sound now, with your mates at Action House.' She gestured for the others to leave. 'Except you,' she said to Vernon. 'I'll need your help.'

'Is it bad?' Jack asked as the others left. He touched his face. 'Oh God. Sbad, ain't it?' He began to weep.

'Buck up, mate,' Vernon said, avoiding Jack's eyes. He could not very well tell Jack the truth: that he would be scarred for life and that his face would be forever set in a gruesome rictus.

Zoe retrieved a bottle of laudanum from her bag and handed it to Vernon. 'Give him thirty drops of this in a glass of water.'

Vernon did as he was told.

As Jack's breathing slowed and his eyes grew heavy, Zoe cleaned his wounds with antiseptic. The instant he was asleep she prepared a suture. With the needle threaded and inserted in its holder, she pierced the flesh at one corner of Jack's mouth and pulled the needle through. She did this again and again, until she reached the earlobe, where she tied the suture into a knot. Then she repeated the same procedure on the other side of his face. 'There,' she said when she finished. She looked solicitously at the sleeping Jack. 'You're as good as new.'

'You've got a soft touch,' Vernon remarked.

'I darned my father's socks as a girl. It's not much harder than that.'

The two of them cleaned up and sterilised the medical equipment and then went out onto the verandah for a smoke. It was past dusk. The moon and the stars shone brightly overhead.

'Will he be all right?' Vernon asked.

'He'll pull through,' Zoe said. 'Though I can't say the same for his self-esteem.'

'The poor bugger.'

She lit a cigarette and took a deep draw and looked up at the brilliant night sky. 'I'm ready for that drink whenever you are.'

//

He got disorientated as he surfaced from the Oxford Circus Tube station, unsure whether he was facing Oxford Street or Regent Street. Bodies jostled him this way and that. He was a head taller than most of the people surrounding him, but he still was unable to see what he had been told to look out for: the girl in the white Grecian dress.

Someone called his name. He turned and through the throng caught a glimpse of Zoe's face. She was standing on her tiptoes and waving at him.

He forced his way through the sea of people. 'Look at you!' he said when he finally reached her. 'Who'd have thought?'

She was dressed in a way he had never seen her before, and she was stunning in white. She could no longer be said to be just one of the boys, even with her Eton crop. 'I almost didn't recognise you either,' she said. She laughed with pleasure at the way he was looking at her. Pretending to be coy, she trailed a finger down the lapel of his coat. 'Why, Mr Price, you're in mufti.'

He doffed his fedora and kissed her hand. 'So what do you think?'

'You look brilliant in a suit.'

They walked down Regent Street amid the neon lights and surging people. Even at this late hour, cafés and clubs and milk bars and restaurants brimmed with life. So much light poured from the shops, it made the streetlamps superfluous. To the south the Piccadilly Circus billboards illumined the skyline.

'Don't you just love it here?' Zoe said.

'Wait till you see where we're going.' Vernon sounded almost giddy. He loved Soho too. It was like nothing he had experienced before. A different, a brave new world—one of the few places during his three years in London he had felt at home. Soho had the seediness and grime of the East End and the glamour and sophistication of the West End. And its night-time denizens came from all walks of life: the rich and the poor, immigrants and natives, Jews and gentiles, coloured and white. Some were dressed to the nines, while others looked like streetwalkers or tramps. But it was the freedom and lack of self-consciousness that Vernon loved most. People were here to have fun—and to hell with everything else.

At a street corner Vernon took Zoe by the hand and whisked her down a side lane and into a court.

'Have you been here before?' she asked as they hurried along.

He said he hadn't—at least, not to the particular place they were going. It was a members-only club, and a friend had pulled some strings to get them in.

They came swinging up to the club, hand in hand and breathless from their dance through the court. A doorman stood at the entrance in black tie and a top hat. Above him a neon marquee read 'The Bottled Lightning'.

'I'm a friend of Saul Maccabee's,' Vernon said. 'He should've phoned earlier.'

'Indeed he did, sir,' said the doorman. 'Please come in.' He opened the door. 'The Maccabee party,' he announced.

'Good evening, sir, madam.' The maître d' stepped from behind a stand and took Vernon's hat. 'We have been expecting you.' He disappeared into a cloakroom and then returned and said, 'This way, if you please.'

Vernon and Zoe followed the maître d' past the booths and bistro tables of the club's main lounge. The place was rather mysterious and elegant. There was no lighting except for hurricane lamps on the tables and post-mounted gas lanterns on either side of the bar, which was made entirely of glass block. The floor was a zigzag-patterned black-and-white marble, and aluminium mosaic tiles, with floral and geometric shapes, covered the ceiling. Club patrons sat here and there on velvet-upholstered stools and benches, eating hors d'oeuvres and drinking cocktails. Wisps of cigarette smoke filled the air.

Zoe tugged on Vernon's coat sleeve. 'How *mod*,' she said sotto voce.

The maître d' led them to a private room off the lounge. In its centre was a zebrawood coffee table surrounded by black-leather settees. Wall sconces and votive candles provided ambient light, and on the table stood a cheese platter, a couple of tumblers, and a bottle of gin.

'Here you are,' the maître d' said. 'A waiter will be with you shortly.'

Vernon glanced at Zoe, nonplussed. 'I don't understand,' he said to the maître d'.

'What don't you understand, sir?'

'All of this.' With a flick of his hand, Vernon indicated the contents of the table, the room.

'Compliments of Mr Maccabee, sir. You may order anything you like. The bill has already been settled.'

'Anything we like?' Zoe asked. She gave Vernon a nudge.

'*Anything*,' the maître d' repeated. 'Now if you'll excuse me.' He bowed and backed from the room.

Vernon and Zoe sat down on a settee.

'Topping!' she said, kicking off her sandals. 'Who's this friend of yours, anyway? He must be minted.'

'He is,' Vernon said. 'We met at LSE a couple of years ago. He made his money speculating in gold and currency markets, and now he lives in a white-stuccoed mansion in Belgravia.'

A waiter appeared with a tray of tonic, ice, and lime wedges. 'Hallo,' he said in an Italian accent. 'I am here to serve you drinks.' He prepared the cocktails, set them onto silverplated coasters in front of Vernon and Zoe, and proceeded to enumerate the items on the platter. 'The gouda there is the only cheese not of Italian origin,' he said proudly. 'The others are Gorgonzola, Stracchino, Parmigiano-Reggiano, and Pecorino-Romano' — he pointed to each cheese as he named them — 'all imported from *Italia*. And the spread is what in Italy is called *mostarda di frutta*.' He picked up the tray. 'If there is nothing else, *buon appetito*.'

As soon as the waiter left, Zoe stretched out voluptuously on the settee. 'A girl could get used to this.'

The waiter's talk of Italy made Vernon think of the Jackboots and the direction they were heading. He and Zoe had yet to finish their conversation about that. And now things were escalating. Jack the lad and his Glasgow smile. It portended no good. 'Did you mean what you said the other night about the Fascist Party?'

'Let's not talk about that now.' Zoe closed her eyes and laid her head in his lap. 'I'm positively knackered.'

All right, he thought, and shrugged. He would let the subject drop, then. There would be time enough for talk in the future. Besides, he could do worse than sit silently with a woman like her. He looked down without self-consciousness at her bright, youthful face. By God, she was gorgeous. And she was with *him*, and they were enjoying the good life together at someone else's expense. He leaned back contentedly, felt the weight of her body nestle into him. He could get used to this sort of life, too.

//

Ever since that day he gave Saul the Billie Holiday record, Vernon was determined to help him re-enter society. This became even more imperative after Saul's generosity at The Bottled Lightning. Vernon could not allow Saul to waste away in grief. But what to do? Social calls and gifts of records would go only so far, and he could not compel Saul to act against his will.

It occurred to Vernon that perhaps a mutual friend of theirs, Georgina Wilson, could help. He knew her through her role as editor-in-chief of *The Masses*, the magazine of the radical socialist organisation the Scipian Society. She often solicited writing on economics and politics from LSE professors and their students. Vernon himself had contributed several articles related to his doctoral thesis about colonialism and plantation economics.

Saul knew Georgina socially. He had moved in the same circles as her, before Esther's death. She was a spinster in her mid-sixties but had an unearned income and so was part of the upper middle class. She and Saul first met after he came down from Cambridge and was flirting with the Fabian Society, a less radical precursor to the Scipian Society. Back then, she was still hobnobbing with the 'Old Gang' of Fabians, which included George Bernard Shaw. Saul had been attracted to the personalities, the intellectualism, and the Society's liberal ideals. He was especially attracted to Georgina. She was only in her forties then and had a magnetic effect on men, both young and old. She had dark glowing eyes and a profusion of black hair, which she wore in a pompadour. One of her grandmothers was thought to have been Jewish.

Part of her appeal for Saul, beyond her appearance, was that she was full of contradictions. To an impressionable young man, her enigmatic nature made her seem more alive, more human. She was prim and proper, and yet she freely fraternised with East Enders. During the Nineties, when she was barely twenty years old, she had gone slumming in the East End to investigate the sweating system. And yet, despite her advocacy for the poor, she remained a snob. She was repulsed by people who dropped their aitches and considered slum dwellers to be 'the wild races of darkest England'. She described the East End as if it were a creature that had crawled out of the Thames, covered in muck and pustules. By the time of her association with the Fabians, she viewed unfettered capitalism as evil, and yet through her father, who had been a wealthy merchant, she lived off the fruits of the Industrial Revolution. Her social service and East Ending were open rebellions against Victorian mores, and yet she suffered, like most Victorians, from a guilty conscience over her sexuality and her abandonment of God.

Saul was enthralled. He dove head first into his activities with the Fabians. His first employment in London, before he and Esther were married, was with the stockjobbing firm Wedd Jefferson. When he was not working, he would meet other Fabians at coffeehouses to discuss the latest political theories, or he would join Georgina on her trips to the East End. He wrote articles for local newspapers about his ideas and experiences and slowly made a name for himself as a serious social reformer.

Then the Great War came. Saul tried to join the army but was certified medically unfit because of his congenital hand tremor. With impotent desperation, he watched his friends being deployed, one by one, to the Continent. As more and more men died in the trenches, and as the ranks of the Fabians became depleted, many of the socialists questioned the gradualist creed of Fabianism. The war was proof, they said, that the Fabian notion of 'the inevitability of gradualness', which was rooted in the Victorian belief in evolutionary progress, was daft. Science and the accretion of socialist policies were not enough to bring about the perfectibility of man in the foreseeable future. More radical changes were needed.

The controversy led to in-fighting among the Fabians. Georgina and the Old Gang were on one side, and the extreme-left Fabians were on the other. Saul found himself in the middle, trying to mediate between the sides. He distrusted Marxist ideology and continued to believe in the gradualist approach to change so long as it stayed within the capitalist system. He *was*, however, willing to suppress his scruples to some extent if it would mean keeping the Fabian Society intact. But his mediating did no good. Meanwhile the war raged on and millions perished. Even the staunch defenders of Fabianism began to lose faith.

When in 1917—as Lenin and the Bolsheviks were seizing power in Russia—Georgina voiced concern that the socialists had failed to create the new moral order that the Old Gang envisioned, it spelled the beginning of the end for the Fabian Society. Soon rumblings were heard that the Fabians had been named after the wrong general, the Roman Fabius Maximus, whose slow, harassing tactics against Hannibal proved successful. It was pointed out that Fabius had not in fact defeated Hannibal; that honour had gone to another Roman general, Scipio Africanus, who was not afraid to engage the enemy in pitched battles. Georgina and the extreme-left Fabians suggested forming a splinter group modelled after Scipio's strategies. Hence the Scipian Society was born.

As the parent organisation receded into the background, the Scipians took their ideas about labour unrest and social planning to greater and greater extremes. Increasingly they sounded like cranks and elitists, and Saul grew disenchanted. He borrowed a device from the socialists' bag of tricks and agitated. The Scipians were contemplating forced sterilisation of the 'unfit' as part of a eugenics program and held a meeting to discuss the issue. Saul, feigning interest, turned up at the meeting and plied the moderators with questions. Who would decide whether someone was fit? And what, pray tell, would make someone 'unfit'? Would *he* be unfit because of his hand tremor? His sarcasm offended many of the Scipians in attendance, and instantly he was blackballed. Georgina came to his defence, but the damage had already been done. In a final salvo, he got into a heated debate with Shaw and called him a dull, empty windbag.

Vernon learned of Saul's history with the Fabians during their many meetings at the Corner House during 1934 and 1935. As it happened, Georgina was the cause of their first argument. It came to light that they both knew her, and Saul went off on a tangent about how she had become fanatical in her old age.

'Socialism is a kind of religion for her,' he said. 'She can thank Herbert Spencer and other progressive Victorians for that, I suppose. They believed evolution could become a conscious process: man's a risen ape and not a fallen angel, etcetera etcetera. Their church was dedicated to the service of man instead of to God.'

It seemed to Vernon that something of the spurned lover was evident in the way Saul talked about Georgina and the socialists. 'But at least,' Vernon responded, 'she's doing something to achieve social justice, misguided or not. Didn't you once say yourself that that was a laudable political aim?'

Saul set down his teacup. 'I did, yes. And I stand by that. It's not Georgina's aims I take issue with.' He looked away for a moment, lost in thought. The orchestra were playing Gershwin's 'Rhapsody in Blue' mezzo-forte. 'Let me put it this way,' he said eventually. 'Georgina believes the government should provide every individual with a minimum of civilised life, correct?'

'Correct.'

'That's a good intention, and as an aim, I support it wholeheartedly. What I take issue with is not her intentions but her paternalistic attitude. The road to hell, after all, is paved with good intentions. Georgina and other socialists like her have the attitude that as privileged members of the governing class, they have the right — nay, the duty — to do the thinking for the untutored masses. It's almost messianic, this mission of the enlightened expert, the disinterested elite, to regenerate society and govern the people for their own good. Of the early Fabians, Shaw was the worst of the lot in this respect. For years he saw himself as a messiah, preaching a kind of secular salvation. He used to refer to administrative saviours as supermen, an apparent misreading of Nietzsche's idea of the *Übermensch*.'

Vernon sat back, shaking his head. He could not so easily disregard Georgina's lifelong dedication to social justice. She was a person of goodwill, genuinely interested in overthrowing class distinctions. Was that so wrong? What did her wealth and snobbery and paternalism and potential delusions of grandeur matter if she devoted her time and energy to the betterment of society? Many of the leisured class were motivated to provide social services simply out of fear, fear of a working-class uprising. That was not Georgina's motivation. She had a genuine desire for human solidarity and sociability. Vernon articulated some of these thoughts about Georgina to Saul.

'Now hold on a minute, old chap,' Saul said. 'You misunderstand me. The problem goes back to human nature. Georgina may be pure of heart, but you can't generalise from her to all other political activists. If you were to hand over the reins of the British government to an elite core of organisers, the result wouldn't be a utopian society. It would be something closer to fascism. A demagogue would emerge from the elites — someone like Shaw who fancies himself a messiah — tradition and continuity would go the way of the dodo, and before long there would be a "tremendous smash-up of existing society" similar to that of the French and Russian Revolutions.'

'You exaggerate,' Vernon replied.

'Do I?' There was a striking similarity, Saul said, between the Scipian's position vis-à-vis Parliament and that of the political right-wing. Like the fascists, the Scipians believed that extreme competition in ideas led to deadlock and that therefore the 'dithering Parliament' should be replaced by people who could get things done. From that standpoint, both the Right and the Left were on the conservative end of the political spectrum. The only difference was that the socialists wanted Parliament replaced by a group of elite bureaucrats while the fascists wanted it replaced by a strongman.

'And "orthodoxy and complacency are diseases of civilisation",' Vernon said. 'I've heard Georgina say that as well, and it's true.'

'It *is* true, I give you that.' Saul laughed. 'In the same way that neuroses are a disease of civilisation.' He was thinking of Georgina; she had become neurotic, as well as fanatical, in her old age. At any rate, he could see that it would take more than a well-formed argument to persuade Vernon that Georgina's political views were dangerous. Vernon was as enamoured of her as Saul had once been.

'On the matter of Georgina, my fine young fellow,' Saul concluded, 'you and I will just have to agree to differ.'

Chapter 4

Kicking against the Pricks

In Georgina's view, Saul was suffering from an acute case of *Weltschmerz*, or world weariness, and the best thing for that was a good old clipping round the ears. She said this to Vernon outside the offices of *The Masses* on Kemble Street early one Sunday morning. She had planned to spend the day working, but when Vernon told her about Saul's depression, she dropped everything and suggested they visit him at once.

Vernon made excuses because he had in mind she would go alone. 'If we go together,' he said, 'Saul will see our visit for the intercession that it is.' Vernon checked his watch. It was almost ten o'clock. 'Besides, I have schoolwork to do.'

But Georgina would have none of it. 'Two are better than one, as the Good Book says,' she replied, appealing to Scripture. The Bible, she once told Vernon, was wisdom literature, even if the writings of Darwin and Spencer made religious faith seem like superstition. She added now, 'And a threefold cord is not quickly broken. What's the Sabbath for if not to help a friend in need?'

Before Vernon could object any further, he and Georgina were getting into the back seat of her Bentley. She instructed the driver to take the usual route to Grosvenor Place and on to the Maccabee's.

'Yes, ma'am,' the driver said, and away the car went.

As they drove down the Strand, Georgina retrieved a powder box from her purse and examined her face in the mirror. 'An absolute fright,' she said, touching the bags under her eyes. 'But it will just have to do.' She sighed. 'I haven't been to Saul's in … My word, has it really been six months since Esther's wake?'

'It has,' Vernon said.

'Time certainly does fly.' A look of nostalgia came into her eyes. 'Only yesterday, it seems, I was attending their wedding. Esther was such a beautiful bride.'

They arrived at Saul's house and went up to the door and rang the bell.

Sidney answered. For some reason he made eye contact only with Vernon and more or less ignored Georgina. 'Good morning, sir,' Sidney said warmly. 'If I might be so bold, sir, your last visit here'—his voice dropped to a whisper—'it did Mr Maccabee a world of good. He talked of little else for days.'

'I'm glad to hear it,' Vernon said. He detected something of the snob in Sidney's behaviour toward Georgina. Perhaps it was on account of her clothes. Vernon had become so accustomed to her bohemian ways himself that he no longer paid much attention to how she dressed. But today, he now noticed, she was particularly dowdy. She wore a rolled-brim cloche hat, a drab-looking crepe blouse, and a skirt with a large stain on the front of it.

Sidney finally acknowledged her and said matter-of-factly, 'Madam.'

Not to be outdone, Georgina curtly brushed past him into the entrance hall. In the process her hat went askew on her head, revealing some of the wispy and untidy hair beneath. She righted her hat in a fury. 'Where's your employer? We have to see him.'

'Asleep, I am afraid.'

'Asleep? At this hour?' She seemed be having one of her bilious attacks. 'Go wake him, please. Vernon and I will show ourselves to the drawing room.'

As they waited in the drawing room, Georgina grew impatient and busied herself dusting the furniture with a doily. The house had gone to seed in Esther's absence. 'For heaven's sake,' Georgina said, picking up a ball of fluff from the floor and showing it to Vernon. 'An absolute disgrace.'

'I told you things were bad.'

Sidney came in with the tea.

'Does no one clean here anymore?' Georgina asked him.

'Mrs Grant does her best, madam. It has not been easy looking after Mr Maccabee since —' Sidney broke off.

An awkward silence followed.

'There's a good fellow,' Georgina said eventually, patting Sidney on the arm. 'I dare say it hasn't been easy.'

Another twenty minutes went by and Saul still did not appear.

'The impertinence,' Georgina said as she finished her second cup of tea. '*Weltschmerz* or not, there's no excuse for keeping us waiting like this. I've half a mind to drag him out of bed myself.'

'No need for that,' Saul said, entering the room at last. He was clean-shaven and nattily dressed. 'Forgive me, but I couldn't see you as I was.'

'Hello, Saul,' Georgina said. She went to him, and they kissed each other on the cheeks. From her expression, it was clear that all had been forgiven.

Saul turned to Vernon. 'How was your night out with your lady friend?'

'It exceeded expectations. I owe you a debt of gratitude.'

'We can call it even, then,' Saul said. 'A kindness for a kindness, let's say.' A brown-leather chesterfield and matching chairs surrounded an Oriental-style rug in the centre of the room. He sat on a chair and motioned for the others to sit on the chesterfield. He would have served himself a cup of tea, but he suspected that whatever remained of it in the teapot had long since grown cold. 'So, what brings the two of you here?'

'To make a proposition,' Georgina said.

'Aren't you getting a little old for propositions, Georgina?'

'Don't be cheeky.' She smiled in spite of herself. Then she tilted her head and touched her hair and said, 'I'd like you to come write for me at the magazine. We're in need of good writers, and you have such a facility with language. Now that you're no longer working — or now that you no longer need to work, I should say — it's such a shameful waste of talent for you to be doing nothing.'

'You know how I feel about the Scipian Society.'

'But that was such a long time ago. Can't you let bygones be bygones?'

'This isn't an expression of interest, but won't some of your colleagues take exception to my involvement with the magazine? I didn't exactly part ways with the Society on good terms.'

'Leave that to me. I wield a lot of influence these days.'

A painting on the wall caught Saul's eye. It was Esther's final completed work. He had forgotten it was there. How long had it been since he last entered the drawing room? He could not remember. Months had gone by in an impressionistic blur, one day bleeding into the next. How was he going to manage without Esther? He could hardly bear to be in the same room as her painting. His eyes resettled on Georgina. 'It's a nice gesture,' he said, 'but I don't think I'm up for it, if I'm honest.'

'Come on, Saul,' said Vernon. He had read some of Saul's old articles, and they were brilliant. Writing for *The Masses* might be exactly what Saul needed to get him active again — and to get him out of his depression. 'If you're worried about stepping on someone's toes, don't be. Plenty of the contributors to *The Masses* don't see eye to eye. That's what keeps the magazine's content fresh and relevant.'

'Let me think about it,' Saul said. He was not averse to the idea of writing for *The Masses*, but he refused to be ganged up on.

'What's there to think about?' Georgina asked. 'Have you been reading the papers lately?' There was a sense of urgency in her voice.

'You mean the international papers and this Wallis Simpson business?' Saul said in jest. 'It's appalling, I agree. Sin is always so much worse when someone else commits it.' He knew how to get under Georgina's skin. Unlike her, he had never had a crisis of faith.

Even in his youth, he had no sense of sin, no guilty conscience for having turned his back on organised religion. He had only one lingering guilt, and that was his not having served in the Great War.

'You really do try one's patience,' Georgina said. 'I don't give a fig about King Edward and his concubine. I'm referring to what's happening on the Continent. The remilitarisation of the Rhineland, to name but one issue of concern.' In the past, she had made no secret of her disdain for what she characterised as the draconian Versailles Treaty. She was convinced another European war was coming. The Germans had been backed into a corner, and like most caged animals, they would be forced to bare their teeth and lash out. 'War is a very real possibility. You mark my words. And now more than ever, we need voices like yours, voices of reason. It's not too late for you to make a difference, Saul. The pen's mightier than the sword.'

'I'm surprised to hear you say that,' Saul replied. 'Not so long ago you were singing the praises of the Soviet Union.'

'You may not believe this, but, like the human race, I've evolved.'

Saul sat back with a smile and crossed his legs. 'I don't doubt *you've* evolved. You're an enlightened person. But the human race? That remains to be seen.'

//

From the door of the study, Saul had watched her put the finishing touches on her painting, a pyramidal composition of naked women swimming in a lake. The painting was colourful as usual, with a variety of purples and reds and yellows and greens. One of the women in it stood alone near the shoreline beneath a tree, her back to the other swimmers, her head lolling to one side. A vine appeared to be entangled round her neck.

Saul asked what the woman represented.

Esther stepped back from the easel, the palette still in her hand. She had a serious look on her face as she thought of what to say. A minute passed in silence. It was a self-portrait, she said eventually. Did he remember the time they went to Windermere and saw the girls swimming in their maillots? He had been offended, had said the girls might as well be swimming in the nude. She had laughed at that. It was such a prudish thing to say. She had thought, What if the girls *had* been nude? That would have been a lark. And what if *she* had been one of those girls? How liberating it would have been! Then she had thought of Cezanne and Matisse and their theme of women in the open air, and a seed had been planted. Now here the seed was, grown into a painting.

Saul went over and stood next to her and studied the composition more closely. All the swimmers were impressionistic save for the figure of Esther. The other women were like nondescript spirits, but Esther, along with the tree and the vine, were as detailed as a photograph. Her body was submerged in water up to the waist, and though her face was not visible, it was obviously Esther. Saul could see that from the curvature of the back, from the pinned-up curls of the hair. There was something unnerving about it all, and also dreamlike.

As he stood there, Esther told him she had decided to call the painting *Swimmers in a Landscape*. It was for Ernst, she said. She'd give it him next time she saw him. Perhaps they could invite him for Hanukkah this year once the business of his arrest was cleared up. She hadn't seen him for over two years, not since he started writing for the *Lippische Landes-Zeitung*. It had been his dream to work there. He had been pouring his heart and soul into the job — before his arrest, that was. As Esther spoke, she grew increasingly spirited and her words came out faster and faster.

Saul realised she was becoming euphoric. Now that her painting was finished, her energies would have to be diverted elsewhere.

She took him by the hands. She had almost forgotten, she said. Ernst might have difficulty paying his way to London. He was a poor journalist, after all. She and Saul could defray some or all of the cost for the trip from Detmold, couldn't they?

They certainly could, Saul assured her. He kissed her on the cheek. He was proud of her, he said. The painting was her best work yet. Did she know she was his *belle juive*?

She said she did. How could she not? He said it often enough. She started laughing hysterically.

It made him happy, and just a little bit afraid, to see her that way.

//

The morning after Esther received the letter about Ernst's arrest, Saul followed through on his promise to make enquiries at The Odd Fellows Club. He decided to broach the subject with Sir Addington over a game of billiards. Late in the game — they were playing to one hundred, it was Saul's turn, and the score was tied at ninety-five — it occurred to Saul that it would be undiplomatic for him to beat his opponent while asking for a favour. He would have to throw the game.

He chalked his cue tip and walked round the table to get a proper angle on his shot. At the top of the cushion, the other cue ball and the red ball were lined up directly in front of a corner pocket. It was an easy combination shot and such a shame to waste: if he had wanted to, he could have potted all three balls in a single go and won the game decisively.

'Looks like you've got me by the bollocks,' Sir Addington said, sitting sidesaddle on a tall stool next to the table. He was a fleshy, imposing man with an Edwardian moustache, and he had changed little since his time in the Queen's Own Hussars.

Saul smiled confidently and set the chalk onto the rail. Addressing his ball, he pretended to aim for the combination shot but instead, at the last second, made an adjustment and hit the ball off centre. It missed the other cue ball entirely, skidded off the red ball, and rattled into the corner pocket.

'Rotten luck, old boy,' Sir Addington said with a smirk, none the wiser about what Saul had done. The old hussar took his cue ball and played in-hand from behind the balkline. His moustache twitched as he aimed and sighted in his shot. The cue ball struck the red ball perfectly and pocketed them both for a winning hazard. It was the end of the game.

'Nicely played,' Saul said, laying it on thick. As he set his cue onto the table, his expression turned serious. 'Neville' — Neville was Sir Addington's given name — 'I'm hoping you could pull a few strings for me at the Foreign Office, if it wouldn't be too much trouble. I need an audience at the German embassy. It's a rather delicate matter involving my brother-in-law. The German authorities have falsely charged him with sedition.'

'That's not good.' Sir Addington inserted his cue into the rack on the wall and then turned back to Saul. He was still smiling from his win. 'It would give me the utmost pleasure to be of help, Maccabee old boy. One of the German Ambassador's underlings, a chap by the name of Hans Otto, owes me a favour, as it happens. I could arrange a meeting for you as early as this afternoon if you like.'

'Anything you could do would be greatly appreciated,' Saul said.

'I should forewarn you, though. Don't expect much from the bloody Hun. Diplomatic relations with them have been frosty since the advent of the *Deutsches Reich*. They've got the bizarre notion that *we* owe *them* something after the Great War. You'll very probably smell burning martyr when you go to the embassy.'

Sir Addington was as good as his word and arranged a meeting between Saul and Hans Otto for four o'clock that very afternoon. Prussia House, the German embassy, was a Corinthian-columned building in St James's district. When Saul arrived there a few minutes before four, a clerk ushered him to an upstairs room and asked him to wait. Herr Otto would be with him shortly, the clerk said. The room had book-lined walls and a picture window overlooking Waterloo Gardens. Saul went to the window and looked out. It was a sunny day. A clump of beech and oak and chestnut trees marked the boundary of the gardens. Pedestrians walked jauntily along Carlton House Terrace. The statue of John Fox Burgoyne stood at the corner of the gardens, and on Waterloo

Place, partially discernible through the foliage, was the equestrian statue of Edward VII. The Germans had done well, Saul thought, to select this site for their embassy. Perhaps they were not so uncivilised, after all. Indeed, up until the Great War, they had been better known for their rich tradition in art and literature and music than for their barbarism.

His eyes were drawn to the books on the shelves. He took one at random and leafed through its pages. It was Nietzsche's *The Birth of Tragedy*, in the original. At Trinity College he had read the book in translation. He was underwhelmed by its ideas then, but a quotation stuck in his head all these years: *Knowledge kills action; action requires the veils of illusion.* A shibboleth for the man of action. No wonder the fascists were so enamoured of Nietzsche.

'You know German?' a man's voice asked from the doorway.

Saul turned. The man was Aryan-looking with close-cropped hair. '*Ein bisschen,*' Saul said and returned the book to its shelf.

'You are Mr Maccabee, the friend of Neville's?'

'Yes.'

'*Guten Tag.* I am Hans.' He came over and shook Saul's hand. 'It is a pleasure.'

'The pleasure's all mine.'

'Shall we?' Hans said, indicating a pair of tub chairs near the window.

They went over and sat down.

'Neville tells me you are seeking information about your brother-in-law, Ernst Rosenblum, who was arrested.'

'I realise it's an imposition, but my wife has been worried sick — '

Hans raised a hand in apparent objection. 'I must stop you there, Mr Maccabee. It is beyond my power to help you or anyone else in such matters. If I were to do so, I would soon be under suspicion myself.'

'How do you mean?'

The door to the room was slightly ajar. Hans got up and closed it and returned to his chair. 'You did not hear this from me,' he said, 'but the Nazis are brutes. They are destroying the Fatherland. When they suspended freedoms under the Constitution last year, it was merely a ploy to eliminate political opposition. They have created a reign of terror and intimidation. No one dares speak out against them because agents and informants are everywhere. Neighbours denunciate neighbours for the merest trifle. I would not be surprised if the Gestapo had tapped the telephones here in the embassy. Suspicion runs that deep. And now that the secret police are under the auspices of Himmler and the *Schutzstaffel*, they have intensified their efforts to quash dissent. I fear your brother-in-law may have been caught up in that. If he had the temerity to criticise the Nazi Party—. I daren't say what they might do to him.' Hans stood up to go. 'I wish I could help you, Mr Maccabee, truly I do. But I have my own family to think of.'

Saul's head was spinning as he left the embassy. What was he going to tell Esther? If even half of what Hans said was true, Ernst would be lucky to escape the firing squad. The knowledge would devastate her. She and Ernst were more than brother and sister; they were one another's alter egos. Not only did they look alike, but they also had similar personalities and shared an inseparable bond. They were like two halves of the same soul. They even claimed to be able to feel each other's pain. Esther told Saul a story once about how as teenagers she and Ernst were on the frozen river Werre playing *Eisstockschiessen*, a winter version of shuffleboard, when the ice broke and Ernst fell into the water. He was rescued instantly but later developed pneumonia and for days lay in bed. Somehow Esther fell sick, too. The family doctor thought her symptoms were psychosomatic but could not explain her phlegmy cough or her high fever. It was one of those inexplicable mysteries and suggested an empathic connection between brother and sister. The Germans had a word for it, *Einfühlung*, or 'feeling into', which meant more than empathy; it implied an ability to engage emotively with art and literature and music as well as with people. *Einfühlung* was the source of Esther's artistry, what Saul referred to as the soul in her paintings.

When he got home from the embassy, he told her that a high-ranking diplomat was personally looking into Ernst's case and would get back in a few days with any news. Some truths, Saul had decided, were best left unsaid.

Chapter 5

Cloak and Dagger

His student lodgings were on Drury Lane, five minutes' walk from LSE. He was in the habit of waking early each morning, doing some reading, and then spending several hours at the LSE library. He was beyond the stage in his doctoral programme of taking classes and teaching, so his only responsibilities included working on his thesis and occasionally meeting with his supervisor. His evenings were spent at Jackboot rallies or at Action House or, more and more frequently, with Zoe at various places round London.

One afternoon, after returning to his room from the library, he found a note under the door. At first he was confused because the paper was completely blank. Then he realised what it was. Hurriedly he shut the door and went into his room. By the mattress on the floor was a shadeless lamp. He switched it on and held the paper over the bulb. The words *Hyde Park Wellington Monument midnight* slowly appeared. He crumpled up the paper and set it alight in an ashtray and watched it burn. He had been expecting this moment: his first communication from the District Secretariat.

He was due to meet Zoe for dinner at eight o'clock. They were going to the West End again, this time to an Anglo-Indian restaurant on the Mayfair side of Regent Street. He would have plenty of time, he thought, to eat dinner, walk Zoe home, and get to the dead-drop point by midnight.

Shortly before eight, he met Zoe under the Victory House arch on Swallow Street. His pulse quickened when he saw her. She wore a pink floral shift. With each meeting she seemed to become more and more feminine. He took her by the hands and squeezed them tightly. 'You look first-rate as usual,' he said, eyeing her shift.

'You mustn't keep spoiling me like this. Indian food? It's all so exotic.'

'That's what I was aiming for. There's something I must tell you, and somehow fish and chips didn't seem right for the occasion.'

She kissed him. 'Aren't you mysterious?'

A *darwan* in a Punjabi turban and uniform opened the door for them to Victory House. 'Please to enjoying your meal,' he said in broken English.

Vernon and Zoe took the lift up to the mezzanine floor. The maître d', a lanky Englishman, stood in the restaurant's entryway. 'Good evening,' he said. 'Do you have a reservation?'

'Price, for two,' said Vernon.

The maître d' checked the reservation list. 'Right. Follow me, please.' He led them to a bistro table beneath a glass chandelier and pulled out Zoe's chair for her.

As Vernon sat down, he glanced round the place. Its décor was a mingling of Mughal latticework and British colonial furnishings. Framed posters of the Indian actress Sulochana and of other famous Eurasians adorned the walls. He had been here once before, with friends from LSE, and had liked its ambience. It reminded him of home.

'Bhimrao will be your waiter tonight,' the maître d' said, handing them their menus. 'He is from the Central Provinces. I hope everything will be to your satisfaction.'

Vernon and Zoe smiled.

As the maître d' returned to the entryway, Zoe said, 'The restaurant's rather authentic, isn't it?'

'Everything except the maître d',' said Vernon, and they both laughed.

The waiter arrived with their water.

'*Śubha sandhyā*,' Vernon said. 'We hear you're from India.'

'Yes, sir, I am. You know Hindi. *Namaste*.' The waiter put his hands together and bowed slightly.

Zoe stared at Vernon. 'You're full of surprises.'

'It's what I needed to tell you. About my past.'

The waiter asked if they wanted anything else to drink before they ordered their food.

'I'll have a pint of Carlsberg,' Vernon said.

'A sidecar for me,' said Zoe, still staring at Vernon.

'A Carlsberg and a sidecar coming right up,' the waiter said, then went to fetch the drinks.

Zoe gently kicked Vernon under the table. 'Go on, then. You've built up the suspense so that I can hardly stand it.' She crossed her arms. 'What is it you've been hiding? That you're a genius and speak a dozen languages?'

Vernon laughed. 'No, nothing like that. I don't even know Hindi, not really, just a few phrases I picked up in Delhi when I was there at university. What I needed to tell you is where I'm from.'

'You're from India?' Zoe said animatedly. 'I was wondering about your accent. It sounded — it sounds — colonial, but I couldn't quite place it, and I didn't want to pry. I assumed your father had been stationed in a British colony somewhere.'

Vernon was encouraged by her response. 'I'm not from India, but I am from that part of the world.' He glanced round again, his eyes settling for a moment on the Sulochana poster. 'There's a reason I brought you to this particular restaurant. The original owner was the grandson of an English general and an Indian princess. He decorated the place to suit his tastes, put up pictures of other Eurasians like him. … He and I share a similar ancestry. Like him, I come from the Indian subcontinent. Except that I'm not from India. I'm from Ceylon.'

Zoe looked at him, at his light-coloured skin, at his brown hair.

Vernon continued, 'I know what you're thinking: I look like any other Englishman. But I'm not an Englishman. I was born of a European father and a Sinhalese mother. In the eyes of the British, I'm not European, and in the eyes of the Ceylonese, I'm not Ceylonese. I'm what the British call a Eurasian and what the Ceylonese call a Burgher. I'm a mix-breed. A half-caste.'

Zoe remained silent. She seemed to be weighing the information in her mind.

The waiter returned with a tankard of beer and an amber-coloured cocktail and asked if they were ready to order their food. Vernon ordered the kedgeree; Zoe, the mulligatawny soup. As they ordered, they both had embarrassed looks on their faces, as if they had been caught having a lovers' tiff.

Even after the waiter had gone, Zoe remained silent about Vernon's origins, and he now regretted having told her. He had thought that she of all people would understand him and would accept him for who he was. She was liberal-minded, despite her affiliation with the fascists. Only two days ago she told him she was weary of their violent ways and was intending to leave them. The incident with Jack had been the final straw. She had decided to return full time to nursing at London Hospital. It was a sign, Vernon had thought, of her human decency. But perhaps he had been wrong. Perhaps he could not trust her, after all. 'Repeat to no one what I've just told you. As it is, only Saul and a few administrators at LSE know my history. My life depends on your keeping it a secret.'

Zoe kicked him under the table again, much harder this time. 'You're crackers,' she said, offended. She had been surprised by his revelation, that was all. 'I don't care a pennyworth what your ancestry is, whether you're a full-blood or a mix-breed or even a human ragbag. You need to get that through your clever little head right now.'

He laughed, and inwardly breathed a sigh of relief, secure in the knowledge that his secret was safe with her.

//

On his way from the Hyde Park Corner Tube station to the Wellington Monument, Vernon did not encounter a soul. He turned into the south-eastern edge of the park and walked up to the statue of Achilles. Bathed in moonlight, it stood over thirty feet tall, a sword and a shield in its hands, a cloak draped over one shoulder. So far as Vernon could see, no one was about. Nor was there any sign of a drop.

The Clock Tower began to chime the Westminster Quarters. *Midnight,* Vernon thought. He circled the statue's mound to make sure he had not missed anything. But still there was no package. Where *was* the bloody thing? He hoped to God it had not been intercepted. That would be brilliant, if his orders ended up in the wrong hands. How would he explain *that* to the District Secretariat?

Big Ben stopped chiming, and Vernon had an unnerving thought: that perhaps there was no package at all and coming here was a trap. It would mean that someone had found out who he was and had lured him here with the note. His eyes flitted nervously round the park. Again there was no one. He felt relieved. Perhaps his fears were unwarranted. He needed to calm down, he told himself. If coming here *were* a trap, it seemed likely that the perpetrator would have shown himself by now.

He decided to wait another minute and then leave. He was not cut out for this cloak-and-dagger business. Besides, there were other things he would rather be doing. Sleeping, for one. Or getting to know Zoe better. Earlier that night, he had walked her to her flat, and for the first time she invited him in. He gave an excuse about having a prior engagement. She did not press him for an explanation, but skirting the truth with her made him feel wretched.

He heard a noise now and whirled round.

A man appeared from the opposite side of the statue. He wore a flat hat and a vest, and his shirtsleeves were rolled up. Vernon did not recognise him. 'A friend,' the man said in a low voice as Vernon grabbed him by the throat.

'Prove it,' Vernon said, tightening his grip. 'What's the password?'

'Justice,' the man choked out.

Vernon loosened his grip and released the man. 'Why are you here? I was expecting a dead drop.'

'There was a last-minute change of plan,' the man said. He rubbed his throat. 'They said you were as strong as an ox, but I didn't believe it till now. Good to finally meet you, comrade. I'm Spartacus, your handler.'

'Sorry for roughing you up.'

'No fear.' Spartacus shook Vernon's hand. 'Let's get down to business. Don't ask any questions because the less you know, the better. All you need know for now is that the Jackboots have been spreading black propaganda. Your orders are to track the nightly movements of one of their directors, Conor Walsh, and report back to me on his activities. He's a dangerous bastard, so be careful.'

Vernon did not like the sound of that. What if his cover were blown? He had spent weeks associating with people whose worldviews he despised, and that would all be for naught if his identity were uncovered. His expectation from the start was that he would simply pass along information about the goings on at Action House. Never did he imagine he would be shadowing the Jackboot leadership. Whatever Director Walsh was suspected of doing, however, must be important if the District Secretariat were willing to risk a live meeting between operatives like this.

'If you are compromised in any way,' Spartacus went on, seeming to read Vernon's mind, 'abort the mission immediately. Gather what information you can and get out.' He handed Vernon a piece of paper. 'Conor Walsh's address.'

Vernon slipped the paper into his trouser pocket. Then he watched Spartacus slink away like a thief and vanish into the trees.

//

Every night for a week, Vernon surveilled Walsh's tenement in

Stepney Green. Nothing notable happened. On one occasion, Walsh went to Action House, but otherwise he stayed at home.

Vernon was contemplating giving up when on the eighth night his luck changed. It was nine o'clock, a half-hour past sunset, and he had just taken up position in the shadows of the tobacconist's shop down the street from Walsh's tenement. Suddenly Walsh appeared on his front stoop, dressed in a cloak. He looked up and down the street. For a moment he seemed to sniff the air, which smelled of rain. Then he lifted the cloak's hood over his head, stepped off the stoop, and made his way south toward Whitechapel. Vernon followed at a distance.

Walsh took backstreets all the way to the Isle of Dogs. At Blackwall Basin, he stopped on the boardwalk and lit a cigarette. Vernon ducked behind a parked lorry outside a warehouse. Between draws at his cigarette, Walsh gazed into the water, the surface of which reflected the city's lights. He seemed to be mulling something over.

Vernon could not understand why Walsh had come here, of all places. He would not have walked over four kilometres just to have a smoke. Or was he simply taking an evening constitutional? But then why the cloak and in the middle of August?

Presently Walsh put out his cigarette and was on the move again.

Vernon started to follow but almost immediately stopped. Someone was approaching along the boardwalk from the direction of Poplar Dock, heading straight for Walsh. As they passed each other, Walsh handed off an envelope. Vernon strained to see the stranger's face, but it was too dark. He would have to change tack, he thought, and shadow the stranger. Whatever it took, Vernon had to find out what was in that envelope.

There was a flash of lightning and a thunderclap and it began to rain.

The stranger double-timed down the boardwalk toward Vernon, who took cover under the lorry. He lay on his stomach and peered out into the darkness. Less than a half-minute later, it was raining buckets and the stranger came sloshing past the lorry. At ground level, all Vernon could see were the stranger's steel-capped boots, but there was something familiar about them. Where had he seen them before?

He rolled out from under the lorry and got to his feet. The rain was so intense, he could not see more than a few metres in front of his face. Already he had lost sight of the stranger. He continued his pursuit as far as the West India Docks. Stopping at the edge of a lock, wet to the bone, he stood there staring through the pouring rain. It was no use, he realised. The stranger was gone.

But then Vernon remembered where he had seen the boots. Morley. They belonged to Morley.

//

She came to him in the night. He had just lain down to sleep when he heard someone tapping on his door. He was expecting it to be one of the neighbours asking for matches or some such trifle. Instead, it was Zoe, her clothes sodden, crying.

'It happened again,' she said. 'My last day with the Jackboots and it happened again.'

'What happened again?' he asked, helping her to a chair.

'Another attack.'

He wiped the tears and rain from her face. 'I want to know everything,' he said, 'but let's get you dry first.' He went to the bathroom and brought back a towel and a handkerchief and sat down in a chair beside her. 'Now, tell me what happened.'

She recounted the story. The attack this time was at Action House, on a guard at his post. There had been a noise in the trees, and the guard had gone to investigate. He must have been hit over the head because he could not remember anything after that. One of the other guards found him unconscious, a Glasgow smile carved into his face.

Zoe put a hand to her mouth and held back a sob. 'I've never seen so much blood, and I'm a nurse. The viciousness of it. His face was worse than Jack's. It was all I could do to sew him up.'

Vernon reassured her, but he, too, was troubled by the attacks. He wondered what the ritual disfigurement signified. It was the type of thing gang members did to rivals, not antifascists to fascists. He recalled what Spartacus said about black propaganda. Perhaps Spartacus meant the business with the Sicarii, and somehow Walsh was implicated. It seemed like too much of a coincidence that on the very night Walsh and Morley met in secret, the Sicarii struck at Action House. 'What time did the attack occur?' Vernon asked.

'I don't know. Sometime between nine and nine-thirty, I suppose. Why?'

'Only curious.' The timing was off, he thought. Walsh could not have been the perpetrator because he was in Whitechapel and the Isle of Dogs between nine and nine-thirty. What about Morley? He would have had time to get from Action House to Blackwall Basin if he had left by nine-fifteen. But what was his motive? He showed genuine concern after Jack's attack. Or was he simply playacting?

'I worry about you,' Zoe said. 'What if *you* get attacked?'

'You needn't worry. I can handle myself.' Vernon had been thinking the same thing about her. He was glad she quit the Jackboots.

'How can you be so sure?' She grasped his hands. 'Promise me you'll be careful.'

'I promise,' he said and kissed her.

She blew her nose with the handkerchief, then dried her hair with the towel and glanced round the room, at the sparse, thrift-shop furnishings: the mattress on the floor, the shadeless lamp, the rickety table and chairs. She had seen the outside of the university housing a few times before but never the inside.

Vernon read the shock on her face at his modest accommodations. 'I spend what little money I have on the important things. Like you, for instance.'

'I told you not to spoil me.'

'You're worth every penny.'

There was a silence between them. The only sound came from

the rain pulsating against the windowpane.

'Perhaps you should stay the night,' he suggested.

She considered this for a moment. Then, 'I'd like that.'

He switched off the lights and took her by the hand and guided her to the mattress. They kissed and fumbled at each other's clothes in the dark. Her hair was still damp and redolent of rain. When they were finally in a state of nature, he could hardly contain himself. He had wanted to touch her for so long. He kissed her breasts and the soft part of her stomach round her navel. He moved lower, but before he could kiss her there, she stopped him and pulled him up toward her. Then she rolled him onto his back and got on top. He had never done it like this before and found it titillating. They made love, hurriedly and a little awkwardly, to the syncopated rhythm of the rain.

Afterward, they both craved a cigarette but were too lazy to get up. They lay back contentedly, holding hands, and stared at the ceiling as if it were a starry sky.

'A penny for your thoughts,' she said.

He was thinking of how, despite her avowed acceptance of his origins, she might react differently if she were to see Ceylon firsthand. It might prove too foreign for her. The food, the climate, the languages, the people — she would not be the first Westerner to experience culture shock in the East. But the culture of Ceylon was an integral part of who he was. If she rejected that, she rejected him. He rolled toward her. 'I was thinking of how gorgeous you are,' he said and smothered her face and neck with kisses.

Chapter 6

In Memoriam

Saul's deception about his trip to the German embassy only delayed the inevitable. Eventually the truth came out. A year or so after Ernst's arrest, word reached Mr and Mrs Rosenblum in Detmold that their son had been interned at Dachau. They made an official request to see him but were denied. Ernst was a traitor to the state, they were told, and was scheduled to be executed along with several other political prisoners.

The parents notified Esther to that effect. She and Saul were having afternoon tea in the drawing room when Sidney delivered the telegram on a silver tray.

'Oh, how nice,' Esther said, not for a moment suspecting the news of Ernst. It was one of her good days. Cheerfully she took the telegram from the tray. As she read, she turned pale.

'You should go,' Saul urged Sidney.

'Yes, sir.' Sidney quietly closed the door behind him.

'What is it, my dear?' Saul asked.

Without speaking, she handed him the telegram.

He read it. 'Good God.' His worst fears had been realised. It was the kind of stressful event he worked tirelessly to protect her from. He scrutinised her face to see how she was taking the news. She was still pale but otherwise seemed fine. 'Can I get you anything?' he asked. 'Some Aspirin perhaps?'

'No, no.' She looked exhausted all of sudden. She lay back on the chesterfield.

Saul adjusted the pillows and cushions to make her more comfortable. 'That's right, have a good rest. I'll be here if you need me.'

'Yes, a rest,' she repeated distantly. She closed her eyes and drifted off to sleep.

A few minutes later, she sat up abruptly, a maniacal look on her face. 'Do you think Sir Addington could intervene again on Ernst's behalf? You said he has influence with that minister at the German embassy.'

Saul blenched. He had been dreading this moment, when he would have to tell her the truth about the conversation he had with Hans Otto. As well as he could, he sugar-coated the details.

She listened impassively, and even after he had finished, she did not respond. He worried about her the rest of the day.

Later that evening, she complained of a migraine and retired to bed early. Her doctor was called in, but he could find nothing wrong with her. He prescribed a sleeping draught and advised rest.

She did not sleep, however. In the middle of the night, she rushed into Saul's room, hysterical.

'What the devil?' Saul said, scrabbling for the switch on the bedside lamp.

'There's something on my neck!' she cried, hovering above him like an apparition. She would not stop swaying.

'Keep still,' he said, and grabbed hold of her. He squinted in the lamplight, and, lo and behold, there was a faint indentation on her neck. He touched it. 'Does it hurt?'

'It's like fire.'

He got up and helped her onto the bed. 'Wait here.' He left the room and came back with an Aspirin tablet and a glass of water.

She took the medicine and instantly relaxed. 'I love you,' she said. 'You know how much I love you, don't you?'

'Of course I know. I love you too.' He gently positioned her onto her back and tucked her under the duvet. 'You'll stay with me the rest of the night,' he said.

Only later, with perfect hindsight, did he understand the significance of her question.

//

Mrs Grant was the one to discover the body, hanging limply from the attic ceiling, a stool tipped over beneath it.

Downstairs, Sidney and Saul heard a scream and ran up to the attic.

They found Mrs Grant lying in a heap on the floor, wailing. 'I did try to get her down,' she said between sobs. 'I did try.'

Together the two men unloosed Esther's lifeless body from the rope. Saul was shaking so uncontrollably, the operation took longer than it should have. At last they got her down and placed her onto the floor. Saul squatted next to her and examined her body. She was not breathing. On her neck were bruises and abrasions; on her face, a network of purplish red, spiderweb-like streaks. He felt for a pulse but could not find one. Instead of panicking, he became almost catatonic. Over and over he held her wrist in his hand and released it, held her wrist in his hand and released it.

'Mr Maccabee,' Sidney said, touching Saul's arm.

There was a protracted silence.

Eventually Sidney said, with an anguished look on his face, 'Mr Maccabee, she's gone.'

Saul did not hear. Once more he picked up Esther's wrist and held it.

Sidney left him alone with Esther and went to Mrs Grant and lifted her from the floor. Then he led her downstairs to the kitchen, where he settled her into a chair with a snifter of brandy before telephoning the operator and asking for Whitehall 1212.

When the police arrived fifteen minutes later, Saul was still in the attic next to Esther, on his knees rocking back and forth, her wrist in his hand. 'My *belle juive*,' he was saying. 'My *belle juive*.'

II

Nothing he did, no amount of absinthe or sleep, exorcised that moment from his mind. He could not get over why she took her own life. The implication was that she valued death more than she valued him. Otherwise, why had she been willing to leave him this side the grave?

And then there were the suddenness and finality of the act. One moment she was there; the next … She had told him she loved him, but that was no proper goodbye. She did not even leave a note. Her paintings, her clothing, the furniture and bric-a-brac in the house, the flowers in the garden—those were the only traces left of her now. He remembered how Georgina once defended, in the heyday of her time with the Fabian Society, people's right to suicide. A 'voluntary withdrawal from life', she had called it. But what about the loved ones who were left behind? What rights did they have?

Not since his father's death, when Saul was only eleven, had he felt so abandoned. His father had been a successful barrister, despite prejudice against Jews, and his untimely death in his forties left his family—his wife, Saul, and three younger children—utterly destitute. Saul, not yet old enough to shave and two years before his bar mitzvah, suddenly became the man of the house. He developed a carapace as a result, to hide his Jewishness and his intellectualism as well as his grief. At every stage in his adulthood—after he went up to Cambridge, after he became wealthy, after he lost Esther—he added yet another layer to the carapace, to the point that it became as thick as armour. But still, Esther's suicide was more than even he could bear. The constant thought of it eroded his carapace from the inside out.

Visiting her grave was one of the few things, besides listening to music, that brought him solace. He had chosen a simple headstone and plot at Highgate Cemetery. It was near an immense oak tree, surrounded by ferns and a thicket of briars. Soon after her burial, the headstone was covered in ivy and moss. The sight of it all—and the damp, earthy smells — soothed his nerves. He liked to walk among the overgrown plots and read the inscriptions on crosses, obelisks, tombs, urns, until he got to Esther's headstone, where he would place flowers from his garden and read aloud the inscription. *Esther Maccabee, An accomplished artist and a loving wife, 1893 - 1936.* It was as though, during his time at the cemetery, he were communing with the dead.

//

Esther's memory was now the only thing preventing Saul from writing for *The Masses*. He had got it into his head, in the month or so since Georgina and Vernon paid him a visit, that taking up the pen again would be a betrayal of Esther, the work a sign that he had stopped mourning. Georgina, however, was unsympathetic to the reason for his demurral.

'Rubbish,' she said to him when he turned up unannounced one afternoon at the magazine's offices. She sat at her desk proofing an article.

He stood to one side of her, examining a framed photograph of Leon Trotsky on the wall. 'I know it's irrational, but —'

'Balls, balls, balls,' she interrupted and set down her pencil and looked at him with exasperation. 'Now you listen to me. The torture you've put yourself through during the past seven months is more than irrational. It's masochistic — the behaviour of a flagellant, not a mourner.' She glanced at Trotsky's grizzled and bespectacled image. 'He and I don't see eye to eye on everything — his doctrine of the "permanent revolution" is a bit extreme — but we do agree that clinging to the past is unhealthy. There comes a time when we must accept change in our lives and move on. If we don't, we become reactionary and retrograde.'

'What I was about to say is, I feel as though I need Esther's blessing. It was political activism, after all, that got Ernst killed.'

Georgina sighed. 'No one's asking you to organise a march or support a parliamentary candidate. All I'm asking is that you write the occasional article. … Oh, I almost forgot. There's something I'd like to show you.' She opened a desk drawer and pulled out a stack of grainy, black-and-white photographs. 'Do you remember that VPK camera I used to carry round way back when? I found these the other day. They're of you in the East End. In 1915, I should think.' She handed him the photographs.

He thumbed through them. They were all rather unexceptional, save one. In it, he was on the deck of the Tower Bridge. He had on a coat and a tie and a boater hat from his Cambridge days. Next to him on the walkway a screever was chalking what appeared to be a caricature of Prime Minister Asquith. A moment of placidity, Saul thought, in an otherwise turbulent time. Long-forgotten memories of the war years suddenly flashed through his mind.

'You were such an earnest young man,' Georgina said. 'Whatever happened?'

'I put away childish things.' With an air of melancholy, Saul returned the photographs to the drawer. 'Life has a way of delivering you googlies. Sometimes not even pads can protect you. And if you get hit hard enough or often enough, you start to crack.'

'Aren't we all just a little bit broken?' She gave him a warm-hearted smile. 'Don't give up on life, Saul. You have too much to offer. You also have friends who care about you and who want to see you return to your old self. Think of your writing, should you choose to do it, as honouring Esther's memory, not betraying it.'

Saul sat down in the chair opposite Georgina. He was ready to make official his commitment to the magazine. 'Suppose I do decide to work for you. Would you allow me to write on any subject I choose?'

'As long as it's connected to social justice, you may write on any subject you choose, yes.'

'Then I'll begin this evening.' Ideas for his first article were already swirling round in his head. A few days before, stories about Jesse Owens's spectacular feats at the Berlin Olympics had started coming out. To Saul, Owens was proof that the Aryan race was not superior to Negroes or anyone else, proof that Hitler's *Mein Kampf* was the twaddle of a small, uneducated mind. If Owens could outrun the best of the Aryans, then the Nazi definitions of the 'weak' and the 'strong' were patently false.

And writing about Owens would be only the beginning. What Saul really wanted to write about were the contributions American Negroes and Jews had made to jazz, the most original and iconoclastic music in the history of music. Nothing a Nazi had invented could hold a candle to jazz. Jazz was free, improvisational, soulful—an art form to which Negroes and Creoles and Jews, the so-called 'weak' of society, had contributed disproportionately. Why was that? Saul could scarcely name all the relevant musicians, there were so many of them. Louis Armstrong. Duke Ellington. Billie Holiday. Benny Goodman. Teddy Wilson. George Gershwin. Bessie Smith. Count Basie. Sidney Bechet. Buddy Bolden. Buddy Rich. Eddie Cantor. Artie Shaw. Lionel Hampton. Fletcher Henderson. Earl Hines. Tommy Ladnier. Jelly Roll Morton. Joe Oliver. Kid Ory. Charlie Parker. Fats Waller. The names rolled off the tongue like the swinging syncopations of a jazz song.

//

'Welcome back to the world of the living,' Vernon said as he and Saul took their seats at the Corner House. They were there to celebrate the completion of Saul's first article for *The Masses*. The article was especially meaningful for Saul because he had dedicated it to Esther.

'I missed our tête-à-têtes,' Saul replied. 'And coming here.' He looked over at the orchestra. They were playing Shostakovich's 'Tahiti Trot'.

A waitress came by, holding a pad and a pencil, with a linen draped over her arm. 'What can I get you two gentlemen?'

'Tea for two,' Saul said, smiling at his own witticism. But the remark failed to elicit a response from either Vernon or the waitress. Apparently neither of them was aware that 'Tahiti Trot' was an orchestration of the Broadway song 'Tea for Two'.

'Tea it is,' the waitress said and nipped away.

'Tahiti Trot' came to an end, and the orchestra started up Gershwin's 'I Got Rhythm'.

Vernon lit a cigarette. 'Georgina tells me your article for *The Masses* is a *tour de force*.'

'I wouldn't go that far,' Saul said. 'But she did accept it without changing a word, so she must have been pleased.'

'When's it coming out?'

'October, I think.'

'I look forward to reading it.'

Saul waved a hand dismissively. 'Enough about me. Let's talk about you. We have so much to catch up on. How are things with your thesis, with your lady friend, with the Crown colony of Ceylon?'

'We'll be here for hours if I tell you all of that.'

'So be it.'

'All right,' Vernon said with a smile, delighted to be the centre of attention. He gave a brief overview of his thesis. Generally the research was going well. He had got halfway through the section on plantation labour and was on schedule to finish the whole thing by the end of Lent term.

'As soon as that?' was all Saul could think to say, the words more a statement than a question. His descent into depression seemed to have caused him to lose all sense of time. He knew the day would come when Vernon would finish his studies and return to Ceylon, but it did not seem possible that that day was already less than a year away.

'It's hard to believe, I know,' Vernon said. 'It caught me by surprise, too.' He tapped the ash from his cigarette into an ashtray. 'As for Zoe, she's working a fifty-hour week at London Hospital now, so I only see her on her days off. I wish I could see more of her, but what to do? I can't ask her to sacrifice her future for my sake.'

The waitress returned and poured them each a cup of tea.

Saul waited until she had left, then asked, 'Do your parents know about Zoe?'

Vernon shook his head as he took a long drag of his cigarette. 'I'm afraid to tell them—well, Amma anyway. I don't think Pater would mind. But Amma? She wants me to marry a nice Sinhalese or Burgher girl. Yesterday I received a letter from Minnette saying Amma's trying to arrange a marriage for me. To some girl I don't even know.'

'Remind me. Minnette's your sister, the poetess?'

'Yes. This past May she graduated from a women's college at the University of Delhi, where I got my undergraduate degree. She's back home in Kandy now, and Amma's driving her mad. She says she can't wait for me to return, if only to distract attention away from her.'

'Your mother sounds exacting.'

'It's not that I don't love her dearly, but this is 1936, and the days of arranged marriages are a thing of the past, or at least they should be. She should know that. She married for love herself.'

'As did I,' Saul said. He lifted his cup to his lips and held it there for a moment, staring wistfully into space. Vernon's remark had reminded him of his introduction to Esther's parents on a trip to Detmold shortly after his wedding engagement, of how he had been treated coldly at first because he was a 'foreigner'.

'I hope I didn't say something to offend you,' Vernon said.

Saul emerged from his reverie. 'On the contrary. Talking to you is restorative.' That was why he enjoyed Vernon's company so much, he thought. He could speak openly when they were together, and let his carapace slough away. He adjusted his spectacles. 'Tell me how the rest of Ceylon is doing. The last we spoke about it, you said the country was reeling from economic depression. You also spoke of drought and flooding and a malaria epidemic, if memory serves.'

Vernon stubbed out his cigarette. 'All that has improved—but only just. It's the reason I have to go back. My people need me. In the last year, the independence movement has gained steam. Even a socialist party—the Lanka Sama Samaja, or Equality, Party—has formed. Minnette is thinking of joining them. And here I am, over eight thousand kilometres from home, doing nothing.' He had yet to tell Saul of his political activities in London.

'Do you think independence would solve Ceylon's problems?'

'I don't know. Things aren't as black and white as people suggest. The British talk of the white man's burden, and as distasteful as that sounds, there's some truth in it. Ceylon wouldn't be where it is today if the British hadn't invested in transportation, education, sanitation, and the like. There's also no denying that *Pax Britannica* brought peace and social stability to Ceylon, which prior to 1815 had been mired in war for three centuries. But many of those who want independence deride the British Empire because they say it's based on exploitation, not on free commerce and other liberal ideals. They see the malnourished in Ceylonese villages — crammed into tiny huts, dying like flies — and it makes their blood boil. It makes *my* blood boil. People see this injustice and they want change. They want accountability. And they want someone or something to blame — someone or something other than themselves and chance, that is. For that, for a scapegoat, the British and imperialism fill the bill nicely.'

As he listened to Vernon's impassioned words, Saul felt like he was back with the Fabians, in a coffeehouse discussing the evils of the East End. 'Political and social conflict are the same the world over, it would appear.' A similar debate between the Left and the Right, he added, had been raging at Westminster for decades. In England the culprits simply went by different names: foreigners and capitalism. And Ceylon's villagers had much in common with London's East Enders. Both populations lived hand to mouth, in appalling and perfectly damnable conditions, malnutrition pinching their faces and rotting their teeth. It *was* something that made one's blood boil, and it *was* something that ought to be changed. From England to Ceylon, the poor were being squeezed at both ends: given slave-wages and charged extortionate rents. That was one constant across space and time. *The rich got richer and the poor got children*, as the saying went.

Chapter 7

The Cockroach

During his most recent conversation with Saul at the Corner House, Vernon left out one important detail about Minnette's letter. It concerned the rising tide of nationalism in Ceylon and the accompanying discrimination against Burghers, Europeans, and mixed-race couples like his parents. An incident had occurred, in which his parents were refused service by a local merchant in Kandy. The news deeply distressed Vernon, but he kept it to himself at the Corner House because he did not want to be seen to complain.

After returning to his room later that morning, he drank a shot of Scotch and then lay down on the mattress and reread Minnette's letter.

Dear Vernon,
I hope this letter finds you well. Ammi and Thathi and I are fine —
that is, as fine as can be expected under the circumstances. Did
you receive my last letter? I only ask because letters have been
known to get lost in the international post. And when you didn't
respond, I was concerned you hadn't received it. We really ought
to do better about keeping in touch. Please don't take that as a
recrimination. It is only a wish. You know as well as I do that we
drifted apart after you left for university, and it is my fault as

much as yours.

So much is happening here, I scarcely know where to begin! You probably have heard about the LSSP. I am on the fence about joining. I have read their manifesto and find it all rather intriguing, but I am not keen to get involved in politics at the moment. Dr de Silva, the Party president, visited Thathi the other day. The LSSP are looking for whites to speak at rallies, and Thathi has agreed to do it. When Dr de Silva learned that I was back from university, he asked me to work for him at the LSSP headquarters in Colombo. It was rather unexpected. I told him I would have to think about it. What do you think? Should I do it? Could you see me as a Ceylonese Mahatma Gandhi, fighting for our own purna swaraj?

I would just as soon not have to tell you this, but things are getting worse in Ceylon. Ammi and Thathi and I went to Mr Arunasalem's last week and the old codger refused to sell us produce. He said our kind were not welcome there. Thathi was livid. What kind were those, he wanted to know? Fisticuffs nearly broke out. If Ammi and I hadn't been there, Thathi might have split Mr Arunasalem in two. You know how he gets when he is cross. Needless to say, we won't be going to Mr Arunasalem's anymore. It makes me sad. You and I have known Mr Arunasalem all our lives.

On a lighter note, Ammi is up to her old tricks. Do you remember Ramona Bolling? She was in the same form as me. Ammi has told her you are coming home in May and has invited her to dinner all these months in advance. Don't be cross with me, but I am so very glad Ammi's focus has been transferred to you for a change. She has been inviting boys to the house ever since I came back from Delhi, and I am sick to death of it. They are all halfwits, every last one of them. I impatiently await your return.

Love,
Minnette

PS Enclosed is my latest poem. It recently appeared in Dekho, an Indian magazine. And wouldn't you know it, the magazine has since ceased publication. So yet again I am in search of an outlet for my work.

Vernon got up and went to the kitchenette and had another shot of

Scotch. Every time he read the part in Minnette's letter about the greengrocer, he became enraged. Thathi *should have* split the old codger in two. He would have been within his rights. No wonder he was willing to speak at LSSP rallies. For years he had shied away from politics. *Render unto Caesar the things which are Caesar's*, he used to say. But people like Mr Arunasalem had driven Thathi to take a stand. Vernon wondered what was happening to Ceylon. There had always been racial prejudice, but never was it this overt in recent memory and never against Europeans. He had to get back home, to do something to stem the tide. Perhaps he would even join the LSSP himself.

Minnette was right to say they had drifted apart. He *had* received her previous letter but for weeks put off writing back. There was always something or other that took precedence: his thesis, Zoe, Saul, the work for the District Secretariat. He had got so absorbed in finding his way in London and in life generally that he forgot the importance of family. He would have to rectify that once he got home. In a small way, he could start now, by writing to Minnette.

He got out a fountain pen and some stationery and sat down at the table. He wrote:

Dear Minnette,
I must apologise. I did receive your letter from a month ago, and
my only excuse for not responding is that I've been busy. Will you
forgive me? It's true we've drifted apart, and I would like very
much for that to change. Perhaps it will be some comfort for you to
know that I think of you and Ammi and Thathi often. I have
friends here, but it's not the same as being round all of you and at
home, in the country I love.
I'm saddened, like you, about what happened with Mr
Arunasalem. I wish Thathi had given him a thrashing. It would
have served him right. The nationalistic fervour is bringing out
the worst in people. This race hatred smacks of fascism. That's
why, if you're going to support any political party at all, it should
be the socialists. They don't care about the colour of your skin or
the nationality of your ancestors. We are all human, they argue,

and as humans, we share a common purpose.

I am of course in favour of your joining the LSSP, but you must decide that for yourself. And yes, I could see you as a Ceylonese Gandhi. I know you're a pacifist at heart and disapprove of violence.

Congratulations on your poem. I read it with pleasure. It's brilliant, Minnette. The imagery. The sensuousness. I could almost smell the cinnamon and nutmeg you describe. My first thought was of love cake, and it made me nostalgic for home. Where does it come from, I wonder, your aesthetic sense? Certainly not from Ammi and Thathi.

Vernon turned over the piece of paper and continued writing.

I have a suggestion. You mayn't like it, but I'll offer it up anyway. I know the editor-in-chief of a magazine here in London called The Masses. It's a socialist magazine, but each issue includes a selection of poetry on issues concerning social justice. Would you be interested in contributing to it? Perhaps you could write a poem about what it means to be Burgher in a British colony. I would be happy to put in a good word for you with the editor. Just a thought.

Oh, one last thing. You'll be pleased to hear I have a new sweetheart. Her name is Zoe Tilston, an English girl. I know you would like her. She's a year older than you and is a nurse and is incredibly modern. We've been seeing each other for close on two months now, and things are getting serious. You can't tell Ammi and Thathi, though. I would never hear the end of it. I'm enclosing a separate, sanitised letter for them. Please see that they get it. And mum's the word about Zoe.

Your Loving Brother,
Vernon

He wrote the letter to his parents and then prepared an envelope and went out to the blue pillar box on Drury Lane. The postman would have come already, but it made Vernon feel better to drop the envelope into the box, as if relations with Minnette would be re-established that much sooner. Before returning to his room, he stood there on the street for a moment looking toward India House on Aldwych, the same direction the airmail would go if it were to travel as the crow flies. It was marvellous to think that the post would reach the Indian subcontinent, a quarter of the globe away, in only a week.

//

On one of her days off, Zoe came over to Vernon's for the evening. They had grown tired of going out and so planned to stay in and cook together. For the meal, Vernon decided to make cheese curry, something he used to eat regularly at university in Delhi because it tasted so good and because it was so easy to prepare. Earlier in the day, he had gone to the Indian restaurant on Regent Street to ask where he could find *paneer* and chickpeas and various spices. It turned out that much of what he needed was unavailable and that he would have to improvise. He spent the next three hours peregrinating all over Soho in search of ingredients. At a Greek delicatessen, he bought chickpeas and strained yoghurt and *halloumi*, a Cypriot cheese that could substitute for *paneer*. From a street stall, he bought a Jewish flatbread called *malawach* to use in place of *naan* or *paratha*. The balance of the ingredients he bought at Sainsbury's.

He got home from shopping shortly before Zoe arrived and arranged the groceries on the table. It was quite the collection of foodstuffs, representing multiple ethnicities and coming from several parts of the world. Zoe, he thought, would be enchanted. She had raved for days about the food at the Indian restaurant.

'It smells scrummy in here,' she said when she came into the room.

'Wait till the cooking starts.' He went to the window and opened it. 'That's for the neighbours. To keep the building from smelling like an Indian market.'

She took off her bolero jacket and draped it over a chair. 'Look at all this,' she said, inspecting the items on the table.

'I hope you appreciate the trouble I went to.'

She sidled up to him with a coy smile. 'How would you like me to show my appreciation?'

He burst into laughter. 'A kiss will do.'

'You're too easy,' she said and pecked him on the cheek.

As she pulled away, he noticed her fingertips. 'What's this?' he asked.

'A surprise for you.' She gave him her hand to examine. In preparation for the evening, she had given herself a half-moon manicure and painted her nails black. She was always accessorising in interesting ways. 'Do you like it?'

'I do. Perhaps you shouldn't cook. You might ruin your nails.' He let go of her hand.

'Don't be silly,' she said as she rolled up her sleeves. 'Now, what can I do?'

'You can slice the cheese into cubes. About a half-inch square should do it.'

'All right.'

Knives and cutting boards were already on the counter. She cut the *halloumi* while he diced an onion and some garlic cloves. Then she chopped the coriander leaves and fenugreek, and he sautéed the onion and garlic in a pot on the hob. She watched as he stirred in dried chillies and the chopped herbs and the rest of the curry base: black pepper, cumin, flour, paprika, salt, and turmeric. Finally he added the chickpeas and water and turned the heat to low.

'How heavenly,' she said, breathing in the smells. 'What's next?'

'While this simmers, we fry the cheese.' He transferred the cheese to a pan and fried it, turning the cubes over occasionally. The fried cheese along with sugar and yoghurt were the last items to go into the pot, which he removed from the hob. 'All we need to do now is heat up the bread.' He warmed up four pieces of *malawach* inside the cooker and then dished out two platefuls of curry.

They took their plates to the table and sat down.

Zoe glanced quizzically from the table to Vernon. 'We forgot the cutlery,' she said.

'No, we didn't. We eat with our fingers in Ceylon. Here, I'll show you.' He tore off a segment of bread, used it to scoop up some of the curry, and put the ball of food into his mouth.

With an uncertain look, she followed his lead. No sooner had she done so than her eyes lit up. He had been worried that the amount of chilli in the curry might shock her English palate, but now she leaned across the table and said, 'Will you cook for me *every* night?'

'I gather you like it, then?'

She arched her eyebrows as if his question were absurd and then resumed eating.

After dinner, he made a couple of black and tans and they drank and smoked and talked well into the night. Neither of them wanted their time together to end. But she had a six o'clock shift at hospital the next morning and needed a good night's sleep.

She was reluctantly gathering up her jacket to go when a noise came from outside. They both glanced toward the window, which was still open. It was a moonlit night. Somewhere out on Drury Lane an owl was calling shrilly, making a kew-wick sound. Zoe listened to the owl with an abstracted air. Eventually she set her jacket back down and looked at Vernon and asked, 'Do you *have* to return to Ceylon?'

The question caught him off guard. He hardly knew what to say. It had never occurred to him to stay in London after graduation. The truth was, he viewed his time at LSE as a stepping-stone to entering politics back home. Life in the West, and a woman, played no part in that calculus. And yet his involvement with Zoe was more than just a passing love affair. He thought enough of her to mention her to Minnette, did he not? 'You could come away with me,' he said before he knew what he was saying.

'Oh, I couldn't possibly. What would I do there?'

'You could be a nurse like you are here.'

Her face brightened for a moment, then darkened again. 'I wouldn't fit in.'

'Why not? There are plenty of Europeans who have acculturated to Ceylon. My pater—' He stopped. He could see from her expression it was no use.

'Will you write to me?' she asked quietly.

His heart went out to her then. 'Things aren't as desperate as all that, are they? Of course I'll write to you. In the meantime, we have months to enjoy each other's company.' He had the urge to unburden himself. There was so much he wanted to tell her, to ease her pain and to cast off the weight of the secrets he had been keeping from her. He got up and took her by the hands. 'There's something else I must tell you. Another confession of sorts.'

She squeezed his hands as he lowered his eyes. 'What is it?'

When he looked up again, he said, 'I'm not actually a fascist. I never was. I've been working for the communists to gather intelligence on the Jackboots.'

She regarded him. 'You *are* crackers.'

'I'm not a member of the Communist Party,' he said, as if that were the source of her concern. 'It's just that the communists are the only ones willing to stand up to the fascists.'

'Even if you're not a communist, you're an antifascist mingling with fascists in their own lair. Do you want to get yourself killed?'

'I won't get killed.'

'What else haven't you told me?' she said, withdrawing her hands.

He took a deep breath—relieved to finally be through with the lies—and told her everything.

//

His real name was Vernon Prins, and Johannes Prins, his pater, was Dutch, not English. When Vernon joined the Jackboots, he adopted the anglicised surname Price in order to disguise his ancestry. The name was a play on words, based on the maxim *Eternal vigilance is the price of liberty*. Everything else he had said about himself was more or less true, even the part about his pater's having served in the Great War, except that his pater had not been a Royal Marine but rather had fought alongside Indians and Anzacs at Gallipoli.

Vernon had paternal ancestors in Ceylon going back to the period of Dutch colonisation during the late eighteenth century. A great-great-great uncle had acquired land in the hill country near Kandy town and cultivated coffee. What started as a smallholding slowly grew into a sizable plantation. The Dutch colonial administration ceded power to the British in 1796 and still the hard-working Prins thrived in Ceylon. For over a century the plantation was passed down from generation to generation. Even the coffee blight of the 1870s did not deter them. They replaced the coffee with tea and developed new markets for their product. The decline of the Ceylon Prins was not due to laziness or the caprices of fate but rather to a blind devotion to racial purity. Each subsequent generation found it progressively difficult to entice marriageable women from the Netherlands. When Luuk Prins, the last of the male heirs, died in the Nineties, he had no wife and no direct descendants, and so the entirety of his estate went to Johannes.

At the time, Johannes was a twenty-year-old living in Amsterdam. The moment he learned of his inheritance, he jumped at the chance for adventure. He had been raised hearing romantic tales about the Ceylon Prins and had read stories and poems about the British Raj. On globes and on world maps he had gazed with wonder at the equatorial island of Ceylon, dangling tantalizingly like a teardrop from the tip of India.

The events of Johannes's transition to life in Ceylon became part of the Prins family lore. Within a fortnight of receiving the news of his inheritance, he packed his meagre possessions and set sail on the *SS Uitheems*. It took him over a month to reach Ceylon, and he was in awe of the place when he got there. Disembarking from the launch in Colombo harbour — amid the windy sea air and humid heat — was like stepping onto another planet. He passed through customs to the crowded, alien streets of Colombo Fort. The architecture of the buildings and the dress of the Europeans were familiar to him, but everything else was utterly strange. The only vehicles to be seen were bullock carts and hackeries, rickshaws, and the occasional horse-drawn carriage. Enormous rain trees lined the streets. Swarms of crows scavenged rubbish here and there, cawing obnoxiously. People of many races co-mingled and went in and out of the shops. Before going to the Fort Railway Station, Johannes tarried awhile on the streets with his single piece of luggage, looking at the wares on display in shop windows and trying not to stare at the brown-skinned Ceylonese women and men: the women in brightly coloured saris; the men in long white skirt-like costumes, their hair in buns like Victorian ladies, held up by half-moon-shaped tortoiseshell combs.

At the railway station later that night, a young Ceylonese porter took Johannes's trunk, hoisted it onto his shoulders, and ran ahead, threading his way through the crowds and sleeping bodies on the platform. Johannes got to his sleeper compartment to find his trunk already stowed. He gave the porter a tip and immediately lay down on the berth. It was a night-mail train. He was so exhausted from his travels, he slept the entire five-hour journey. He awoke shortly before the train pulled into Kandy Station. The sun had not yet risen, and all he could see through the compartment window were the dark shapes of trees and shrubs as the train wended its way through virgin jungle.

His uncle Luuk's *periya durai*, or plantation superintendent, was waiting for him at the station. He was a middle-aged Tamil man and went by the name of Mr Dawson. They greeted each other tentatively. Mr Dawson had not expected Johannes to be so young and sturdy: six foot six and weighing sixteen stone. For his part, Johannes was still in a state of culture shock. Mr Dawson salaamed and called Johannes *mahattaya*, or gentleman. Johannes said 'Hello, it is nice to meet you' in Dutch and warmly and rather forcefully shook Mr Dawson's hand. There was an awkward moment of incomprehension before Mr Dawson relieved Johannes of his trunk and led him to the carriage.

They set out for the plantation on a rutted cart-track. The sun was just beginning to rise. Johannes took in his surroundings like an explorer discovering a new world. Kandy town itself was like an

English hamlet transplanted in the middle of a jungle. He had so many questions he wanted to ask, but it became evident that the only way he and Mr Dawson were going to be able to communicate was through broken English.

After bumping along the dirt road for more than an hour, they rounded a bend, and suddenly the jungle opened to verdant, terraced hills blanketed in miles and miles of tea shrubs. For Johannes it was like something out of a dream. A light rain was falling, and the hilltops were enshrouded in mist. In the distance the Knuckles Mountain Range rose up toward the heavens. Mr Dawson struggled to explain to Johannes in English that the peaks had been so named by the British because they resembled the knuckles of a clenched fist.

They came to a signpost that read Eden Estate. Mr Dawson drew up the carriage in front of a factory building, where eighty-odd servants and plantation-hands stood on the muster ground in the mizzling rain. The two men got down from the carriage, and Mr Dawson directed Johannes to take his place before the labourers. The head overseer of the plantation stepped forward first and introduced himself. Then one by one the labourers stepped forward, genuflected, and worshipped at Johannes's feet, as if he were a god. He was so embarrassed that by the fifth labourer, he begged Mr Dawson to stop them. Once the labourers were back in formation, Johannes gave an awkward speech in English, which Mr Dawson translated into both Sinhala and Tamil. There would be no more grovelling, Johannes said, while he was the owner of Eden Estate. The only subservience would be his, to the labourers and the plantation. And it was not right that they had been made to stand in the rain. He reiterated his commitment to the plantation before dismissing everyone.

In the weeks and months to come, he kept his word. For the next ten years, in fact, he dedicated every waking hour to improving the plantation and the lives of the labourers. He introduced artificial fertilisers, mulch, and compost and planted nitrogen-fixing grasses and trees between the tea rows. Yields increased to a thousand pounds made tea per acre. With the profits, he built a community school and a dispensary, and each labourer received a small house on plantation land. Eden Estate became a village unto itself.

During all this time Johannes had no eyes for women, or at least that was the official line. Privately, he admitted — to Vernon, on his sixteenth birthday — that he had frequented prostitutes in Kandy town for years until he met Amma. The fateful meeting occurred in 1906. Late one afternoon, Johannes was driving to town for supplies when an axle on his carriage broke. He pulled off to the side of the road and got down to have a look. The damage was severe enough that it would require the services of a blacksmith. He unhitched the horse and led it by the reins through a stand of sal trees toward Kandy Lake, a shortcut that would halve his time to the blacksmith's.

He saw her as he was watering his horse along the shoreline of the lake. She was bathing alone, in a *diya redda*, or water cloth, wrapped tightly round her body. She looked like a goddess. Her long black hair was wet and slicked back, glistening in the afternoon light. Languorously she tilted her head to one side and wrung the water from her hair. Johannes remained motionless, watching her. A gulp of Indian cormorants — seemingly watching her, too, with their piercing blue eyes — stood perched on a half-submerged tree branch in the lake. Nothing existed for Johannes in that moment except the girl and the cormorants and the shimmery green water.

After he had finally moved on, he could not stop thinking about her. He asked after her at the blacksmith's, giving a brief description, and immediately the blacksmith knew who she was: the eighteen-year-old daughter of a local rest-house owner. Her beauty preceded her, the blacksmith said. Her name was Kamala Thalwatta. She was Sinhalese and unmarried. The blacksmith gave a knowing wink and suggested that Johannes stay the night at the rest-house until the work on his carriage was done.

Johannes remonstrated, but in the end, he followed the suggestion. That night at the rest-house, however, he was sorely disappointed, as there was no sign of Kamala. The next morning, he returned to the blacksmith's, not expecting to see her again. But the blacksmith had yet to finish the work on the carriage, and so Johannes had to stay another night at the rest-house. This time she was there, helping serve food in the dining area for the evening meal. Johannes waited until he had her alone at his table before speaking to her. He told her in Sinhala how he had come upon her while watering his horse at the lake, how he could not stop thinking about her. He thought she would bristle at his words. Instead, she lowered her eyes and smiled. She seemed pleased by what he said. He was encouraged and asked if he could see her again. Perhaps they could go for a carriage ride? She said she would like that but would have to get permission from her parents first.

Initially Mr and Mrs Thalwatta objected to Johannes's advances because he was a *suddha*, a white man. But then they discovered he was a wealthy tea planter and had a change of heart. The courtship lasted a year. Johannes and Kamala were married in July 1907, in a private ceremony on Eden Estate. Vernon was born five years later and Minnette three years after that.

So Vernon and Minnette were what the locals referred to as Dutch Burghers, people of Dutch and Ceylonese descent. Despite their mixed parentage, they had magical childhoods on the plantation. They were treated like royalty by the servants and by their maternal grandparents whenever they visited. Once he was old enough, Vernon attended boarding school at Trinity College, Kandy. Whites and other Burghers were there, as well as Muslims and Sinhalese and Tamils from affluent families. To the extent that racial prejudice existed, it was subtle or hidden entirely from public view. Overt racial slurs in the island—such as the one about Eurasians having 'a lick of the tar brush'—were generally confined to colonial administrative outposts and to expatriate circles in distant Colombo.

But attitudes toward Vernon and his family changed during the Twenties. The cataclysm of world war left Great Britain weak, and its influence in the Crown colonies began to wane. Meanwhile

Johannes returned from the Gallipoli peninsula a broken man. Eden Estate suffered in consequence. Economic turmoil and the eventual worldwide depression were the final nails in the coffin of the Prins family prosperity. Their status as upper-class Ceylonese came into question.

In April 1929, with events looming in America that would send the world into a downward spiral, and just months before Vernon left for university in Delhi, he had his first taste of overt racism. He had been seeing a Sinhalese girl on the sly. She was a student at the Girls' High School in Kandy. Whenever they spent time together, Vernon would walk or bicycle her home to a secluded spot a half-mile from her house, where they would part ways to avoid being seen by her parents or the neighbours. One weekend, after spending the morning together at the Royal Botanic Gardens, Vernon took her home on his bicycle as usual. But when they reached the drop-off spot, the father was there waiting for them. He had a scowl on his face and was slapping a cricket bat against the palm of his hand.

'Go home!' the father shouted at his daughter in Sinhala.

She scrambled off the back of the bicycle and gave Vernon a quick side-glance, with tears welling up in her eyes.

'It'll be all right,' Vernon said. 'Go.' He could hear her sniffling as she ran home.

The father came toward him. 'No daughter of mine is going to associate with a lowly cockroach.'

Everything happened so fast, Vernon did not have time to be scared, so he held his ground. He had never been called a cockroach before, but he understood the word's connotations. Cockroaches were vile creatures, living in filth, and those that dwelled in the dark for long periods of time underwent a moulting process that rendered them an off-white colour. On exposure to sunlight, they got progressively darker, browner. It was similar to what happened to the skin colour of the progeny from interracial marriages. And the Dutch translation for the Sinhala word *kärapottā*, or cockroach, was *kakkerlak*, which also meant half-caste.

The bat was swinging toward his head when he caught it in mid-air and wrested it from the father's hands. He tossed it into a nearby thicket of lantana. The father fell back, stunned. Standing at six feet five inches, Vernon was well over a head taller than the father, and weighing fifteen stone, he also was much heavier. In school he had earned the nickname Nandhimitra, the strongest of King Dutugamunu's legendary giant warriors described in the *Mahāvaṃsa*, a fifth-century epic poem about the history of Ceylon.

'Do your worst,' Vernon said, and raised his fists to the low-guard position.

The father turned tail and ran, cursing as he went.

Vernon never saw him, or the daughter, again.

//

He received a change of orders from Spartacus: to spy on Morley instead of Walsh. Morley was one of the permanent residents at Action House, so it would be relatively easy to search his room. Vernon chose his moment carefully, on a night when he had guard duty and when Morley and the other Jackboots were off-site at a rally.

He arrived early for duty and stopped off at the house.

The guard on the verandah snapped to attention and saluted. 'Hail Leader.'

'Hail Leader,' Vernon said, saluting back. He went to the front door. 'I have to use the loo.' Inside the house, he crossed the bay, pretended to go into the lavatory, and then sneaked upstairs to Morley's room.

The blinds were closed. He could barely see in the dark. He swapped out his gauntlets for the torch in his pocket and switched it on. His heart pounded as he shone the light round the room.

He started his search with the campaign desk. The pigeon holes were crammed with materials: articles from the Jackboot propaganda organ, *Jackboot News*; several Jackboot communiqués, including the one about the Sicarii; the Jackboot manifesto; a leaflet entitled 'Ten Points of Fascism'; a brand new copy of Mussolini's *My Autobiography*; and the May 1934 issue of the German newspaper *Der Stürmer*. The newspaper headline read *Jüdischer Mordplan gegen die nichtjüdische Menschheit aufgedeckt*. Vernon was not fluent in German, but he knew that *jüdisch* meant 'Jewish' and that *nicht* meant 'not', and there were enough similarities between German and Dutch that he could decipher the rest. Roughly the headline translated to: 'Jewish Murder Plan against the Gentile Humanity'. On the bottom of the newspaper's title page, beneath what looked like a caricature of two Jewish men, was the line '*Die Juden sind unser Unglück!' The Jews are our misfortune!*

Vernon saw red as he folded up the newspaper and returned it to the desk. A murder plan? Who would believe such tripe? As if the Jews had nothing better to do. Vernon had seen the Jews in the East End. Some of them could barely put food onto their tables, let alone find time to conspire against gentiles. Such a conspiracy theory was even more outlandish than the one about the Hidden Hand. And yet there had to be people who believed it. *Der Stürmer* would not exist otherwise. The irony was that an *actual* conspiracy was happening in Germany: the Nazis, not the Jews, were the ones with the murder plans. They hated anyone who did not conform to their idea of the master race. That included cripples, lunatics, and the mentally deficient, as well Jews, gipsies, and all others of colour, even half-castes like Vernon. Fascism threatened individuality and cultural pluralism. It threatened Vernon's very identity.

He searched the closet next. Evidence of antisemitism was not enough to link Morley to Walsh, Vernon realised. He had to find something more. There was a shelf above the clothes rack, but it contained only hats and gloves. On the floor was a line of shoes. He got down onto his hands and knees and checked along the insole of each shoe. Still nothing. He was about to move on when he noticed a tin box at the back of the closet. He aimed the torch on the lid, which read 'Cherry Blossom boot polish outfit'. Opening the box, he saw that it contained the usual polishing paraphernalia but also an envelope. *Right*, he thought, and drew out the envelope. Perhaps it was the same one Walsh had given Morley. Inside was a stash of five-pound notes, a hundred pounds' worth at least. Where would Morley have got so much money? He was on the dole so far as Vernon knew.

A loose piece of paper fell out from among the fivers and fluttered to the floor. Vernon picked it up and held it under the torchlight. The only writing was a series of numbers: 021036. Were the numbers a code? The combination to a safe? A date?

He heard a floorboard creak, from the direction of the stairs. His heart missed a beat. Quickly he put everything back in its proper place, switched off the torch and pocketed it, and positioned himself behind the clothes. The footfalls grew nearer and seemed to stop outside Morley's room. Vernon shut his eyes. *This is it*, he thought. His cover was about to be blown. So much for his promise to Zoe. She would be distraught if she knew what he had got himself into. He opened his eyes and steeled himself for a fight. If this was going to be the end of his time with the Jackboots, he wanted to go out with guns blazing.

But then the footfalls resumed and a door down the hallway opened and closed.

Now was his chance. He would be pushing his luck if he stayed any longer. He slipped out from the closet and made for the door. No one was in the hallway. He hurried downstairs, his heart still racing, and used the banisters to lighten his weight on the creaky steps. On the ground floor, he went into the lavatory and closed the door behind him. The light above the washstand was on. He stared at himself in the mirror. His cap was crooked, so he straightened it. The rest of his uniform appeared to be in order. As a diversion he flushed the water closet and ran water in the basin. Then he put his gauntlets back on and went out to the verandah.

The guard was smiling waggishly. He glanced at his wristwatch. 'You must have had some spring cleaning to do.'

'Something like that,' Vernon said and headed for his post.

Chapter 8

Things Happen for a Reason

He had not touched a drop of absinthe for over a fortnight, and he was thinking more clearly now than he had for months. He could thank Vernon and Georgina for that. They had come to his aid when he needed it most and had shown generosity, kindness, loyalty. If he had been a praying man, he would have lifted his eyes toward heaven and said amen.

It was the writing for *The Masses* that did the trick. The process of organising and transcribing his thoughts onto paper — a kind of secular rite — gave him focus and a creative outlet. He started his first article by jotting down ideas into a leather-bound notebook. Then he sat down at the desk in his study and typed. Esther's easel and painting materials and an unfinished landscape were there in the room with him. From time to time he looked up from the typewriter, saw the perspective lines and vanishing point drawn in pencil on Esther's canvas, and had a flash of inspiration — and the words came flowing.

He wanted to be a writer from an early age. Life, however, had had other plans for him. His father's untimely death, and his family's concomitant reversal of fortune, had thrust upon him the responsibilities of adulthood. From then on, he cast aside his aspirations and devoted his energies to the pursuit of wealth. At St

Paul's School, he worked tirelessly to win scholarships, and when he went up to Cambridge, he did the practical thing and read economics instead of literature. After graduation he continued with steely determination to do everything necessary to provide for his mother and his siblings. He despised stockjobbing, but it was a means to an end. His dalliances with the Fabian Society and with journalism were momentary distractions from his ultimate goal. Even marriage did not sidetrack him.

During the mid-Twenties, an opportunity arose, and he seized it. Leading up to the 1924 general election, London's *Daily Mail* printed a letter in which Moscow's Comintern purportedly ordered the Communist Party of Great Britain to engage in seditious activities. The letter, which only later was proved to be fraudulent, created antisocialist sentiment among voters and swayed the election so that the Tories came to power in a landslide victory. Saul suspected what would follow: in their misguided belief in the pre-war glory days, the Tories would re-instate the gold standard at an inflated level. So he bought gold bullion and short sold American dollars against pounds sterling. His speculation turned out to be correct. As Great Britain's economic woes deepened, he grew rich.

But he found himself moving farther and farther away from his origins and even farther away from his aspirations. By 1930, when the rest of the world was in the throes of economic depression, he was able to reduce his hours at Wedd Jefferson and semi-retire from working life. He thought the change would bring him respect, but instead it brought him resentment—from his employer, his peers, his siblings. Money, it seemed, could buy everything but friendship. In 1931, he pulled off another financial coup speculating on the Bank of England's abandonment of the gold standard and decided to retire fully. How much bread and honey did one need? he asked himself. There was a point beyond which the size of one's bank account became obscene, and at any rate he was through with money-grubbing. With a clear conscience, he resigned from Wedd Jefferson and also made a substantial donation to the Save the Children Fund.

It was then the shunning began. At The Odd Fellows Club, Sir Addington and the other elders treated him as before—still referring to him as that 'strapping young lad' who was a whizz with money—ostensibly because they had already made their mark in the world and so did not view Saul as competition. But Saul's peers were a different matter. They sowed malice born of envy and spread off-colour jokes about his Jewishness. He was a money-mad Jew, they said. He most certainly had acquired his wealth through dishonesty. To desire wealth to gain freedom was all very well if one were in one's fifties or sixties, but in one's thirties or forties, it was unseemly. Saul was unorthodox; he was 'other'. And his eccentric, artistic wife stirred up even more obloquy against him.

This was his situation from 1931 onwards. He consoled himself by spending more time with Esther and putting his faith in her painting. He became her promoter and organised exhibitions of her work at art galleries in London and in Edinburgh. She won modest acclaim, and for the first time in years, he had something other than his wealth to be proud of.

Then she, too, abandoned him. There was no one left for him to turn to. He was estranged from his siblings, and his mother, with her stoical Victorian mindset, would never understand the convolutions of an existential crisis. But after Esther's death, he felt he had no choice but to seek his mother's help.

She lived in a house he had bought for her in Richmond upon Thames. In the days following Esther's wake, he went there and sat with her in her parlour. They both were dressed in full mourning: he in a black frock coat and matching waistcoat and trousers; she in a black bombazine dress. They had not said more than a few words to each other since taking their seats in the stiff, straight-backed chairs. The room had a northern exposure and so was stuffy and poorly lit. But Saul did not mind; the atmosphere suited his mood.

Jessie, the parlourmaid, entered with a tea service and a plate of currant buns. 'Good day, sir,' she said, setting the crockery onto the coffee table. She was all smiles whenever Saul came to the house. Every year for Christmas he gave her a pudding and a ten-pound note.

Mrs Maccabee folded her hands in her lap as Jessie went about serving the tea. 'That will do,' she said after Jessie had finished.

'Yes, ma'am.'

Saul was alone with his mother again, and he had the impulse to lay bare his troubles, to tell her how lonely he felt without Esther. 'Mamme—' he started to say, but words failed him.

She looked away. There was pain in her eyes. Saul knew she could not bring herself to accept what Esther had done. Suicide was a crime in England, as well as a violation of Jewish law. The week before, a rabbi had to deem Esther of 'unsound mind' so that he could perform her burial rites.

Saul got up to leave.

'So soon?' Mrs Maccabee said. 'But you hardly touched your tea.'

'I beg your pardon, Mamme.' He kissed her on the cheeks.

She held his face between her hands and said, 'You must keep a stiff upper lip, *zeeskeit.*'

He left the house feeling no better than when he came.

From that day onward, he coped as well as he could by hiding behind his carapace in the presence of others, though it was not enough to stave off paralysis and insomnia. He began to hole himself up in his bedroom for days on end.

In his darkest hour, before he turned to medicating with absinthe, he attempted suicide. He had been taking bromides for the insomnia, but he still could not sleep. One night, in the early hours, he got up from bed and went to the bathroom and switched on the light. He stood before the mirror, glaring at himself. With his beard fully grown by then, he looked like a tramp. His eyes were bloodshot, and there were signs of eczema on his face and neck. He opened the medicine chest and took out the bottle of bromides and emptied it into his hand. Eight pills were left. 'Bottoms up,' he said aloud, and swallowed the pills dry. They edged down his throat one by one. He returned to his room and crawled into bed and closed his eyes, thinking with an unnatural calm *It will all be over soon.*

The next morning he awoke, very much alive. He felt nauseous and physically weak, but goddamn it, he was very much alive.

Another seven months elapsed before he realised he could not shuffle off his mortal coil any more than he could shuffle off his past or his Jewishness or his intellectualism. When he began writing for *The Masses*, it was as if a prayer had been answered. He finally was becoming who he had always wanted to be, and it gave him a reason to live, even without Esther. His ideas about Providence had long since been replaced by ideas about fate and destiny, but lingering at the back of his mind were notions of the Chosen Race and God's will, that things happen for a reason. God, he thought — whatever 'God' meant in this day and age — was looking out for him.

It did not seem to bother him that he was regressing to the thought patterns of his childhood. He often contemplated now the books of the Tanakh — especially Job and Ecclesiastes — and the inscrutable mystery of God. He did not know what possible reason there could be for Esther's death or for his or Job's or anyone else's suffering, but there had to be a reason. He was tempted to pray, to say Kaddish for Esther, to gaze wistfully toward the east as it were. Was not the purpose of prayer to self-reflect and change one's destiny? Vernon and Georgina came to his aid for a reason. Whatever God meant in twentieth-century terms, He certainly was not dead, as Nietzsche suggested. Emasculated, perhaps, but not dead.

//

Have you heard about the rabbi who specialised in circumcisions? He slipped and got the sack.

That was the latest joke going the rounds at The Odd Fellows Club. It was tame compared to what Saul had grown used to. In the months since Esther's death, his ill-wishers had taken pity on him and toned down their derogatory remarks. Sir Addington also took it upon himself to shame the offending club members into submission. They were all odd-fellows to a man, he said, and it was unworthy of them to act like rabble from the East End. If they kept up their behaviour, they might find themselves associated with the Jackboots and the Nordic League and the bloody Hun. Was that what they wanted? His question had the desired effect. The last thing the aristocracy wanted was to be associated with bigots and hooligans and other riffraff.

Sir Addington's concern was well founded, in light of what was happening on the streets of London. By the summer of 1936, fascist propaganda was spreading at an alarming rate, and Jackboot rallies were becoming bigger and their rhetoric more virulent. He was particularly concerned about escalations in Jew-bashing and the possible consequences for Jewish communities in the East End. One day in late August he invited Saul to the club to discuss the matter.

They met in the bar, a rich Victorian room overlooking the Marble Arch. It was midday, so an abundance of seating was available. They chose a table next to the fireplace, surrounded by horseshoe chairs. On the wood-panelled walls hung paintings of fox hunts and of various dignitaries. The painting above their table was a portrait of Prime Minister Baldwin, the latest member to join the odd-fellow ranks.

A barman in black tie stood behind a counter in the corner of the room. Sir Addington called out to him, 'A glass of port, my good man.' Saul ordered a glass of sherry; he was still abstaining from absinthe but thought a little wine would do him no harm.

The two men exchanged a few trivialities, mostly about the weather, and then they both lit up, Saul his pipe and Sir Addington a cigar. Through the miasma of tobacco smoke, Saul asked, 'Well, Neville, to what do I owe this pleasure?'

'You don't beat about the bush, do you, old boy? I won't either, then.' Sir Addington tapped the ash from his cigar into an ashtray. 'I expect you've seen the papers?'

'You mean about the fascists, I suppose. You're the third person to ask me that.'

'I'm not surprised.' Sir Addington watched as the barman approached the table with their drinks. 'Ah, here we are. Thank you, my good man.' He set down his cigar and swirled his glass of port and took a sip. 'What you perhaps don't know,' he resumed, lowering his voice, 'is what has been happening behind the scenes here in London. The Commissioner of Police is a good friend of mine. He tells me—in the strictest confidence, mind you—that the Yard have been working round the clock to stop the vandalism in the East End. They haven't been able to prove it yet, but they think the Jackboots are the hooligans responsible.'

'What vandalism?'

Sir Addington's eyes narrowed. 'So you're even more in the dark than I thought. The papers have limited their reporting to Jackboot rallies and other headline-worthy stories. It seems synagogues and businesses in the poverty-stricken East End aren't important enough.'

'Are you saying synagogues and Jewish businesses in the East End are systematically being vandalised?'

'That's precisely what I'm saying, old boy. And it's not simply the harmless graffiti stuff either. The perpetrators have been nailing pigs' heads or rashers of bacon to doors and chalking swastikas on walls. The East End is starting to look like Berlin's Barn Quarter.'

Saul held his glass of sherry to his lips for a moment without drinking. He had heard about the posters plastered all over the East End—ones that read 'Christ Killers' or 'Perish the Jews'—and the desecration of religious sites—churches and synagogues alike—had become almost commonplace in recent years. But widespread, targeted affronts against Jewish establishments in London was something new, something worrisome. He drank a bit of the sherry. 'You say Scotland Yard are on the case?'

'Yes. And Special Branch. They view the Jew-bashing as dangerous.'

'Why are Special Branch involved? I thought their remit was restricted to threats of subversion.'

'The vandalism is serious enough it has become a matter of

national security. There's fear at Whitehall and MI5 that if something isn't done soon to pre-empt hostilities, the Irish and the communists will band together with the Jews and there'll be mass riots from one end of London to the other.' Sir Addington seemed ill at ease just talking about the prospect. He picked up his cigar and took a draw.

'The government should ban the Jackboots outright,' Saul said, furrowing his brow. 'They're a menace to the public peace.'

'I agree, and there are MPs who would agree with you, too. But Westminster's hands are tied because of freedom of political expression. No matter how despicable they are, the Jackboots have the right to conduct rallies and march in the streets, and the police are required by law to protect those rights whenever they're threatened. It's probably no consolation for you to know this, old boy, but the BBC have unofficially banned fascists from wireless talks. And Parliament are considering a ban on the wearing of political uniforms in public places.'

'You're right, that's no consolation. But I appreciate what you've told me, Neville. It has given me some food for thought.' Vernon's dire warning, Saul now realised, had not been far off the mark. He was not sure what *he*, a single individual, could do, but he had to do something. He emptied the ash and dottle from his pipe and downed the remainder of his sherry. 'If you'll excuse me,' he said, getting up to leave, 'I have to see for myself the current state of the East End.'

//

Sidney was outside the club waiting for him in the Rolls-Royce. Saul got into the back seat, and they drove from Marylebone to Shadwell. Where Royal Mint Street turned into Cable Street, the road narrowed and became more crowded and infinitely grubbier. The shops, and the tenements above them, were run-down and soot-stained. People on the pavements, predominantly in grey or black clothing, had careworn expressions on their faces.

At the sight of it all, Saul's mind leapt backwards more than twenty years, to his first time East Ending with Georgina. He remembered stopping in Whitechapel to listen to a man playing a barrel organ. To someone with Saul's ear, the music was dreadful, but he was so taken with the organ grinder's capuchin monkey, he gave the performance his full attention.

'Does your monkey do tricks?' Saul asked after the song had ended.

The organ grinder snapped his fingers, to which the monkey chirped. The next thing Saul knew, the animal was on his shoulder, purring and picking at his bowler hat.

Bystanders gathered round.

'It's adorable,' Georgina said.

'Perhaps too adorable,' said Saul, embarrassed at the spectacle he was making of himself.

The organ grinder snapped his fingers again, and the monkey climbed down from Saul's shoulder, squatted on the ground in front of him, and stretched out a hand.

To the sound of laughter and clapping, Saul gave the monkey a farthing.

Later that day, in Petticoat Lane, Georgina asked Saul for the time. He reached into his waistcoat pocket and was startled to find it empty. His watch had been nicked. The cheeky little bastard, he thought. A masterful trick, that.

Now, as the Rolls-Royce continued east on Cable Street, Saul did not see any inflammatory posters or pigs' heads or rashers of bacon. It occurred to him that perhaps the situation was not as bad as Sir Addington had made out. And if Jew-bashing were going on anywhere in London, this would be the place. Shadwell was one of the most densely populated Jewish districts in the East End. Of course, the Jackboots knew that. Why else would they stage so many of their rallies on Cable Street?

The shops along the road slowly metamorphosed. Bakeries, bootmakers, capmakers, haberdashers, kosher butchers, and milliners—with names like Abrahams, Goldstein, Klyman,

Markovitch, Rodinsky—gave way to grocers, pubs, ship's chandlers, and tobacconists, with names like Higgins, Kelly, O'Brien, Reilly, Sullivan.

Saul told Sidney to stop the car at the earliest opportunity.

They came to a small car park next to St George's Town Hall, and Sidney pulled into it. 'Are you sure this is a good idea, sir?' he asked, turning and giving Saul a doubtful look.

'I won't be long,' Saul said. He handed Sidney a one-pound note. 'Help yourself to a little something at O'Brien's while I'm gone.'

Saul let himself out of the car and made his way to the pavement on the south side of Cable Street. He had not gone a block when a gang of waifs came out of Angel Mews and accosted him.

"ello, guv,' one of the boys said. 'Give us a ha'penny?'

Saul instinctively felt for his watch. It was still there in his pocket. 'I'll do better than that, boys,' he said, relieved not to have been pickpocketed. He gave them each a shilling.

'Cor,' the boys said in concert. 'Fanks, guv.'

'That's for not stealing my watch,' Saul said under his breath as he resumed his walk.

He had yet to see a fascist poster, but as he reached Dellow Street, a loudspeaker van, with the Jackboot insignia emblazoned on its side, came round the corner, blaring vitriol.

'Nationalise the wealth of the Jew banks!' a voice boomed. 'Expel all Jews from the country!' 'Send them to Dachau!' There was no cohesion or logic to the words. The hatred spewed out ceaselessly. 'Down with the Jews!' 'Perish Judah!' 'The Yids, the Yids, we gotta get rid of the Yids!'

A crowd of East Enders spontaneously formed on the street and blocked the van. As the van came to a stop, its back doors opened and several uniformed Jackboots spilled out, carrying rubber truncheons. They moved toward the crowd with arms swinging.

More East Enders joined the blockade, and before Saul could back away, he found himself in the midst of it. He was pushed and elbowed. All round him punches were being thrown to defend against the truncheons. For a moment he came face to face with one of the Jackboots, who stared at him as if he were sub-human. He felt a chill go down his spine. The Jackboot started to swing his truncheon at Saul's head, but just as this was happening, the crowd swelled and sent Saul headlong to the ground. His hands and feet were trampled on. No one heard his repeated cries in the gathering tumult.

The crowd could not be overpowered, so the Jackboots retreated to their van.

'Fucking Fagins!' one of them shouted before the van doors closed. 'Go back to Moscow!' Apparently it was of no consequence that most of the people in the crowd were Irish.

The van went into reverse, backed onto Dellow Street, and then sped away in the other direction on Cable Street.

With the Jackboots gone, the crowd dispersed.

Saul got to his feet and limped to the pavement, examining his scuffed and bruised hands as he went. On the pavement, he fixed the dent in his homburg and shakily brushed the dirt from his suit.

An Irishman in a flat hat approached him. 'Looks like things went a mite arseways for you.'

'That they did,' Saul said, putting his homburg back on. He glanced in the direction of the departing van. 'Are they here often?'

'Yeah. We don't want 'em here, but the guards're in bed with the fascists. So we take matters into our own hands. Same as the Jews.'

'How do you mean?'

The Irishman told of a story going round the East End about a secret society of Jewish vigilantes, known as the Sicarii, that had been striking the fear of God into the fascists. 'Jaysis, those Sicarii are tough blokes. I've seen for myself what they can do. They bloody well carved up some of the Jackboot lads like Christmas geese.'

'Carved up how?'

'A proper Glasgow smile,' the Irishman said. He ran his fingers up the sides of his face and made a throat-cutting sound.

'Good God.' Could it be true? Saul wondered. The story

sounded like an antisemitic canard, one of those blood-libel superstitions that had been perpetuated against Jews for centuries. But perhaps the Sicarii were real. If people were pushed hard enough, they had a tendency to push back. Look at what the Shadwell community just did to the Jackboots and their van. 'My eyes have been opened,' Saul said, lifting his homburg. 'Much obliged.'

The Irishman touched his hat and nodded. 'Go way outta that.'

Satyagraha

Vernon still did not know what the numbers on Morley's note meant. He had passed the information along to Spartacus but had been given no further orders. He was told only to keep an ear to the ground. He thought the numbers were most likely a date, but what was the significance of Friday, 2 October? It was not a bank holiday. Did it have something to do with the Jewish calendar? He would have to ask Saul about that the next time they met.

More importantly, if the numbers *were* a date, what was Walsh planning then? It had to be something serious, or why the secrecy? There was talk recently at Action House of a planned rally to trump all rallies, in which thousands of shock troops would descend upon the streets of London, to break the backs of the antifascists for good and all. But that was rumoured to be scheduled for the 4th of October, not for the 2nd. The District Secretariat were already aware of this possible 4 October rally and intended to prepare a counter-demonstration as soon as details were confirmed. Again Vernon was told simply to keep an ear to the ground.

Days passed as he waited for intelligence on the Jackboot front, and in the meantime, he received a large envelope from Minnette. It contained a letter, a poem, and an article from the *Journal of the Dutch Burgher Union of Ceylon.* Zoe was with him in his lodgings when the envelope arrived. She was anxious to learn the contents of the letter, as she knew Vernon had mentioned her to Minnette.

They sat at the kitchenette table.

'Do you think she'll approve of me?' Zoe asked.

'I don't see why not,' he said. 'She has no reason not to.' He read the letter aloud.

Dear Vernon,
Of course I forgive you, although there is nothing to forgive, not really. It is quite understandable that you have been busy.
I am glad you are as eager as I am to strengthen our relationship. It will be wonderful, will it not, when you return to Ceylon? There are so many places I want to see with you, places we have not been to since we were children. Do you remember? The Aluviharaya rock temple, the trails in the Knuckles, the Gerandi Ella waterfall. I have such fond memories of touring the hill country with you and Ammi and Thathi.

Zoe made a slight movement in her chair. Vernon looked up from the letter to see her eyes watering. No doubt the reference to his returning to Ceylon, and the things he would do once he got there, reminded her that their time together was nearing an end. He leaned over and kissed her, then read on.

They were thrilled, by the way, to get your letter. You do not know how much it means to them to hear of your exploits in London. Thathi is always saying to Ammi, 'Who would have thought a Prins would be getting a PhD? And in economics and politics, no less.' He calls you 'the big man about London'.
I took your advice and joined the LSSP.

'What's the LSSP?' Zoe interrupted, dabbing her eyes with a napkin.

'A new socialist party in Ceylon. Their name means equality in Sinhala.' Vernon noticed that Zoe's purple eye shadow had smeared. 'May I?' he said and took the napkin and wiped the discolouration from beneath her eyes. 'You can't go out in public looking like the bride of Frankenstein.'

She gave a mirthful little laugh and swatted him on the arm. 'Do I look perfectly awful?'

'It would take more than smeared makeup to spoil your gorgeous face.' He resumed reading.

There is not much for me to do just yet, but Dr de Silva has asked me to go to Colombo next week for training. The LSSP headquarters is in the Maradama industrial section of Colombo, on Panchikawatte Road. I plan to stay with my friend Lena in Cinnamon Gardens during the training. I think you met her once. She is Sinhalese and has the most beautiful black hair and fair skin. Through the LSSP, I hope to be a force for positive change. If I can educate even one Mr Arunasalem in the world, it will be worth it.

    You, a new sweetheart? And an English one at that? Zoe. What a lovely name. I wish I could meet her. You have always had such good taste in girls. Tell her for me that I am jealous of the time she gets to spend with you. Could you send me a photograph of her? If not, you must at least tell me what she looks like, or I shall be obliged to use my imagination. And you know where that will lead. In my mind's eye, I can see her already. She has red hair and freckles and breasts the size of mustard seeds and crooked teeth and a gammy leg and possibly even a goitre. How is that for a picture? Is it anywhere near the truth?

'Your sister's dotty,' Zoe said with a burst of laughter.

'Yes, she is. But I'm sure if you met her, you'd like her all the same.'

'I already do.'

Of course, [Vernon flipped over the letter] I would not dream of telling Ammi about Zoe. She would go straight to an astrologer and have them read your horoscope and badger them until they told her what she wants to hear, which is that you are destined to marry a Ceylonese girl from a good family and never, never a foreigner (even though she married one herself) and certainly not a nurse.

    I have enclosed a poem. It is a political one as you suggested and is entitled 'Satyagraha', the Sanskrit word for Gandhi's philosophy of confronting injustice through nonviolence, a fancy way of saying civil disobedience. Please do submit the poem, if it would not be too terribly inconvenient. I have never seen The Masses magazine, but beggars cannot be choosy. Did you mean what you said about my Dekho poem? There are certain of my pieces that I have especial fondness for, and the Dekho poem is one of them. In addition to 'Satyagraha', I have enclosed an article from the DBU journal that might be of interest to you. It gives a sense of the struggles we Burghers are facing in Ceylon. Thank you so much for responding to my last letter. And thank you for submitting my poem.

Love,
Minnette

Vernon returned the letter to its envelope. 'Do you have a photograph I could give her?'

'Nothing recent,' Zoe said.

'You'll have to get one taken, then. Only, I don't know where.'

'There's a photographic studio on Bovay Place in Holloway.'

'You could go there. Or we could have Georgina Wilson take one of the both of us. She has a camera she uses for the magazine. It takes excellent black and whites. Shall we go see her together next weekend? I know she would be delighted to meet you, and I have to give her Minnette's poem anyway.'

'That would be nice.' Zoe picked up the poem but immediately set it back down. 'Would your mother really be so set against me?'

Vernon was quiet for a moment. Then he said, 'In the abstract, perhaps. But she would get over her prejudices the instant she encountered you in person. She would realise you're not as evil as she imagined, and then you would be welcomed into her presence with open arms. She's fickle that way.'

Zoe did not appear convinced but said nothing more. She read Minnette's poem to herself and then handed it to Vernon. 'It's quite good,' she said.

Vernon read it as well and agreed. It was about Gandhi's Salt

March. 'I don't know how she does it. You can see Gandhi — with his frail body and shaved head, wrapped in a lungi and wearing steel-rimmed spectacles — travelling the four hundred kilometres amid the heat and dust of India. Georgina's going to love this.'

Zoe glanced at Vernon's bedside clock on the floor. 'I should be going.' She had to work a night shift at hospital.

'Must you?'

'I must.'

They kissed and he walked her to the front of the building and they said their goodbyes.

Back in his room, he sat down at the table again and read the DBU journal article. It was from the 'By the Way' column and was written by someone called Niemand.

A studied campaign of misrepresentation has been waged for some time against the Dutch and their descendants in Ceylon. It is apparently due, to a large extent, to an 'inferiority complex'. It may also be due to the outburst of a nationalism which is too excited at the moment to think calmly and soberly. Or it may be due, in a few cases, to mere envy and malice — two of the deadly sins which blight the progress of all communities and have invariably been their ruin.

But if this campaign is not withstood vigorously and at once the prospects for the future of the Community are dark. One purpose of these notes is to draw the attention of the younger members of the Community to their danger and their duty.

They must not look to the older men any longer; it is a vain, and generally a selfish, hope. Some of them, following the example of Mr R. G. Anthonisz, have freely done what they could, and have at least shewn what might be done in regard to those things that ought to be done. Many, however, of the older generation are indifferent both to the danger and the duty. All is well with themselves, they imagine, and therefore all will be well to the end of time! An occasional rude shock to their complacency is soon forgotten. But the shocks are becoming more frequent and more severe.

It is thus for the younger members of the Community to rouse themselves to a clear understanding of the situation in which they are placed, or they will find no place, except as hewers of wood and drawers of water, in the new condition of things. Even to enjoy the cinema and the dance we must have money, and money comes from work. If our young people will but stop to consider what chances they have, and will have, of securing work — work, that is, for others who employ them, and pay them, and dismiss them — they will learn something to their advantage.

Vernon felt a thrill go through him. The article was a call to action. Bravo, Niemand! The stuff about work was laying it on a bit thick, but Vernon appreciated where Niemand was coming from. Young Burghers *did* need to do more to improve the lot of the Community.

The days of rich and easy-going fathers are now no more. Except in a few instances the fathers themselves find life a pretty hard struggle for existence. One of the most painful experiences of recent years has been the sight of fathers who won good positions and lived in well-to-do circumstances, but whose old age was passed in gloom and often in want.

Vernon thought of his pater, of how he was a shadow of the man he used to be. What the Great War had not done to him, the worldwide economic depression *had*. These days were a time of tea overproduction, so the International Tea Regulating Board had put estates on a quota to support prices. It spelled the doom of Eden Estate. Thathi had been forced to sell out and retire from the proceeds. Ammi and Thathi were not exactly impoverished, but they had fewer servants now and their bungalow in Kandy town was a major step down from the one they used to have on the plantation.

No one should shut his eyes to the social and political revolutions which are openly taking place in our midst, though their working might be in secret. Feudalism is a lost cause. Wealth avails nothing. Personal reputation does not count. Ancient lineage and high office are matters of derision. This is the day of the many against the few, of the humble against the exalted, of those who have not against those who have, of those who are against those who would be.
What then? Shall we fold our hands in despair, and be silent and inactive? It is these who perish in the struggle. Those who win

are those who have the courage to fight, to face heavy odds, whose heads under the bludgeoning of chance are bloody but unbow'd.

It is rare to see any of our young men strike out in a new direction, or even 'on their own' in an old direction. A few who have done so have made good, rising from very small beginnings to respect, independence, and affluence. But their example is not followed. We all cherish the beaten path. We all want to be paid by others, to depend on others for our maintenance.

None of that applied to Vernon, he thought. *He* had struck out in a new direction and had forsaken the beaten path.

It is fashionable nowadays to smile at Smiles' Self-Help, *but it would be a good thing if that book were put into the hands of our young people. An active self-help committee or society would be of real value, and of far more use than a mutual admiration club.*

These observations on the general outlook for our young people were necessary before indicating the special need for preserving the Community and its good name. Both are in danger, and the danger lies not so much in the veiled or open hostility in certain quarters as in the strange but fatal indifference of the Community itself and of those who seek to lead it. That is a reason for the younger generation, for our young men and (here is more hope) our young women, to awake, to study, to contrive, and to act. This, they say, is the age of youth; let youth then prove itself — if it can.

Well said, Niemand. Minnette will prove herself, of that you may be certain, you old bugger.

If there is no anxiety to preserve the Community, so be it. But that would be a curious reflection on the first fathers of the Community. Even more is it a reflection on the existing members of the Community. In these days of assertive nationalism everybody is anxious to know who everybody else is; what race or nation he belongs to, and what place that race or nation holds in history. No respect or consideration attaches to 'nondescripts without race or language'.

True, but you are missing the point, Niemand. Bigots and

nationalists view the world the same way they view race: there is black, and there is white, and there is nothing in between.

As a first step to self-respect and unity, our young people should know their own history, the history of themselves; that is, the history of the Dutch in Ceylon from 1640 onwards. This is all-important, as the prevailing ignorance on the point is astonishing, in spite of the many valuable articles on the subject which have appeared in the Journal *from the beginning. That ignorance explains much of the indifference which is apparent. There is no need to make a detailed study of the history; the essential outlines will suffice to start with, but a certain minimum is necessary. We ought to know in what circumstances the Dutch came to Ceylon; how the maritime provinces came under their rule; how they governed these provinces; how they were dispossessed; and how their descendants have fared since. In this way a Dutch descendant will at length know his own people as a Sinhalese or a Tamil (not to speak of an Englishman) knows the race to which he is proud to belong. We investigate genealogies and print them. It is not mere vanity that prompts this course. What we need quite as much, if not more, is the 'genealogy' of the Community as a whole, not from 1796, but from 1600 at least, about which date the Dutch East India Company was founded. How many of us can write down the Dutch name of that company, or tell us what the three distinctive letters stand for which we see on Dutch coins?*

When a party of schoolboys sit on a Buddhist statue in the jungle, there is a storm of indignation leading to public meetings and representations to government. The same thing happens if the picture of a dagoba is woven on a railway map, or a racehorse is named Buddha. If a cartoon of the Prophet appears in a Ceylon book or newspaper, the Muslim world resents the outrage, and reparation is made. When Hitler sneers at the Indians, the Indians everywhere hit back. But when the children of the Dutch descendants in Ceylon are compelled to learn that the Dutch were a nation of sordid instincts, and that their own parents are no better — then what happens?

The whole question of the text-books used in our schools and approved or actually set for use by the Department of Education requires urgent examination and revision. It is too large a question to be considered here. But the main point urged in these notes is that the matter is serious yet scarcely touched by those whose business it is to investigate and to act.

Vernon rolled up the article and slapped it against the palm of his hand. A wasted opportunity, he thought. The Dutch name of the Dutch East India Company was *Vereenigde Oostindische Compagnie,* but did knowing that make you a better person? And Dutch guilders were not even used in Ceylon anymore, so what did the inscriptions on the coins matter? Vernon was in favour of having Dutch Burghers learn Dutch history but not for the sake of memorising facts or to differentiate themselves from the rest of humanity. It was not what you knew but how you used your knowledge that mattered. Once again, Niemand missed the point. By focusing on the plight of Dutch Burghers, to the exclusion of Buddhists and Hindus and Muslims and everyone else, he was no better than the people he derided for racism. Besides, being Burgher meant by definition that you were part Sinhalese or Tamil or Moorish as well as part European. The truth was, *everyone* had a right to his own identity and to co-exist without discrimination. It was more important to study the history of mankind than the history of one's immediate ancestors. If only we would do so. If we *would,* we would soon discover that at root all humans are essentially the same, no matter their colour or creed.

//

On Saturday morning, Zoe met Vernon at his lodgings, and together they walked down Drury Lane to the offices of *The Masses.* It was a cloudy and dreary day, not the ideal conditions for a photograph, but it seemed to Vernon that waiting for a sunny weekend in London during the month of September would be like waiting for a blue moon.

As they neared Kemble Street, it started to rain.

'Oh bother.' Zoe pulled up the hood of her mackintosh.

Vernon knew how much time she had spent preening herself for the photograph. Marcelling her hair and sculpting her eyebrows, alone, took her over two hours. He opened his umbrella and handed it to her.

'What about you?'

'You have more to protect,' he said, indicating her makeup. 'Besides, we're almost there.'

They hastened to the magazine's offices.

In the vestibule, a young man, one of the sub-editors, was going out just as they were coming in. He noticed the umbrella and Vernon's wet clothes and hair. 'Drat, I forgot the blooming brolly this morning.'

'Sorry about that,' Vernon said. He and Zoe wiped their shoes on a rug and hung their coats and the umbrella on a rack.

The sub-editor hovered in the doorway, debating whether to dart out into the rain.

'Where can we find Ms Wilson?' Vernon asked.

'Room 40,' the sub-editor said.

Vernon gave him a blank look.

'Up the stairs, second door on the left. Room 40 is where we do all our planning. It's named after the British intelligence operations during the Great War.'

Vernon and Zoe went upstairs and down the hallway.

Georgina was alone in Room 40 attaching drawing pins to an enormous map on the wall. She had her back to the door and did not hear Vernon and Zoe come up behind her.

'Are you planning the next magazine issue or a second world war?' Vernon said.

'Goodness.' Georgina put a hand to her heart and spun round. Her frown turned to a smile upon seeing Vernon. 'Why, darling, it's you! You shouldn't scare an old lady like that.' She looked at Zoe. 'Hello, my dear. Now I know why he has kept himself out of sight for so long.'

Vernon laughed awkwardly. 'Georgina, this is Zoe Tilston. Zoe, this is Georgina Wilson.'

Georgina and Zoe kissed and embraced.

'It's good to see you again, Georgina,' Vernon said, kissing and embracing her in turn. He went up to the map. It was of East London. 'Seriously, what *is* all this?'

'Impending Jackboot marches and rallies.' Georgina stood next to him in front of the map. 'As the fascists step up their activities, so do we. Their next rally will be at Trafalgar Square on Friday. The Scipian Society and other antifascist groups are planning a counter-demonstration.'

'Where did all this information come from?'

'I wouldn't be a very good journalist if I divulged my sources, now would I?' She glanced back at Zoe, then said to Vernon, 'Why don't the two of you attend the counter-demonstration. We need all the help we can get.'

Vernon begged off. He said he had work to do for his thesis. In actuality, he was already scheduled to attend Friday's rally at Trafalgar Square, as a Jackboot, not as an antifascist. It would be disastrous, he thought, if he were to encounter Georgina there. He would have to watch out for her and keep a low profile. What lengths he was having to go to maintain secrecy! The whole thing was too absurd. 'Speaking of Jackboot rallies,' he added by way of diversion, 'does the date 2 October mean anything to you?'

'I can't say it does,' Georgina said. 'Why?'

'Nothing of importance.' He took out Minnette's poem from his trouser pocket and handed it to Georgina. 'This is one of the reasons I came. It's a poem of my sister's.'

She unfolded the paper and began to read. '"*Satyagraha*". Where have I heard that word?'

'In connection with Gandhi, no doubt. It means non-violent protest. Do you think *The Masses* might be interested in publishing it?'

'Yes,' she said, still perusing the poem, 'we might. I'll run it by the board of editors. What's your sister's name?'

'Minnette.'

'You said "one of the reasons" you're here. Is there another reason?'

'Well, I wanted you to meet Zoe, of course. But we were also hoping you could take our photograph. Minnette has asked for one of Zoe.'

'I'd be happy to.' Georgina went over and touched Zoe's face. 'That explains why you're so nicely done up, dear. And here I was thinking it was for my sake.' She left the room and came back with her camera. 'Let's see,' she said, looking for the best spot to take a photograph. She pointed to a bare section of wall, opposite a window. 'Stand over there, why don't you.'

Vernon and Zoe moved to where they were directed.

It was still raining outside, so there was little natural light in the room. Georgina improvised and set up a floor lamp, aiming its bulb at the couple. 'That ought to do it.' She stood in front of the window and pulled open the camera's lens board and put an eye to the viewfinder. 'Say *satyagraha*,' she said and, grinning childishly, pressed the shutter-release button.

//

Overhead, an enormous flock of pigeons carved a zigzag pattern in the sky, momentarily blotting out the sliver of the setting sun that was visible through the clouds. Like a military procession, they moved in tight formation and changed direction on a sixpence. Eventually they swerved east, then as quickly north—with the portico and spire of St Martin-in-the-Fields as a backdrop—and landed en masse on the roofline of the National Gallery, its dome and turrets becoming a fluttery profusion of feathers.

The Jackboots and their supporters had taken over the pigeons' usual gathering place in Trafalgar Square. So many people had shown up at the rally, some of them were forced to climb atop the fountain ledges to make space. The Leader had already spoken for almost an hour. He stood before the pedestal of Nelson's Column, his voice booming over the microphones, his hands moving with the studied precision of an orchestra conductor. The audience were bewitched.

Vernon was positioned on the southern perimeter of the square, between Nelson's Column and the statue of Charles I. He and other shock troops had been tasked with helping the police keep the antifascists at bay. A cordon of sawhorses surrounded the square, the words POLICE LINE - DO NOT CROSS painted on the horizontal bars in large white letters. Mounted police patrolled the cordon, swatting antifascists with wooden truncheons if they came too close. Every now and then a young antifascist would sneak past the police and scale a sawhorse, and Vernon or some other Jackboot would seize them by the scruff of the neck and toss them back over the line.

To his relief, Vernon had not yet seen Georgina amid the crowds, although members of the Scipian Society were definitely there. A short time earlier, a small group of them had approached the cordon and attempted to distribute pamphlets. And one of the Scipians, a young woman, had dared to reach across a sawhorse. No sooner had she done so than the truncheon of a mounted policeman came crashing down onto her head. Again and again the truncheon struck, and with each blow, the horse did a little dance, moving laterally with rapid footfalls as if it were spooked. Vernon wanted to intervene and put an end to the brutality, but he could not. He looked on helplessly as the young woman shielded her head from the blows and fell to the ground. Moments later, her comrades carried her away. Georgina was not among them.

Now the shouts from the antifascists intensified. Above the din of The Leader's voice, the words 'Down with fascism!' could be heard. Big Ben's chimes added to the cacophony, travelling unobstructed down Whitehall and mingling dissonantly with the sounds of human discord and hate.

Then Vernon saw Georgina. She stood on the other side of the cordon next to the mounted policeman who had beaten the young woman. They were having a heated discussion. Vernon could not hear what they were saying, but he got the gist of it from Georgina's wagging finger. She did not appear to be intimidated by the truncheon or the towering height of the horse.

Vernon retreated into the crowd. He had to avoid being seen.

'Pardon me,' he said repeatedly as he navigated toward Duncannon Street. None of the people he passed took their eyes off The Leader. They simply grimaced as he went by and grudgingly made way.

He was level with the statue of King George IV when someone said his name, or rather his alias. He turned to see Fitch. They were close enough that Vernon could smell the tobacco on Fitch's breath.

'You look like you're on a mission,' Fitch said.

'I am of sorts.' Vernon put a hand on his stomach. 'Feeling a bit iffy.'

'Quiet, you!' a nearby man yelled, staring daggers at Vernon and Fitch.

'Oi!' Fitch yelled back. 'Show some respect for the ill.' To Vernon he said, 'Follow me' and then pushed his way to the north-eastern edge of the cordon. 'Make way for Jackboots! Make way!' At the cordon, Fitch helped Vernon over a sawhorse and beckoned to one of the mounted constables. 'Could you get this lad here safely through the Bolshies?'

'Yes, sir,' the constable said. He released his foot from the off-side stirrup and, with an outstretched hand, pulled Vernon up onto the horse's croup.

'Get well, mate,' Fitch said.

Vernon saluted.

The constable took the reins and turned the horse into the crowd of antifascists, who parted but not without expressing their disdain. They booed and hissed and grabbed at the constable's and Vernon's uniforms. The constable fended them off with savage swings of his truncheon.

At last they broke through the crowd onto Duncannon Street. The horse trotted past St Martin-in-the-Fields to within a stone's throw of the Strand before the constable tugged on the reins. He glanced over his shoulder. 'You should be safe here.'

'Many thanks,' Vernon said. He got down from the horse, crossed the road, and headed up Adelaide Street.

It was getting dark. The sun had dipped down behind the National Gallery, and now the entirety of the churchyard lay in shadow. Vernon had barely walked fifty metres before a capless Jackboot staggered out from the path that ran along the north side of the church.

'Help me,' the Jackboot struggled to say, then immediately collapsed.

Vernon ran over and knelt down. 'Christ almighty,' he said, falling back onto his haunches. Even in the failing light, the Jackboot's freshly incised face was ghoulish.

A police whistle sounded from the other side of Adelaide Street, followed by shouts and the tramping of feet.

Vernon just sat there, too stunned to move, as the police surrounded him.

//

'Now, tell me again what you were doing in the churchyard,' Detective Chief Inspector Quinn said. He had a thin angular face and greying hair. He sat at a table opposite Vernon in a Scotland Yard interview room. Beside the door, a uniformed constable stood guard.

Vernon removed his gauntlets and stacked them neatly next to his cap on the table. 'I was going home.'

'You're a student living in Covent Garden, I think you said?'

'That's right.'

'Why were you going home when you were? The rally hadn't finished.'

'I was feeling poorly.'

'And now you're feeling better?'

'Apart from being here, I am, yes.'

'Do you know the victim?'

'No.'

'You've never seen him before tonight?'

'Not that I recall. There are tens of thousands of Jackboots in London. And there are new recruits daily.' As Vernon spoke, he saw in his mind the victim's disfigured face. He picked up his cap from the table and wrenched it in his hands. 'Is he all right, the man who was attacked?'

DCI Quinn narrowed his eyes. 'He's in hospital, since you ask. He lost a lot of blood before he was brought in, but the doctor says he'll pull through.' The inspector paused and jotted something down onto a pad of paper. 'When you were passing the church, did you see anyone else besides the victim?'

'No.'

'No one on Adelaide Street or in the churchyard?'

'No one.'

'Did you hear anything?'

'Only the noises from the square.'

'What do you make of the Sicarii?' DCI Quinn asked, suddenly changing tack.

Vernon gave a start. Why was the inspector asking about that? Perhaps he knew more than he was letting on. 'It's a lot of rot,' Vernon said with feeling.

'Why do you say that?'

'I don't countenance conspiracy theories. The Jews are like everyone else, just trying to make their way in life.'

DCI Quinn glanced at Vernon's jacket, at the Sam Browne belt, at the armband on his sleeve. 'You don't sound much like a fascist.'

'Not all Jackboots are prats.'

'No,' DCI Quinn said, 'I suppose not.' He opened a file folder on the table and pulled out a photograph. It was of Morley. 'Do you recognise this man?'

Vernon felt his hands go clammy. 'Yes. He's a Jackboot. His name is Stewart Morley.'

'What do you know about him?'

'Nothing much, only that he's a former stevedore and is on the dole.'

'Did you know he has a criminal record?'

'No.' So Morley was an old lag, Vernon thought. That figured. Morley always did seem as if he had something to hide. 'What did he do?'

'Never mind that.' DCI Quinn returned the photograph to the folder and then stared at Vernon in silence for a moment. 'Care for a fag?' he asked eventually.

'I would, as a matter of fact,' Vernon said, glad for anything that would help calm his nerves.

DCI Quinn motioned to the constable, who produced a packet of Woodbines.

Vernon took one, and the constable lit it for him. 'Are you going to charge me with something?' Vernon asked the inspector between puffs on his cigarette.

'We've nothing to charge you with.' DCI Quinn picked up the file. 'You're here as a witness, not as a suspect, and you're free to go. We have your name and address should we need anything further from you.' He turned to the constable. 'Will you please show Mr Prins out.'

Vernon stood up so quickly he almost knocked over his chair. 'Thanks for the fag,' he said awkwardly and, holding the cigarette between his pursed lips, gathered up his cap and gauntlets and followed the constable out.

Chapter 10

The Sicarii

Saul had lived in his ivory tower for so long, he became oblivious to the state of the poor in the East End. Naturally he was even less aware of the London underworld—not just the activities of pickpockets and prostitutes and organised criminals, but also the machinations of political zealots like the fascists and the communists and, lately, the Sicarii. The Irishman believed that the Sicarii were Jews. Whether that was true or not, the attacks had been instigated by *someone* and they were politically motivated. Why else target Jackboots?

The name Sicarii was familiar to Saul. He had not studied Latin for over two decades, but he was fairly certain the word *sicarius* meant ruffian or killer or something of that sort. Perhaps he came across the word at St Paul's. He read classics there and was stuffed to the gills with useless Latin and Greek trivia, part of the so-called lower division of the *Artes Liberales*. That was why he studied sciences at Trinity College: to cleanse his palate of the trifles he learned in public school.

It occurred to him now that the one place he could find out more about the Sicarii was the London Library. His membership there had long since expired, but now that he was writing again, he thought it might be useful to renew it. With this in mind, the morning after his visit to Shadwell, he and Sidney drove to St James's Square.

'You'll steer clear of the fascists this time, won't you, sir?' Sidney said as he pulled up the Rolls outside the library.

'Your concern is touching, Sidney, but there aren't likely to be any fascists where I'm going.' Saul got out of the car and went up to the front door of the library. There was something dignified in his step, as though he were approaching hallowed ground.

The inside of the library was exactly as he remembered it, and he felt a twinge of nostalgia. Dust particles radiated sunlight from the windows above the entrance. The librarians behind the reference desk, awash in the same light, moved along the bookshelves that spanned the length of the twenty-foot wall, the upper sections of which were accessible only by a steel staircase. Infusing the air was the faint acidic odour of aged paper, that ambrosia of the scholar.

An elderly librarian assisted him at the reference desk. Her hair was pulled into a chignon, and she had a pince-nez on the bridge of her nose. They spoke in undertones for a minute. Then he filled out the necessary paperwork while the librarian searched the card catalogue for books on the Sicarii.

'There isn't much, I'm afraid,' she said upon returning to the desk. 'Only three books contain direct references to the Sicarii: the *Jewish Encyclopaedia* and two others, both by the same author.' She lifted her pince-nez and held up a piece of paper close to her eyes. 'What were they again? Ah, yes. Titus Flavius Josephus's *Antiquities of the Jews* and *History of the Jewish War against the Romans*. I also found a cross-reference to the Zealots in the Talmud.'

'Four sources might be enough for my purposes,' Saul said.

The librarian smiled. 'If you'll wait in the reading room, I'll get them to you in two shakes.' She scurried off to the bookstacks.

In the reading room, Saul sat down in the last remaining chair at the end of a table. He glanced round. Everyone was busy reading or taking notes, in absolute silence. The man to his immediate left had a thick moustache and thinning hair and was dressed in a tweed suit. In immaculate handwriting on the notepad in front of him was a series of quotations. Saul discreetly read the first of them: 'We are perfide Albion, the island of hypocrites, the people who have built up an Empire with a Bible in one hand, a pistol in the other, and financial concessions in both pockets.' It sounded, Saul thought, like the kind of sentiment Vernon might express.

Seated to Saul's immediate right was a thirty-something woman in a plain black frock. She had a string of pearls round her neck, tightly curled hair, and a long, pink face. She was reading what appeared to be a book of American nursery rhymes, open to a page with the title 'Ten Little Niggers'. She must have felt Saul's eyes on her because she suddenly grabbed the book and drew it to her chest, as if she had been caught reading pornography. He averted his eyes, just in time for the librarian to arrive with his books.

'Here you are, sir,' she said in a low voice, setting the books onto the table.

'Very much obliged.' He scooted his chair closer to the table, pulled the chain on the banker's lamp in front of him, and took up the first of the books, the *Jewish Encyclopaedia*.

As he read, he recalled where he had heard the name Sicarii: at Torah study in synagogue when he was a boy. The Hebrew word *Biryonim* had come up in a Talmud passage the students were reading, and Saul asked the teacher what the word meant. The teacher said the literal translation was 'boors', but in this case, *Biryonim* was referring to a group of Jews known as the Zealots, who rebelled against the Roman occupation of the Holy Land during the first century AD. Saul was curious to know what it was that made the Zealots boorish. Didn't non-Zealots also fight in the Great Revolt? he asked. Non-Zealots fought too, the teacher said, but it wasn't the act of fighting that made the Zealots boorish; it was their tactics. The Zealots included a sub-group called the Sicarii, who were trained assassins. They would surreptitiously stab Romans and Hebrew Roman sympathisers at public gatherings and then disappear into the crowd. Saul was silent upon hearing this. The history of Jewish rebellion was infinitely more interesting than the dry teachings of the Torah. For the rest of the study session, he daydreamed about what it would be like to be an assassin.

The *Jewish Encyclopaedia* contained other minutiae, definitions and whatnot, that refreshed as well as confirmed his memory. For example, his guess at the meaning of the Latin word *sicarius* had been correct. Over the centuries it variously meant 'dagger man' or 'violent man' or 'murderer'. The Sicarii got their name from the fact that they carried *sicae*, or small daggers, concealed in their cloaks to carry out assassinations. According to the encyclopaedia, they were the 'upholders of the Fourth Philosophy' on behalf of the Zealots.

For more information about the Fourth Philosophy, Saul turned to Josephus's *Antiquities of the Jews*. He decided to skim it because it was eight hundred pages long. The word Zealot never came up, and the Sicarii were mentioned as robbers, murderers, and ruffians but not as a sub-group of the Zealots. Josephus referred only generally to a 'fourth philosophic sect'. Up until the time of Christ, there were three Jewish sects: the Pharisees, the Sadducees, and the Essenes. Then a fourth philosophic sect was founded. Josephus wrote of this sect that they 'agree in all other things with the Pharisaic notions; but they have an inviolable attachment to liberty, and say that God is to be their only Ruler and Lord'. Of course they would say that, Saul thought. It was a way of justifying their attacks on anyone who disagreed with them. 'They also do not value dying any kinds of death [...]' So they were martyrs too. They were like modern-day anarchists or the more radical elements of the Scipian Society, with their emphasis on liberty and their repudiation of authority and their fearlessness in the face of death. And doubtless the Sicarii of old viewed themselves the same way anarchists viewed themselves today: as freedom fighters and not as terrorists.

Saul stood up and stretched. His back ached. He had read for three hours already and needed a break. The woman who had been sitting across from him was gone, as were most of the other people who had been in the reading room. He went to the window overlooking the garden. Shafts of sunlight streamed through the clouds, like Jacob's Ladder, turning the plants a brilliant green. He entertained the thought of going to the garden for a smoke, but then he remembered the library's lightwell. He switched off the lamp and made his way there.

As he opened the door to the outside, a pigeon flushed from a windowsill, dislodging one of its feathers. Saul watched the feather flutter, then catch an air current and circle and twirl all the way to the ground. No one else was in the lightwell. He sat down on a stone bench and packed his pipe and lit it. It was the lunch hour, and though he should have been hungry, he was not. The excitement of being in the library again and reading about the mysterious Sicarii had caused him to lose his appetite. He did not know how much more he could possibly learn, but he intended to continue reading at least through the afternoon. He had told Sidney to be back at the library by four o'clock, so four o'clock it would be.

He crossed his legs, took a deep draw at his pipe, and held the bit meditatively in the corner of his mouth. None of his reading thus far, he realised, had shed any light on the present-day Sicarii who were targeting Jackboots. Who were they? And if they were not Jews, how did they come to know so much Jewish history? A part of him—the same part that as a child had revered the original Sicarii—hoped they *were* Jews. Even now in his imagination he could see them moving stealthily among the Jackboots: striking without warning, escaping undetected, exacting their pound of flesh.

//

Georgina came into the study, where Saul was typing away at his desk. She had the galley proofs of the October issue of *The Masses* in one hand and an edition of the *London Morning Post* in the other. She waved the proofs about and set them onto the desk. 'A superb issue, if I do say so myself. No small thanks to you. Look over your article when you have a chance, please. We'll go to press in three weeks or thereabouts.'

Saul did not stop typing. When inspiration came—and the

thoughts were flowing as they were now, like water from a sieve — he had to keep going, or, he worried, the flood of ideas might evaporate into thin air. His eyes remained fixed on the typewriter for several more carriage returns, until he got to the end of a page. But instead of stopping, he said 'Apologies,' inserted a new piece of paper, turned the roller knob, and continued on, at the brisk pace of fifty words a minute.

'I'll just make myself comfortable, shall I?' Georgina said. She went to Esther's unfinished painting and stood before it. Only the pond — in blues and blacks and greens and whites — had been painted. The rest of the work was still in the sketch stage. 'I've never seen one of Esther's works in progress. It's like seeing into the mind of a genius.'

At last he stopped typing and looked up. 'That's my muse. It's of a farm in Suffolk. We went there early in our marriage. She had this idea that one day we would leave London and retire to a place like that.' His voice was full of regret.

Georgina came over and put a hand on his arm. 'I'm so sorry.'

'Keep a stiff upper lip, my mother would say.' He indicated his typing. 'Staying busy is the important thing.'

'What is it you're working on?'

'Some Jewish history.' He smiled up at her.

'Would it be appropriate for *The Masses*?'

'It's for my own edification, really.'

'Well, if you should have an idea for another article, I'd love to hear it. You have an open invitation, you know, to submit to the magazine.'

'That's kind of you, Georgina.' He picked up the proofs and perused the table of contents. His article, 'Jazz and Issues of Race', was on page 43, between something about the Aid Spain campaign and a piece entitled '*Satyagraha*'. 'What's "*Satyagraha*"?'

'A poem. About Gandhi's Salt March. Vernon's sister wrote it.'

'Minnette?' he said with sudden animation. He had heard so much about her, he felt he already knew her. He turned the pages to the poem and read. It was in the form of a narrative, very visual and intense, and reminded him of Robert Frost's 'Out, Out—'. Gandhi came to life on the page. There he was, vividly setting out from his *ashram* and drawing crowds into his orbit as he marched, mile upon mile, to the Arabian Sea. There he was, also, standing on the salt flats of Dandi, shading his eyes against the sun, which sat low in the western sky and appeared as though it were about to fall off the edge of the earth. And there he was in his final act of defiance, a withered hand reaching down and slowly plucking from the mud the forbidden lump of salt.

Saul closed the proofs. 'She's a rising star.' He felt even closer to Minnette than before. He had had a similar feeling eighteen years ago when he first saw one of Esther's paintings, and he was discomfited now to think that another woman could reproduce such an intimate moment from his past.

'The editorial board think so, too,' Georgina said. 'Do you know they voted unanimously in favour of publication? If you happen to see Vernon before I do, please don't tell him the news. I want to surprise him with it myself.'

'Very well.' He tapped the newspaper in her hand. 'What's this you've got?'

'Something you should see.' She opened the paper to page B1 and held it out in front of him, pointing to the headline 'Jews behind Spate of Attacks on Jackboots'.

He read the article to himself.

A concerted effort is afoot to harass and intimidate law-abiding members of the Fascist Party. Three Jackboots, in three separate incidents, have been brutally attacked since June. Witnesses have stated that all of the attacks were unprovoked. The most recent attack occurred on Friday near Trafalgar Square during a Jackboot rally. The victim, a twenty-eight-year-old ship repairer, was released from hospital on Sunday and is said to be recuperating at his home in Canary Wharf. When questioned about the incident, a spokesman for the Metropolitan Police, Detective Chief Inspector Nigel Quinn, declined to comment.

Is this what Great Britain has come to? Are we to lose our right of free speech and are we to be cowed into submission by enemies of the State? Under the common law, every Briton has a right to freedom of expression. But we have reached the woeful point in this country in which that freedom is largely a thing of the past.

It has come to the attention of the editors of this paper that the Hidden Hand – a Jewish cabal who control international finance, cinema, and the majority of the press – are funding a terrorist organisation behind the aforementioned attacks on Jackboots. To date, both Parliament and the police have done nothing to stop this grave miscarriage of justice. It is time for action. It is time to stand up to those forces that would rob us of our sacred freedoms. It is time to follow the example of fascism and accept the challenge of Jewry. […]

Georgina said, 'There should be a law against the deliberate reporting of lies.'

'So you don't believe the bit about the terrorist organisation?' Saul asked.

'Certainly not. Or the Hidden Hand nonsense. Or the complicity of the police in suppressing fascism. I was at that Jackboot rally on Friday, and I assure you, the police did *not* side with the antifascists.' She shook the paper. '"It has come to the attention of the editors of this paper" for shame! The lack of attribution and the advancement of conspiracy theories go against every journalistic standard of which I'm aware.'

Saul thought of his writing about the Sicarii. He agreed that the notion of a Jewish cabal acting like a puppeteer in a Punch and Judy show was a load of rubbish, but the Sicarii? There was a historical precedent for them. Even the Irish in Shadwell believed that the Sicarii were Jews, and the Irish had no antisemitic motive for doing so. 'Supposing this terrorist organisation were real,' Saul said. 'Could you blame them for lashing out against the Jackboots, who clearly have it in for the Jews?'

Georgina closed the paper and set it down and leaned forward on the desk. 'Did you know,' she said, ignoring Saul's question, 'the owner of the *Post*, Sir Thomas Davies, and the Jackboots are as thick as thieves? Word has it, Sir Davies contributed a large sum of money to the Fascist Party. There's your journalistic impartiality for you.'

An idea struck Saul. 'We ought to fight fire with fire.'

'Meaning?'

'Meaning, in the same way that Sir Davies is funding the Jackboots, we should fund the opposition.' Saul had never donated to a political organisation before, but, to paraphrase Hippocrates, desperate times called for desperate measures. 'We could also take a lesson from Gandhi and hit Davies where it hurts: his pocketbook. The Jewish community won't take kindly to this latest assault on their religion. I'll contact the Jewish People's Council and the owner of *The Jewish Chronicle* and push for a boycott of the *Post* and a withdrawal of all advertising. After that, Sir Davies would be a fool to continue publishing rubbish about the Jews.'

Georgina was visibly moved. 'Why, Saul, bless my soul.'

'I've surprised myself, to be honest. But I suppose this is my calling now. Let me start by making a donation to the Scipian Society and *The Masses*.'

'I wouldn't hear of it,' she said.

He pulled out his chequebook from a desk drawer. 'Will a thousand pounds do?'

//

The atonality and fragmentation of Schönberg's Third String Quartet was the musical equivalent of Bolshevism, Saul thought. He sat by himself at a Corner House table, watching and listening to the two violins, the viola, and the cello express their individuality and also trade and expand upon each other's ideas.

Vernon returned from the lavatory and sat down and poured himself another cup of tea. 'There's something I've been meaning ask you.'

'One moment,' Saul said, raising his pipe, not taking his eyes off the orchestra.

The first movement of the quartet had ended, and now the second movement began with a slow, plaintive three-bar violin duet, with the viola and cello adding commentary. The music was disturbing, kaleidoscopic, its atmosphere like air from another planet. For some reason as Saul listened, he pictured a member of the Sicarii weaving their way through a crowd of Jackboots, keeping their head down, a hand clenching the dagger in their pocket. Each pluck of an instrument's strings seemed to presage the assassin's strike, and in the movement's final development and coda, Saul could see, as plainly as he saw the musicians before him, the victim bleeding out and the assassin's stealthy escape.

Saul turned from the orchestra and noticed that his pipe had gone out. Lightly tamping the tobacco, he moved a match in a circular motion round the bowl and then took a series of shallow puffs. 'Sorry,' he said to Vernon. 'You were saying?'

'I was just wondering what Jewish holidays are coming up.'

'Well, let's see.' Saul held his pipe in the corner of his mouth for a moment and then said, 'Rosh Hashanah is later this week, Yom Kippur is next week, and Sukkot is the first week of October.'

'What's Sukkot?'

'The Feast of Tabernacles. It marks the end of harvest time and commemorates the Israelites' exodus out of Egypt. Why the sudden interest in Judaism, old chap? Are you thinking of converting?'

Vernon laughed. 'No, nothing like that.' He looked over at the musicians, who were passionately bowing and plucking their instruments. The music had become livelier, more light-hearted, but it was still haunting. 'Do remember when you asked how I knew so much about the fascists?'

'You were at my house at the time, if memory serves.'

'Right. And instead of answering your question, I directed you to the headline in the *London Morning Post*?'

'Yes.'

'I was trying to hide from you the fact that I had joined the Jackboots.'

Saul suppressed a cough. '*Joined*? How do you mean "joined"?'

'I mean infiltrated. I'm a stool pigeon. A spy.'

'Good God,' Saul said round the stem of his pipe. 'Are you mad?

Do you want to get yourself killed?'

'You sound like Zoe.'

'I've reason to be concerned. Jackboots on a rampage aren't a pretty sight.' Saul glanced at his hands. There were still faint signs of bruising from the trampling he had received in the East End.

'I can handle myself,' Vernon said, echoing his words to Zoe. From his expression, however, it was clear he was not so sure. 'In any case, it's you I should be concerned about. Since when have you seen Jackboots on a rampage?'

'There was a bit of a scrum over in Shadwell the other day. A van of Jackboots turned up looking for a fight, but the East Enders showed them what's what.'

Vernon gave Saul a quizzical look.

'I wanted to see for myself what's happening in the East End. A friend at The Odd Fellows Club said the Jackboots have been stepping up their provocations.'

'And you got more than you bargained for,' Vernon said, as though he were thinking out loud. He took a sip of his tea. He seemed to have something on his mind. 'What you saw in Shadwell may be a drop in the bucket, Saul.' Vernon's expression had become serious. 'The Jackboot leadership are planning something, something big. A rally to end all rallies and perhaps something else besides. That's why I was asking you about Jewish holidays. Somehow the 2nd of October is relevant to the Fascist Party's plans.'

'You think they're planning to target Jews in some way?'

'I do, yes.'

It occurred to Saul that perhaps the Sicarii were aware of the same plans and were stepping up their own activities in anticipation, as a form of self-defence. He said, 'You might be interested to learn that I've been doing some research on an organisation called the Sicarii. Are you aware —?'

'What kind of research?' Vernon interrupted with a look of concern.

'You've nothing to fear. It's only library research.' Saul laughed. 'I've no intention of infiltrating them, for example.'

Vernon sat back in his chair, regarding Saul. 'You don't actually believe in that bollocks, do you?'

'You mean that the Sicarii are Jews? I don't know what to believe.' Saul paused, then said, 'You didn't seem very much surprised just now when I mentioned the Sicarii. What do you know of them?'

'Only what I've seen of their handiwork. And what I've read of them in a Jackboot communiqué.' Vernon refrained from mentioning his interview at the Met.

Saul's face lit up. 'This communiqué, when was it issued?'

'Sometime in June, I believe. Why?'

'I see.' Saul looked over at the orchestra again. Schönberg's song was coming to an end. The fourth movement was faster and more strident until the last seven bars, when the song suddenly turned quiet. In the relative silence, Saul's hands remained suspended above the table, in a curious prayer-like posture. Smoke curled and danced from his pipe.

Homeward Bound

Vernon was now in regular contact with Spartacus. On one occasion, they rendezvoused at The Green Park under the cover of night, and Vernon told Spartacus what Saul said about the Sicarii: that the timing of the Jackboot communiqué and the subsequent attacks on Jackboots were too much of a coincidence. It confirmed Vernon's own suspicions that the Sicarii business was only a smokescreen.

'It's time you were extracted,' Spartacus replied in a stage whisper. Behind him the gilded wrought iron of Canada Gate, and beyond that the gilt-bronze wings of the Victoria Memorial, shone in the silvery light of the crescent moon. A nippy breeze was blowing. Spartacus lifted up the lapel of his reefer coat and inclined his head. 'If what you say is true, we're dealing with lunatics.'

Vernon was conflicted. He did not want to end up with a Glasgow smile, obviously, but at the same time, he was so close to a breakthrough. 'You can't do this,' he said. 'Not after all the work I've done.'

Spartacus shook his head. 'The risks are too great. I couldn't have it on my conscience if you were attacked.'

'How are the risks any greater now than they were before?'

'It's not only the risks to you personally. There's the Communist

Party to consider. We don't need the police breathing down our necks or having them think we're allied with the Sicarii, real or not. If they're on to Morley, they might be on to you, as well.' Spartacus glanced furtively round the park, then added, 'I'll confer with the District Secretariat about it, but I'm certain they'll agree with me.' He made a fist and discreetly kept his arm at his side, in a mock communist salute. 'Long live the revolution.'

'Long live the revolution,' Vernon echoed and then retraced his steps back across The Broadwalk in the chill night. *So this is it*, he thought. After three months of ingratiating himself with people he despised, this was it. His efforts seemed so abortive. He put his hands into his coat pockets and, looking both ways along Piccadilly, crossed the street. Night owls were still out and about on the pavements, but the road itself was deserted.

At Piccadilly Circus, the billboards and the streetlamps coalesced into a blaze of light. Vernon glanced at his watch. It was close on midnight. He suddenly felt tired. He could use a good night's sleep. No doubt that was something he would have more of now. Sleep and time. What an utter *waste of time* his intelligence gathering had been. What did he accomplish? Nothing, unless he counted seeing the inner workings of the Fascist Party as an accomplishment. He was not at all sure what he expected, but certainly this was not it: to be, three months on, haunting the streets at night without a shred of useful information about the Jackboots.

Actually, to be fair, he could not say he had come away from his experiences completely empty-handed. He had met Zoe, after all. She was a ray of moonlight in this mad, mad world. There was *that*, at least, he told himself reassuringly as he wended his way home.

//

The next day he received a cable from his mother. His vision blurred as he opened the red envelope and saw the single line: 'THATHI VERY POORLY'.

He gave the telegram messenger a thruppenny bit, then went

back into his room, plopped down onto a chair, and closed his eyes. The world seemed to be caving in round him. *Very poorly.* What did that mean? *Whatever* it meant, it had to be serious, or Amma would not have cabled. Was Thathi dying? How could that be? Minnette mentioned nothing of a serious illness in her last letter, and she wrote barely a fortnight ago.

Of all the times for this to happen. There were seven months left before graduation, and he would have to excuse himself from university if he were to return to Ceylon. The succinctness of his mother's cablegram made him angry. He knew she did it to save money, but he suspected she also did it to put the onus on him to decide what to do. The passage to Ceylon was no small matter, and she would not have wanted him to feel pressurised. But that was precisely what he *did* feel. If he stayed at LSE through Lent term, and in the interim his pater died, Vernon would have no one but himself to blame.

Somehow he could not even imagine his pater dead. The eventuality seemed so remote, even with the spectre of illness looming. As a man, Thathi was larger than life. Physically he was massive, and he had survived so much: emigrating to Ceylon, two bouts of malaria, and even the Great War, in which millions of others had died. And after all that, to be cut down so suddenly by an invisible enemy?

There was nothing for it, Vernon concluded. He would have to take a sabbatical and go to Ceylon as soon as possible. He was fairly certain his supervisor and the LSE administration would be understanding given the circumstances. Now that he thought about it, leaving London for a while might actually be a godsend. It would allow him to fully extricate himself from the Jackboots. And he would come back for the Michaelmas term next year and tackle his thesis with fresh eyes and renewed energy.

He was in such a perturbed state of mind, he almost forgot about Zoe. What was he going to tell her? He had been dreading the day when he would have to say goodbye, and now that day was perhaps less than a fortnight away. He did not want to part with her any more than she wanted to part with him. He would have to work out exactly what to say and exactly how to say it. She deserved the best valediction he could devise.

But first things first. He had to cable Amma a response. It was midday in London, so it was late afternoon in Kandy. Time enough yet for him to shoot off a cablegram. He grabbed his coat, went outside, and headed for the post office. Before he reached Tavistock Street, he settled on the message he would send: short, to the point, and sufficiently vague: 'HOMEWARD BOUND VERNON'.

//

Just to be safe, to make sure there was no confusion as to the meaning of his cablegram, he wrote a follow-up letter to Minnette. He had so much to tell her, in any case — including the good news about her poem. Earlier that day he had gone to the offices of *The Masses* to pick up the photograph of him and Zoe, and Georgina surprised him with the magazine's October galley proofs. He was so excited that afterward he had difficulty concentrating on his research at LSE. He ended up cutting short his time at the library and scuttling home. Zoe was coming over for the evening, and he was keen to share the news with her.

She was already in his room sitting at the table when he got back. She had a key to the door now and had let herself in. 'Hello,' she said, beaming. She had come straight from hospital and so was wearing her nurse's uniform. Her clutch and white nurse's cap and pinafore apron lay on the table.

'I was hoping you'd be here,' he said.

She got up and kissed him.

He pulled from his school satchel the photograph and the magazine proofs. 'Look,' he said, opening the proofs to Minnette's poem.

'Oh how marvellous! Minnette will be ever so pleased.' Zoe snatched the photograph from Vernon's hand and scrutinised it. '*This*, on the other hand, will make her gorge rise. I look positively awful.'

'No, you don't.'

'Do you *have* to send it to her?'

'Honestly, you look fine,' he said and lifted his satchel over his head and set it onto the table along with the proofs. 'More than that, actually: you look gorgeous.'

She scrutinised the photograph again. 'You're just saying that.'

'For what purpose?'

'Don't pretend you don't know,' she said, pressing the photograph to his chest and laughing. 'To get into my knickers, of course.'

'How ever did you guess?' He let the photograph fall to the floor and then, at the same time that he kissed her, undid the collar of her dress.

She kissed him back, and little by little they undressed each other and tumbled onto the mattress. Their love-making was animalistic in its concupiscence. In no time at all, they both climaxed in quick succession. They were utterly spent afterward. For a while they just lay there entangled in one another's arms, sweating profusely and breathing heavily and feeling the rapid pulsations of their hearts.

After he caught his breath, Vernon got up and put on his underclothes. He had been thinking of home, of his pater. 'Would you mind if I write a letter to Minnette?'

'Of course not,' Zoe said. She was still naked on the mattress, her nubile body exquisite in its shapeliness. She rolled onto her side and rested her head on a hand. 'I'll watch you while you write.'

He felt an unwanted tumescence coming on. 'Now look what you've done.'

She giggled.

Half-smiling and sitting slightly hunched at the table, he began to write.

Dear Minnette,
I've so much to say and ask, my letter may be a bit garbled. Let me

start with the most urgent matter. How's Thathi? Is he really doing as poorly as Ammi's cablegram suggested? I have a few loose ends to tie up here, but I should be able to get home by the end of October. I've booked passage on the Orient Line's SS Oronsay, which leaves from Tilbury Docks on 11 October. Everyone at LSE has been so understanding. I asked for a year-long sabbatical, and it was granted immediately. I must have impressed someone along the way. No doubt it helped that I framed my trip as a fact-finding mission, as well as a mission to see Thathi. I plan to visit Eden Estate or some other estate while I'm there and do additional research for my thesis.

On a more positive note, The Masses accepted your poem! It will appear next month. I'll bring the galley proofs with me when I come. You should have heard what Georgina Wilson, the magazine's editor-in-chief, had to say. Evidently it was the first time in the magazine's history that the editorial board voted unanimously in favour of publishing a poem. I'm so proud of you, my sweet little sister.

Enclosed is a photograph of Zoe. She's gorgeous, no? Your imagination was a smidgen off. Her teeth and hair and legs and everything else about her are absolutely perfect.

He stopped writing and leaned over and retrieved the photograph from the floor. He looked at Zoe's black-and-white image, then at the colour, three-dimensional version on the mattress. She really was gorgeous, with or without colour and in two dimensions or three. As he admired her naked body, she smiled at him, in that convivial way she had, and it struck him that he was in love with her. His heart palpitated. Was it really true? He had never loved a woman quite like that before. He turned over the piece of paper and resumed writing.

You know, I think I'm in love with her. It occurred to me just now, as I was writing this letter, that I can't live without her. Isn't that what love means? It seems to me it is. On a whim last month, I suggested to her that she come away with me to Ceylon after I graduate from LSE, but she said that that would be impossible. Suppose, instead, I were to return to London from my sabbatical and stay here for good, or at least until I can convince her to go to Ceylon. I realise you and Ammi and Thathi would be unhappy with my returning here, but at some point I have to do what's best for me, no? Of course, if I were to return to London for good, my dream of becoming a Ceylonese politician would be forever lost. That's life, and economics, for you: one difficult decision after another. What to do?

Your idea of travelling round Kandy while I'm there sounds brilliant. I can think of scores of other places I would like to see besides Aluviharaya, the Knuckles, and Gerandi Ella. Are you up for a whirlwind tour of the island? We could borrow Thathi's Austin and drive it about recklessly like a couple of psychopathic toads.

How was your LSSP training in Colombo? I must say I'm glad you joined them, and I've no doubt you'll be a force for positive change.

By the way (and pardon the joke), if you should ever come across this Niemand character — the author of the DBU journal article you sent me — tell him that I relished reading his article but that I have a bone to pick with him. His views on race are as blinkered as the nationalists' are.

Your Loving Brother,
Vernon

He set down his pen and stared out the window. The light on Drury Lane was beginning to fade. And to think, a month from now he would be in Kandy, sitting on the verandah of his parents' bungalow watching the sunset, drinking toddy and listening to the hoo-hoo of the wood pigeons in the surrounding jungle.

Zoe came up behind him and put her hands on his shoulders. She was wearing his shirt now. 'Could I read it?'

He flinched. He had not yet told her about the sabbatical. He was planning to wait for the right moment, but perhaps this was it. His written words expressed his feelings better than he ever could orally. 'I was going to have to tell you sooner or later,' he said, handing her the letter.

She took it and sat down at the table. As she read, her eyes filled with tears.

He could not tell whether she was happy or sad or both. He waited in suspense for her to finish reading.

When she finally did, she said, 'Do you mean it?' and managed a smile through her tears.

He leaned over and kissed her. 'Every last word.'

//

A letter from Minnette arrived a week later. She apologised for the shock Ammi's cablegram must have caused. But she and Ammi had got their wires crossed: Ammi assumed Minnette already told Vernon about Thathi's illness, and Minnette assumed Ammi would not want anything said until Thathi's illness was properly diagnosed. Then after they realised their mutual mistake, Ammi wired Vernon before Minnette could post him a letter.

I told her to hold off on sending a wire, but these days, she simply does not know her right from her left. She has become ill herself from worry and exhaustion. Dr Fernando is coming every day now to attend to Thathi, but it is not enough. Ammi and I take turns at night keeping vigil by his bedside. He cannot keep food down any longer and has lost so much weight so quickly, it is frightening. If only he had not been such a stubborn fool and had allowed us to ring up Dr Fernando sooner. Thathi had been complaining of a dicky stomach for weeks, but when Ammi pressurised him to see a doctor, he refused. Surgery might have been an option then, but not now that the cancer has spread. We should have known something more serious was wrong after what happened at the LSSP rally last month. Thathi was giving his speech and midway through rushed off the stage to be sick. A troop of LSSP chaps had to help him to the Austin, and I had to drive us home. He and Ammi sat in the back seat with his head resting in her lap.

Ammi says she is sorry for not writing to you herself, but she [...]

Vernon heard a noise come from the hallway outside his room. He stopped reading. There was a murmur of voices, then a fist beating out a tattoo on his door. It was an odd time of day, he thought, for someone to be calling. He got up from the table and opened the door.

DCI Quinn and another policeman stood there, in plain clothes and with their hats in their hands. 'Hello, Mr Prins,' DCI Quinn said. He held up his Special Branch warrant card. 'You remember me, I trust?'

'Of course,' Vernon said. 'Do come in.' He made way for them to enter.

DCI Quinn stepped inside and glanced round the room. 'Sorry to trouble you, but we'd like to ask you some additional questions if we may.' He pointed to the other policeman. 'This here's Detective Sergeant Smillie.'

'How do you do?' DS Smillie said to Vernon with an outstretched hand.

Vernon realised he was still holding Minnette's letter. He set it onto the table and then shook the sergeant's hand.

'I hope we're not interrupting anything too important?' DCI Quinn said. He studied Vernon's face. 'You look like a rainy day in Seathwaite.'

'Some bad news from home,' Vernon said vaguely. He had not quite grasped yet that his pater was dying. He sat down at the table and motioned for the two policemen to sit as well.

'Where's home?' DCI Quinn asked as he pulled up a chair and set his trilby onto the table.

'Ceylon.'

'Really? The good old British Raj, eh?'

Vernon simply nodded. He did not have the energy to explain that Ceylon was not technically a part of the British Raj.

'You're a long way away from home,' DCI Quinn added.

'Yes, I am.' The mere mention of home left Vernon feeling hollow inside. He drummed his fingers on Minnette's letter for a few moments before collecting himself. 'Do you fancy a cuppa? I have a Ceylonese brand.'

'Don't trouble —' DCI Quinn started to say, but DS Smillie spoke over him and said Ceylonese tea would be jolly good.

Vernon got up and put the kettle to boil and then returned to his chair at the table.

'Some information has come to light,' DCI Quinn said. He looked at DS Smillie, who retrieved from his jacket pocket a small diary and fumbled through it for a half-minute before settling on a page that contained copious notes. DCI Quinn shook his head as the sergeant spent still more time reviewing the page.

'Right,' DS Smillie said finally and set down the diary. 'We've interviewed a number of other Jackboots in connection with the attack at the Trafalgar Square rally, and not a single one of them has heard of the name Prins. Would you care to explain? We have our own theory as to what that might mean, but we're hoping to hear it from the horse's mouth.'

Vernon saw no point in hiding the truth from the police anymore. What did it matter now that Spartacus was extracting him from the Jackboots? 'I'm only posing as a fascist,' Vernon said.

DCI Quinn regarded him. 'We thought as much. You're playing with fire, you know.'

'What would you have me do?' Vernon responded. 'You lot aren't helping.'

'You're wrong there,' DCI Quinn said with a scowl. 'Not all coppers are fascist sympathisers.' Then he smiled crookedly and added, 'Just like not all Jackboots are prats. Your involvement with these hooligans is your affair. There doesn't appear to be anything illegal about what you've been doing, but we took an oath to protect the British citizenry, and by posing as a Jackboot, you're putting yourself in serious danger.' He rapped the table with his knuckles. 'Forewarned is forearmed.'

'I appreciate your concern,' Vernon said, 'but—'

'A new witness has come forward,' DS Smillie interjected.

DCI Quinn frowned. 'Yes, yes, Smillie, I was getting to that.' He sighed and then said to Vernon, 'The evening of the incident at St Martin-in-the-Fields a deacon saw someone in a cloak running away from the churchyard.'

Vernon's ears pricked up. 'Say that again?'

At that moment the kettle, which until then had been steadily building up steam, let out a shrill, pregnant whistle.

Chapter 12

Atonement

Everything was hazy and impressionistic. What sounded like a Gregorian chant could be heard somewhere in the distance, first a single voice and then multiple voices with elaborations. Esther was dressed in a white-lace gown, a veil over her face and a baby's-breath halo in her hair. Saul also wore white and had a skullcap on his head. She circled him seven times, swaying and twirling, like a maiden of old. Then her movements slowed, and, lifting her veil, she stopped entirely and stood beside him, at which point his mother came over and draped a prayer shawl round his and Esther's shoulders. A glass of wine appeared out of nowhere, suspended in air. He took hold of it, and together he and Esther drank. Finally he placed the empty glass on the ground and smashed it with his foot, to general rejoicing and shouts of *'Mazel tov!'*

Saul awoke. He lay in bed for a time in that semi-conscious state between dreaming and waking, the steady thrum of rain on the windows lulling him into a torpor. It was the morning of Yom Kippur, the day of atonement. He had been considering going to synagogue and wearing a *kittel* but ultimately decided to limit his observances to fasting and introspection.

He got out of bed. As he dressed, his thoughts returned to

Esther. She haunted his waking hours as well as his dreams. He wondered if her 'sin' could be forgiven and if she had a soul. Was she wandering the spirit world now, or—he could not help the thought—was she looking down upon him from the heavens above?

His stomach growled while he straightened his necktie in front of the dressing table. He had not eaten since before sunset the previous day. He was not in the habit of fasting, but he had been raised to believe that an occasional abstention from food and drink was good for the soul, in the same way that a tête-à-tête was good for the soul. He thought back to his time in Torah study. The word soul, he seemed to recall, appeared multiple times in the Yom Kippur section of the Torah. According to Scripture, the soul was the life force of the body, and the purpose of fasting was to deny the body and in turn deny the afflictions of the soul. The resulting pain created empathy for others. *Einfühlung*, as the Germans called it.

He finished dressing and then went to the kitchen to remind Mrs Grant that he would not be eating breakfast or any other meal that day.

'Will you be having tea, sir?'

'Not even tea.'

She put a palm to her forehead. 'What a dunce I am, Mr Maccabee. Please do forgive me. I very nearly forgot what day it is.' She started for the door that led onto the garden. Saul was planning to visit Esther's grave, and Mrs Grant knew he liked to take flowers with him whenever he went. 'You'll be needing flowers. Dear me,' she said, seeing the rain and fog through a window. She called out to Sidney to bring an umbrella.

The two servants went out to the garden, and Sidney held the umbrella while Mrs Grant picked the flowers. They returned to the kitchen a few minutes later with a large bouquet of asters, chrysanthemums, cockscomb, Japanese anemones, naked ladies, and snapdragon—all the multifarious colours of autumn.

Mrs Grant shook the water from the flowers over the kitchen

sink before wrapping the stems in parchment paper. 'An arrangement fit for a queen,' she said, handing Saul the flowers.

He bowed his head in thanks. He was in good spirits — feeling at one with the world as it were — and did not care that the flowers were slightly droopy from the damp.

'Shall we go, then, sir?' Sidney said. 'I suggest galoshes and a mackintosh on a day like today.'

They drove the Rolls to the cemetery, and Sidney parked on Swain's Lane. It was still raining. With the bouquet in one hand and an umbrella in the other, Saul made his way down the sinuous, muddy paths. Fog, like wisps of smoke, wafted through the trees. The air smelled of autumn leaves and sodden earth, and the gravestones and ferns exuded atonement, melancholy, and the remembrance of things past.

He was approaching Esther's grave when out of the corner of his eye he saw something move. He turned to the sound of a blood-curdling shriek, like a woman in distress. He nearly jumped out of his skin. Another movement caught his eye, and an animal with auburn fur showed itself for an instant, then disappeared into a thicket.

Only a fox, Saul thought. Somewhere in that dense undergrowth must be a fox's earth and a litter of cubs. Even amid all this death and decay, life went on.

Beneath the oak tree the rain was less intense. He knelt before Esther's grave. A surge of emotion overcame him as he read the headstone's inscription. Nine months on and he still had not got over her suicide. If she *had* been such a loving wife, why did she do it? Why did she leave him to fend for himself in this godforsaken world? For Ernst's sake? Was he, Saul, not enough?

And yet he knew it was unfair to judge her by society's standards when at the end she might not have been in her right mind. Not to mention that she was a genius, and geniuses did not think and behave the same way the herd did. Allowances had to be made.

He looked up at the raindrops dripping from the branches and leaves of the oak tree. As he did so, recollections of the early days of his marriage came flooding back: of Hanukkah celebrations and picnics and nights out and trips abroad. And later, after they moved to Belgravia and became more comfortable with each other: dinner parties and evenings in the garden and orchestra performances at the theatre — all the trappings of sophisticated, upper-class life.

'Esther,' he said aloud. With every fibre of his being he wanted her to be alive, to experience those days with her again. Even one day would suffice. 'Esther.' Her name reverberated through the trees.

He placed the bouquet of flowers at the base of the headstone and, in the continuing rain, unconsciously said the final lines of the mourner's Kaddish: 'He who creates peace in His celestial heights, may He create peace for us and for all Israel; and say, Amen.'

From the depths of his heart he loved Esther still, and he could forgive her anything.

//

He was sitting on the chaise longue in his bedroom with his eyes closed, listening to Schubert's String Quartet No. 14. The first variation of the second movement had just begun. A lilting violin descant floated above the theme. At the same time, the second violin and the viola played in pulsing triplets; the cello, in pizzicato. It was as though, Saul thought, the instruments had voices and wills of their own. There was a kind of freedom, one might even say egalitarianism, in the varied melody and the independence of play. With a little improvisation, it seemed to him, the quartet could be called jazz.

A knock at the door interrupted his train of thought. 'Yes?'

Sidney entered. 'Pardon me, sir, but you are wanted on the telephone.'

'By whom?'

'Mr Prins, sir.'

'I'll be right there.' Saul switched off the gramophone and went to the entrance hall, where the telephone handset lay off the hook on the console. He picked it up and said, 'Vernon, old chap. Must be something important if it couldn't wait until our next meeting at the Corner House.'

'I've received news,' Vernon said. 'From home.'

Saul was expecting some elaboration, but all that followed was silence. He thought perhaps the connection had dropped. 'Vernon? Are you still there?'

'I'm here. My pater —' Vernon's voice caught.

'You mean to say …?' Vernon had told Saul of Johannes's illness.

'Not yet … but … Sorry, Saul. It suddenly struck me —'

'No need to apologise, old chap. I know a thing or two about these things. Just the thought of the death of a loved is sometimes enough to break one's heart.' Saul paused, thinking with a pang of Esther and of his own father. 'You'll be leaving for Ceylon soon, I expect.'

'In a fortnight or so. I've been granted a year-long sabbatical.'

Saul took a moment to process this. For purely selfish reasons he did not want Vernon to go. Eventually he said, 'You'll be sorely missed.'

'You could always come with,' Vernon said on an impulse. It was the second time in as many months he had invited someone to Ceylon. He seemed intent on surrounding himself for as long as possible with the people he loved.

'You make it sound so simple,' Saul said, 'as though you were inviting me on a weekend excursion to Brighton.' He found Vernon's invitation amusingly quixotic.

'But it *is* simple, in a sense. You have no commitments to prevent you from going. And you have the time and the money. That's more than most people can say.'

'What about Sidney and Mrs Grant? I couldn't very well leave them here to run the house on their own.'

'You could, actually, if you chose to.'

'Could I?' Come to think of it, Saul thought, perhaps he could. Other than Sidney and Mrs Grant — and perhaps his mother and

Georgina and Sir Addington—no one would miss him, really. His absence from London would be only temporary at any rate. Not to mention that he had never been to the Orient. Romantic images, *à la* Rudyard Kipling, flashed through his mind. Scenic hill stations. Magical bazaars. Monkeys clattering over iron roofs. And of course Minnette would be in Ceylon. Dear dear Minnette. The rising star. Meeting her, alone, would make a trip to Ceylon worthwhile. 'Yes, perhaps I could,' Saul said. 'I'll think it over.'

'Brilliant.' As an afterthought, Vernon added, 'One more thing. A development has come to my attention—with the Jackboots and the Sicarii. I can't say more, except that something significant is about to happen.' Before Saul could probe, Vernon rang off.

//

The rumour of a Jackboot rally to end all rallies was gathering pace. It was assumed now, by all opposition parties, that a rally or a march or something of the sort would occur on 4 October. Opposition forces mobilised. The Jewish People's Council petitioned the Home Secretary to ban the Jackboot event, and the *Jewish Chronicle* released a warning for Jews to stay away from certain areas of the East End. Preparations also were made for counter-demonstrations. The Communist Party cancelled an Aid Spain rally in Trafalgar Square that had been planned for 4 October and instructed its supporters to hold antifascist demonstrations instead. Even the Labour Party got involved, touring a loudspeaker van through the East End and encouraging residents to block access to the Jackboots.

The Scipian Society did its part, as well. Saul was pleased to see his money being put to good use. Georgina called a special 'war-cabinet' meeting at the offices of *The Masses* to work on a four-page antifascist supplement to be included at the last minute in the October issue. The supplement urged counter-demonstrators to mass in their tens of thousands and erect barricades at Cable Street, Gardiners Corner, Leman Street, St George Street, and wherever else possible. London was to be awash with antifascist leaflets and 'white with chalked and whitewashed slogans': 'The fascists are provoking civil war in East London'; 'Protest against the fascist's military operations'; 'We want no Hitler torture or Franco brutality here'; and 'End fascist hooliganism in East London'.

Saul wrote two of the leaflets himself, one about the dangers of fascism and one about the scourge of racism. The day after Yom Kippur, exactly a week before the expected Jackboot event, he went in to the offices of *The Masses* to help typeset the leaflets. Georgina was there in Room 40 rallying the editorial troops.

'Come now, ladies and gents, chop-chop,' she was saying when Saul came in. '"We few, we happy few, we band of brothers" … and sisters.'

Staff were going to and fro, listening to Georgina with half an ear.

'You'd think it was Saint Crispin's Day,' Saul said to her.

'I have to motivate them somehow.' She looked at her staff with pride. 'We have two days before the October issue goes to press. And until Friday, at the latest, to print and distribute the leaflets.'

There was a kerfuffle near the doorway. A group of staff had gathered round one of the sub-editors, who held in front of him the Sunday edition of *The Times*. 'Bloody brilliant,' someone said.

As Georgina and Saul joined the group, the sub-editor smiled and pointed to the front page of the paper, the headline of which read: 'Jackboot Director of Propaganda Arrested'. Accompanying the article was a large photograph of a man with a scarred face.

'What does the article say?' Georgina asked.

'It says Director Walsh is alleged to have orchestrated attacks against his own men. Special Branch have taken him into custody.'

Saul smiled to himself. The 'development', he thought. So that was what Vernon had been talking about.

Georgina glanced at Saul. 'Why would he do such a thing?'

'To further the fascist conspiracy theory of a "Jewish world-hydra",' Saul said. 'What better way to provoke your followers to violence against Jews than to create a factitious enemy and name it after an actual organisation from Jewish history.'

'What better way, indeed.' Georgina grabbed the newspaper, tore the article and Walsh's photograph from the front page, and shredded it to bits. 'Good riddance to bad rubbish,' she said, tossing the bits into the air. The paper scattered like confetti, to the delight of everyone in the room.

Chapter 13

Playing with Fire

'We have a traitor in our midst,' Captain Goodheart said.

He was standing on a soapbox in the bay at Action House. Twenty-odd Jackboots—including Fitch, Jack the lad, Morley, and Vernon—surrounded him. They all eyed each other at the captain's pronouncement.

'Wait till I get my hands on the bastard,' Morley said. 'He'll rue the day he was born.'

A chorus of 'Hear hear!' went round the room. Vernon joined in, pretending as much outrage as he could.

'Pipe down!' Captain Goodheart said. 'I haven't finished what I came here to say. This nark—whoever he is—is an informant for the police and is responsible for Director Walsh's incarceration. We received an anonymous tip that a Jackboot—one of our own, a two-faced traitor—gave false information to the police, and shortly thereafter the Director was arrested.'

Vernon could not understand what Captain Goodheart was on about. Who would have provided an anonymous tip? The only person he could think of was DS Smillie. No one else would have had reason to remain anonymous. Rarely did the police shy away from making public their fascist sympathies. Or was Captain Goodheart just trying to create a red herring and the Jackboot leadership already knew who the nark was?

'No offence, sir,' Fitch said, 'but wouldn't it have been wiser to keep quiet about the nark?'

'Perhaps. But his identity is still unknown. The Leader determined that it would be best to let the nark know we're on to him and smoke him out that way.'

Vernon kept perfectly still. All he had to do, he told himself, was to stay calm and act like everyone else. He had made it this far without giving himself away.

Jack cleared his throat. 'Sir, is there really nuffin' in what the papers say? Director Walsh ain't the one who done this to me?' He touched his scarred face. He was close to tears.

Captain Goodheart stiffened. 'Now you listen to me, Jack.' The captain paused and looked at the others for a moment. 'And this goes for the rest of you, too. We all know who controls Fleet Street. You read for yourselves the article in the *Post*, the only paper not in the enemies' hands. What *The Times* said about Director Walsh is a pack of lies. Pure and simple. A fabrication to smear the reputation of the Party. And the Fagins and Shylocks won't stop there. They're bent on destroying us. Only last week the Jewish People's Council petitioned the Home Secretary to ban our upcoming march. Will you stand by and allow this travesty of justice?'

'Never!' Morley shouted, and several voices, including Vernon's, echoed the indignation. 'Never! No, never!'

Arms went up in salute. A savage chant followed. 'Hail Leader! Hail Leader! Hail Leader!'

'That's more like it,' Captain Goodheart said once the shouting died down. 'As you were, gents.' Then he stepped off the soapbox and left the bay.

Everyone dispersed. Vernon seemed to be safe for now.

Out on the parade ground, Jack pulled him aside. 'Do you believe what the Captain said 'bout Director Walsh?'

'Keep your voice down,' Vernon said, looking nervously in the direction of the verandah. No one appeared to have heard. He thought it an ill omen—after all the talk of a nark—that Jack was looking to him for counsel. But perhaps Jack could be of service. What did he, Vernon, have to lose in any case? He already had one foot out the door. Spartacus and the District Secretariat had decided to extract him on 4 October, after the rally. Besides which, he would be leaving for Ceylon soon. 'Come with me,' he said to Jack, grabbing him by the shoulder strap of his belt. Together they headed for the trees. As soon as they were far enough away from the house, Vernon asked, 'Why are you questioning Captain Goodheart's integrity?'

Jack grimaced. The gashes on his face, however, made it seem like he was smiling. Vernon could hardly stand to look at him. Jack said, 'I heard 'em talkin',' and the words sounded like an accusation. Evidently he was not the same starry-eyed recruit of a few months ago.

'Who?' Vernon asked. 'Who did you hear talking?'

'Good'eart and Morley. I was in the crapper, and they didn't know I was in there. I heard 'em talkin' outside the door.'

'What were they saying?'

'They was up to somefin'. Good'eart said for Morley to stick to the plan. Bout following Director Walsh's orders this Friday. What do you s'pose it means?'

Friday was the 2nd of October, Vernon thought. The note on the piece of paper in Morley's closet might correspond to a date, after all. Despite Jack's confidences, however, Vernon knew he still had to be careful. 'There's probably a simple explanation,' he said with as much detachment as he could muster. At the same time, he was thinking that whatever the significance of 2 October was, he had every intention of finding out.

//

For three days Vernon kept a close eye on Morley. The only thing out of the ordinary was that Morley seemed more antagonistic than usual. On Friday morning, during formation, he had an altercation with Fitch. Fitch said 'Bullshit' in response to a remark of Morley's, and Morley misheard it as 'Bolshevik'.

'No one calls me a Bolshevik and gets away with it,' Morley said. He broke ranks and clocked Fitch in the face with such force, it sent him reeling.

'Stop buggering about!' the drill sergeant bawled. 'Get back in line!'

Fitch put his tongue to his bloodied lip, and a glimmer of defiance came into his eyes. 'Is that all you've got? I may be an old man, but I can paste the likes of you with one hand tied behind my back. I didn't survive the Great War to be beaten up by a pansy. That's right, Stewart. You're nothing but a Mary Ann. I bet the misses is mighty pleased with the housework you do while you're cadging money from the PAC. Oh, right, I forgot, your misses kicked you out, didn't she? That's why you're living here.'

Laughter erupted from the column.

Morley coloured. 'You better watch what you say, or —'

'Or what?' Fitch cut in. Turning aside, he winked at the others in formation.

'Or I'll kill you!' Morley said in a rage, and fell upon Fitch.

As they exchanged blows, they knocked each other's caps off and trampled them underfoot.

The entire column collapsed then and gathered round the two men. Exhortations of 'Fight, fight, fight, fight' resounded across the acreage.

'Stop it! Stop it right now!' the drill sergeant shouted, rushing into the fray. He wedged himself between Morley and Fitch and held them at arm's length.

'Out of my way,' Morley said. 'I've no quarrel with you.'

The drill sergeant let go of Fitch and got into Morley's face. 'Stand down, or I'll have you flogged to within an inch of your life.'

'All right, all right,' Morley relented. He stepped back and spat a gob of blood and spittle onto the ground and wiped his mouth with a jacket sleeve.

Fitch unclenched his fists and picked up his cap, slapping it against his thigh to remove the dirt and grass. He had a disaffected look on his face.

The drill sergeant glared at each of them in turn. 'Now shake hands. A momentous evening and weekend await us, and we should be fighting the enemy, not each other.'

Leaving their gauntlets on, the two men shook hands grudgingly.

'Right, back in line, all of you!' the drill sergeant barked. 'Seventeen hundred hours will be here before you know it.' A mock run of Sunday's march through the East End was scheduled for five o'clock that evening. It was to be an all-hands-on-deck affair.

After morning formation, everyone went about Action House making preparations for the march. By five o'clock, all but a few stragglers had left for the various rendezvous points in the East End. Vernon and Fitch and two guards were the only ones to stay behind.

'Shouldn't you be going?' Fitch asked Vernon.

They stood on the verandah, watching the sun drop below the tops of the beech trees. It was a rare spot of sunshine for this time of year.

'I could ask you the same thing,' Vernon said. He removed his gauntlets and retrieved a packet of cigarettes from his jacket pocket and offered one to Fitch.

'Don't mind if I do.' Fitch kept his gauntlets on. His upper lip was so badly swollen, he held the cigarette loosely in the corner of his mouth.

They both lit up, and their gazes returned to the glowing sky beyond the trees.

Vernon took a fierce drag and expelled the excess smoke with a flick of his tongue. He thought he had better enjoy the sunset while he could. It might be the last one he would see in London for a while.

'I'd rather be here, truth be told,' Fitch confided, indicating the view. He laughed scornfully. 'Instead of marching like a Joe Soap through the streets.' It seemed Jack was not the only one to be losing faith in the fascists.

Vernon wanted to say as much to Fitch but refrained. Instead he said, 'We should be off. Which march are you in?'

'St George Street.'

'Leman Street myself. Cheers, Arthur.'

Fitch held up his cigarette. 'Yeah, cheers.'

Vernon glanced at the horizon one more time before descending the verandah stairs. On the parade ground, he toed out his cigarette and put his gauntlets back on. He would rather be here too, he thought—or anywhere else, in fact—than marching through the bloody streets. But what to do? It occurred to him as he continued to cross the parade ground that his contingent of marchers would be forming at Aldgate East Tube station right about now. If he hurried, he could catch them up before they reached Wapping High Street.

He was passing Bethnal Green Gardens when he saw Morley slinking through a wood, in the direction of Action House. Vernon ducked behind a hedgerow. Morley scaled the fence at the edge of the wood and dropped onto the pavement along Braintree Street. He appeared not to have noticed Vernon, and moved swiftly up the street.

Vernon waited for a minute and then followed at a distance. He was fairly certain Morley was returning to Action House, but why? How could that be part of Walsh's plan? The only thing Vernon could think of was that Walsh wanted Morley to continue the attacks on Jackboots. More attacks while Walsh was in police custody might exonerate him—or at least allow for renewed accusations that the Sicarii were responsible. And as for the logistics of an attack, a lone guard would be an easier target than someone marching amid scores of troops.

On Cornwall Avenue Vernon spotted a telephone box and considered ringing up DCI Quinn, but there was no time. An attack would be over in the blink of an eye, and Vernon could not in good conscience let that happen when he had the power to prevent it, even if he hated fascists with a passion.

Morley turned onto Globe Road. He was definitely going to

Action House. As Vernon rounded the street corner himself, so many people were on the pavement, he lost sight of Morley. With a sense of urgency, Vernon navigated through the people, but just when he caught a glimpse of a Jackboot uniform a block or so away, sirens suddenly started up at the Bethnal Green fire station and amplified to a wail. A crowd amassed, obstructing the path across Roman Road. Then three fire engines zoomed by. Vernon watched helplessly and cursed under his breath.

The nee-nah of the sirens receded into the distance, and finally the onlookers went their separate ways. Vernon crossed the street and broke into a run. Within minutes he was rushing through the trees surrounding Action House. He encountered one of the two guards at the far edge of the trees and came to a stop. 'Have you seen Morley?' he asked, catching his breath.

'No,' the guard said. 'Should I have?'

'Come with me.'

'But I can't leave my post.'

'Morley's planning another attack,' Vernon said with a grim expression.

'What do you mean?'

'There's no time to explain.' Vernon raced to the house. He could hear the guard's panting and heavy footfalls behind him.

On the verandah, the second guard lay prostrate by the front door. The back of his head was bleeding. He groaned.

'See that he's all right,' Vernon said to the other guard and then went into the house.

He heard a commotion upstairs. He got to the bottom of the staircase to see Fitch confronting Morley on the landing.

'You're the nark, aren't you?' Morley said with hatred in his eyes. He held a burning match between thumb and forefinger.

'If you believe that,' said Fitch, 'you're barmier than I thought you were.'

Vernon started up the stairs.

'Ah, Price,' Morley said, 'you're just in time to witness justice being served.'

'Don't come any closer,' Fitch warned, waving Vernon back. 'He's about to light this place to kingdom come.'

It was then Vernon saw, in the dim light of the stairwell, the can with 'Shell Motor Spirit' in yellow block letters on its side. He stood perfectly still and looked down at his feet. The steps were wet, and the sickly sweet smell of petrol filled his nostrils. He looked up just as Fitch lunged for Morley's hand and the match went twirling through the air. There was a cracking sound as Morley and Fitch crashed over the balustrade. In the same instant the petrol vapour ignited and a fireball swept along the landing and down the stairs. It whooshed between Vernon's legs, singeing his jodhpurs. He turned and slipped and tumbled. At the bottom of the stairs, he got to his feet with an effort, cradling his left arm. His cap lay smouldering on the floor.

The fire burned all round him now. He could feel its intense heat against his face. Even so, his instinct was to find Morley and Fitch. He covered his mouth and nose with a gauntleted hand and peered into the black, rolling smoke. The outlines of a pair of jackboots were just visible to one side of the staircase. He got down onto his hands and knees and crawled below the smoke. He reached Fitch first. Morley lay unconscious a couple of metres away.

'My leg,' Fitch complained. 'I think I've broken my leg.'

'Get on my back,' Vernon said, dropping to his stomach. After Fitch climbed on, Vernon belly-crawled toward the door of the bay. His eyes stung as he strained to see through the smoke, which swirled and eddied above them. They had not gone far before Fitch was seized by a coughing fit. 'Just a little farther,' Vernon encouraged.

At last they reached the threshold of the door, and Vernon helped Fitch to his feet. 'Lean on me,' Vernon said, and for a split second before they took their first step, he looked back through the smoke and saw the entire staircase engulfed in flame.

The uninjured guard met them halfway across the bay. 'What happened?' he asked as he lent a hand with Fitch.

'Morley started a fire,' Vernon said. He nodded toward Fitch.

'Get him to safety.' Then he turned round and headed back to the staircase.

'What are you doing? You can't seriously —'

But Vernon had already disappeared into the smoke. He went to the lavatory and removed his jacket and doused it in water from the tap. With the jacket draped over his head, he ran heedlessly into the conflagration.

He threw off the jacket at the side of the staircase and, holding his breath, grabbed Morley by the arms and dragged him to the bay. Only after he had cleared the smoke did Vernon finally gasp for air. His lungs were near to bursting. He backed out the front door and let go of Morley and fell onto the verandah. He saw the guard's face hover above him for a moment before losing consciousness.

//

He came to on the parade ground, wheezing like a concertina. His head ached abominably, and his hands throbbed, the fire having burned through his gauntlets.

Fitch lay next to him. 'There he is. You don't sound so good, mate.' Fitch's words sounded to Vernon like they were coming out the wrong end of a loud-hailer. 'Actually, you don't look so good either. Your face is blue.' He gave a strange little laugh. 'If it makes you feel any better, my leg hurts like a son of a bitch.'

'I think I'm going to be sick,' Vernon said and turned his head away. He vomited until everything vacated his stomach.

'Poor blighter. Hang in there. An ambulance is on its way.'

Vernon rolled onto his back. The air was thick with smoke and ash and the acrid smell of burning wood. He remembered the fire then. Morley. What happened to Morley? Vernon must have uttered the question aloud because Fitch responded.

'He didn't make it. The bastard broke his neck. Bloody ironic, eh? You risked your life for a dead man.'

The words only half-registered in Vernon's mind. It was getting hotter, the air more stifling. Dazedly, he looked up at the grey-tinged sky. Flecks of ash fluttered overhead like apocalyptic snow. He closed his eyes. Dead man. The phrase seemed to be devoid of all meaning. A wave of nausea washed over him. He felt as if he might vomit again.

Moments later—or perhaps minutes, he could not tell—he opened his eyes and heard the sound of a siren. Voices followed, and footfalls, amid flashing lights. Ambulance crew appeared. Roughly and without ceremony, they lifted him off the ground and put him onto a stretcher.

'Careful, you brutes,' Fitch said. 'That's precious cargo you've got there. I'll live to see another day because of him.'

The smoke began to clear. As Vernon passed in and out of shadow, the temperature became appreciably cooler. For a moment his blurry vision came into focus. He was amid the trees. Above, sunlight trickled through the cathedral-like branches and illumined the multi-coloured leaves. It hardly seemed possible that only a hundred metres away Action House was a blazing inferno.

In the ambulance, he was transferred from the stretcher to a steel bed. A mask was drawn over his nose and mouth. Almost immediately his breathing improved. Then the doors slammed shut and the siren began to wail and the ambulance was on the move.

Something pricked his arm. 'To help with motion sickness,' a voice whispered into his ear. Soon his eyes grew heavy. The last thing he remembered was Fitch, on the bed across the way, asking when it would be his turn for some of that good stuff.

//

'I told him he was playing with fire,' DCI Quinn said light-heartedly, in an apparent attempt to cheer Zoe up.

They and another nurse stood next to Vernon's bed in a ward at London Hospital. They thought Vernon was asleep, but he was only pretending. He had awoken earlier to the sound of hushed voices—Zoe's, DCI Quinn's, and that of another nurse—on the other side of the curtain surrounding his bed. He had kept his eyes closed as the curtain was drawn back because he did not want to talk to anyone but Zoe.

DCI Quinn's pun seemed to have missed the mark because Zoe did not respond. From what Vernon could gather, she was in no mood to talk to the others, either. He overheard her say before the curtain was drawn back that she had had a tremendous fright when he was brought in to hospital. She had been on duty and several times had sneaked off from her rounds to keep vigil at his bedside.

'He should come round any moment,' the other nurse said now as she went about changing Vernon's dressings. 'The sedative only lasts a few hours.'

Until then, Vernon had felt no pain in his hands, but the moment they were exposed to air, they suddenly felt raw, as if the skin had been peeled away. He held back a wince.

As the nurse finished up with the new dressings, she said to Zoe, 'Everything will be all right, dearie. The doctor says Mr Prins is a hardy young man.'

'If what Arthur Fitch says is true,' DCI Quinn put in, 'Vernon's more than that.' To Zoe he added, 'I should be off. I'll only be in the way when he wakes. Give him my regards, if you wouldn't mind.'

'I will,' Zoe said. 'Good night.'

'Good night.' DCI Quinn followed the other nurse out.

Zoe sat on the edge of Vernon's bed. 'You bloody fool,' she murmured lovingly, running her fingers through his hair.

He opened his eyes.

'Oh.' She withdrew her hand.

'Am I really such a fool?' he said, his voice raspy but playful.

'Have you been awake all this time?'

He could see the vexation on her face. 'Sorry. I didn't have the energy to talk to DCI Quinn just now. It sounded like he had already spoken to Arthur, in any case.' He sat up and looked round. 'Where *is* Arthur, by the way?'

'In another ward.'

'Is he all right?'

'He's fine. Not even a leg cast has stopped him from entertaining the nurses and other patients with jokes and war stories.'

In the silence that followed, Vernon suspected what Zoe was thinking—that he had been foolhardy and reckless—and she was right. He had almost died. And for what? To save a dead man, who in life was a stark raving lunatic. What did Morley hope to accomplish by starting a fire, anyway? And why did Walsh put him up to it? Another self-inflicted wound to blame on the Jews? The economist and political scientist in Vernon could not make any sense of it. Perhaps there was nothing to make sense of. It would be like trying to rationalise the motivations behind fascism. Some human behaviours had no basis in rational thought.

'You're not invincible, you know,' Zoe said, sensing Vernon's contrition.

'I know.'

She gently took one of his bandaged hands in hers. 'You bloody fool,' she murmured again. 'You gave me an awful fright.'

//

The next morning Saul paid Vernon a visit in hospital. Zoe had telephoned him, he said.

When he arrived, Vernon was eating breakfast, or at least attempting to. He was forced to hold his fork like a shovel because of the bandages. Immediately he stopped eating and set down the fork, glad for the distraction. 'Wonderful to see you, Saul— although you needn't have taken time out of your busy schedule.'

'What nonsense. You would have done the same for me. In fact, you already have, and more than once. I'll never forget that, old chap. Not for as long as I live.' Saul had a posy in his hand. 'Where would you like these? They're from my garden, to brighten up the place.'

'For me? I thought you might've found yourself a sweetheart.'

Saul laughed. 'Don't be ridiculous.' He placed the flowers onto a side table. 'There you are. A bit of colour.' Gesturing to Vernon's breakfast tray, he said, 'Eat. You mustn't stand on ceremony on my account.'

'It's all right,' Vernon said. 'I've had enough, anyway.' He moved the tray from his lap to the other side table. 'So how are you?'

'Never mind me. How are you?' Saul glanced at Vernon's bandages. 'You look like you've been in the wars, if you don't mind my saying.'

'I got myself into a bit of a scrape.'

'So it would seem.' Saul refrained from saying anything critical. Zoe had apprised him of the events at Action House, and from the looks of it, Vernon needed no reminding of his stupidity. Saul said, 'I was going to say you missed all the excitement last night, but you had some excitement of your own, didn't you?'

'What excitement did I miss?'

'Haven't you heard?'

Vernon shook his head.

'The antifascists answered our call. I wish you could have seen it, old chap. It was magnificent.' Saul's voice had become animated. 'There were four thousand counter-demonstrators by some estimates. We marched through the East End and right into fascist strongholds in Bethnal Green. Communists and Scipians and Jews and gentiles and rich and poor — they were all there to stand up to the Jackboots. So many counter-demonstrators were out on the streets, the fire engines had difficulty reaching Action House. From what I hear, it very nearly burnt to the ground.'

A chill went through Vernon. He thought of what Zoe said about not being invincible. He could have gone up in smoke along with Action House.

'Everyone is determined to prevent Sunday's march,' Saul added. 'We spent the night building barricades, using anything we could get our hands on: old bedsteads and bedsprings, tables and chests of drawers, packing cases, fish boxes from Billingsgate fish market, absolutely anything. The barricading is still going on as we speak.'

'I was wondering why you looked so haggard. Have you really

been up all night?'

'I have, indeed.' Saul smiled like a devious child.

'You're inspiring,' Vernon said with sudden emotion. 'Will there be room for one more agitator in tomorrow's counter-demonstrations, do you think?'

'Why not? The more the merrier.' Saul's face suddenly clouded. He realised his enthusiasm had got the better of him. 'On second thoughts, perhaps you shouldn't. You're far from recovered.'

'Don't let the bandages fool you. I'm perfectly fine. The doctor only wanted me here for twenty-four hours for observation. Besides, it's high time I put away my Jackboot uniform and marched on the side of justice, no?'

Saul smiled uncertainly. 'So long as you don't jump out of the frying pan into the fire.'

Chapter 14

The Battle

It was Sunday, 4 October. The Home Secretary had denied the petition of The Jewish People's Council, and so the Jackboot march was going ahead as planned. No one from the Jackboot leadership or the *London Morning Post* commented on how such a thing could happen if a Jewish cabal controlled the government.

That morning Saul awoke early, ate a full breakfast, listened to some music, and then had Sidney drive him to Gardiners Corner. Vernon and Zoe and Georgina and a small army of Scipians were there. Many of them held placards that read 'Bar the Road to Fascism' or 'They Shall Not Pass'. Barricades had been set up, blocking passage to Commercial Street to the north and Whitechapel High Street to the east. It looked, Saul thought as he joined the crowd, like a scene from the French Revolution.

Georgina greeted him with an embrace. 'You slept well last night?'

'I did.'

'Good. You'll need your wits about you today.'

Vernon and Zoe came over. He appeared much improved since his release from hospital. His hands were still bandaged, but the superficial burns on his face were scarcely noticeable. He introduced Zoe to Saul, since they had only ever spoken over the telephone.

'Hello, Mr Maccabee,' she said, smiling. She gave him her hands, and they kissed each other on the cheeks.

'Vernon speaks very highly of you, my dear. And please, call me Saul.'

Shouts—'The police are coming, the police are coming!'—intruded on their exchange of pleasantries. Everyone turned to see a group of young men and women running up Leman Street. One of the men was a sub-editor from *The Masses*. The group surrounded Georgina, excitedly talking over each other.

'One at a time,' Georgina upbraided them. To the sub-editor, she said, 'What on earth is all this about? I told you to do some reconnoitring, not start a riot.'

'The police are coming,' the sub-editor repeated, gasping for breath. 'Up Leman Street. Thousands of them. The entire mounted regiment and every constable in London, by the looks of it.'

'Good gracious,' Georgina said.

'They'll remove the barricades,' said Vernon. 'We can't allow that.'

'No,' Georgina said, 'we can't.' She turned to the sub-editor and asked where the reinforcements were. Any moment now hundreds, if not thousands, of antifascists were expected to march along Whitechapel Road toward Gardeners Corner.

'The last I heard, they had only just left Whitechapel Station.'

She frowned. 'Then it will be five minutes or more before they arrive. We'll have to stall the police. Get the word out that there's a change of plan.'

Murmurs of an impending confrontation with the police passed like a convulsion from protestor to protestor. In a matter of minutes, an immense human barrier formed across Leman Street.

'The police wouldn't dare attack us, would they?' Zoe asked as she and the others took up positions at the head of the formation. Her question went unanswered. Everyone was too preoccupied watching the police column draw nearer. It was less than a quarter-mile away now. Navy blue uniforms and custodian helmets were visible down Leman Street for as far as the eye could see. The initial excitement among the protestors fast turned into panic.

'There really must be thousands of them,' Saul observed soberly.

An inspector — the only one of the mounted police with a black band on his peaked cap and Bath stars on the epaulettes of his tunic — rode at the head of the column. Thirty yards from the protestors he raised his hand, and the column came to a halt. Then he and two constables dismounted and walked up to the protestors. 'Who's in charge here?' the inspector asked brusquely.

Georgina came forward. '*I* am.'

The two constables exchanged glances and smirked.

'You're disturbing the peace,' the inspector said. 'Tell your followers they're breaking the law and they should clear the streets and go home before somebody gets hurt.'

'We have every right to be here,' Georgina said, unintimidated. 'This is a peaceful demonstration against the brutality of fascism.'

'You may have the right to demonstrate, ma'am,' the inspector said, 'but you've no right to block the streets. Get your people to move, or we'll move them for you.'

An old man suddenly leapt from the crowd, holding up a British Legion standard. He wore a poppy on the lapel of his overcoat. 'Honour our ex-servicemen!' he howled maniacally, waving the standard in the air. 'Denounce fascism!' Before he could say another word, the constables prised the standard from his hands, tore the fabric into pieces, and snapped the pole in two. The old man, at a loss for words, gaped at the debris on the ground.

Saul was incensed. 'That's your way of keeping the peace, is it?' He could not remain silent while the police abused their power.

'You're wasting your breath, Saul,' Georgina said. 'The police are no better than the fascists they're protecting.'

Boos and catcalls issued from the protestors.

The inspector sniggered. 'Consider yourselves warned.' He and the constables returned to the column and re-mounted their horses. Orders were communicated. A squadron of mounted police detached from the column and trotted their horses toward the protestors.

'They're going to charge,' Vernon said. He grabbed hold of Zoe. 'Stay close to me.'

At that moment pandemonium broke out. A flood of antifascists poured through the barricade on Whitechapel High Street. 'The reinforcements have arrived!' someone cried. Bursts of cheering mingled with the sound of bobby whistles and the galloping of horses. The protestors braced themselves for an onslaught from the police. In one thunderous voice they shouted over and over again, 'They shall not pass!'

The first line of mounted police reached the protestors, who stood their ground, shouting and waving placards. Several of the horses reared. One of the policemen slid off his horse and landed on his backside. Some of the protestors went to his aid, helped him to his feet, and asked him if he was all right. As soon as he said he was, they confiscated his truncheon and his helmet and told him to shove off. He limped ignominiously after his horse, which had bolted down a side street. Meanwhile the rest of the police's advance guard retreated back to the column.

The protestors cheered. There were a few thousand of them now, stretching from Leman Street to the intersection of Whitechapel High Street and Commercial Road.

As they watched the police regroup, Saul and Vernon stood shoulder to shoulder, like brothers in arms. The repelling of the police had been intoxicating for Saul. It was the first time he had participated in an act of civil disobedience, and the experience gave him a greater appreciation for what Gandhi must have felt while leading the Salt March. That was what true leadership was, Saul reflected: the inspiring of others. Vernon had said Saul was an inspiration, but to Saul, Vernon was the inspiration. Everything Saul had done to support the antifascists, he did because of Vernon. Saul looked at him now standing courageously by his side. Vernon exuded strength, resilience. In spite of his hospitalisation, he looked healthier and stronger than ever.

'They're preparing to charge again!' Vernon yelled.

This time three or four squadrons set off from the column at a gallop. Their truncheons were drawn. A collective shudder went through the protestors.

'For justice,' Saul said, digging in his heels.

'For justice,' Vernon echoed.

The police's ire had been provoked. They charged with redoubled force. Reigning in their horses just short of the protestors, they rode half-pass and swung their truncheons as they went. Vernon managed to fend off the incoming blows for a minute or two, but the assault was too fast and furious. Protestors dropped like flies. Saul was among them. A truncheon swiped him across the face, knocking him over.

'Saul!' Georgina screamed.

He saw stars for a moment as he lay supine on the ground. *So this is what it's like to be done over*, he thought. Aside from the pain in his jaw and the ringing in his ears, it was not so unpleasant. He had been in worse pinches playing rugby at St Paul's; more than once, he remembered, he had found himself at the bottom of a ruck. And then there was the recent incident in Shadwell. By comparison his current situation was a walk in the park. Protestors scurried past and avoided treading on him. Between the passing bodies he caught glimpses of thin, wispy clouds in the sky.

Suddenly the faces of Georgina and Zoe appeared above him.

'His eyes are open,' Georgina said. 'Saul, can you get up?'

He did not respond. Together the two women and the sub-editor dragged him to safety.

The scene had become chaotic. Protestors ran this way and that, with mounted police in chase. Most of the protestors had fallen back behind the barricades. A flatbed lorry formed part of the barricade across Whitechapel High Street. The seriously injured, half a dozen of them including Saul, were carried to the bed of the lorry to receive treatment. A doctor moved in their midst, tending to injuries. Zoe lent a hand. She was examining Saul's face when he inexplicably sat bolt upright.

'Hello there,' he said as though emerging from a fog. 'No need to worry about me. I'm right as rain.'

'I'll be the judge of that.' She put a hand to his forehead. 'How does your head feel?'

'Like a million pounds.'

'I'm being serious. You might be concussed. Do you remember what happened earlier?'

'A beautiful young lady, a heavenly angel, touched my face.'

'No,' she said, trying not to laugh, 'before that.'

'A policeman bludgeoned me.' Saul looked abstractedly at Leman Street where his bludgeoning had occurred. Protestors were still running round, parrying blows from the police. A lone figure on horseback, majestic in the morning sunlight, came ambling out of the mayhem and cantered toward the lorry. 'My sainted aunt,' Saul said. 'How ever did he manage that?'

Somehow Vernon had stolen a policeman's horse. 'Couldn't let your attacker get away scot-free,' he said as he pulled up alongside the lorry. 'So I nicked his horse. He didn't seem to have much use for it in any case, seeing how he was handcuffed to a lamppost.'

Saul guffawed. 'You didn't!'

'I *did*.'

'That'll teach him to beat up unarmed protestors,' Zoe said.

'Just the man I was looking for,' came a familiar voice from behind Vernon. Vernon turned in the saddle. It was Spartacus, with a couple of his deputies. Spartacus made a fist and raised his arm in the communist salute. 'I have one last mission for you, if you're interested.'

'Depends on what it is,' Vernon said guardedly, shooting a glance at Zoe.

'The Police Commissioner has directed the Jackboots to change their route. They're going to march on Cable Street instead of Whitechapel Road. We've just come from where they're congregated on Royal Mint Street, and they appear to be waiting for The Leader to arrive before they depart. If enough of us could get to The Mahogany Bar Mission area in the next half-hour, we could stop them passing. There's only one problem: a cordon has been set up at the intersection of Alie Street and Commercial Road. Several hundred foot police are there blocking the way.'

'And you want me to help break through.'

'Yes. Will you join us?'

Vernon glanced at Zoe again.

'You'll resent me the rest of your life if I hold you back,' she said.

'I promise I won't do anything overly reckless.'

'You had better not.'

'Will you look after her?' Vernon asked Saul.

'Me after her? I dare say it should be the other way round.'

//

The protestors split into two groups, one to protect the barricades at Gardeners Corner and the other to march down Commercial Road. Instructions to avoid violence were disseminated among the protestors, as the District Secretariat did not want their members to be branded hooligans like the fascists.

Spartacus commandeered Vernon's horse to lead the march. Some two thousand protestors followed him on Commercial Road. At Alie Street, he dismounted and, accompanied by Vernon, went up to the cordon to confer with the police.

'You can't go any farther,' one of the constables threatened as they approached.

'We only want to exercise our God-given right to demonstrate against fascism,' Spartacus said. 'Would you deny us that right?'

'We know what you want, you Bolshie bastard, and we won't allow it.'

'Especially not after you pinched one of our horses,' another constable chipped in.

'You're welcome to the horse,' Vernon said, 'if you allow us to pass.'

'Piss off.'

'Right.' Spartacus turned to go. Vernon followed him in silence. 'You heard them, Prins,' Spartacus said the moment he was back on the horse. 'They want to do it the hard way.' He gave a signal to the protestors that the march would be moving forward.

Placards were handed up to the front line to shield against truncheon blows. Vernon took one that read 'Unite against the Bigotry and Hatred of Fascism'. He held it up high and, swaying it back and forth, began to chant 'Down with fascism!' Others joined in. For the first time in months Vernon was free to openly demonstrate against fascism, and it felt invigorating. His days of agitating in the shadows, he thought, were finally over.

Spartacus stood in the stirrups of the horse and raised a fist. 'Forward, march!'

The protestors advanced toward the cordon. None of the police backed down, and the foremost of them belligerently twirled their truncheons as the protestors drew closer. Volleys of abuse passed from side to side. Soon truncheons were smashing into outstretched placards. The antifascist interdict against violence had given the police the upper hand. One placard after another fell to the ground. Vernon held onto his longer than most, but with each truncheon blow, bits of paper tore off until all that remained of the slogan was the word 'Unite'. He tossed the mangled placard into a gaggle of police, then lifted his arms to protect his head. Those on the front line followed his lead. They surged forward in a body.

The cordon collapsed. As the police scattered, some of them blew their whistles in a futile attempt to restore order.

Vernon pushed his way to a clear path on Commercial Road.

'We've no time to lose,' Spartacus said, riding up behind him. 'Get on.' He reached down and locked arms with Vernon, who bounded alongside the horse for a few strides before swinging up onto its croup.

They loped to Gower's Walk and then on to Back Church Lane. A minute later they were at Cable Street. The road going west, however, was impassable. Rubbish of all kinds blocked the way. Nearby, men with pick-axe handles were pulling up paving stones to reinforce the barrier.

Spartacus strode over to them. 'Are you friends or foes of the masses?'

'Who's askin'?' one of the men said in a Cockney accent. He wiped the sweat from his forehead and held up a hand to shield his eyes from the sun.

'A friend,' Spartacus said.

The other men stopped working to listen in.

'How do we know you ain't coppers?' the Cockney asked.

'Do we look like bloody bluebottles to you?' Spartacus replied.

'No, s'pose not, but you're sittin' on one of their 'orses, ain't ya? So either you're clever blokes, or you're a couple of coppers in disguise.'

'I'm neither, as it happens.' Spartacus pointed a thumb over his shoulder. 'This here's the clever one. He took the horse right out from under a bluebottle bastard.'

'Is that so? Then as I live and breave, you're friends of ours.'

Spartacus and Vernon dismounted. Then Spartacus slapped the horse's rump, sending it bolting back up the lane.

The East Enders resumed their work on the barrier.

'Have you seen any Jackboots come this way?' Spartacus asked.

'No,' the Cockney said, standing up again and holding the pick-axe handle in both hands. 'But from what we 'ear, they bloody well intend to. We'll be ready for 'em, if they do. The fuckin' fascists. They fink they can goad us like cattle. But they ain't seen what we East Enders can do. It was mostly our women who captured those cuntstables earlier.'

The other workmen laughed.

'What do you mean "captured"?' Vernon asked, ignoring the portmanteau.

'See for yourself,' the Cockney said. He lifted his chin toward the other side of the barrier.

Vernon and Spartacus climbed to the top of the rubbish heap and looked over. Twenty to twenty-five policemen — gagged and bound and clad in nothing but their smalls — lay squirming in the middle of the street. Oddly, the area was otherwise abandoned. Doors of shops and windows of tenements were open, and the ground was covered in refuse, as if a riot had occurred and then people had vacated in a hurry. In the distance, a large crowd loitered on Royal Mint Street.

'You should've seen it,' the Cockney proceeded to explain. 'The coppers came and started givin' orders like they owned the place. We 'ad to clear out, they said. To make room for the Jackboots. We told 'em to sod off. This was our home, and we didn't want no fuckin' fascists muckin' it up. They got pushy, said for us to clear out or else. Or else what? we said. Then one of the women threw a piss-pot from a window. It hit a copper in the 'elmet and knocked it clean off his head. He 'ad piss runnin' down the front of him like the inside of a crapper. We damn near died laughin'. The coppers weren't too pleased wiv that, but there was nuffin' they could do. Faster than you could say "bottles and stoppers", we pelted 'em wiv broken paving stones, and missiles rained down on 'em from above: piss-pots, lumps of wood, rotten fruit, old bedding, you name it. You'd've fought it was Armageddon. The coppers took cover in shops. So the women came down onto the streets and 'elped us bash the doors in. The coppers didn't put up a fight after that. They came out wiv their 'ands up. We 'ogtied 'em then, and they've been there on the street ever since.'

As the story came to an end, Spartacus and Vernon stood there smiling at each other for a moment. Then Spartacus said to the Cockney, 'I couldn't help noticing the inhabitants of Cable Street are gone. Where'd they go?'

'Over to Royal Mint Street. They're goin' to give the Jackboots 'ell before they march. They might even stop 'em cold if they can. Sbound to be a good show. You ought to get over there to see it. We'd go ourselves, but someone has to stay 'ere and guard the place, 'aven't they?'

'We wouldn't miss it for the world,' Spartacus said. 'Godspeed, my friends.' He and Vernon scrambled down the other side of the barrier, then hastened through the hogtied police and on to Royal Mint Street.

The crowd was making an awful din. They numbered in the

thousands. East Enders stood on one side and Jackboots on the other, with the police in between. The Jackboots were chanting, 'L-E-A-D-E-R, we want The Leader!' to which the East Enders were shouting back, 'So do we, dead or alive!'

'We're in luck,' Spartacus said as he and Vernon began to intermix with the East Enders. 'The Leader isn't here yet.'

'*Look* at this,' Vernon said, taking in the spectacle. 'It's brilliant. The locals are holding their own.'

'L-E-A-D-E-R ...' the chanting continued.

Spartacus and Vernon made their way to the edge of the police cordon.

'That's far enough,' a policeman said, jabbing Vernon in the chest with a truncheon.

'What now?' Vernon asked. But when he turned, Spartacus was gone. He scoured the crowd. There was no sign of Spartacus anywhere.

Something was happening on the other side of the police cordon. The Jackboots suddenly went quiet. A motorcar and some motorbikes could be heard puttering along the road. The Jackboots nearest the cordon gave way, and the motorcar, with shock troops on the running boards and with a motorbike escort, appeared and parked in front of the stage. The Leader had finally arrived.

He stepped from the car and took the stage with his entourage. Cheers burst forth from the Jackboot rank and file. 'L-E-A-D-E-R ...' they began to chant again. On the stage, a rostrum had been set up with a cluster of microphones. Numerous amplifiers lined the edges of the platform. The Leader went to the rostrum and snapped to attention and gave the fascist salute. Immediately the cheering stopped and his followers saluted back. The sound of several thousand jackboot heels clicking together — followed by the rallying cry 'Hail Leader!' — echoed eerily across Shadwell.

The Leader motioned for silence. He waited until every arm dropped and every voice hushed. Then he said venomously, 'These Jewish rascals —' But before he could say another word, the East Enders shouted 'Down with fascists!' so loudly that, even with the microphones and the powerful amplifiers, his voice was drowned out.

'Down with fascists! Down with fascists! Down with fascists!'

Vernon yelled the words, too, with the conviction of a religious mantra. No other words so precisely expressed what he felt at that moment. Fascism, he thought—and those who promoted it—needed to be confronted, needed to be stopped. Such a worldview had no place in civilised society, was antithetical to equality, and to liberty, and to progress, and to hope.

'Down with fascists! Down with fascists! Down with fascists!'

Still nothing The Leader said could be heard. He gesticulated and moved his lips in an absurd pantomime, like a demented marionette.

Suddenly a rock catapulted from somewhere on Vernon's right, flew overtop the police, and skittered across the stage. Vernon thought he glimpsed Spartacus's flat hat in the vicinity of where the rock had been thrown, but when he looked closer, all he saw were the grey, drawn faces of East Enders. The Leader's bodyguards rallied round him. A whole barrage of rocks followed then. One struck its target true. The Leader tottered, covering his face with his hands. His bodyguards helped him to the car, which reversed to one side of the stage, waited for the Jackboots on the street to make way, and then drove off with the motorbikes in tow.

Even as The Leader departed, the shouting of the East Enders did not let up. It became ear-splitting. Distant voices seemed to mingle with nearer ones. A plurality of voices, Vernon thought. The voices of the future, not of the past. He stood on his tiptoes and looked back over the crowd. People were coming from Cable Street. The protestors had passed through the barrier! All two thousand of them, shouting and raising their fists as they marched!

The police began to make a hasty retreat, whether because of The Leader's departure or the protestors' arrival, Vernon could not tell. But the police were definitely retreating. There would be no fascist march today. Vernon wished Zoe and Saul and Georgina could have been here to witness the victory. As he watched the police, as well as the Jackboots, withdraw from the street, he too raised a fist—and yelled the mantra at the top of his lungs.

'Down with fascists! Down with fascists! Down with fascists!'

Part 2

Kandy, Ceylon

Chapter 15

Homecoming

The train chugged up the track into hill country and, mile by mile, snaked its way toward Kandy. Vernon and Saul had a compartment to themselves. While Vernon read a book, Saul gazed out the window, transfixed by the scenery. Everything in the countryside—the trees and grasses and paddy fields and tea terraces—was lush and shockingly green. Saul understood why Vernon was so fond of Ceylon. It was like living in the Garden of Eden.

On the outskirts of Balana village, as the sweeping Alagalla Mountains appeared on the horizon, the sky suddenly opened up. It was a deluge of biblical proportions, obscuring everything in sight outside the train. Saul remarked on how the monsoon rains of Ceylon made England seem like a desert island by comparison.

Vernon lowered his book. 'It's really only a matter of degree,' he said a little defensively. He was tired and hot and irritable. Besides which, he was having difficulty concentrating on his book, worried as he was about his pater. He had telephoned Minnette from the Grand Oriental Hotel in Colombo, and something in her voice had been amiss. Watching the rain now come down in buckets, he added, 'It rains almost as frequently in London as it does here. Only here, the volumes are greater.' He turned away from the window and, continuing in the same vein, said that if he were given the choice between living in England or Ceylon based solely on the weather, he would choose the latter hands down. In Ceylon, things stayed green year round, while in London from November to March, there were no leaves on the trees and everything looked dead and bleak even when it was not raining or snowing. His first year at LSE had taken some getting used to because London was perpetually cold and cloudy. Sunny days in Ceylon, on the other hand, were truly sunny days: the sky was endless blue; the sun, enormous and brilliantly white. Such weather made you glad to be alive, even if it *was* devilishly hot.

'You're quite right,' Saul said, not taking offence at Vernon's vehemence. 'There's something oppressive and dank about the British Isles. It explains why so many of us Brits escape to the Mediterranean each year.' He had a theory about Great Britain's climate and the effect it had on the temperament of its inhabitants: the limited sunshine increased the amount of melancholy. He thought perhaps Esther herself had been affected by London's dreary weather. Her moods almost always improved on sunny days.

The train's whistle blew, and a moment later, their compartment went dark.

'What the devil?' Saul said. He fumbled for the matchbox in his jacket pocket on the seat next to him and struck a match. It gave off just enough light for him to see Vernon's face.

'It's only a tunnel,' Vernon said, grinning.

'And what, may I ask, is so funny?'

'That we should be talking about sunlight and Britain right before everything goes black, in a tunnel built by the British as part of the white man's burden.'

'Yes,' Saul said, blowing out the match as the flame reached his fingertips and returning the compartment to darkness. 'I suppose that is funny.'

Again the whistle sounded, and as the train emerged from the tunnel, sunlight flooded the compartment. Saul looked out the window. The rain had let up. Through the mist, he could see the hills stretching to the horizon. Somehow — the evidence from his eyes beggared belief — the verdure had become an even brighter shade of green.

An hour later they arrived at Kandy Station. A porter helped them off the train with their trunks. Vernon thanked him in Sinhala and tipped him generously. As the train pulled away, Saul and Vernon stood there bewildered for a moment in the sultry midday air. They were the only passengers to have deboarded.

Saul turned and noticed that the station building behind them was nothing more than a terracotta-roofed hut in the middle of the jungle. 'So this is Kandy?' he said without any inflection in his voice.

Vernon did not respond. He was looking up and down the track for Minnette. She was supposed to be meeting them at the station. When he telephoned her from Colombo, he had informed her of their arrival time in Kandy. It was uncharacteristic of her to be late. He went inside the hut to ask after her.

In Vernon's absence, Saul observed the environs of the station. All round, the jungle teemed with life. He recognised some of the tree species: palms and plumeria and ironwood. He fancied himself an amateur naturalist, having studied botany and ornithology at Cambridge. And he had spent the best part of his time on the *SS Oronsay* reading *The Fauna and Flora of British India*, which he acquired at Hatchards bookshop before leaving London.

He listened closely to the birds in the trees. There were so many of them, it was like being in an aviary. He had trouble isolating specific calls. The only bird he could identify with certainty was the parakeet. A small flock of them were roosting in one of the larger ironwood trees, chattering raucously. He also thought he heard, deeper in the jungle, the metallic, rolling call of a barbet and the fluty, synchronised calls of a pair of babblers. Individually and in concert, the birdcalls were music to his hears.

It started raining again, lightly. Almost instantly the birds stopped calling.

Vernon emerged from the hut. 'No one has seen her. Something important must have come up.'

'I hope it's nothing serious,' said Saul.

'So do I.' Vernon said nothing more. He was chary to speculate about what might have delayed Minnette.

A man with an umbrella appeared some distance away on the other side of the track. He was beckoning to Vernon and Saul.

'I presume you know who that is?' Saul said.

'It looks like Mr Gunaratne, a neighbour of Ammi and Thathi's. Minnette must have sent him.' Vernon glanced up at the sky. 'There's nothing for it, we'll just have to get wet.'

With a trunk in each hand, they crossed the track and walked to Mr Gunaratne in the mizzling rain.

Mr Gunaratne was a short Ceylonese man with a round face, and he was almost as black as the Africans and West Indians Saul had seen in Soho. 'Hello, young man,' Mr Gunaratne said to Vernon in a singsong voice.

'Hello, Mr Gunaratne.' Vernon did not introduce Saul. 'Where's my sister?'

'We had best get out of the rain,' Mr Gunaratne said with his eyes averted. 'I'll explain everything on the drive home.' He smiled at Saul, then tiptoed through the mud for a few yards before veering off into the jungle. 'Come,' he said over his shoulder.

Vernon and Saul followed him through the trees. It was rough walking. A dirt path had been broken in in the undergrowth, but it was muddy and lined with thorny shrubs. Saul regretted not having worn his galoshes.

Shortly they came to a tan Humber parked alongside a dirt road. Mr Gunaratne took their trunks, one by one, and crammed them into the back seat. 'I'm afraid it'll be a rather tight fit for whoever sits in the back,' he apologised.

'No problem at all,' Saul said and quickly squeezed in next to the trunks.

Vernon protested.

'It's only fair, old chap. After all, I'm half your size.' Saul also was thinking it would be better for Vernon to have a modicum of privacy when Mr Gunaratne explained why Minnette had not come herself. Whatever the news was, it was unlikely to be good.

Mr Gunaratne started up the Humber and pulled onto the road. The rain intensified, pelting the windscreen. He turned on the wiper and concentrated intently on the road as the Humber built up speed.

Meanwhile Vernon just sat there staring out the passenger-side window. The tension in his body was unmistakable. Finally he lost patience. 'What was it you were going to explain?'

'Your father … He's not long for this world, I'm sorry to say. Your mother and sister asked me to get you home at once.' Then Mr Gunaratne floored the accelerator. The needle quivered up to thirty-five, and clumps of mud flung in the Humber's wake.

//

Dr Fernando, the family doctor, came out of Johannes's room seconds after Vernon rushed into the bungalow. Their eyes met, and Vernon knew immediately it was too late. Neither of them spoke. Dr Fernando simply opened the door to Johannes's room, put a hand on Vernon's shoulder as he went by, and left the family to grieve.

Vernon thought his heart would break as he quietly entered the room. Kamala and Minnette were kneeling next to the four-poster, weeping. On the bed, Johannes's eyes were closed, his hands folded on his chest. He had a thick white beard, and beneath it, his face was jaundiced and emaciated. He must have suffered a great deal before his death, Vernon thought. Even the effort to get out of bed and shave had been too much.

A half-minute passed before Kamala and Minnette noticed Vernon.

'Darling!' Kamala said, wiping her tears and getting to her feet. She embraced him tightly. She had aged, he noticed, since last he saw her. She was still beautiful, even at fifty, but her hair was greyer and thinner, and she had wrinkles on her forehead and crow's feet at the corners of her eyes.

Suddenly his heart overflowed with shame. He should have been here, at home, to relieve some of her burden. He had a chance to come sooner. Why did he not? There were more important things in life than careers and politics. 'I ought to have come sooner,' he said, berating himself.

'You're here,' Kamala murmured. 'That's all that matters now.'

Minnette joined them. She had dark circles under her eyes, as if she had not slept for days. She started to cry again when Vernon embraced her. 'Hello, Brother,' she said through the tears.

'Hello, Sister.'

She gave him a loving look as they parted. 'It's good to see you.'

'It's good to see you too.'

'Come,' Kamala said to him. 'Now that you're home, you must say goodbye to your *thatha*.' She went to the bed and gestured for Vernon to follow. 'Doesn't he look peaceful?' She stroked Johannes's beard and then kissed his forehead.

Vernon knelt down, taking Johannes's lifeless hand in his. But he could not bring himself to say goodbye. That would have to wait, until the sting of loss had abated and he could summon the strength. For now, he simply pressed his cheek to Johannes's hand, and wept with abandon.

//

While Vernon attended to family matters, Saul went to Mr Gunaratne's house up the road. They sat down in a pair of planter's chairs on the verandah and silently and rather sombrely watched the rainwater cascade off the roof. Before they could strike up a conversation, a rather good-looking chap with an umbrella in one hand and a doctor's bag in the other came walking up the stone path to the verandah. He wore a tropical wool suit and had close-cropped hair and European-like features.

'Dr Fernando,' Mr Gunaratne called out. 'What news?'

Dr Fernando shook his head gravely as he mounted the stairs. On the verandah, he dropped his umbrella and bag onto the floor and slumped into a chair. Despite his appearance and his Portuguese surname, he was as dark-skinned as Mr Gunaratne. The doctor sighed and said, 'It never gets any easier, losing patients.'

'I should think not,' said Mr Gunaratne. He glanced in the direction of the Prins's bungalow. 'Poor Kamala. And the children.'

'How's Vernon?' Saul ventured to ask.

Dr Fernando looked at him absently without responding.

Mr Gunaratne sat forward and gripped the arms of his chair. 'How obtuse of me. I didn't introduce you. Dr Fernando, this is Mr Saul Maccabee, a friend of Vernon's from London. Mr Maccabee, this is Dr Bernard Fernando, Kandy town's esteemed physician.'

Dr Fernando still had an absent look in his eyes. 'Bernie's fine,' he said, putting a thumb and middle finger to his temples. He closed his eyes and scrunched up his face as if he had a headache. 'You'll forgive me, Mr Maccabee, if I don't shake your hand. I've had a most trying afternoon.'

'Of course,' Saul said. 'And you may call me Saul.'

'And I'm Romesh,' Mr Gunaratne put in. 'Now that we're on first-name terms, shall I brew a pot of tea? We could have ourselves a cosy little chat while it rains.'

'Perhaps some other time, Romesh,' Dr Fernando said. 'I only stopped by to recover myself before I make my last house call of the day.' He stood up and turned to Saul. 'As for the young Mr Prins, I can only say that he has had a terrible shock, as have his mother and sister. They'll need all the friends they can get at a time like this.'

'Indeed,' Saul said. He understood all too well the exigencies of loss.

'It was a pleasure to make your acquaintance, Saul. Good day.'

'Yes, good day.'

Dr Fernando gathered up his umbrella and his bag and stepped out into the rain.

Romesh waited for him to recede from view, then said, 'I fear his solicitousness toward his patients will be the death of him one of these days. He has taken the Hippocratic oath to dizzying heights.' A conspiratorial look formed on Romesh's face. 'Of course, in Kamala's case, he had special reason to be attentive.'

'How do you mean?'

'The two of them were sweethearts once. A long, long time ago. Before Johannes came along and impressed her with his wealth. She dropped Bernie like a ton of bricks, and after that he devoted himself to his medical studies. He's happily married now — to one Celine Fernando — or so he would have us believe. I'm not much taken myself with the notion of conjugal bliss.'

Saul had already drawn the conclusion that Romesh was a confirmed bachelor. Earlier, as they first came onto the verandah, Saul got a glimpse of Romesh's inner sanctum through an open shutter. The upholstered furniture was in tatters, and books and papers and other sundries lay strewn about the floor and on tabletops. There were no signs whatsoever of a woman's influence. It reminded Saul of his own house after Esther had gone.

Vernon suddenly appeared on the verandah stairs. He looked like he had been put through a wringer. His hair and clothes were sodden, and his face was flushed. 'Is Mr Gunaratne gossiping again?' he asked as he stepped onto the verandah. He could not have heard much of what Romesh had been saying, so the implication seemed to be that Romesh had a reputation as a gossip.

'Ah, look who's out and about,' Romesh said. 'A good sign. A good sign, indeed.'

Saul got up from his chair and clasped Vernon's hand. 'My condolences, old chap.'

Vernon nodded but avoided Saul's eyes.

'I was thinking,' Saul added, 'that under the circumstances, perhaps I should stay at an hotel.' It was one thing, he thought, to provide emotional support; it was quite another to get under foot at a time of crisis.

'Bosh!' Vernon responded. 'You're to be my guest, and that's flat.'

Saul was taken aback. 'See here, old chap, the last thing you need is an interloper insinuating himself into your personal affairs.'

'You're not an interloper, Saul. I consider you a comrade and one of my closest friends.'

Saul blushed. 'All the same, I think it would be best if I made myself scarce just now.'

'Perhaps I could be of assistance,' Romesh offered. 'There's a solution, a middle path, that might be amenable to you both. It would avoid the inhospitality of sending Saul to an hotel and also keep him close to home. Saul could be *my* guest—for a fortnight, say. It just so happens I have a spare room and am in want of company.'

To Saul the idea of staying in the home of someone he barely knew was *not* amenable. But he did not think he could say as much without seeming rude.

Vernon, for his part, interpreted Saul's silence as assent. 'I'm amenable if Saul is,' he said. 'Are you sure you wouldn't mind, Mr Gunaratne? You've been awfully generous already.'

'I wouldn't mind at all,' Romesh said and clapped his hands together as though the decision were final.

//

'Let me look at you, *putā*,' Kamala said, looking up at Vernon and cupping his face in her hands. She wore a red-and-gold Kandyan sari, and her long black hair, flecked with grey, hung loosely on her shoulders and down her back.

He had just finished putting away the things from his luggage when she came into his room. Moments earlier, he once more had given himself up to grief, as he hung his clothes in the wardrobe, knowing his pater would never again share with him the sights and smells and sounds of home.

'You're the perfect likeness of your *thatha*.' Kamala became meditative. 'You know, he kept asking after you. He held out hope that he would see his son—"the big man about London"—one last time.'

'Oh, Amma.' Only *one* day, Vernon thought. That was all he would have needed to have seen Thathi alive. Only one day. He felt another prick of conscience.

'Did you find what he left for you?' she asked.

Vernon shook his head, holding back the tears.

She opened a chest of drawers, in which three velvet cases were stored.

'His campaign medals!' he said excitedly. The medals were for Johannes's service in the Gallipoli campaign: the 1914-15 Star, the British War Medal, and the Victory Medal. 'He used to refer to them jokingly as Pip, Squeak, and Wilfred.'

'Yes. He remembered how you liked to look at them as a boy.'

At random Vernon selected one of the cases and opened it. Inside was the Victory Medal. It was bronze, coin-shaped, with a winged figure on the front, and was attached to a rainbow-coloured ribbon. Just looking at it conjured up an assortment of memories for Vernon, of his time in London and his childhood: Spartacus at their meeting in The Green Park, the Victoria Memorial glinting in the moonlight; Thathi at a gathering of ex-servicemen on Galle Face Green in Colombo, wearing the three medals round his neck; and he and a friend, at perhaps the age of ten, sneaking into Thathi's bureau to get a peek at the medals and, if at all possible, hold them in their hands.

'He left you other things, as well,' Kamala said. 'His paradox gun. And his old howdah pistol that he cherished. But there'll be time to discuss that later.'

Minnette entered the room and saw what Vernon was holding. 'Thathi's medals.' She became meditative in the same way that Kamala had earlier. It was a constant complaint of Kamala's side of the family—that Minnette looked nothing like a Thalwatta and everything like a Prins—but there was no mistaking now the resemblance between mother and daughter. 'He wanted you to have them because he said you were as brave as he was, gallivanting all over the world, first to Delhi, then to London. He said he wanted you never to forget the price that was paid in the Great War, the price that continues to be paid to this day.'

'I won't forget,' Vernon said with an air of solemnity, as if he were duty-bound never to forget. No, he thought, he would never forget the price of war. Nor would he forget the price of peace — which was eternal vigilance. Reverently he closed the case and returned it to the drawer.

Kamala cupped his face in her hands again. 'You'll always be my little boy. It seems like only yesterday you were still wearing nappies. I never used to mind changing you, even though you had an *ayah* to do that, because you were such a cute baby, with your head shaved like a monk. Of course, we couldn't tell you that then. You would have got the evil eye.' She smiled at the remembrance. 'We were rather superstitious in those days.'

'I'm not a little boy anymore, Amma.' Vernon withdrew her hands from his face.

'I know,' she said with sadness in her voice. As an afterthought, she added, 'You'll be having children of your own soon.'

Minnette shot him a glance, and he repressed a smile.

Kamala appeared not to have noticed the exchange between brother and sister. 'I'll leave you two to catch up.' She hesitated in the doorway for a moment and glanced at Vernon. 'Whatever became of your friend Mr Maccabee? The guestroom was made up for him.'

'He felt he would be intruding, given the circumstances. I told him that that was bollocks, but he wouldn't listen. Then Mr Gunaratne offered to let him stay at his house for a spell, and it was agreed upon.'

'How considerate of them.' An artful expression crossed Kamala's face. 'We must repay their thoughtfulness. Let them know, will you — when next you meet — that they must come for dinner one evening, after things are settled with Thatha. Let them know too — and you must be very explicit about this — I won't take no for an answer.'

Chapter 16

Serendipity

Saul's stay at Romesh's house was not going well. The guestroom had no wardrobe or even a chest of drawers; its ceiling fan was broken; the bed's mosquito net was moth-eaten, with holes the size of a fist; and the adjoining bathroom did not have running hot water. Then when Romesh came in to put clean linens on the mattress, an intrusion of gigantic cockroaches scurried out from under the bed. Romesh pretended not to notice, muttered enigmatically 'A bloody curse', and went about changing the linens while Saul looked on in horror. After Romesh had finished and left the room, Saul was beside himself. He expected to forgo certain creature comforts in Ceylon, but he drew the line at sharing a bed with arthropods.

He needed some air. Rifling through one of his trunks, he pulled out a pair of binoculars and his pipe and tobacco pouch and then hurried outside. It had stopped raining. According to what Romesh said earlier, there was a half-mile-long path that ran from the back of the bungalow down to the Mahaweli River. Saul found the path and set out for the river. The ground was sopping wet, but it was of no consequence because his shoes were already caked with mud from the walk at the railway station.

As soon as he was in the thick of the jungle, he stopped and looked up through the bamboo and the mass of trees: fig and breadfruit and many other species of which he could not identify at a glance. It was still overcast. Crepuscular rays lit up the western sky. He estimated it to be about an hour before sunset.

Continuing on, he listened to the sounds of the jungle. The tree canopy was alive with birdcalls. There were so many of them that, similar to the environs of the railway station, he had difficulty identifying individual birds. Variously he heard chirrups and clucks and screeches and warbles and what sounded like the coos of a dove. And he saw flashes of brilliant-coloured feathers, like the palette of one of Esther's paintings: reds and yellows and greens and blues. As he approached the river, a pair of yellowish birds flew from tree to tree among the lower branches. One of them alighted on a nearby granite outcrop. Saul felt a rush of exhilaration: he was about to get his first close-up look at a tropical bird. But before he could remove his spectacles and focus the binoculars, the bird was gone.

With the naked eye, Saul stared at the spot where the bird had been. Not all was lost, he thought. Indeed, the bird had given him an idea: he could get a better view of the jungle atop the granite. He hung the binocular strap round his neck and circled the granite until he found its gentlest slope and then clambered up. At the top he could see the river and across it to the opposite bank. The surrounding vegetation was unbelievably luxuriant. He sat down on a flat section of rock that was only slightly damp and lit his pipe and enjoyed the view for a while. Everything about the jungle was on such a grand scale. Next to the granite outcrop stood a mature breadfruit tree. Its fruit was ripe, the largest of the ovaries bigger than rugby balls. He almost laughed, the proportions were so absurd. Across the river an immense fig tree dominated the eastern skyline. A movement in its upper branches caught his eye. From a distance it looked like dozens of retracted umbrellas were hanging upside down among the branches. He trained the binoculars on the tree.

'Ho ho!' he said aloud as if he had discovered gold. The objects were not umbrellas; they were a colony of flying foxes. Their brown, fox-like heads and rust-coloured mantles were unmistakable in the fading light. It would not be long, he thought, before they would take to the air and drink from the river on the wing and prowl the night for flowers and fruit. He alternated between watching the flying foxes through the binoculars and smoking his pipe, until, fifteen minutes before sunset, he decided to return to Romesh's.

He was climbing back down to the jungle floor, on all fours, when he heard a rustle in the leaf litter at the base of the granite outcrop. Something was wriggling in the leaves. As he got closer, he thought he saw the markings of a snake. He froze, with his foot hovering inches above the ground. Slowly raising his foot back up and at the same time clutching at pockets in the rock to keep from falling, he squinted at the creature in the leaves.

'For pity's sake,' he said to himself and breathed more easily. The creature was nothing more than an earthworm. But what an earthworm! It was an inch in diameter and nearly two feet long. Saul got down to the ground and picked it up. It writhed in his hands. He wished he had a camera, to memorialise his discovery. No one back home in London would believe that such a thing existed without photographic proof. Mrs Grant certainly would not. She would be incredulous and would accuse him of pulling her leg. An earthworm as big as a snake, indeed! He would not have believed it himself if he had not seen it with his own two eyes and touched it with his own two hands.

He returned the worm to its place in the leaves and then strolled back to Romesh's, more lightsome than on his way out. Before stepping onto the verandah stairs, he stopped to kick the mud off his shoes.

'There you are,' Romesh said from the front door as Saul came up onto the verandah. 'Where have you been? You shouldn't wander off by yourself.'

Saul's mind was in another world. He seemed not to have heard Romesh. 'I've seen the most extraordinary things,' he said dreamily.

'There was this bird. Yellow. It bounced in flight like a woodpecker. I must consult my field guide.' He went past Romesh and into the bungalow and, in the guestroom, exchanged his binoculars and smoking accoutrements for the field guide. Upon returning to the verandah, he stood in front of Romesh and riffled through the book's pages until he got to the colour plates of Ceylonese birds. 'Let's see,' he said, turning one page at a time. He was shaking, not from nervousness or his congenital hand tremor but from pure, unadulterated excitement. 'Here we are.' He ran a shaky finger down the page of yellow-coloured birds, stopping at one with a yellow front and yellow ear tufts and yellow patches below the eyes. 'There. That's it, by Jove. A yellow-eared bulbul.'

'They're as common as crows,' Romesh said, deflating the moment.

'Are they really?' But Saul was only slightly disappointed. For such a majestic creature to be commonplace, it seemed to him, was almost as spectacular as it was for it to be a rarity. At any rate, it was merely a matter of perspective. What to the Oriental might be unexceptional, to the Occidental might be exceptional, and vice versa. Romesh would doubtless find London's Underground, which to Saul was a dirty and humdrum mode of transportation, to be one of the most wondrous things in the world to behold.

'May I?' Romesh said, asking for the book.

Saul handed it to him.

Romesh flipped to the section on raptors. 'If it's a rare specimen you want,' he said, pointing to the picture of a Jerdon's baza, 'this is a rare one indeed.'

There was still enough light in the gathering dusk for Saul to see the hawk's crest and the banding pattern on its underside. It was a magnificent animal.

'A pair of them can sometimes be seen on the edge of the Udawattekele reserve north of Kandy town,' Romesh added. He closed the book and handed it back to Saul. 'Perhaps it would interest you to go there tomorrow to see if we can spot them?'

'It most certainly would. That is, if it wouldn't be too much trouble.'

'Not at all.'

A young Ceylonese woman emerged tentatively from the bungalow and, avoiding Saul's eyes, said something to Romesh in her native tongue.

'Ah, right right,' Romesh said with a quick wobble of his head. He turned to Saul. 'This is Prema, the girl who comes to cook for me. She's asking about dinner. Which is what I came to ask you about myself—but which, like a dullard, I promptly forgot. Will you be all right eating what I eat? My usual fare—curries and sambals—is rather spicy.'

'When in Rome,' Saul said agreeably.

Romesh relayed to Prema what Saul said.

She smiled with lowered eyes, then went back into the bungalow.

'Shall we go into the sitting room while we wait?' Romesh asked, opening the door for Saul.

Prema had prepared the sitting room for their arrival. The ceiling fan hummed overhead, a mosquito coil smouldered on the floor, the wicks of hurricane lanterns flickered from the walls, and two uncapped bottles of beer stood perspiring on the coffee table.

'Straight from the icebox,' Romesh said, picking up both bottles and handing one to Saul. 'It's a Ceylonese beer. Brewed not far from here in Nuwara Eliya.' He clinked his bottle against Saul's. 'Cheers.'

'Cheers,' Saul echoed and took a sip. He did not normally drink beer, but on this occasion, he found the cold, hoppy beverage exceedingly refreshing. After the long train journey, and in the heat, he was not peckish so much as parched. He took another, more substantial drink. 'Thanks, Romesh. Just what the doctor ordered.'

The smell of chilli peppers and spices wafted in from the kitchen. It was so intense, it made Saul sneeze.

'Bless you,' Romesh said. He laughed. 'I told you the food's spicy.'

A silence ensued. Saul racked his brains for a topic of conversation but came up empty. They looked at each other awkwardly and exchanged smiles.

Then Romesh said, 'I say, some music would be nice.' In a corner of the room was an old gramophone and a box of records. He set down his beer and scampered over to the gramophone and put on a record.

It was a movement from one of Schubert's impromptus, for solo piano. Saul knew the piece well. Its melody was languid, hauntingly prayerful, with a fluttering broken-chord pattern. To Saul's mind, the hands on the keyboard conversed in a way that was far superior to any extemporaneous conversation he and Romesh could have had. 'You're a man after my own heart,' Saul piped up above the music. His mind coloured as he went on listening. Perhaps staying at Romesh's would not be so objectionable, after all.

//

Vernon was in two minds about whether to tell Minnette of his involvement with the Jackboots. Now that she was a member of the LSSP she might sympathise with his own political activism. But she was likely to be as unimpressed with his recklessness as Zoe and Saul and DCI Quinn had been. Vernon also did not want to have to explain why he waited until the second week of October to set sail from London. He could hardly admit to himself that while he was off playing spy games among the fascists, his pater had been at death's door. Besides that, during his first private moment with Minnette after returning to Kandy, all she could talk about was how scheming Kamala was.

'Did you see the look on her face?' Minnette asked him after Kamala had given instructions to invite Saul and Mr Gunaratne to dinner. 'That's how she gets when she's plotting something.'

Vernon was tempted to point out that Minnette often got the same look on *her* face, but he held his tongue. Somehow it did not matter now, any more than Kamala's plotting mattered. He had become more forgiving of other people's frailties in the wake of

Johannes's death. 'Leave her be,' Vernon said. 'She has done neither of us any harm.'

'You won't be saying that when one of her plots involves you. You heard her hint about grandchildren. She'll be inviting Ramona Bolling over for dinner next, you wait and see. Even while Thathi was deathly ill, she was inviting boys over in the hope that I'd fancy one of them. But they were all such poor specimens, it made me sick. Do you know that the beastliest of the lot, Lionel Hingert, tried to kiss me? I had gone to the loo after dinner and was coming out the door and there he was on the threshold blocking my way, with his lips puckered and without so much as a by your leave. So I kneed him in the groin.'

Vernon let out a bellow of laughter. He could see as plain as day Lionel doubled over, the blighter's hands covering his injured bollocks, and Minnette storming off in disgust.

'It's not funny.'

'I'm laughing at what *you* did, not what Lionel did.'

'Still, you don't know what I've been through because of Amma, and I wouldn't wish the same on anyone, least of all you.'

'I'll handle her diplomatically if it should come to that.' Vernon was still laughing inside at what Minnette had done to Lionel. It felt good to give himself up to merriment instead of grief.

'For your sake, I hope she doesn't invite Ramona for dinner. Personally I don't set much store by gossip, but in this case, I think the gossip's true. Ammi says it can't possibly be true because Ramona comes from a good family, but since when has that been a bar to wickedness?'

'What gossip?'

'You'll have to ask Mr Gunaratne that. He knows all the tawdry details.' Minnette produced from her trouser pocket an envelope with airmail postage on the front and handed it to Vernon. 'It's a letter from your sweetheart. I intercepted it from the postman before Amma could see it.'

Vernon flushed. 'I told her not to write till after I arrived in Kandy.'

'Keep it hidden from Amma's prying eyes,' Minnette warned and left the room.

He tore open the envelope. He was cross with Zoe for being so careless, but he also was eager to read what she had to say. He had written to her thrice while on the *SS Oronsay* and had cabled her once after his arrival in Colombo, but he had not received word from her since leaving London. He read her letter keenly.

My Dearest Love,

I know you said not to write until after you arrived in Ceylon, but I simply couldn't wait any longer. I received the letters you sent from the ports of call on your voyage out and they were so sweet and loving my heart ached for you as I read them. Oh, when will you come back to me? I am counting the days already.

Nothing much has changed here since you left. I am not sure whether that is a good thing or a bad thing. Perhaps it is both. Or neither. It could just be that it is what it is, life being one big muddle.

You may have read of this in the papers, but the week after you left London, the most dreadful thing happened. The fascists carried out another antisemitic attack. Just telling you of it is almost more than I can bear. It was on Mile End Road and seemed to be retaliation for the 4 October antifascist demonstrations. A group of Jackboot youths set fire to cars and smashed windows and looted Jewish shops and attacked anyone who so much as appeared to be Jewish. There was a razor-slashing and one Jew was picked up and hurled through a plate-glass window and after him a four-year-old girl was thrown in. Have these thugs no shame? I know I told you I abhor violence, but when I heard the news, all I wished for — besides the wellbeing of Mr Maccabee and our other Jewish friends — was that you were here to exact vengeance on the Jackboots. Was that vile of me? Am I no better than the fascists for thinking such thoughts? Tell Mr Maccabee, please, that I apologise on behalf of all the gentiles in England for this latest outrage against his faith.

King Edward is up to his shenanigans again. Rumours are swirling about London that he has installed Mrs Simpson in a house he rented for her in Regent's Park. In all honesty, I find it rather silly that people make such a fuss. The King should be able to do what he pleases in matters of the heart, just like you and I should be able to do what we please together regardless of our ethnicity or our nationality or our social status or our religion or our politics or anything else. And just like Jews should be able express their faith and their identities howsoever they please. I know I am preaching to the converted in telling you this, so I will say no more on the subject.

Do write to me again soon. I very much want to hear the rhythm of your voice, and catch the scent of your hand, even if it is only on paper.

Thinking of You Always,
Zoe

Vernon had no idea Zoe was so philosophical. He read the letter through a second time. She was right to be concerned about Saul's reaction to the 'Mile End Road Pogrom', as the antisemitic incident came to be called by the British press. It had been reported on widely while Vernon and Saul were travelling on the *SS Oronsay*. After Saul first learned of it, he was distressed for days. From Port Said, he cabled his mother, to say that she and other London Jews were in his prayers. It would give him no end of pleasure now, Vernon thought, to hear of Zoe's concern for him.

Vernon returned the letter to its envelope and hid it beneath his smalls in the chest of drawers. He would delay writing back to Zoe for a few days, he decided. He might break down weeping if he were to tell her of his pater's death any sooner than that.

As he made his way to the dining room — with the familiar smell of curries filling the air — he wondered where she was at the moment. There was a five-and-a-half-hour time difference between England and Ceylon, so presumably she was on a shift at London Hospital. He imagined her making her rounds from ward to ward, wearing her blue-and-white nurse's uniform, as gorgeous as ever. He was glad she had written, despite his initial irritation. He missed her terribly.

//

Saul and Romesh rose at dawn and drove to Sangamitta Mawatha and footed it to a grassy clearing on the southern edge of the Udawattakele Forest Reserve. Saul wore a pith helmet, a khaki shirt and shorts, woollen socks, and country boots. On his back was a rucksack containing his birdwatching kit: a field guide, binoculars, and a canteen of water. They got to a stand of cinnamon-tree saplings and knelt down in the undergrowth, watching for any signs of a Jerdon's baza in the clearing. It was a splendid morning. The horizon east of Kandy was like a brightly coloured sari, with bands of yellow and orange and pink.

They were there for only a few minutes when a small deer appeared on the opposite side of the clearing and began to graze. Saul looked at it through his binoculars. It had a reddish-brown coat, and black markings ran the length of its face and head.

'A barking deer,' Romesh whispered.

Saul had read about the deer in his field guide, which referred to it as an Indian muntjac. He remembered it because it was unique among deer species for being omnivorous. Besides feeding on plants and fruit, it ate bird eggs and small animals and occasionally even scavenged on carrion. The males also had canines for fighting during the rut. Saul lowered his binoculars. The thought of a meat-eating deer with eye teeth made his entrails contract.

He and Romesh continued to scan the sky above the clearing for the elusive raptor, alternately swatting mosquitoes from their bodies and wiping perspiration from their faces. For the best part of an hour they did this, until their knees ached. By then, the deer had disappeared back into the jungle, and the only birds they had seen in the clearing were a storytelling of crows feeding on the carcass of a dead animal. Finally Saul stood up and stretched.

Romesh did the same. 'I seem to have made a pig's ear of our expedition,' he apologised.

'No matter. All in a day's work for a birdwatcher.' Saul took a swig from his canteen and, to show there was no ill will, handed it to Romesh.

'Just so we don't totally waste the day,' Romesh said between drinks, 'shall we take a stroll through the reserve? You can't fail to see birds in there, and the paths are well travelled.'

'Yes, why not.'

They exited the trees and rounded a bend and came to a path that led to the depths of the jungle. A trail post read 'Byrde Lane'.

'It's only about a mile from here to the royal pond,' Romesh said, turning up the path.

'What's the royal pond?' Saul asked.

'The forest was once a pleasure garden of Kandyan kings, reserved for them alone, and they bathed in the pond. It's no longer used for that, but it attracts animals from all over the area.'

Either side of the path the jungle was overgrown with vegetation. Among other plants, there were cinnamon and fig and ironwood trees as well rattan and climbing palms, and entwined in the branches of the larger trees were vines and creepers. A variety of orchids grew from tree trunks or, in places where sunlight reached the ground, from rocks. Orangeberry and coffee shrubs and ferns comprised much of the understory.

They had not gone up the path more than a hundred yards before Saul's senses were overwhelmed by birdcalls and colour. Back at the clearing, he had heard calls coming from deep within the jungle, and mynah birds had made a din high up in the trees — with their gurgles and screeches and wails and whistles — but he did not see any of them. Now, so many birds were visible to the naked eye, it beggared description. There were babblers, barbets, emerald-coloured doves, leafbirds, parrots, thrushes. Saul kept peering through his binoculars every few feet. After he stopped for the umpteenth time, he apologised to Romesh.

'That's why we're here, isn't it?' Romesh said.

The path continued to meander. Every once in a while, they saw an animal cross the path several hundred yards ahead of them, mongooses and deer for the most part. At one point a sounder of wild boar crossed, and Saul and Romesh had to stop to let them pass. Eventually the path veered north, and its name changed to Lady Horton's Drive. Saul commented on the name change.

'One hundred years ago,' Romesh explained, 'the then-governor of Ceylon, Sir Robert Wilmot-Horton, built the path as a remembrance to his wife. If I'm not mistaken, she was buried in Garrison Cemetery to the west of here.'

Saul was glad to be getting an education in British colonialism as well as one in tropical wildlife. But he was not sure whether to be impressed or cross with his compatriots. The British seemed determined to leave their mark on the countries they colonised in ways that went far beyond their administrative remit. Local cultures, crops, languages, place names, even names of birds — all of these things had been influenced in one way or another by the British. The Jerdon's baza itself was named after a Brit — the surgeon-naturalist Thomas Jerdon — as though the natives had failed to discover the hawk themselves until Jerdon came along. 'The white man's burden, indeed,' Saul said, his past conversations with Vernon on the subject of colonialism coming to mind.

'Beg pardon?' Romesh said.

'Nothing, old fellow. I was merely thinking out loud.'

A blue flycatcher flitted by.

'Did you see that?' Romesh said, stopping in his tracks and following the bird with his eyes.

Saul stopped too. He trained the binoculars on the thicket of shrubs into which the bird had flown. It was now perched on a branch, making a series of short, metallic clicks. 'A Tickell's blue flycatcher, I believe,' Saul said as the bird's blue and red colours came into focus. It was named after the British ornithologist Samuel Tickell, Saul recalled. He seemed to recall, too, that a number of other birds, in Burma and India, were saddled with the man's name. Yet another instance of a Brit sticking his nose where it did not belong.

'Right right,' Romesh said, waggling his head, 'I see what you mean.' He did not seem to be referring to the bird at all, but rather to Saul's earlier remark about the white man's burden. There was a gleam of amusement in his eyes. He smiled and gestured for Saul to lead the way up the path.

In a quarter-mile, the path forked, with a new segment running north-south. A clump of ironwood trees formed a bower overhead. Saul hesitated, uncertain whether to go right or left. Romesh came up behind him.

'Which way do we go?' Saul asked.

Romesh looked up and down the path to get his bearings. 'I do apologise. I haven't been here for a while.' He pointed northward. 'I believe that way leads to the cave dwellings.'

'Cave dwellings?'

'Yes. They're abandoned now, but they were once used by hermit monks.' As he spoke, Romesh screwed up his eyes and stared across the intersection of the paths. 'Right.' He seemed to have recognised some feature or other. 'The pond's just here.'

Before they set out, a branch above them broke. They both looked up.

'I say,' Saul said. In the trees a troop of toque macaques climbed among the branches or sat grooming each other. The moment the monkeys realised they were being watched, they grew restless. Saul watched them warily watch him. The monkeys seemed almost human in their expressions and behaviour. Saul was reminded of Darwin and Spencer and the theory of evolution. It was incomprehensible to him, in this day and age, that anyone could believe humans to be descendants of angels and not of apes.

'They're rather curious-looking, no?' Romesh said, referring to the monkeys. 'I sometimes imagine them — owing to their pink faces and ludicrous whorls of hair on their heads that look like bad wigs — to be reincarnations of eighteenth-century British politicians. Or perhaps someone from our own time — ignoring its transmigratory impossibility, mind. That one there, for instance.' He pointed at one of the uglier monkeys. 'Wouldn't you say it looks an awful lot like Prime Minister David Lloyd George?'

Saul laughed. 'You're quite the humorist, Romesh.' He looked more closely at the monkey. 'Now that you mention it, I do see a slight resemblance. The same hairdresser may be at work, if nothing else.'

At that they both laughed heartily. And they continued to laugh as they crossed the intersection and stepped through a narrow breach in the vegetation, pushing aside vines and gnarled branches, until the putrid odour of stagnant water hit them in the face. Saul was tempted to pinch his nose, the smell was so overpowering. Soon they were at the edge of the pond, a muddy-brown cesspool. Saul could not imagine anyone's being desirous to bathe in it. Nevertheless, there was something beautiful about the wildness of the place, with its dense tangle of plants and its dappled light filtering down through the trees. Doubtless it provided a refuge for animals from the heat.

Silently Romesh motioned to a bird perched on a tree branch less than twenty feet away. It was so close and colourful, Saul did not need his binoculars to see it. And he knew instantly what it was: a kingfisher. Its feathers were a dazzling mix of black, blue, orange, red, yellow, white, and a seventh colour that could only be described as violet. Even more interestingly, it had something in its beak, but Saul could not tell what it was. He reached for the binoculars round his neck.

'It was worth coming here, no?' Romesh said under his breath.

The word 'here' at once triggered in Saul's mind thoughts of Ceylon and Kandy and the forest reserve as well as of the pond. 'Yes,' he said, 'yes, indeed,' at the very instant that he saw through the binoculars the head and legs of a small frog protruding from the kingfisher's bright-orange beak.

//

Saul had laughed at Romesh's witticism about the macaque and Lloyd George, but not because he thought the idea of reincarnation laughable. He was well aware that the belief in 'rebirth' had a long history in the West as well as in the East. The likes of Plato and Socrates believed in it, as did many Orthodox Jews, even some up to the present day. As far as religious ideas went, it had a certain elegance, and though it was implausible, it was no more implausible than the Judeo-Christian notions of heaven and hell. Rather than a spirit's free-floating to some mythical place in the cosmos as it was thought to do under Judeo-Christian doctrine, under reincarnation, a soul—or a chain of 'causal connections', in the language of early Buddhism—was thought to transmigrate to another being here on earth or in some other realm. Whether that occurred in a Schubert or a cockroach was a matter of good or bad karma, similar to the way in which a Christian or a Jew or a Mohammedan would enter the Pearly Gates or be cast into the fires of hell depending on his good works or on the grace of God.

Among the musty books in Romesh's library was one on the tenets of Buddhism. Romesh had recommended the book to Saul after they returned from the forest reserve. Saul took it now, along with a cup of tea Prema made for him, and sat alone on the verandah and read. He was in a contemplative mood. As he read, his mind kept wandering to thoughts of Esther. He knew it was not very Buddhist, this wandering of the mind, this dwelling on the past. But he had yet to reconcile himself to her death, and it now occurred to him that the teachings of the Buddha might be useful in that regard. Esther would have encouraged him in such studies. She was well read in philosophy and religion. When they were newlyweds, they often discussed the prospect of an afterlife, though they stopped short of discussing reincarnation. He wondered what she would have made of such an idea, whether she would have dismissed it outright or would have entertained its possibility. He still did not believe in the existence of a soul himself, not in the literal sense at least. There were the figurative senses of empathy and artistic feeling, certainly, like the *Einfühlung* in Esther's paintings. But a literal soul that roamed the afterlife? Or one that transmigrated from living being to living being? It went without saying that the existence of a soul would be preferable to the alternative: the spiritless body returning to the dust from whence it came. He liked to think, if the soul *were* real, that Esther's was now inhabiting some brilliantly coloured bird on a heath or in a wood somewhere in England. She could be a kingfisher, perhaps—Britain's very own, the common or Eurasian kingfisher as it was called, with its turquoise back and rufous chest. Saul smiled to himself at the thought.

It was no use reading now, he realised; he could not concentrate for more than half a page at a time. He had read one passage several times and still had not registered its meaning. He closed the book and set it onto the arm of the chair, then drank the remainder of his tea and listened to the birds in the trees. It had been a long time since he lived such a carefree existence, and he had to admit it was rather pleasant. Gone were the daily worries of the householder. No perpetual reviewing of *The Financial Times* to monitor his investments. No attending to repairs on the house or the Rolls. No nagging from Mrs Grant about the week's menu or his untidiness or his sleeping in late or how much food he was or was not eating. In Ceylon he could do as little or as much as he liked. He could live the life of a monk, if he chose, and forsake the world entirely. And no matter what he chose to do, he would be blissfully isolated from the machinations of fascists in Britain and on the Continent. Of course, he missed Sir Addington and their games of billiards at The Odd Fellows Club, and he missed Georgina and his affiliation with *The Masses*, but the temporary loss of these things was a small price to pay for freedom from worldly cares.

The sound of voices on the road jolted him from his reverie. Vernon and a young woman were coming toward Romesh's bungalow. Saul sat up and waved. 'Hello, there!' he said jovially, not ready just yet, it seemed, to forsake the world.

He got up from his chair and met the visitors as they reached the top of the stairs. The young woman was tall like Vernon, five-foot-eight at the least, and had the same olive-coloured skin, full lips, and brown eyes and hair. She wore white culottes, a printed dolman-sleeve blouse, sandals, and a sun hat. She was quite captivating, Saul thought. 'Minnette I presume?'

'How do you do?' she said. 'I've heard so much about you, I feel I already know you.'

'And I you.'

They took each other by the hands and kissed.

'Please tell me you've heard only good things,' he said, glancing at Vernon with an expression of mock concern.

'You presume too much,' Vernon said. 'I've told her you're a scoundrel.' His voice sounded different to Saul's ears, more high-pitched, more colonial, as though he were unconsciously dropping his London accent and reverting back to the Ceylonese way of speaking.

'I dare say it's better to know the truth up front,' Saul said lightly, at which Vernon and Minnette laughed. Saul was glad for the repartee. He had been apprehensive of meeting Minnette because of the feelings her poetry aroused in him back in London. But now that he was seeing her in person, and now that she was laughing at his wit, he felt perfectly at ease. He gave her an appreciative smile.

Vernon and Minnette came up onto the verandah. 'A little light entertainment, eh, Saul?' Vernon said, noticing the book on the chair.

'What I managed to read of it is quite interesting. I should like to discuss it with you sometime, if you'd be so inclined.'

'By all means,' Vernon said. 'But I must forewarn you, I'm not much of an expert on the subject. Pater was an atheist, and Amma's never been one to proselytise, so Minnette and I very rarely went to temple as children.'

Minnette sat on a chair. 'That may be about to change.' She sighed and removed her hat. As she did so, her hair, which had been tied up in a side bun, came undone and fell down about her face. 'Ammi's talking of having a *dānē* for Thathi. If she goes through with it, she'll be going against his wishes. He lived a simple life, and he wanted a simple burial.'

'What's a *dānē*?' Saul asked.

'An almsgiving,' Minnette said, tilting her head to the side and retying her hair. 'Monks come to the house and say prayers for the dead, and we give them food and other alms.'

'You can see it for yourself next week,' Vernon said before Saul could ask further questions. 'And you won't be intruding. Our dearest friends and family will be there.' He picked up the book, quickly skimmed the table of contents, and set it back down. 'In any case, I'm glad you're making yourself at home. After I left you here yesterday, I was worried I had made an error of judgment. Mr Gunaratne's house isn't exactly up to your standards.'

'No worries on that score,' Saul said, concealing the truth. In fact, he had had an abominable night's sleep, what with the perspiring and having to fend off mosquitoes, and in the morning he had to shave and bathe with tepid water. But he did not want to seem ungrateful. 'Romesh has been most generous, and Prema is an excellent cook. Her meals are to die for. I've even ventured to eat with my fingers, if you can believe it.'

'Have you?' Vernon said, surprised at Saul's adventurousness.

'I most certainly have. And then this morning Romesh and I —'

'Did I hear my name?' Romesh said, coming out the front door. 'Oh, hello, dear,' he said to Minnette. 'I'm terribly sorry for your loss.'

She smiled faintly. 'Thank you, Mr Gunaratne.'

'How does your mother do?'

'She's well. It was at her behest, actually, that we've come to see you. And Mr Maccabee. She wishes both of you to come to dinner next week.'

'And she expressly said she won't take no for an answer,' Vernon added.

'We wouldn't want to cross your mother,' Mr Gunaratne said. He clasped his hands behind his back. 'Would she like us to bring anything? I could have Prema whip up her speciality, eggplant curry' — he shot Vernon a quick smile — 'because I know how much you like it.'

'That would be nice, Mr Gunaratne,' Minnette said. 'So I'll tell Amma you'll both be coming, then?'

Romesh deferred to Saul with an enquiring look.

'Yes, very well,' Saul said. 'It would be our pleasure.'

Chapter 17

Rebirth

It was decided after Johannes's cremation that the ashes would be buried in the Thalwatta family plot at the Mahaiyawa Cemetery. The plot was in a secluded area far from other graves, in the shade of sal trees draped in fig lianas. Johannes had requested on his deathbed that he be buried there. In his last moments, as he lay gasping in pain, a wistful look came into his eyes and he said with a struggle that the plot reminded him of the wood near Kandy Lake, where all those years ago on his way to the blacksmith's he had caught his first glimpse of the heavenly vision that was Kamala.

Vernon had seen the burial plot before. The remains of his maternal grandparents were there, as were those of an uncle, the older of Kamala's two brothers. Vernon remembered going to the plot, once, before his grandparents and his uncle died. He must have been seven years old at the time, when he and his family were still living on Eden Estate. He and Minnette went to stay on holiday with their grandparents, Seeya and Aacha Thalwatta, in Kandy town. One day during their stay, Seeya took Vernon to the cemetery. On their walk over, Seeya said there was something he wanted to show Vernon, something he had had built for the family. It was a secret, he said. Not even Aacha knew about it yet.

They arrived at the plot containing the Thalwatta burial vault, and Vernon glanced round, confused. There was nothing in the vicinity except a stone slab, a blank headstone, and some grass and trees. He stared for a moment at the biggest of the trees, as if someone might jump out from behind it in surprise. 'Is this it, Seeya?' he asked innocently in Sinhala. 'Is this all you wanted to show me?'

Seeya patiently explained the purpose of the burial vault. As Vernon listened, the implications of what was being said slowly dawned on him. He waited until Seeya finished speaking, then scrunched up his eyes and asked if one day the headstone would have writing on it like all the other headstones in the cemetery.

'Yes,' Seeya said gravely. 'My name will be on it one day. And your *aacha's*. And your uncles'.'

'And Amma's,' Vernon said, filling in the omission.

Seeya remained silent, and Vernon knew then that his *amma's* name, too, would be on the headstone one day, and perhaps even his *thatha's*. He suddenly wanted to cry, but before the floodgates could open, he felt a reassuring hand on his shoulder and heard Seeya's soothing voice talk of rebirth and the impermanence of life and the importance of not clinging to the things of this earth.

At Johannes's burial service, seventeen years later, Vernon thought of this moment, and it gave him solace, although he still wanted to cry when he saw the name of his pater etched into the granite headstone along with the names of his grandparents and his uncle. The service was a low-key affair with no formal ceremony, consistent with Johannes's wishes. Besides Vernon and Minnette and Kamala, two cemetery caretakers were the only others in attendance. The three family members stood round the burial vault and quietly watched the caretakers draw back the vault stone. Kamala held the urn that contained Johannes's ashes. In the brick-lined vault were four small wooden boxes, one of which was open and empty.

Kamala knelt down to set the urn into the open box and was so overcome with emotion, she fainted.

'Amma!' Minnette cried.

In the nick of time Vernon caught Kamala and the urn in his arms. He helped her to her feet, and Minnette consoled her.

'I'm all right,' Kamala said, gently pushing her children away.

Vernon knelt down and placed the urn into the box himself. As he did so, he had a vision of Johannes on his deathbed, with his gaunt face and white beard, looking like an old mariner adrift at sea. It was not the first time Vernon had such a vision. It had recurred numerous times during the past two days, and he was beginning to think he would never be rid of it. He stood up and stepped back between Kamala and Minnette and took each of them by the hand. His heart rose to his throat as the caretakers covered the box and closed the vault. An important chapter in his life seemed to have ended.

That evening, the family went to temple, the first time in years they did so together. Vernon invited Saul to go along as well. For the occasion, they all dressed in white: Kamala and Minnette in white saris; Vernon and Saul in white shirts and sarongs. Vernon had told Saul he could wear a pair of linen trousers if he wanted to, but Saul insisted on following Buddhist tradition to the letter. 'When in Rome,' he said. So he borrowed a sarong from Mr Gunaratne, which was several inches too short, and in the evening shuffled over to the Prins's house with a self-deprecating smirk on his face, as if he were parading round in a woman's skirt.

Before they all got into the Austin to go to temple, there was a moment of awkwardness as Vernon introduced Saul to Kamala. Vernon could not tell the reason for this — neither his mother nor Saul was bashful in the company of others — unless perhaps his mother had been expecting Saul to be a younger man. Vernon had never mentioned to her Saul's age, and it may have been a shock for her to learn that she and one of her son's closest friends were of the same generation.

They arrived at temple just after sunset. As they removed their sandals and got out of the car, Saul remarked on how splendid Ceylon was in response to a question of Minnette's, and she accused him of exaggerating. She could be fiery sometimes like Johannes.

Saul shook his head. 'A few minutes ago, perhaps I would have agreed with you, but not after seeing this.' He gestured toward the temple grounds. 'No, I don't believe I exaggerate.'

Vernon nudged Saul. 'Best not to row with her.'

'Look what you've done, dear,' Kamala said, adjusting the fall of Minnette's sari. 'And please don't start a row, not here of all places.'

'I'm not starting a row,' Minnette said with a pout. 'I merely wanted Mr Maccabee to explain himself, and he has done so.'

They walked across the car park and under an archway. The grounds were dimly lit, with only a few outdoor electrical lamps. A stupa and a bodhi tree stood to one side of the image house. Incense sticks and oil lamps burned on a stone altar round the tree — which, Vernon remembered, were meant to purify the area and illumine the darkness of ignorance. White frangipani flowers lay everywhere: round the tree, at the base of the stupa, on various pedestals, and along the paths between the image house and the other shrines. Worshippers and monks moved silently about the grounds. Overhead, flying foxes filled the night sky.

In the silence and the relative darkness, amid the smells of coconut oil and sandalwood, the place had an atmosphere of piety and spirituality. For Vernon it brought back a surfeit of memories. He recalled, among other things, facts he once learned about the temple. He whispered to Saul that the stupa was nearly six hundred years old and was reputed to have been built by a Kandyan king. Saul seemed unable to break himself away from the shrines. He stood there in the centre of the grounds for a while taking it all in, first in front of the bodhi tree and then in front of the stupa.

Eventually Vernon motioned that it was time for them to go to the image house. Saul followed reluctantly. Upon entering the house, they bowed before a lotus-pose Buddha statue. Minnette and Kamala, along with a few other worshippers, were already there, kneeling at the altar. Vernon and Saul knelt down, as well, and made an offering of the frangipani flowers Minnette had given them earlier.

Vernon knew he was supposed to worship, but he had not done so since he was a boy, and he was not sure he remembered how. He folded his hands and awkwardly rested them on the altar rail and closed his eyes. He ought to have had thoughts of his pater, pleasant thoughts of precious moments they had shared, and he ought to have said a prayer, to bestow merit on his pater's next life. But all he could think of was how he had waited too long to return to Ceylon. And all he could see, repeatedly and mercilessly, was the vision of his pater's deathly face. His heart raced and he began to sweat. He opened his eyes and looked round. He was the only one in the image house not praying. Even Saul was. Vernon closed his eyes again and laid his head and arms onto the altar rail and listened to the rhythmic pounding of his heart. As if in accompaniment, from outside the image house came the familiar hum of monks chanting *pirit*.

//

Saul stood before the full-length mirror in Romesh's guestroom. A borrowed sarong was tied round his waist, and his hairy legs were visible up to the lower part of his shins. He turned and looked at his reflection in profile and nearly laughed out loud. Not since he was an unbreeched boy had he looked so absurd.

But the sarong would have to do. He had never been to a Buddhist temple before, and he was not about to let a trivial thing like his appearance prevent him from going.

'How does it fit?' Romesh asked sheepishly as Saul came out of the room, ignoring how obviously ill-fitting the sarong was.

'I should be lying if I said it fits well,' Saul said. 'Indeed, it would be more apt to say I look like one of those Elizabethan actors playing the part of a woman.'

'Surely not.'

'You're too kind, Romesh. At any rate, no matter. I've made up my mind to see the temple, and I aim to do so as properly as I can.'

The plan was for Saul to meet the Prins family outside their bungalow at six o'clock sharp. He left Romesh's shortly before the appointed time and walked down the road in his sarong and sandals with a halting gait. It was a lovely evening. The humidity from the recent rain had dissipated, and a light breeze now took the edge off the heat from the setting sun.

At the Prins's bungalow, Vernon and Minnette and an older woman, whom Saul presumed to be their mother, were sitting on the verandah. Saul waved to them as he approached. When they saw him, they got up and came down off the verandah and joined him on the road. They were a handsome family: Vernon tall and lithe; Minnette and Kamala smartly dressed in white saris. There was a sense of warmth and geniality in their mannerisms.

Vernon introduced Saul to his mother.

'Pleased to make your acquaintance,' Saul said. As he leaned in to kiss Kamala on the cheeks, he noticed her eyes settle for a moment on the four inches of exposed leg beneath his sarong, and felt blood rush to his face. He quickly put a hand onto the tie of his sarong lest it should come undone and, after kissing Kamala, stepped back.

'Good of you to be here,' she said after an awkward silence.

Saul continued to hold the tie of his sarong. 'Words cannot express the sympathy I feel for your loss. I recently lost my wife, and—' He stopped short. 'Perhaps I've said enough.'

'Yes, you have,' Minnette said, smiling. 'The tenderness in your voice speaks for itself.'

Saul smiled back, grateful for the morsel of kindness.

The family motorcar was parked on the road. Vernon went to it and opened a back door. 'Shall we go, then?' he said, signalling for Saul and Kamala to get in.

On their way to the temple, they exchanged pleasantries, the kind of small talk Saul normally would have considered palpable nonsense. But since Minnette was doing most of the talking, he found the conversation less objectionable. At one point she asked him what his impressions were of Ceylon. She was always curious, she said, to know how foreigners viewed the country.

Saul thought for a moment before answering. It was his inclination to give an honest opinion—enumerating some of the bad things about Ceylon, such as the heat and the lack of running hot water and the accursed insects, as well as some of the good things—but he did not want to say anything that might cause offence. On the other hand, if he were to say only good things, everyone would see through his disingenuousness instantly. Vernon, certainly, would demur; he disliked false sentiment as much as Saul did. Saul was about to give his answer—a balanced opinion, with greater emphasis on the good things—when the motorcar pulled into the temple car park. The view, even in the semi-dark, took his breath away. There was an old-world quality to it that made the medieval monasteries of England seem comparatively new. An immense spired dome stood in the centre of the temple grounds, its base lit up by candles and lamps. Against the white of the dome, silhouettes of flying foxes could be seen crisscrossing the sky. All over the temple grounds, devotees in white and monks with shaven heads and wearing saffron robes paid silent homage to the Buddha.

'Ceylon puts Britain to shame,' Saul said sententiously as he stepped from the car and went round to the other side to open the doors for Kamala and Minnette. He opened Kamala's first. She took his proffered hand and thanked him.

Minnette did not wait for him to open her door. She got out, strapping her handbag across her body. 'Surely you exaggerate?' she niggled him.

'A few minutes ago, perhaps I would have agreed with you,' he said, taking the criticism in his stride. 'But not after seeing this.' He gestured to the dome and the environs of the temple. 'No, I don't believe I exaggerate.'

'Best not to row with her,' Vernon said, nudging Saul.

In the process of strapping her handbag round her body, Minnette had dislodged the drape of her sari. Kamala noticed it and said, 'Look what you've done, dear.' She came over and re-pinned the drape. 'And please don't start a row, not here of all places.'

'I'm not starting a row,' Minnette responded. 'I merely wanted Mr Maccabee to explain himself, and he has done so admirably.' She retrieved something from her handbag and practically thrust it into Saul's hand.

He could not see what the thing was in the wan light. He removed his spectacles and looked more closely. It was a spray of delicate white flowers.

'For inside the image house,' Vernon explained. 'To make an offering.'

They walked across the car park and entered the temple grounds and, for Saul's sake, looked round a bit before going inside the image house. No one they passed, devotees or monks, spoke above a whisper, similar to what one would find in a European church or library. Saul was captivated. He went to the peepal tree to examine it. Its heart-shaped leaves appeared glossy in the artificial light. He had read about the tree, in his field guide and in Romesh's book on Buddhism. It was a member of the fig family, and some of the hardier specimens reportedly lived for up to three thousand years. It had particular religious significance — hence its alternate name the 'sacred fig' — because the Buddha was said to have attained enlightenment under one.

As Saul moved on to examine the dome, Vernon came up behind him. 'I knew you'd like it here,' he said in a whisper. 'Did you know the stupa's nearly six hundred years old? It's reputed to have been built by a Kandyan king.'

'Indeed?' Saul said, gazing up at the stupa, which was over a hundred feet tall. He would have stood there for several more minutes had Vernon not tapped him on the shoulder and motioned for him to follow.

'We should be going,' Vernon said. 'Amma and Minnette are already in the image house.'

Once they, too, were inside the image house, they bowed, then knelt down beside Minnette and Kamala at the altar and made an offering of flowers. A number of other devotees were there, praying like Minnette and Kamala before a large marble statue, which Saul presumed to be a rendition of the Buddha in a state of meditation.

When in Rome, Saul thought, and closed his eyes and folded his hands. He had never meditated before, not in the Oriental sense, but he knew generally what it entailed: clearing the mind of distracting thoughts and focusing on the present. He recalled something in Romesh's book about breathing techniques that purportedly aided in the practice of meditation. He focused his mind on his inhalations and exhalations of breath, but there was nothing for it. Minnette, who was kneeling next to him, brushed against his arm, and the next thing he knew, thoughts of her intruded into his mind. He suddenly had the desire to ask her about her poetry, to discover what she was working on at the moment, and to tell her how much he admired her poem 'Satyagraha'. He had wanted to discuss these things with her during the drive to the temple, but somehow it seemed inappropriate, when the family were still in mourning, for the conversation to take such a turn. Not to mention that the motorcar, with Vernon and Kamala there, was no place for a tête-à-tête.

A movement next to Saul caused him to open his eyes. Vernon had shifted his position and was now resting his head on the altar. Saul closed his eyes again. He thought it absurd that his mind wandered so easily, like that of an inattentive child. Clearly he was not cut out for this sort of thing. He would make a poor Buddhist, indeed, if he were to try to follow the religion's tenets.

Just then what sounded like plainchant from a Catholic liturgy started up outside the image house. A different set of voices soon followed, adding to the chant's harmony. Saul listened intently. The melody, it seemed to him, bore a striking resemblance to a medieval organum.

//

After Vernon had gone to temple, his visions of Johannes moderated, but his guilt over having arrived in Ceylon 'too late' did not. To distract his mind, and as a sort of penance, he poured himself into helping prepare for the *dānē*. Part of the ceremony was to feed the monks a meal, a form of almsgiving which, like prayers, bestowed merit upon the departed. Typically more food was made than the monks could eat—the more generous the offering, it was thought, the greater the resulting merit. Making an abundance of food would not have been a problem on Eden Estate, when the Prins family had a household of servants, but now that they lived in reduced circumstances in Kandy town, they were forced to rely on a daily to do their cooking and cleaning. Her name was Rani, and she was a brilliant cook. Despite her cooking abilities, however, she could not be expected to make a breakfast banquet herself in only a few hours. So for the *dānē*, the entire household contributed to the effort.

Well before sunrise on the morning of the event, the Prins's kitchen pullulated with activity. Kamala and Minnette chopped ingredients for the curries, while Rani did the frying and Vernon steamed the rice. All four hotplates on the hob were going at once. The air smelled of fried chillies and sautéed onions and vegetables.

Vernon had been put in charge of the *kiribath*, or milk rice, a staple food for special occasions among the Sinhalese. Every time he lifted the lid off the saucepan to check the rice's consistency, steam and the nutty aroma of basmati wafted up. The smell reminded him of his childhood, evoking thoughts of *dānēs* and the Sinhalese New Year and full-moon days. He remembered how, when he was a small boy, his family used to eat *kiribath* for breakfast on the first day of each of month, a way of ushering in auspicious beginnings throughout the year.

Once again he lifted the lid off the pan, and aromatic steam rose up into his face. The grains of rice round the edges of the pan, although fattened with water, had a slightly desiccated appearance. Rani saw this and made a stirring motion with her hand to signal that the rice was ready for the next step. She and Vernon often resorted to sign language to communicate with each other. She had a smattering of English, and he had a smattering of Tamil, but they were both shy to speak each other's languages.

He stirred the rice with a coconut-shell spoon. Then he retrieved a cup of fresh milk—from the coconuts Rani had grated and pressed—and poured it over the rice and put the lid back onto the pan. Within minutes the rice had a thick, glutinous texture. He took the pan off the hob and scooped the steaming rice onto a platter covered with banana leaf, which when heated released an odour evocative of tropical forest. Using another part of a banana leaf, he flattened the heap of rice and shaped it into a large rectangle and left it to cool. Once the rice was set, he cut it into little squares. Later the cakes would be served to the monks with lentils and various vegetarian curries.

Rani and Kamala and Minnette, hovering over the platter now, each picked up a cake and tasted it. Vernon held his breath as he awaited their verdict. Rani, instead of responding, simply giggled.

'It's that bad?' Vernon said, crestfallen.

Kamala shook her head. 'You misunderstand her, dear. Her laughter is her way of saying you've become quite the cook. Ceylonese men aren't known for their cooking abilities, even with simple things like rice, because they consider it women's work. So you're not the average Ceylonese man. You're a cut above.'

Minnette snorted. 'Don't let it go to your head.'

Kamala took another bite of her cake with a look of approval.

Since there was nothing left for Vernon to do in the kitchen, he went to his room and shaved and bathed and got dressed in anticipation of the monks' arrival. He still had time to kill, so he decided to write to Zoe. Something about making *kiribath* had been cathartic, and he now felt he was in the right state of mind to tell her of his pater's death.

Dear Zoe [he began],
I'm sorry for not writing to you sooner. But I think you'll forgive
me when you know the reason. I arrived in Kandy last week to
find Thathi had passed away. To tell you this in such
straightforward terms seems almost callous, but I assure you, I've

never felt the passing of a loved one so keenly. Not even the deaths of my maternal grandparents, to whom I was very close, elicited such sorrow. I keep seeing Thathi on his deathbed. It's a ghastly image. Have you ever seen a photograph of Darwin in his old age? That was what Thathi looked like, except worse because his illness had left its ravaging marks on his face. I don't want this to be how I remember him, but I can't seem to get the image out of my mind. What I need, I think, is work. Idle hands are the devil's tools, as the proverb goes. This morning I helped prepare for a Buddhist ceremony for Thathi, and it seems to have got me out of my funk, at least for now. I'm able to write to you as a result.

In the coming weeks, in addition to working on my thesis, I might join the LSSP like Minnette. There have been rumblings recently of anti-imperialist agitation in Colombo, and if I were to join the LSSP and travel to the coast, I could see for myself what it's all about and determine whether I want to lend the movement my support. That's what the Buddha taught: never to accept the opinions of others, even his own, simply on trust.

I've yet to tell Saul of your well-wishes — there hasn't been an opportune moment, and I have to be careful what I say within earshot of Ammi — but I will soon. I know he'll be happy to hear you're thinking of him.

With regard to the Mile End Road Pogrom, you're not vile for reacting as you did. Saul and I had similar reactions, all the more so because we were helpless to do anything about it thousands of miles away at sea. And you are better than the Jackboots. Don't ever forget that. Your hatred of them is motivated by love for your fellow man and concern about the plight of the Jews, while their hatred is motivated by malice and bigotry and ignorance.

I'm not sure I have an opinion about King Edward's behaviour. (I do, of course, have an opinion about the monarchy: it's an outmoded form of government and has no business existing alongside a parliamentary system. Besides which, I've never been impressed by royalty. They're people like everyone else, only they've been given positions of power based on historical accident and dumb luck, not on merit. It's a sad state of affairs, indeed, that the favours of this world are so rarely distributed according to merit.) Actually, I take back what I said about not having an opinion about King Edward's behaviour because I agree with you that his love life is his business and not the business of the general public. He should be able to choose his lover freely and without

*censure — like countless people have done before him, including
Ammi and Thathi, and like countless others, including you and
me, I hope, will do in the future.*

I love you dearly, Zoe. And I miss you more than I can say.

Forever Yours,
Vernon

He folded the letter and slid it into an envelope and hid it in the
chest of drawers. As soon as he could, he thought, he would hand-
deliver the letter to the postman. Perhaps after the *dānē* was over he
would be able to sneak out unnoticed. He could not be too careful
when it came to Ammi and her prying eyes.

//

The Prins family stood in their front yard in the early-morning
sunlight, waiting for the ceremony to commence. Mr Gunaratne
had driven to the temple to pick up the monks because it was too
far for them to walk. Everything was prepared for their arrival. Rani
had finished making the last of the curries, and the sitting room,
where the ceremony was to occur, had been immaculately arranged
in white. Saul and two other guests — Kamala's younger brother
Agit and his wife Shanthi — had arrived earlier and were now
conversing in the sitting room to pass the time.

A minute before seven o'clock, Mr Gunaratne's Humber came
puttering up the road. It stopped in front of the Prins's house, and
Mr Gunaratne got out and opened the door for the three monks.
They stepped from the car primly in their saffron robes. Vernon felt
a pang of compassion when he saw that the oldest of them was only
in his early twenties. Possibly they had been given to the temple as
children because their families could not afford to care for them.
With the onset of the economic depression, such an occurrence was
all too common among the Sinhalese poor.

Mr Gunaratne and the Prins family folded their hands and
bowed to the monks in a show of respect. Vernon thought it

incongruous to have to be reverent toward someone so young, but what to do? A strict hierarchy existed in Buddhism in which the priesthood outranked the laity, regardless of age or caste or social status. As a matter of course, monks were considered to be more pious than laypeople, and it did not matter that individual novices were sometimes forced into the priesthood by their parents.

The oldest monk held a relic casket with a white cloth beneath it. He came forward and gave the casket to Vernon, who balanced it and the cloth atop his head and went into the house. In the sitting room, Saul and Agit and Shanthi stopped talking when Vernon came in and watched him as he set the casket onto a table. He signalled that the monks would be entering momentarily, then went back outside.

It was a part of the ceremony to wash the monks' feet before they entered the house. For that, a ewer of water and a white cloth had been placed at the bottom of the verandah stairs. Vernon poured the water over the monks' feet and then Mr Gunaratne dried them with the cloth. After this, everyone went inside.

All the laypeople bowed as the monks entered the sitting room. Floor pillows and reed mats comprised the seating for the ceremony. The monks sat on the pillows, and the laypeople, with their shoes removed, sat on the mats. Once everyone was seated, the oldest monk delivered a sermon in Sinhala on the Three Refuges and the Five Precepts. The sermon was followed by a short address about Johannes and the significance of the occasion. Throughout all this, Saul appeared to be lost at sea — which did not surprise Vernon in the least, as the ceremony was both arcane and in a foreign language.

After the monk finished speaking, Rani brought in the food on a large tray. Kamala stood up and folded her hands and bowed, saying in Pali, 'These alms, along with other requisites, we offer to the whole community of monks.'

The oldest monk said a blessing over the food, and the household went about serving each dish to the monks, who ate sparingly. They received so much food from the laity during *dānēs* that if they were to eat it all, they would become corpulent, in direct violation of their vows. As Rani took away the remaining food, the household returned to their mats.

Then the oldest monk retrieved a spool of *pirit* thread from the folds of his robe. He held the loose end of thread in his fingers and handed the spool to the monk next to him, who in turn held the thread taut and passed the spool to the third monk. In this way the spool went round the room, passed from person to person. When it reached Vernon, he motioned to Saul to avoid letting the thread touch the floor. Saul took the thread carefully but firmly. He seemed more at ease now, and Vernon wondered if it was because the ceremony shared something in common with Jewish ceremonies. Or perhaps Saul had simply accepted the fact that the Buddhist ceremony, like most religious ceremonies, was beyond the average layperson's comprehension.

For several minutes the oldest monk chanted a blessing in Pali. Then, with Kamala's help, he wound the thread back onto the spool and one at a time called up the laypeople and tied a band of thread round their wrists. When this was over, Kamala presented each of the monks with a gift of new robes. The ceremony ended with one of the younger monks administering a thanksgiving in which all the laypeople were requested to partake of the merits of the ceremony and to transfer those merits to the benefit of Johannes. Finally the monks left the house with Mr Gunaratne, taking with them the relic casket and their alms.

A little later, the Prins family and their guests gathered in the dining room for a post-ceremony celebration. Some of the leftover *kiribath* and curries, along with light refreshments, had been organised on the dining table, and Rani went about serving drinks. In the early stages of the gathering, Agit, a stout and loquacious businessman, dominated the conversation. Through the sheer force of his personality, he cornered Saul and Vernon and Minnette on one side of the table. They all had glasses of freshly squeezed papaya juice in their hands. Kamala and Shanthi stood on the other side of the table, helping themselves to food. Earlier, before the ceremony, Agit had explained to Saul that he was in the export-import business in Galle. Now he was explaining the intricacies of exchange rates between the Ceylonese rupee and foreign currencies, not realising that Saul had made much of his fortune speculating in currency markets. Dealing with exchange rates was a bloody nuisance, Agit complained. He recently shipped a consignment of cinnamon to an Australian company, and the damned Australians misquoted the exchange rate and underpaid him to the tune of several hundred rupees. It led to the most distasteful row and cost him even more money in legal fees. Naturally he would not be associating with that company ever again.

Saul could not get a word in edgeways. 'Indeed?' he said at one point before Agit quickly spoke over him, like an auctioneer shouting down a losing bid.

Eventually Vernon, noticing Saul's discomfort, inserted himself into the conversation. 'In all the commotion this morning, Uncle, I failed to discover where it is you'll be staying while you're in Kandy. All Amma said was that you wouldn't be staying here.'

'At Queen's Hotel, my dear boy,' Agit said, turning from Saul.

'I offered to let them stay here,' Kamala spoke up from across the table, 'but he and Shanthi insisted on going to an hotel.'

Aunty Shanthi tilted her head and patted the bun at the nape of her neck and said, 'We didn't want to impose on you with everything that's happened.' A smear of red lipstick was visible on her teeth as she spoke.

'How long do you intend to stay?' Minnette asked.

'Only through your mother's dinner party, I'm afraid,' Agit answered for Shanthi. 'We must get back to Galle before the week's end.' A philosophical look came into his eyes. 'The export-import business waits for no man.'

Shanthi cackled. 'Goodness me, Agit, you speak as if the bloody thing were alive. Thank heavens it's not. And thank heavens it waits for no woman, either. I sometimes think I would have been far better off marrying a tradesman. At least then I wouldn't have had to listen to your incessant prattling about accounts and market prices and exchange rates.'

'Perhaps you *should* have married a tradesman,' Agit countered. 'I wager my pocketbook would have been considerably fuller if you had.'

Vernon could not remember a time when his aunt and uncle were not at each other's throats. They always seemed to be quibbling and jesting about their marriage. And yet clearly they loved each other.

Shanthi ignored Agit's last remark and said to Minnette, 'You must come to Queen's Hotel one evening while we're here, darling. They have the most delightful dinner buffet. And your mother tells me you're in want of a sweetheart. I've seen some rather handsome young gentlemen passing through the corridors of the hotel.'

Minnette glared at Kamala and shot a knowing glance at Vernon.

'You *would* notice that sort of thing,' Agit reproached Shanthi. 'Be that as it may, so long as you don't bring one of these young gentlemen to our room, I dare say I can't object to your wandering eye.'

'Oh, do hush up, dear,' Shanthi said.

The talk of sweethearts reminded Vernon of Zoe. While everyone else was engaged in conversation, he pulled Saul aside and, under the pretence of asking him about his impressions of the *dānē*, mentioned her letter in an undertone.

'I was hoping she'd write to you,' Saul said, keeping his voice down, as well. 'You seemed to be in need of a restorative.' He took a sip of his juice. 'Tell me, how does she do?'

'She's well. And she expressly sends you her regards.'

'Does she?' As the faintest of smiles formed on Saul's lips, Agit's voice filled the room with 'May I just say —' followed by Shanthi's interruption 'No, indeed, you may not.'

Chapter 18

Ensemble

'Just beyond those trees is where Pater first saw Amma,' Vernon said.

He was driving the Austin. Saul sat in the front passenger seat, and Minnette and Romesh sat in the back. They were on their way to meet Agit and Shanthi for dinner at Queen's Hotel. Kamala had begged off on account of a headache. It was a windy and dusty evening. On Sangaraja Mawatha, each time the car passed a rubbish heap, foraging crows cawed and took wing, sometimes hovering briefly in a gust of wind before landing on the heap again.

Saul looked in the direction Vernon had indicated. Through the swaying sal trees, he could just discern the shimmering water of a lake. 'Very picturesque,' he said. 'How long ago would that have been?'

'Over thirty years,' Minnette answered for Vernon.

Three decades were a long time for two people to be together by anyone's measure, Saul thought. He had been with Esther for nearly two decades, and that had felt like a lifetime. 'No wonder your mother's taking your father's death so hard. My wife and I—' Suddenly he saw himself in the attic of his Belgravia house, futilely trying to revive Esther, and the words stuck in his throat.

'Amma was only eighteen when Pater proposed to her,' Vernon

added, seeming not to have noticed Saul's disquiet. 'She barely knew any other life than the one she knew with him.'

As Saul collected himself, the thought came to him that it must not have been easy for Kamala's parents to accept a Dutchman as a son-in-law. Saul had had difficulty enough getting his German Jewish in-laws to accept *him*, a Jew from a country with deep Anglo-Saxon roots. He would have broached the subject of race without hesitation if he and Vernon and Minnette had been the only ones in the car, but he did not know how Romesh might react. Racial tensions, after all, were high in Europe and its colonies — the Nazi's, with their bigoted Nuremberg Laws, had gone so far as to prohibit marriage and sexual relations between Aryan and non-Aryan races — and from what Vernon said about the white man's burden and growing animosity toward the British, Ceylon was no exception. At any rate, perhaps a motorcar was not the best place for Saul to voice his opinions on such a weighty subject.

Romesh said, 'I think you underestimate Kamala. Feeling the loss of someone is not the same as falling to pieces under the weight of grief.' His tone, it seemed to Saul, suggested he spoke from experience.

Vernon smiled but said nothing. He turned the car onto Kandy Road, alongside which a plague of stray pie-dogs dozed in the swirling dust. On the pavement outside Queen's Hotel, a lamplighter was attempting to light streetlamps with apparent difficulty because of the wind.

'Actually, Romesh,' Saul said, thinking of his own experiences with his father and with Esther, 'you're quite right.' Kamala by comparison was conducting herself admirably. He was reminded of Nietzsche's expression 'what does not kill one makes one stronger'. Nietzsche, like Saul, lost his father in childhood, so he was no stranger to devastating loss. But Saul questioned whether the expression could be applied to the death of a loved one. It depended, he supposed, on the definition of 'stronger'. Only if the word meant that one became inured to the pain of loss could the expression in any sense be correct, and that would be a perverse sort of strength, indeed.

Vernon parked the car, and they all went into the hotel. Across the marbled and chandeliered lobby was a doorway with a fanlight above it. There, a maître d' greeted them and asked if they were with the Thalwatta party. Vernon said they were, and with a beckoning gesture, the maître d' said, 'Right this way, if you'd be so kind' and led them to their table.

The restaurant was like any in London's West End, save the scattering of potted palms. Its ceiling and walls and pillars were a chalky white, and its floor and chairs and door- and window-frames were a rich mahogany. Burgundy and white linens adorned the tables. All the patrons, most of whom appeared to be European, were dressed in evening wear: the men in suits or black tie; the women, save the natives who wore saris, in flowing gowns.

An arcade ran the length of one side of the restaurant. Agit and Shanthi were already seated at a large round table next to an archway. As Saul and the others approached the table, Agit stood and waved and called out to them. 'Come,' he said rather loudly. The other patrons turned and looked, but Agit took no notice. 'Good evening, one and all. My dear boy, my dear girl, you scrub up well. Mr Maccabee, Romesh, how do you do?' He gestured to the empty chairs at the table. 'Do have a seat.'

The maître d' pulled out Minnette's chair for her, and everyone sat down. Saul ended up in a chair between Vernon and Minnette and directly across from Agit.

'That's a beautiful sari, Aunty,' Minnette said, admiring Shanthi's red-and-white sari.

'Thank you, dear. And your dress, it's absolutely lovely. Where did you get it?'

'From a dressmaker in Colombo. Amma had it made as a graduation gift.'

Saul glanced at Minnette's dress, which was made of silver beaded mesh and which had a mock neck and cap sleeves. It *was* lovely. And so was she. She could have passed as a model for Coco Chanel. He had had the exact same thought the moment he saw her emerge from the Prins's bungalow earlier.

Shanthi smiled, exposing what looked like a smear of red lipstick on her teeth. 'Sorry she couldn't make it, by the way. I do hope she'll be all right.'

'I think the lack of sleep is finally catching up to her,' Minnette said.

'Poor dear. Will she be up for the dinner party, do you suppose?'

'She should be.' Minnette took up her serviette, unfolded it, and spread it across her lap. 'As Mr Gunaratne says, you shouldn't underestimate her, especially when it comes to entertaining guests. I expect you'll find her revitalised tomorrow.'

Romesh laughed, whether because he found Minnette's paraphrasing him flattering or because he thought her words had hit the mark was unclear.

All this time, the maître d' had stood by with a long-suffering look on his face. Now he said, 'Please enjoy the food.' He pointed to some tables at the back of the restaurant. 'The buffet is just over there. You may help yourselves whenever you like. And a waiter will be with you in a moment to take your drink orders.'

'It's English cuisine tonight,' Agit said, referring to the buffet. 'Steak-and-kidney pies and Yorkshire pudding and that sort of thing.'

Saul liked the sound of that. He needed a break from eating rice and curries.

A waiter came by—dressed in a burgundy waistcoat and bowtie, a white Oxford shirt, and black trousers—and took their drink orders, which comprised cocktails of various kinds. There was an air of gregariousness about the table, even before the drinks arrived. Several conversations progressed simultaneously and consecutively, some involving the whole table and others involving groups of two or three. The weather was discussed, and world trade, and Vernon's thesis, and the plight of tea plantations, and the LSSP and Ceylonese politics, and King Edward VIII. Saul also used the opportunity to banter with Minnette. He was about to express his admiration for her poetry when a voice from across the restaurant said, 'Vernon Prins, is that you?'

Everyone at the table stopped talking at once and turned their heads. A European-looking chap in his mid-twenties and wearing a white linen suit was coming toward them. 'By George, it *is* you!' the chap said upon reaching the table.

Vernon got up from his chair. 'Geoff.'

'Good old Nandhimitra, how are you, *men*? I heard tell you were back in town. How long has it been — three, four years?'

They shook hands vigorously.

'You're looking well,' Vernon said, taking in his friend's bronzed complexion and military-style haircut. He turned to the others at the table. 'This is Geoffrey Overlund, an old classmate of mine from Trinity College.' He introduced them one by one to Geoffrey. When it was Minnette's turn, Vernon said, 'And Minnette you already know,' at which she and Geoffrey exchanged smiles.

Saul looked perplexed. 'Did you say Trinity College?'

'None of the Trinity Colleges you might be thinking of,' Vernon explained. 'The one I attended is a private school for boys. Just up the road from here, actually.' For everyone else's benefit, he said, 'Saul went to Trinity College, Cambridge.'

Romesh emitted a quick inhalation and exhalation of breath. 'How funny.'

'Overlund, Overlund,' Agit said, seeming to search his memory. 'I daresay I know that name.'

'My pater's the president of the Planters' Association,' Geoffrey said.

'Yes, that's right.' Agit glanced at Shanthi. 'I thought I recognised the name.'

'Good for you, dear.'

Several people began to pass by the table on their way to the buffet. Vernon and Geoffrey stepped aside to make room.

'What are you up to these days?' Vernon asked Geoffrey after the people had gone by. 'The last I heard, you had joined the Kandy police force.'

'I'm a detective sergeant now.'

'Congratulations.'

'Thanks.' Geoffrey put a hand on Vernon's shoulder. 'Say, I read your pater's obituary in the *Daily News* the other day, and I wanted you to know I had the utmost respect for him. So did my pater.'

'Awfully decent of you, *machang*,' Vernon said.

'Oh, and before I forget, there's someone who asked after you the other day.'

'Who's that?'

'Ramona Bolling. Do you remember her?'

'Dear dear dear,' Romesh said.

Minnette started giggling. Saul thought perhaps her cocktail had gone to her head. Vernon gave her a reproachful look.

'She was a form behind us,' Geoffrey went on. 'Anyway, when she asked me about you a few days ago, I told her I wasn't sure you were even in town, but she insisted you were and said for me, if I happen to bump into you, to pass along the message that she's keen to see you.'

'Dear dear dear,' Romesh repeated.

Geoffrey glanced across the restaurant, toward his table. 'You'll have to excuse me,' he said. 'I have to get back. The Superintendent and I are entertaining a foreign dignitary.' He clasped Vernon's hand again. 'Perhaps we could go out for a drink sometime while you're in town?'

'Yes, let's do that.'

After Geoffrey had gone and Vernon had returned to his seat, Agit said, 'Did I hear him call you Nandhimitra?'

'That was my nickname at Trinity. Because of my size.' Vernon frowned at Minnette. 'You seem to have forgotten yourself.'

'Sorry.'

He turned from her to Romesh and back again. 'Are you going to let me in on your little secret?'

'It's no secret at all,' Romesh said frankly. 'Well, let's see, how shall I put it?' He paused, apparently for effect. 'Ramona Bolling's a bitch and a whore.'

'Steady on, Romesh,' Agit said. 'Ladies are present.'

'I can't be faulted for telling the truth. But if I've given offence, ladies, please forgive me.'

'No harm done,' Shanthi said.

Agit glared at her.

'What?' she said incredulously. 'I've heard worse at the hairdresser's, if you must know.'

'That's neither here nor there.'

Romesh stood up suddenly, causing his chair to make a scraping sound on the wood floor. 'Excuse me,' he said. 'My drink seems to have gone straight through me.' Then he dropped his serviette onto the table and left.

'Now look what you've done,' Shanthi said to Agit.

'He only went to the lavatory, dear. Besides, he was the one who started the unpleasantness.'

'Still, you ought to be more careful what you say in front of him. He hasn't been the same since his wife left him.'

Saul had been correct to think Romesh's comment about loss on the drive over was born out of personal experience. He recalled a conversation he had had with Georgina at the offices of *The Masses* a few months ago, when he was still highly despondent over Esther's death. He said something to the effect that life had a way of delivering you googlies, and in response Georgina posed the question *Aren't we all just a little bit broken?* He did not think much of it at the time, but now her question seemed particularly apt.

'Romesh isn't the only one with a wagging tongue,' Agit said, winking at Minnette. To Vernon, he added, 'Whoever this lady friend of yours is, my boy, you should take what he says about her with a grain of salt. He has had it out for women ever since his wife cuckolded him.'

Shanthi made a face. 'Don't be cruel, Agit.'

'I can't be faulted for telling the truth.'

'Just to be clear,' Vernon said, 'Ramona isn't a lady friend of mine.'

'No,' Minnette added with irritation in her voice. 'She's someone Vernon scarcely knows who Amma wants to introduce him to as part of one of her matchmaking schemes.'

'I suspected you weren't happy with your mother's "scheming", as you call it,' Shanthi said. 'But you mustn't be too hard on her. She only wants what's best for the two of you.'

Romesh returned from the lavatory, silencing everyone at the table. As he sat back down, he picked up his serviette and cast an eye from face to face. 'You're awfully quiet,' he observed, unaware that he had been the topic of conversation in his absence.

'What do you say we eat?' Agit said abruptly, clapping his hands together.

'I thought you'd never ask,' said Saul. He had been feeling peckish from the first mention of English cuisine.

They all stood up as one and made for the buffet tables, talking volubly as they went.

//

After Saul and Romesh got back from Queen's Hotel, they had a nightcap on the verandah. They sat in the planter's chairs and, without speaking, listened for a time to the sounds emanating from the jungle: croaking frogs and stridulating insects. The wind had died down. Smoke from mosquito coils commingled with smoke from Saul's pipe, which he drew at between sips of coconut arrack. The moon shone above, and the soft glow of candlelight scintillated through the open windows of the sitting room.

Saul felt a sense of contentment he had not felt for nearly a year, not since before Esther's death. He had very much enjoyed the dinner at the hotel. He did not get to talk to Minnette in the way he hoped, but just being with her and Vernon and the others, conversing about everything under the sun, did wonders to raise his spirits. Curiously, he no longer felt any self-recrimination about enjoying himself without Esther. He was not sure what had changed in that regard. Perhaps it was simply because he was so far away from home — and as such, was not constantly reminded of her absence — or perhaps it was the realisation that he was not alone in experiencing grief. Kamala, Vernon, Minnette, Romesh — they all, like Saul, had suffered loss recently. At any rate, his life seemed to have become his own again, free from a sense of sin. And as for the solid, non-spiritual food at the hotel, that had been good, too. It reminded him of Mrs Grant's cooking: eggy pudding and buttery puff pastry and tender cuts of beef smothered in brown gravy. As he thought of all this, he was transported in his mind to Belgravia. He saw himself and Esther in the garden after eating one of Mrs Grant's sumptuous meals, smoking and sharing with each other the highlights of their days. Spring flowers were in bloom, and though he and Esther could scarcely see the petals in the fading light of the terrace, they were palpably aware of the flowers' presence because the air was saturated with a potpourri of scents.

'Could I ask you something?' Romesh enquired, drawing Saul out of his thoughts.

'I beg your pardon?' Saul said, his voice tinged with displeasure. He did not want to let go of the memory so soon.

'At dinner, when I went to the loo, were the others talking about me?'

The question took Saul aback. 'What makes you say that?'

'Just a feeling.'

Saul thought it wise to tell the truth. He did not want to get caught out in a lie, and, at any rate, answering Romesh's question might lead to further discussion on the matter. In spite of himself, Saul was curious to know the circumstances surrounding Romesh's marital woes. 'Well, now that you mention it, Agit did say something about your wife's having left you. But very little was said beyond that.'

Romesh sighed. 'I don't suppose you'd care to hear my side of the story?'

'Only if you're willing to share it. But perhaps it wouldn't hurt. A problem shared is a problem halved, as the Germans say.'

'My wife left me, that much is true.' Romesh had a pained expression on his face. 'Did Agit say why?'

'Not in so many words,' Saul said obliquely, trying to blunt the embarrassment Romesh might feel about being a cuckold.

'She had an affair, right under my nose, with my *kannakapoolie*. That's Tamil for head overseer. Like Johannes, I used to be a planter but was forced to sell my estate when tea prices plummeted. Many estates were running at a loss at the time, and some planters were even on the cart.' Romesh paused, and a faraway look came into his eyes. Flickers of candlelight danced across the near side of his face. 'My wife, I hear, is in Matale now, with her lover, living in sin.' He paused again. 'It really doesn't bear thinking about.'

'No,' Saul agreed. He was sorry he had played a role in reopening an old wound. Romesh's wife may not have died, but he had lost her just the same.

A mournful, mewing scream came from the jungle. Saul and Romesh stopped talking and looked toward the trees. 'An eagle owl,' Romesh whispered as his and Saul's eyes trained on the location from which the sound had come.

The owl remained silent for a minute. Then noiselessly it dropped from a tree and, swooping down to the ground, landed on what appeared to be a large rabbit. A struggle ensued. The owl's huge outspread wings, spanning four feet at the least, flapped frenetically. At last the struggle ended, and the owl, with its prey gripped in its talons, flew off into the darkness of the jungle.

'Did my eyes deceive me,' Saul asked, 'or did that owl just fly off with a rabbit?' The only birds of prey he was aware of in Britain that could do that were the golden eagle and the red kite.

'Not a rabbit exactly, but something similar, I suspect, like a black-naped hare. It's nothing extraordinary, really. The eagle owl is known for catching prey several times its weight. Sometimes even juvenile barking deer.'

'Good God.'

Romesh took a drink of arrack. As he lowered his glass, he stared with an air of mystery at the section of jungle into which the owl had flown. 'Some think the eagle owl and the devil bird from Ceylonese folklore are one and the same. According to myth, the devil bird lives in the jungle and emits bloodcurdling shrieks, not unlike the eagle owl. It's said to be the reincarnation of a woman who was murdered by her jealous husband because he doubted the paternity of one of her children. And now her anguished cries — which are said to be an omen of death — live on forever in the jungle.'

'A rather grim myth,' Saul remarked.

Romesh grinned. 'Yes, I suppose it is.' He was quiet for a moment, then glanced toward the Prins's bungalow. 'I dare say Minnette will be glad of the owl's predation — one less pest plaguing her garden.'

'I wasn't aware she gardened.' For some reason the knowledge that Minnette gardened raised her even further in Saul's estimation.

'She was forced to after the incident with Mr Arunasalem.'

'The "incident"?'

'Mr Arunasalem, the greengrocer? Didn't Vernon tell you?'

Saul shook his head. Surely Vernon had his reasons for keeping him in the dark.

'A row between Johannes and Mr Arunasalem nearly turned violent. So the Prins family stopped going to Mr Arunasalem's shop, and Minnette started growing vegetables of her own.'

'What was the row about?'

'Mr Arunasalem used a racial slur, and Johannes didn't take kindly to it.'

'I see.'

'The incident created a minor stir in town. I've boycotted Mr Arunasalem's shop myself. I don't like imperialism any more than the next man, but the Prins family and their Dutch ancestors have lived in Ceylon for over a century, and Johannes and Kamala, and their two lovely children, have been — or *had* been, until Johannes fell ill — contributing members of Ceylonese society. Their race was, and is, beside the point. In his day, Johannes was a legend among the plantocracy. Did you know he was instrumental in getting a law passed that banned the plantation practice of forcing Tamil labour to pay their cost of transport from India?'

'No, I didn't,' Saul said. He had played his cards right, it seemed, and was getting the discussion of race he had wanted, after all. 'But then, I'm afraid there's a lot about colonial life I don't know. A little enlightenment wouldn't go amiss.'

'It would be my pleasure to be the source of your enlightenment,' Romesh said with a look of sincerity. He took another drink of arrack before proceeding. 'The law I mentioned was passed fourteen years ago. It has its history in the importation of plantation labour. For decades, there has been a chronic shortage of tea pluckers. Men generally find it beneath them to pick tea for a living, and Sinhalese women find the work too taxing. Planters sidestep this by bringing Tamil women from India, and before 1922, it was common for the women and their families to have to pay their way here. Some of them arrived so heavily indebted, they effectively became bonded labourers for life.'

That sounded to Saul like the early history of America in some respects. 'I imagine that's caused difficulties for Ceylonese society.'

'Indeed. As has the importation of labour itself.'

'And this law —I presume there were those who opposed it?'

'Yes. Some planters fought it tooth and nail. But once it passed, most people, especially the plantation labourers, considered Johannes a hero. Of course, in recent times, Mr Arunasalem and others like him have forgotten everything Johannes did. Nationalism is rarely Buddhist or Hindu in its outlook, and its adherents are rarely troubled by the perpetuation of racial prejudice.'

Saul was impressed by Romesh's remarks. 'You're a good man, Romesh. If you were living in London, I'd put you up for membership in the Scipian Society. You seem to espouse a brand of liberalism that's consistent with the Society's views.'

'Is that a political organisation?' Romesh asked. 'I must confess, I'm not a very political animal.'

'I beg to differ,' Saul said, feeling inspired. 'All humans are political animals. Perhaps some more than others, but still, we're all political animals. Was it Aristotle who said that?' Saul looked up at the moon and the stars. When the answer did not come to him, he shrugged and resumed his disquisition on politics. 'At any rate, the best of us seek to improve the commonweal. Human societies will always be hierarchical—there's no denying that—but we have survived through the millennia by cooperating, not by competing and certainly not by exploiting. Without cooperation, without politics, human culture would not have been possible, and, as a species, we never would have risen above the apes.'

As Saul's voice faded into the night, the frogs and insects went on singing with perfect synchrony.

//

Vernon kept telling himself that the dinner party was for only one evening and that its purpose was to honour the memory of his pater. He felt sure that if he were to have a row with his mother about her guestlist—which, to his chagrin, included Ramona Bolling—he definitely would *not* be paying honour to that memory.

The guests began arriving at seven o'clock. By 7.30, everyone except Ramona had arrived and they were all assembled in the sitting room, chatting and eating hors d'oeuvres and drinking toddy.

'Did you see what Mr Gunaratne brought?' Kamala asked Vernon, perhaps sensing his irritation and attempting to distract him. They and Minnette and Saul and Mr Gunaratne stood near the front door. Kamala's question concerned the eggplant curry Mr Gunaratne had brought for dinner.

'I did,' Vernon replied blandly. The attempt to distract him only accentuated in his mind Ramona's imminent arrival. He glanced at the door, listened for the sound of a motorcar outside. What was Ramona playing at? he wondered. In arriving late, she seemed to be intending to make some sort of grand entrance. The mere thought of the predicament he now found himself in was enough to boil his blood. No doubt Aunty Shanthi had been right to suggest that Amma wanted what was best for him, but forcing him to socialise with a woman he barely knew was a strange way of showing it, was it not? He was not a child, to be cajoled into doing something against his will. He recalled Minnette's wish that his presence in Kandy would detract attention away from her. Notably, not a single eligible young man had been invited to the dinner party.

'You look well, Kamala,' Mr Gunaratne said. 'I take it your headache's gone?'

'It is, Romesh, thank you.'

Minnette gave Mr Gunaratne a meaningful look. 'I told you she'd be revitalised. She's in her element at events like these.'

'I'll say!' Agit's voice boomed from across the room, like a percussion instrument. He was sitting on one of the daybeds next to Shanthi and across from Dr and Mrs Fernando. It was less than an hour into the party and already he was on his third drink. 'She was that way as a girl, too. Her friends used to come over to the house and have make-believe tea parties all the time, and she would play the hostess. She was quite the socialite then. Still is.' Even with a drink in his hand, he carved the air like a conductor, as if to suggest that Kamala's playacting was equivalent to the management of an orchestra. Somehow the gesture reminded Vernon of The Leader.

Shanthi grabbed Agit's glass. 'You'll spill your drink, you lout.'

'Bernie will second me on that, won't you, Bernie?' Agit said. Apparently unperturbed by the loss of his drink, he leaned forward and put a hand on Dr Fernando's shoulder. 'You and Kamala and I were chums way back when, weren't we, old boy?'

'Perhaps you've had too much to drink,' Dr Fernando suggested with a smirk and politely removed Agit's hand.

'Nonsense. I've only just begun.'

'That's what we're afraid of,' Kamala put in. 'Please behave yourself, Brother. This isn't one of your old-boys'-club gatherings.'

Mrs Celine Fernando, a middle-aged Burgher woman, smiled gleefully. She appeared to be enjoying the repartee immensely. 'Speaking of people who haven't changed, I seem to recall that you, Agit, were an inveterate lush in your youth.'

'Oh my, yes,' Shanthi concurred.

Laughter—dissonant laughter, like metal striking metal—reverberated through the room.

'I can see you're all having a bit of fun at my expense,' Agit said, feigning a look of self-pity. 'Permit me to share with you my philosophy of life: Eat, drink, and be merry, that's what I say. For tomorrow we die, no?'

'Who knew Agit had the sensibilities of an Israelite prophet?' Mr Gunaratne said.

Again laughter reverberated through the room.

'See what you've got yourself into?' Minnette said to Saul. 'Our family and friends are a bit barmy.'

'Not in the least.'

'You needn't be polite, Saul.' Vernon swirled the milky-white liquid in his glass and then took a drink, with one eye fixed on the door. 'You're among friends here, and you can speak your mind as you like.'

Kamala held up a hand, like the Buddha's blessing *mudrā*, and tilted her head slightly. 'I'm sure Mr Maccabee has seen worse than our lot in London. I've heard there are some rather queer sorts gallivanting round Soho.'

'Where did you hear that?' Vernon asked, mildly offended. Soho—the colourful, vibrant Soho, where he had made so many precious memories with Zoe—was one of his favourite places in the world.

'Why, from you, dear. I think you said it in the first letter you wrote to me after your arrival in London.'

'You seem to have forgotten yourself, Brother,' Minnette said, giggling at her pun.

'We're allowed to change, aren't we?' Vernon snapped. He was less angry with Minnette than he was embarrassed at his former provincial view of the world. But he *had* changed, that was the important thing. Living in the cosmopolitan city of London, and seeing the evil effects of fascism firsthand and doing his damnedest to stand against it, had made him a better man.

'Yes,' Saul said, his expression turning serious, 'we are.' He clapped Vernon on the back. 'You're to be commended, old chap, for your enlightenment.'

Agit cleared his throat. 'May I have your attention, please?'

One by one the voices in the room died away.

'All joking aside,' Agit continued, 'I haven't forgotten why we're here. And I should like to propose a toast.' Having retrieved his glass, he raised it into the air. 'To Johannes,' he said and threw back a drink.

The others followed his lead. There was a moment of silence, during which Kamala's eyes closed and her lips moved in a pantomime of prayer. Watching her, Vernon felt a sudden pang. He had lost his pater, but she had lost her soulmate. It occurred to him that she must be going through what Saul had gone through recently with his wife. Vernon had only an inkling of what that would be like. The closest thing he could imagine would be for him to lose Zoe, and yet even that paled in comparison because he had known Zoe for less than a year, whereas Ammi had known Thathi for more than a quarter of a century. And if Zoe were to die — well, he would rather not contemplate that, but if she *were* to, suffice it to say, a part of him would die, too. As he continued to watch Kamala's lips move, he had another vision, not of Johannes this time but of her: she was kneeling at Johannes's deathbed, weeping. At the sight of this, Vernon almost could have forgiven her for meddling in his love life.

The sound of voices, mingling with each other and of varying pitch, filled the room again. One of the conversations was between Saul and Minnette.

'I've been wanting to tell you how much I enjoyed your poem "*Satyagraha*",' Saul was saying.

Minnette tilted her head slightly. 'It's funny you should say that, Mr Maccabee, because I've been wanting to tell you how much I enjoyed your article.'

'You read my article?' Saul shot Vernon an enquiring glance.

'All I did was give her the proofs of the October issue of *The*

Masses. She found your article on her own. But I'm glad she did. It deserves to be read by as many people as possible.'

'Perhaps I should read it,' Kamala interjected. 'What's it about?'

Saul was giving a synopsis of his article when Rani came in and announced dinner was ready.

'Please excuse the interruption,' Kamala said to Saul. Then to everyone she said, 'Come' and gestured for them to follow her into the dining room.

'We seem destined never to finish a conversation,' Vernon heard Saul lament to Minnette as the two of them tarried for a moment behind the others.

'We must pick up where we left off when I return from Colombo,' she said.

'I had no idea you were leaving town.' Saul sounded disappointed by the news.

'I have to attend some meetings for the LSSP. But I'll be back in a few days.'

'We'll continue our conversation upon your return, then.'

'I look forward to it.'

In the dining room, the table was set for ten. One of the chairs was still empty after everyone had sat down. When Agit commented on the empty chair, Vernon's chest constricted.

'That's for Ms Bolling,' Kamala said. 'I don't understand what's keeping her.' As her eyebrows arched, a thought seemed to strike her. 'It would be rather rude of her to accept my invitation and not show up.'

'It certainly would,' Minnette agreed. Vernon could not be certain, but he thought he saw a shadow of a smile cross her face. 'Shall I telephone her, Amma?' she asked. 'Perhaps something has prevented her from coming.'

'Yes, dear, please do.'

Minnette excused herself from the room. Vernon attempted to make eye contact with her on her way out, but she seemed to deliberately avoid his eyes.

'Enough about Ms Bolling,' Kamala said. 'We're here to enjoy ourselves.'

'Hear hear,' said Mr Gunaratne.

Yes, Vernon thought, *enough about Ramona. For Christ's sake, enough!*

Rani appeared with the food and placed it, one bowl at a time, onto the table. There were bowls of biryani, cashew curry, eggplant curry, Malay pickle, and *raitha.* The intense smell of cardamom and cloves and other spices infused the air.

'You've outdone yourself, Kamala,' Dr Fernando said.

Others paid their respective compliments. Vernon would have added one of his own had he not been preoccupied with thoughts of Ramona. He wondered if perhaps something *had* happened to her. He hoped to God it had—nothing too serious, but serious enough to prevent her from attending the party. It would resolve his predicament at a single swoop.

Minnette returned and took up her seat at the table, next to Vernon. They exchanged glances, but she remained silent. As the others stopped talking in anticipation of what she had to say, Vernon steeled himself for the worst.

'She shan't be coming,' Minnette pronounced.

Vernon breathed an audible sigh of relief.

'Thank the Buddha for small mercies,' Mr Gunaratne added his tuppenceworth.

'Why ever not?' Kamala asked Minnette, at the same time looking askance at Mr Gunaratne.

'She wouldn't say.'

'Never in all my life—' Kamala started to complain.

'No great loss,' Agit broke in. 'More of this delightful food for the rest of us.' He picked up the coconut-shell spoon from the bowl of eggplant and scooped up a large helping onto his plate. As he did so, oil dripped enticingly from the spoon.

A stream of chatter ensued as everyone followed Agit's lead and helped themselves to food and passed the bowls round the table.

When no one was looking, Minnette leaned over to Vernon and whispered into his ear, 'I didn't actually call Ramona just now, you know. But I did call her this morning when I found out she was invited.'

Vernon furrowed his brow as if to ask, 'What do you mean?'

'I could see some intervention was needed,' Minnette continued in an undertone. 'So I used a little persuasion and told her you were already spoken for.'

'You didn't,' he said in disbelief, but he could see from her expression she was in earnest. 'You might have told me sooner. I've been on tenterhooks all day.'

'Where would the fun have been in that?' She laughed. 'I wouldn't have got to watch you sweat.'

Chapter 19

Dissonance

It started with a headache the morning after the dinner party. Saul awoke in Romesh's guestroom to find he could hardly open his eyes, they were so sensitive to the sunlight coming through the windows. He thought perhaps he had drunk too much toddy the previous night, but if so, this was unlike any hangover he had ever had before. His skull felt as though it would crack. He kept seeing flashes of light at the backs of his eyes, and in the depths of his brain was a peculiar drone, like the faint buzzing of an insect.

He dragged himself out of bed to perform his toilet. As he did so, his entire body ached and his hand tremor went into paroxysms. He shivered so badly while shaving, he cut his chin and was forced to stop. The tepidness of the bathwater only worsened his malaise. Upon lowering his body into the tub, he closed his eyes, as though to close out the world, and took a deep breath and fully submerged. It was like being in suspended animation; he imagined he could hear his heartbeat slowing down. When he emerged, a quarter-minute later, he saw the last vestiges of blood from his chin disperse through the water in a cloud of pink. He stared at the vanishing cloud as he mechanically lathered his body with soap. For a fugitive moment he had a thought—something to do with Jewish ritual sacrifice — before it dispersed like blood in water. Perfunctorily he finished his ablutions and got dressed and made his way to the kitchen.

Romesh stood at the cooker frying bacon. On a large platter in the centre of the kitchen table were bangers, fried eggs and onions, tomatoes, and toast. Next to this was a steaming pot of tea. 'Look who's up and about,' he said as Saul entered.

'What's all this?' Saul asked, impressed in spite of the nausea the smells induced. As a secular Jew, he was not opposed to the consumption of pork. Indeed, he often instructed Mrs Grant to fry up a good old English breakfast when the fancy struck him.

'I know how much you enjoyed the meal at Queen's Hotel the other night,' Romesh said. 'So I gave Prema the morning off and took the liberty of making something more to your taste.'

'You're a magnificent host, Romesh.' Saul could not prevent enervation from creeping into his voice. Nor could he prevent light from creeping into his eyes. Squinting, he sank into a chair at the table.

'Whatever's the matter?' Romesh enquired.

'I'm feeling poorly.'

'The result of last night's toddy, do you think?'

'That's what I thought at first. But this is something different.' As Saul said the word 'different', a flash of light pierced the back of his eyes that made him wince.

Romesh came over, unsuspecting, and slid the sizzling bacon from the pan to the platter. Before turning round, he got a closer look at Saul and nearly dropped the pan. 'Good Lord,' he said. 'Your skin's blue.' He hurriedly set the pan onto the hob and then returned to the table and felt Saul's forehead. 'And you're as cold as ice.'

Saul had been fighting the urge to yawn from the moment he sat down. Now it became uncontrollable. He yawned three times in a row.

'Perhaps you shouldn't eat,' Romesh suggested with a look of concern.

'But after all the trouble you've gone to.' In point of fact, Saul was glad of Romesh's suggestion, as he was afraid eating might make him vomit. Just the thought of food made him queasy. 'Excuse me,' he said suddenly and rushed off to the bathroom.

With nothing in his stomach, he only retched, but still, it was exceedingly unpleasant. On his knees, with his face hovering above the water closet, he retched. And he kept retching until his eyes watered.

'Are you all right?' he heard Romesh ask from the hallway. 'If I could be of any assistance …'

Saul did not have the energy to respond. Slowly he got to his feet and stood before the basin mirror. His face was flushed as well as blue. Spittle covered his lips, and his mouth tasted of bile. He splashed water onto his face, gargled, and, without troubling to dry off, went to the guestroom and fell into bed with his shoes on.

He was in and out of consciousness for the next several hours. Early on, he had the vague sense that someone came into the room and removed his shoes and unbuttoned the top buttons of his shirt, but it was only an impression, like the aftereffects of a vivid dream. What was never in doubt was his damnable headache. Each time he would awaken, for a brief moment, he would feel the warmth in his body and the rigidity in his limbs and emit a groan. At one point he startled himself awake with a cry of 'Water!', which seemed to echo for a time before his head was lifted and a glass was put to his lips. Once his thirst was slaked, he fell asleep again. Later, as the room darkened, he thought he heard voices, thought he felt a cold pressure being applied to his chest.

At last the fever broke. He stirred to life and opened his eyes. The blurry image of Romesh's smiling face floated beside him.

'How are you feeling?'

'Better,' Saul tried to say, but his throat was so dry, he enunciated only the first syllable of the word. Nevertheless, he *was* feeling better, drenched in perspiration though he was. His headache had gone, and his body no longer felt as though it were in the early stages of rigor mortis.

'You sound like you could use some of this,' Romesh said, holding out a glass of water for Saul to take. 'And the doctor asked me to give you these when you woke.' In the palm of Romesh's other hand were a couple of white tablets.

'The doctor?'

'Dr Fernando has been to see you. The pills are quinine. You've come down with a case of malaria, my dear friend.'

The peculiar drone came and went. Saul glanced at the mosquito net hanging from the pillars of the bed. Malaria. What a beastly disease. He never really appreciated its virulence until now. He had had a few mild cases of influenza in his life, and scarlet fever as a child, but for the most part, disease had left him unscathed. But malaria—damnable malaria—that was a different thing entirely. He raised himself up against the headboard by an effort of will.

'You do look better,' Romesh said as Saul swallowed the quinine and downed the rest of the water. 'But you may not be in the clear just yet.'

'How do you mean?'

Romesh folded his arms and leaned back in the chair he had drawn up to the bed. 'Sometimes malarial attacks come in bouts. You start to feel better—then, wham, another feverish attack!'

'You mean to say this is only the beginning?'

'Yes, I'm afraid so. That's why it's important for you to rest.'

Saul knew he would have no difficulty with that. He was dead beat; feeling better or not, the fever had drained every ounce of his strength. He handed back the glass and curled up on the bed. Scarcely had he done so than he fell fast asleep.

//

When Mr Gunaratne telephoned to say Saul was ill, Vernon assumed he meant something inconsequential like a head cold or a stomach upset. Mr Gunaratne's initial soft-pedalling of the news seemed to confirm this. At the outset of the call, he said simply that Saul was 'under the weather'. But after a few pointed questions from Vernon, Mr Gunaratne changed his tune and revealed that Saul in fact had contracted malaria. And malaria, he added soberly, was nothing to be trifled with.

No, Vernon agreed, it was not.

In an immediate about-turn, Mr Gunaratne assured Vernon that despite the gravity of the situation, there was no cause for alarm. Dr Fernando had paid Saul a visit yesterday and prescribed medication, and although Saul was still bedridden, he had slept through the night—a very good sign. A very good sign, indeed.

No doubt it *was* a good sign, Vernon thought, but Mr Gunaratne's repeated reversals on the matter did not inspire confidence. He deemed it prudent to make his own assessment of Saul's health. 'Is he disposed to having visitors?'

'I should think he is.'

'Then I'll be there as soon as I can.' Vernon put down the handset and left straight away for Mr Gunaratne's, not bothering to change out of his kurta and sarong.

On the walk over, he encountered Dr Fernando, who was carrying his doctor's bag and who appeared to have come from Mr Gunaratne's. 'Good day, young man,' he said with a nod. 'On your way to see Saul, are you?'

'Yes. How is he? Mr Gunaratne was kind enough to phone me, but I couldn't get a straight answer out of him.'

'He has survived the first course of the disease, thankfully. I've advised him to rest, but I dare say a visit from you would do him good—the fellowship of a friend is its own kind of medicine.' Dr Fernando glanced toward the Prins's house. 'Is your mother at home? I'd like to check on her, if I may.'

'I think you'll find her in the garden.' The thought crossed Vernon's mind that Dr Fernando might have some motive other than solicitude for wanting to see his mother, but he did not pursue the thought any further. There were more pressing concerns at the moment.

They said goodbye and went their separate ways.

Mr Gunaratne had given Vernon permission over the telephone

to enter his house at will, so when Vernon got there, he went in without knocking and made his way straight to the guestroom. Mr Gunaratne sat at Saul's bedside. They were drinking tea and seemed to be engaged in a serious conversation.

'It all goes back to Stravinsky's *The Rite of Spring*,' Saul was saying animatedly. He waggled his free hand, as if in time to some imagined music. 'Jazz wouldn't be what it is —'

'Ah, there you are,' Mr Gunaratne said, noticing Vernon at the door, the interruption in the conversation like a needle skidding across a gramophone record. Mr Gunaratne beckoned Vernon into the room. 'Come in, come in. Pull up a chair.'

'I don't want to intrude,' Vernon said.

'Not at all. We were just having a chinwag about music. Nothing so important it can't wait.' Mr Gunaratne drummed his fingers on the side of his cup. 'Coriander tea? I brewed up some as a therapeutic for Saul.'

'No, thanks, Mr Gunaratne. I shan't be staying long.'

'It's a bit of an acquired taste, I must admit,' Saul said, staring into his cup. 'But it seems to have settled my stomach. I haven't had to visit the WC even once this morning.'

'You're definitely better, then?' Vernon asked. He moved closer to the bed. The windows were shuttered, but even in the dim light, he could see Saul's pallid face and shaking hands.

'I hope your aunt and uncle got off all right yesterday,' Mr Gunaratne said discordantly.

'I've been thinking —' Vernon started to say, disregarding Mr Gunaratne's remark, but before he could finish, Saul interposed with 'And Minnette? Did she get off all right?'

There was a pregnant silence as they all realised they were talking at cross-purposes. It was as if, as a trio, they had been playing solos simultaneously and in different registers. They looked from one to another, like musicians cueing each other in, and erupted into synchronised laughter.

When the laughter died away, Saul asked Vernon, 'What is it you've been thinking?'

Vernon squatted down to Saul's eye level. 'That the moment you're recovered, you should move in with Amma and Minnette and me.' He looked at Mr Gunaratne. 'No offence.'

'None taken.'

'It was never my intention,' Vernon added, addressing Saul again, 'for you to stay anywhere but with us while you're in Ceylon. And now that Amma's "revitalised", you've no reason *not* to— apart from your illness, I mean.'

Mr Gunaratne did not wait for Saul to respond. 'Of course, I'll be sad to see you go. Our conversations have been like manna from heaven.' He paused, as if doubting himself, his eyes settling for a moment on the bed's canopy. 'But perhaps moving to the Prins's *will* be for the best. I can't help feeling I'm somehow to blame for your illness.'

'Nonsense,' Saul said. 'How could you be to blame?' As he posed the question, his eyes, too, momentarily settled on the bed's canopy. 'I've said it before, and I'll say it again: you're a magnificent host.'

Vernon stood up. 'I should go. I only came to see how you're doing, and Dr Fernando said you need your rest. I'll tell Amma, shall I, that once you're on the mend, you'll be moving in with us?'

'Very well,' Saul said. 'If that's what you want, I'd be delighted.'

'Brilliant.' Vernon headed for the door, adding over his shoulder, 'And to answer your questions, yes, my aunt and uncle and Minnette got off all right.' Partway down the hallway, he heard Mr Gunaratne say, 'He's a good lad, eh?' and Saul respond, 'Indeed.'

Outside, it was raining, only moderately but enough to get Vernon's hair and clothes sodden on the walk home. As he sloshed down the road and drew closer to his house, he saw someone coming toward him. He peered into the rain. It was Dr Fernando again. They were almost level with one another when the doctor nodded beneath his upraised umbrella and said, 'You'll forgive me if I don't stop and chat.' Vernon smiled and waved but said nothing and at the same time had the strange sensation that he was watching a moving picture play backwards.

Before he went into his house, he tarried for a minute on the verandah to let his clothes drip-dry. As he stood there looking out at the rain, the old longcase clock in the sitting room began to chime St Mary's. He found the sound comforting, reminding him as it did of his childhood on Eden Estate. The clock, a Prins family heirloom that had been passed down from his great-uncle Luuk, dated back to the 1800s. Some of the clock's features had since been replaced — the dial was now made of brass with Sinhalese numerals, and the case was made of Indian-style wooden latticework — but the inner mechanisms were still the original. Vernon recalled how when he was a boy, he used to help his pater wind the clock's movements every Sunday night. 'Time is a trick of the mind,' Thathi would say as they each inserted a key and wound up the clock. 'The past and the future are only memories and expectations. Reality is the present.' At the time, Vernon vaguely understood the statements to be Buddhist in their logic, but it was not until much later that he understood their meaning. Time was a series of moments, like frames in a moving picture, and Thathi was admonishing him to live in the present, a philosophy of life similar to Uncle Agit's.

The clock struck eleven, and Vernon went inside. By coincidence, Kamala was in the sitting room winding up the clock. She was barefoot and wearing a batik kaftan.

'How's Mr Maccabee, dear?' she asked, turning a key while standing on her tiptoes. 'Bernie told me what happened.'

'He seems to be all right — well enough, at least, to chat and drink coriander tea. I asked him to come and stay with us after he recovers. I hope you don't mind.'

'Of course not. We were expecting him to be here before now at any rate, and it would be nice to have a guest in the house.' Finishing with one key, she moved on to the other. 'With all the commotion during the past fortnight, I forgot to wind up the clock. Do you remember how you and Thatha used to do this' — she paused and laughed — 'like clockwork?'

'I remember.'

'Until you were tall enough, he had to hold you in his arms or lift you up so you could reach the key. It was so cute watching the two of you. You were in such awe of the clock then.'

'What did Dr Fernando have to say while he was here?' Vernon asked, the question striking a wrong note as it came out.

'Oh, nothing, dear. Just to see how I'm doing. And we discussed Mr Maccabee, as I said. Is he *really* all right?' She gave the key one last twist and turned round. 'Heavens, you're soaked! You must change out of those wet things at once. Luckily, Rani brought the laundry in off the line before it rained, so you have several sets of clean clothes to choose from. I ironed them and put them away in your room.' As she said this, Vernon's face turned waxen, but he said nothing. 'I rather enjoyed sorting through your things. It was like when you were still a boy living at home.'

He remained silent.

'What has got into you?' she asked. 'Are you that worried about Mr Maccabee?'

'I think perhaps I am,' he said in deflection and walked away and headed straight for his room. 'Poor darling,' he heard her say as he crossed the house.

In his room, he went to the chest and opened the top drawer and swept aside his smalls. Zoe's letter was still there, but he could have sworn it had been moved. Or did he move it himself when he took out his letter to Zoe and gave it to the postman? He strained to think back to that day, but so much had happened in the interim, he could not remember his exact movements. In any case, if Amma *had* read Zoe's letter, why did she say nothing about it? Was she perhaps waiting to spring it on him when he least expected it? He doubted she was that Machiavellian, but then, there was a lot about her he did not know. He had hardly seen her these past six years.

He changed into a new kurta and sarong and then took Zoe's letter from the drawer and sat down on his bed and read it through again. To read that her heart ached for him made his heart ache for her. But her words, and their cadence, helped calm his frayed nerves, and for a fleeting moment he did not care whether his mother knew about Zoe.

//

Two days later Saul regressed and fell into a coma-like state in which his mind resembled a staticky wireless. Every few hours he would wake with a start, struggle to open his eyes at the same time that he heard crackling noises intermingled with the ambient sound of rain, and then close his eyes and drift back to sleep. Eventually, after the best part of a day, his mind cleared and his fever broke, but not before he had a vivid dream. He was in the attic of his Belgravia house, and in front of him an indistinct form hung from a trolley hook attached to the ceiling. With a sudden, violent jerk of his arm, he reached out. His hand brushed against what felt like flesh and hair. He tried to take hold of it but instead sent the form twirling round and round. What he saw when the twirling finally stopped made him quiver: the snout and floppy ears and deep-set, glowing red eyes of a large black sow.

He awoke in a pool of perspiration. He lay on his back, staring up at the broken ceiling fan. His body still ached, and he felt lethargic, but all his other symptoms were gone. He turned his head slightly and glanced round. Someone had been in the room. He could sense it. The shutters were open, and in the wake of the rainstorm, a cool breeze blew, causing the mosquito net to flutter. On the bedside table were a ewer and a damp cloth. A floral, amber-woody fragrance, like that of an Oriental perfume, lingered in the air.

Voices came from the verandah. They were garbled at first as Saul emerged from his feverish sleep, but the more he listened, the more it became clear that the voices belonged to Vernon and Minnette. She was back from Colombo. Saul's heart skipped at the thought. He was certain she was the one who had been in the room, the one who had nursed him during his fever.

'Dr de Silva is still looking for whites to speak at rallies,' Minnette was saying. 'Do you think Mr Maccabee might be interested? The next rally in Kandy is scheduled for January.'

Saul could only assume she was referring to the LSSP.

There was a long pause. In the silence Saul imagined Vernon taking a drag of a cigarette.

'You'd have to ask him,' Vernon said eventually. 'But perhaps you should wait till he fully recovers.'

'Yes, I'll do that.'

Another pause.

'He'll be all right, you know,' Minnette said. 'You mustn't blame yourself. You couldn't have known this would happen. And besides, it was his choice to stay here.'

'Yeah, I know, I keep telling myself that, but—' Vernon stopped short, as though Minnette had put a finger to his lips.

'I don't care what other people say about you, Brother,' she said, laughing. 'You're a good man.'

'And you're a buer.' Despite the harshness of Vernon's oath, there was levity in his voice.

'I think that's just about the nicest thing anyone's ever said to me.'

Saul stifled a laugh; he could not help being infected by the banter. In his imagination now, he saw Vernon smile and take another drag of his cigarette and expertly tap the ashes over the verandah rail.

Vernon said, 'There's something I must tell you.'

'Let me guess, Zoe's with child.'

'What? No! Why would you say that?'

'To get under your skin.'

'You've succeeded.' Vernon was quiet for a moment, perhaps considering how he might have reacted if Zoe had been pregnant. 'No,' he went on, 'what I wanted to tell you is that you're not the only one in the family with a non-academic interest in politics.'

'You mean you're joining the LSSP?'

'Perhaps, but that's not what I was referring to. I was referring to my time in London. I did more than just write articles for *The Masses*. I agitated against the Jackboots.'

'Truly?' Minnette asked. 'Was it dangerous? Did you take part in the Battle of Cable Street?'

'Yes, yes, and yes.'

'Do tell me about it.'

'One day I will, but not now.' Vernon sighed. Some dark memory, of his near-death experience at Action House perhaps, seemed to weigh on his mind.

'I was right that you're a good man,' Minnette said. And perhaps, just then, she reached out and touched Vernon's hand. 'As long as we're revealing secrets,' she added, 'do you remember that DBU journal article I sent you? The one by Niemand?'

'Are you about to confess to being Niemand?'

'Yes and no. I wrote the article with Thathi. He didn't like to see prejudice toward Burghers and what he called "assertive nationalism". And after what happened with Mr Arunasalem, Thathi wanted more than ever to speak his mind. But he was also afraid of reprisal, so we decided to write the article together under a pseudonym. Then with his illness, he became less concerned about secrecy. It was shortly after the article was published that he agreed to speak for the LSSP. I think he knew he was going to die, and he didn't care anymore what people thought.'

'I didn't know he still had it in him,' Vernon said.

'Nor did I. I thought he had given up on political activism long ago. But now I know better. A desire to agitate for social justice runs deep in our family.'

There was yet another pause, at the end of which Vernon said, 'Shall we go check on Saul?'

Then the front door opened and closed. Saul quickly sat up in bed and wet his fingers in the ewer and ran them through his dishevelled hair. He was leaning against the headboard, with a look of embarrassment on his face, when Vernon and Minnette entered the room.

'Mr Maccabee, you're up,' Minnette said in surprise. She wore a pink silk frock, and as she drew closer to the bed, the scent of Oriental perfume grew stronger.

'How are you feeling?' Vernon asked. 'Could I pour you a glass of water?'

'I'm fine, thank you. Don't put yourself out for my sake.' Saul's throat, in fact, was as dry as dust, but at the moment he was more interested in basking in Minnette's radiance. He found her feminine elegance breathtaking.

'You were restless in your sleep earlier,' said Minnette. 'You kept calling out your wife's name.'

'Did I?' Saul said, remembering his dream. He wondered what it meant. He could not imagine it had anything to do with Esther. 'How, may I ask, do you know her name?'

'Vernon told me. And I also noticed your dedication to her in your article in *The Masses* and put two and two together. You must have loved her very much.'

'Yes.' As Saul uttered the monosyllable, he glanced out the window. The sun had yet to re-emerge after the storm, and the sky was grey. Faint snatches of plaintive birdsong emanated from the jungle.

'Are you sure I can't get you anything?' Vernon asked. 'Food, perhaps? Mr Gunaratne should be back from the fishmonger's soon.'

'Or I could offer you some food for your soul,' Minnette said before Saul could respond. She came forward and handed him a slip of paper.

Saul perused it. It was a poem, entitled 'Il Poya Day'. He got as far as the second stanza and stopped. He wanted to read the rest alone, to savour it in solitude. 'This is one of your own, I presume?'

'You said you wanted to discuss my poetry, so there you are. It's my latest work, and you're the first to read it.' Minnette beamed with pride. 'There are a few things you should know. A *poya* day is a full-moon day, and for Buddhists Il Poya Day signifies the end of a three-month rainy-season retreat, during which time monks consign themselves to temples and don't go out into the community except for *dānēs* and other special events. This year Il Poya Day falls at the end of the month.'

Saul's eyes roamed over the lines of the poem, took in its evocative lotus-flower shape on the page. 'I must say you've piqued my interest, and I look forward to reading it. You don't mind, though, if I hold off until later? I find it preferable to read in solitude.'

'Only if you don't lose it,' Minnette teased. 'It's my only copy.'

'I wouldn't dream of it.' Saul squeezed the paper affectionately. He was about to say he would guard it with his life when he noticed Vernon smiling at him, and suddenly he became self-conscious and bit his tongue. He realised he had allowed himself to get carried away. Heaven knew that dallying with a young woman, and one who happened to be the sister of a friend, was an impossible fancy. To say nothing of the fact that Minnette was half his age.

Chapter 20

Consonance

'Bloody hell,' Vernon muttered as he reluctantly got out of bed to answer the telephone, which had been ringing off the hook for over a minute. The house was dark except for the moonlight streaming through the windows. With his eyes half-open and wearing only a singlet and pants, he groped his way to the sitting room. Before he crossed the threshold, a light came on and the telephone stopped ringing. He entered the room to find his mother there, in her housecoat, holding the receiver to her ear. The longcase clock read 2.22 a.m.

'Who in God's name is it at this hour?' Vernon asked, struggling to keep his eyes open.

Kamala lowered the handset and put a palm over the transmitter. 'It's Romesh. He says to turn on the wireless. There's an unscheduled announcement from the King, it seems.'

Vernon turned on the wireless, selected short wave, and tuned in to the BBC National Programme. The reception was poor, with much crackling, fading, and atmospheric interference. An edition of the *Comic Opera* was on. At intervals choral voices, with orchestral accompaniment, broke through the static. Vernon looked at Kamala and raised his hands and shrugged.

She conferred with Mr Gunaratne, then rang off. 'He says to

wait. The King will be on any moment.'

Minnette came into the room, wearing a lace nightdress. 'What's going on?'

'The King's about to make an announcement,' Kamala said.

Saul was the last to arrive. He came in just in time to catch Kamala's answer to Minnette's question. Bleary-eyed and bespectacled, he yawned and tied the sash of his silk robe. He had been staying at the Prins's for less than a fortnight now, but even in this short time, he seemed to have become a part of the family.

The four of them stood round the wireless, with expectant expressions on their faces. Shortly after the clock struck the half-hour, the music was cut short and the voice of the BBC director general said, 'This is Windsor Castle, His Royal Highness Prince Edward.'

Then the King came on, with his measured, cut-glass accent. 'At long last I am able to say a few words of my own. I have never wanted to withhold anything, but until now it has not been constitutionally possible for me to speak. A few hours ago I discharged my last duty as King and Emperor, and now that I have been succeeded by my brother [...]'

Kamala said, 'Oh my,' drowning out the King.

'Hush, Amma,' said Minnette, 'or we'll miss something.'

'[...] declare my allegiance to him,' the sophisticated voice continued through the static. 'This I do with all my heart. You all know the reasons which have impelled me to renounce the throne. But I want you to understand that in making up my mind I did not forget the country or the Empire which as Prince of Wales, and lately as King, I have for twenty-five years tried to serve. But you must believe me when I tell you that I have found it impossible to carry the heavy burden of responsibility and to discharge my duties as King as I would wish to do without the help and support of the woman I love. [...]'

The signal suddenly went dead.

'Damn it,' Vernon said, grabbing the sides of the wireless and shaking it. He wanted to hear what the King had to say about Mrs

Simpson. 'The bloody thing! Of all the times — !' But his curses were a waste of breath. For nearly a minute the wireless emitted nothing but static. Angrily he switched it off.

'He went and did it,' Saul remarked, re-tying the sash of his robe. 'I never would have believed he'd throw up the throne for the sake of a woman.'

'There are worse things, aren't there, Saul?' Minnette said. She had taken to calling him by his first name of late. Ever since he arrived at the Prins's, his interactions with her had remained formal, but nevertheless a friendly rapport developed between them. Her ministering to him during his illness seemed to have created an unspoken bond.

'You'll have no argument from me on that score. Most certainly there are worse things.'

Once the excitement of the King's abdication was over, they all returned to bed. But Vernon could not sleep. He lay there listening to the whir of the ceiling fan and thinking about the sacrifice the King was making for love. The King, for good or ill, had followed his heart, and, as Minnette and Saul said, there were worse things. Befittingly, well before the King took the extraordinary step of abdicating, Zoe had suggested that the royal affair was none of the public's business and had drawn parallels between that affair and her relationship with Vernon. Now the comparison seemed even more germane. If a king could flout social mores and marry a divorcee, why could Vernon not marry someone of his choosing who happened to be of a different race? He would not be the first to do so. Ammi and Thathi had done it. As had tens of thousands of others under colonialism and the British Empire. And there were prominent examples of controversial relationships in British history and literature, too. Vernon could think of several examples from the books he was compelled to read at Trinity. King Henry VIII and Anne Boleyn. Tamora and Aaron the Moor. Othello and Desdemona. James Achilles Kirkpatrick and Khair-un-Nissa. Queen Victoria and John Brown. Love was blind in more ways than one. It did not see caste or colour or creed or even, sometimes, the worst of a lover's pretty follies.

//

'We have a surprise for you,' Minnette said from the doorway of Saul's room.

Vernon stood behind her, grinning from ear to ear and holding up a paper bag.

Saul removed his pipe from his mouth and invited them in. It was early evening. An oil lamp on the bedside table was lit, and before the interruption, Saul had been considering the meaning of Minnette's latest poem. It had become a kind of ritual for them ever since she gave him 'Il Poya Day': she would give him a polished draft of a poem, he would read it in solitude, and later they would discuss it at length. He set her latest poem onto the side table and sat up in bed. 'What's the surprise?'

'See for yourself,' Vernon said and handed Saul the paper bag.

Saul put his pipe back into his mouth and took the bag and peeked inside. There were several thin red candles that smelled overpoweringly of cinnamon. He was unsure what to say.

'It was Minnette's idea,' Vernon explained.

Then it struck Saul what the candles were for: his menorah. 'Oh, I see. Thank you,' he said over the stem of his pipe, feeling his face turn the colour of the candles. 'You shouldn't have.' The menorah was the only thing he had brought with him to Ceylon that was connected in any way to his religion—sans the candles, for reasons of practicality. On the first day of Hanukkah, four days earlier, he had displayed the candleless menorah in his bedroom window, and Minnette, during a discussion of one of her poems, noticed it. She had not known he was a Jew but seemed to accept the disclosure as a matter of course. Her only response was to say that it would be a pity for him not to light candles over the holiday.

'I spent three days,' she said now, 'searching high and low for the right size. Alas, these scented ones were the best I could do. Besides reeking to high heaven, they're a bit too Christmassy, I'm afraid.'

Saul shook his head. 'Don't apologise. They're splendid.' He set down his pipe, took up a box of matches, said 'Shall we light them now?' and with six of the candles went to the window. He inserted one candle at a time into the menorah, from right to left, skipping the middle nozzle, and then, using the sixth candle, lit the other five, from left to right. When he finished with that, he inserted the sixth candle into the middle nozzle and stepped back to admire the display. 'What do you think?'

'It's lovely,' Minnette said. 'It reminds me of what we do for Vesak, to celebrate the birth, enlightenment, and death of the Buddha.'

'It's interesting you should say that, because the menorah is meant to symbolise universal enlightenment.' Saul, still admiring the display, suddenly frowned. 'I've failed frightfully to follow tradition. The proper thing to do is to light one additional candle each night of Hanukkah until all eight are lit.'

'But you followed it in spirit,' Minnette said. 'That's what's important, isn't it?'

'Perhaps you're right.'

'Of course I'm right.'

'She's nothing if not modest,' Vernon quipped as he made for the door. 'Come, Sister. Let's leave Saul to his reading.'

Minnette glanced at her poem on the table and smiled before following Vernon out.

Once Saul was alone again, he sat back down on the bed and picked up Minnette's poem to re-read. But he could not focus on the words, as his eyes kept wandering to the menorah. The physical act of lighting the candles — something he had not done since he was a boy — brought back a flood of memories. During his marriage, Esther had always been the one to light the menorah. She was more devout than he. Now she was gone — and it was his first Hanukkah without her. Only last December … He could not finish the thought. He felt a rush of anger at Ernst — or rather, at the damned Nazis, as Ernst could hardly be blamed for speaking out. The trouble started with them, the fascists; their ideas were like a cancer metastasising their way through Europe. The PNF, the Nazis, the Jackboots, the Falange — they seemed to be swelling their ranks by the day. And now the fascist swine were forming what Mussolini called the 'Rome-Berlin Axis'. How had the world come to this? Saul felt guilty for living a carefree existence in Ceylon while so many others round the world suffered.

Worse, he felt guilty for being alive, when Esther and Ernst were not. He wished he could turn back the clock. There was nothing more he could have done about Ernst — heaven knew he had tried, using his connections to get a hearing at the German embassy in London. But still, he could have been more vigilant in looking after Esther. She might have lived to see another day if he had.

Again his eyes wandered to the menorah, and despite his anguish, a sense of inner peace came over him. Minnette had been right: he *had* followed in spirit the tradition of lighting the menorah. He must have unconsciously had that in mind all along, an oblique way of keeping Esther's memory, if not her actual self, alive. It was a bittersweet realisation.

//

Yes, Minnette had been right, and what did it matter if modesty was not her strong suit? The truth was, she had a knack for getting to the heart of things. It was her métier as a poet: distilling words and thoughts and images and human behaviour down to their essence. She applied the same insightfulness to the rest of her life and to her observations of others. She was more than a rising star; she was a modern-day sybil, singing the fates from her ampulla.

But as much as Saul wanted to tell her this, he could not. He had made a vow, the moment he moved into the Prins's house, to hide his feelings and to sedulously observe proprieties: it would not do to get romantically involved with a friend's sister under the mother's roof, let alone with someone half his age. For the most part he was able to maintain emotional distance by thickening his carapace in Minnette's presence, by acting more like a teacher than a friend. That, however, was becoming harder by the day. She increasingly sought his advice, often for things that had nothing to do with her poetry, and he did not think he could refuse her attentions without seeming discourteous. On the verandah or in the sitting room, they would discuss politics, religion, science, and anything else that struck their fancies. Once, during one of their discussions, she told him rather tenderly that she understood why Vernon enjoyed his company so much: he was a first-rate conversationalist and impressively knew something about just about everything. Saul blushed and, awkwardly looking away as though a bird had flown by, quickly changed the subject.

So when, on the sixth day of Hanukkah, she invited him to visit a Buddhist temple, he panicked and responded noncommittally. The invitation could not be characterised as an offer to 'step out', as such, but that was what it felt like to Saul, particularly since Vernon begged off accompanying them so that he could work on his thesis, which, he said, he had dawdled over long enough. Saul's feelings were complicated by the fact that he was still thinking of Esther. What would she say—if she *were* observing him from somewhere in the starry firmament—about his behaving like a lovesick schoolboy?

But then a compromise arose with regard to the trip to the temple. Kamala would be accompanying them instead. With the mother acting as chaperone, Saul reckoned, he would be unlikely to forget himself and pour his heart out to Minnette in a moment of passion.

The Temple of the Tooth was more like a museum than a temple. Its main shrine housed a sacred relic: the purported left upper canine of the Buddha. The temple complex was situated to the north of Kandy Lake, nestled among the trees along the western edge of the Udawattakele Forest Reserve. Approaching the complex's entrance on foot was like encountering something out of a storybook. A mossy-brick undulating wall, dotted with holes for displaying oil lamps, flanked the entrance. Behind that stood a white octagonal pavilion with red shingles. And farther back, in the shade of palms and other tropical trees, stretched the main building's hip-and-gable roof.

It was a clear sunny day. Minnette and Kamala were both dressed in semi-formal attire—Kamala in a dark-green sari and Minnette in a blue floral-wrap dress—and they both carried peacock-patterned parasols to shield their faces from the sun. Saul walked with them across the maidan toward the temple entrance. Water birds croaked and squealed on the lake, and from all round the complex came the cacophonous sounds of the jungle. Beyond the maidan, they ascended some stairs, between two large elephant-engraved stone blocks, crossed over a moat, and passed beneath an arched gateway.

At the museum entrance, they removed their shoes and went inside. The museum was a long rectangular hall with a black-and-white marble floor. On both sides of the hall golden elephant heads capped decorative pilasters, and atop pedestals at the base of the pilasters sat Buddha statues. A series of paintings depicting stories from the Buddha's lives spanned the length of the walls. The museum was so crammed with people, it was difficult to move. Short of pushing his way through, Saul could see no way of getting to the shrine at the other end of the hall.

'I forgot it might be like this,' Minnette apologised. 'Shall we wait till the crowd thins out?'

'All right,' Saul said.

They were turning to go when Minnette noticed Kamala had disappeared. 'Ammi?' she called, standing on her tiptoes and scanning the hall. 'She always does this, slipping through crowds with her small frame. I don't see her. Do you?'

Saul shook his head.

'Oh, well,' said Minnette. 'What to do? We'll find her later.' She put her arm in Saul's and led him back out the door, where they retrieved their shoes.

A minute later, after walking down a gallery and descending a flight of stairs, they found themselves in a palm grove interspersed with pink-flowered plumeria.

'Isn't it lovely?' Minnette said, letting go of Saul's arm and doing a half-twirl as she took in the surroundings. 'I haven't been here since I was a girl.' Upon reaching a clearing, she opened up her parasol and sat on a stone bench. Her face was radiant even in shadow. She looked up at him and patted the bench. 'Won't you join me?'

Obediently he sat down. He had not said a word since they left the museum.

'I'd like to ask you something,' she began, smoothing out the skirt of her dress with her free hand. 'I know we haven't known each other for very long — and you're likely to find my asking you this impertinent — but —'

'Perhaps I should speak first,' he interrupted, suddenly finding his voice. It would be bad form, he thought, if he were to leave the asking to her. He started to reach for her hand when he hurriedly drew back because of the expression on her face.

'What did you think I was going to say?' she asked with what seemed to be a flash of understanding in her eyes.

He blushed and cleared his throat. He was at a loss, until he remembered the conversation he overheard from his sickbed at Romesh's. It was a shot in the dark, but it was worth a try. 'You were going to ask whether I'd be willing to speak at an LSSP rally next month,' he ventured. 'And the answer is an emphatic yes.'

She looked incredulous. 'How in heaven's name did you know that?'

'Clairvoyance, I suppose.'

'You're insufferable.' Even as she uttered the criticism, her voice softened. She rested the stick of her parasol on her shoulder. 'Will you really speak at the rally?'

'I'd be honoured.'

'You might face reprisal. Some of our speakers have even received death threats. Thathi did.'

'No matter.' Saul would risk life and limb to please Minnette.

She stared searchingly into his eyes. 'And what was it you were going to say to *me* just now? It was something important, I'm sure of it.'

'Well,' he said, maintaining his composure, 'if you must know, I was going to tell you it's about time you sought publication for "Il Poya Day".' His voice grew increasingly resonant as he spoke. 'You've been tinkering with it for weeks now, and it's not going to get any better than it already is. In fact, as it is, it's magnificent.' He meant every word of what he said, even if it decidedly was *not* what he had intended to say.

She gave him a dubious look as though she did not quite believe him.

//

Vernon was not in fact working on his thesis. Instead, he was writing to Zoe. His concern that his mother would find Zoe's letters had begun to diminish—not once had the subject come up in conversation—but as a precaution he decided to write to Zoe only when his mother was out of the house. He also moved Zoe's letters from the chest of drawers in his bedroom to the medicine chest in his bathroom.

They exchanged letters every fortnight now. The latest one from her had come only yesterday, and he was afraid that if he did not write and post his response to her soon, it might not reach her in time for Christmas. An hour after the others left for the Temple of the Tooth, he completed a draft of the letter and read it over with an editorial eye.

Dear Zoe,
I had a close call yesterday. Ammi happened to be in the garden
when Mr Mendis, the postman, arrived with your letter, and it
was only seconds away from ending up in her hands before I
fortuitously intercepted it. I don't know what I would have done if
she had got to it first. Started weeping, perhaps? I made up a lie
on the spot (about expecting a letter from my LSE supervisor) and
grabbed the post from Mr Mendis and ran off. She must have

thought I was mad.

In any case, it was wonderful to hear from you. I find myself eagerly awaiting your letters, and I send off my responses as quickly as I can to minimise the time it takes for your next letter to arrive. It's strange that London is so unseasonably warm these days, as you mentioned. What do you suppose is causing it? All the smoke belching from chimneys? An absurd thought, I know.

No doubt you've heard about King Edward's abdication. Can you believe it? Who would have thought, when you first mentioned the rumours about the King six weeks ago, that such a thing would come to pass? It just goes to show that love is stronger than the pressures of tradition and society. I thought of you during and after the broadcast of the King's speech (or the Duke of Windsor's speech, I should say). We must follow his example and love each other for who we are and ignore those who would deny us that love for no other reason than racial prejudice. Of course, I'm 'preaching to the converted', as you so often say.

There's something I've been meaning to tell you and might as well now, since we're on the subject of love. Saul and Minnette fancy each other. All the signs are there: the looks, the tenderness, the hanging on every word. The funny thing is, they seem to think they're fooling everyone. But they're not. I think even Ammi suspects something. If so, I can't for the life of me figure out why she has kept silent about it. Perhaps she approves of Saul, because I let it slip one day that he's well minted. I wouldn't put it past her. After all, she married Thathi for his money and only later fell deeply in love with him. You might be wondering what I myself think about the dalliance between Saul and Minnette. I don't mind at all. Saul would make an excellent addition to the family. Just think, if we were brothers-in-law, I would be able to enjoy our tête-à-têtes for as long as we both lived. Oh, what a happy thought! (We had a very interesting conversation about Buddhism the other day. He said something to the effect that the devout Buddhists' goal of enlightenment was similar to the progressive Victorians' notion that evolution could become a conscious process. And it struck me that he was right and that evolution's existence over time, from century to century and from millennium to millennium, is similar to the Buddhist conception of the cycles of rebirth, in so much as it relates to mankind as a whole. In other words, the Buddhist conception of enlightenment could be interpreted as a metaphor for evolutionary processes in man. What do you think? Too farfetched?) But I'm afraid Saul may be too proper, or too conflicted, to tell Minnette how he feels, and I don't dare raise the subject with him myself. Do you know he blushes every time I walk in on him and Minnette during their conversations? I get embarrassed at his embarrassment.

It occurred to me just now that you and I have never discussed Christmas. Do you celebrate it in the traditional way – with paper crowns, Brussels sprouts and goose and mince pies, and the King's message by the fire? My family and I celebrate Christmas because Thathi used to insist upon it even though he was an atheist. But we do things a little differently here. There are no Brussels sprouts in Ceylon, so we have to improvise. One thing we never go without is Christmas cake: our version is just like the British version, with brandy and sherry, marzipan, and various essences and preserves and spices. The number of ingredients the recipe calls for is rather shocking. I looked it up recently because I intend to surprise Ammi with a cake on Christmas Eve. Would you believe there are over thirty ingredients? It's going to take me an age to make. I wish I could be there with you in London over the holidays. I would bake you a cake and shower you with gifts and kiss you ceaselessly beneath the mistletoe.

Forever Yours,
Vernon

The letter seemed fine, so he inserted the folded pages into an envelope. As he did so, he heard the others coming in at the front door. They were back prematurely. He went to the bathroom and hid the envelope in the medicine chest. His mother was in his room when he returned.

'What a wasted trip!' she said, failing to notice the furtive look on his face. 'I've never seen so many people. It was like a zoo. And Minnette and Saul didn't even see the shrine. They went traipsing off somewhere by themselves doing God knows what.'

Vernon smiled almost imperceptibly.

'How did the work on your thesis go?'

'It went well,' he said without elaborating.

'And your professor, what did he have to say?'

Vernon gave her a quizzical look.

'The letter in the post yesterday.'

'Oh, right. Nothing really. He was just checking to see how I'm doing.'

'Speaking of letters—' She noticed Vernon flinch. 'What's the matter, dear?'

'Why?'

'You seem rather troubled.'

He glanced at the window, as if seeking an escape route. 'Perhaps it's the heat.'

'Yes, it is rather hot today.' She lifted up the fall of her sari, used it as a fan for a moment, and then draped it back across her arm. 'As I was saying, I found some old letters the other day, and —'

'What gave you the right to search my things?' he blurted out, his face flushed with anger.

She stared at him blankly.

Realising his mistake, he said, 'You mean you didn't find Zoe's letters?'

'I haven't the faintest idea what you're talking about. Who's Zoe?'

The game was up, he thought. He might as well tell her the rest of it now. 'She's a good friend of mine. From London.'

'A sweetheart?' Her voice sounded hopeful.

'Yes, a sweetheart. If all goes to plan, we'll marry one day.'

'It's that serious? Do tell me about her.'

In a few breathless sentences he told her about Zoe.

'She sounds lovely,' Kamala said when he finished.

'You're not upset?'

'Why would I be?'

'Oh, I don't know: she's English, she's a nurse, she's not Ramona Bolling.'

'I never really liked Ramona, to tell you the truth. She uses far too much henna and paint for my taste. And the most dreadful rumours about her have been flying round Kandy.'

'Good thing she didn't come to the party, then.' It occurred to Vernon that Minnette and Zoe would not believe Kamala's reaction.

He could hardly believe it himself.

'Yes, it was.' She cupped his face with her free hand for a moment. 'I'm terribly happy for you, darling. All that remains is for you and Zoe to bless me with a grandchild.'

'Don't push your luck, Amma,' he said and kissed her on the forehead. 'You didn't finish what you were saying, by the way, about the letters you found.'

'They're love letters from Thathi, when I was only eighteen. I forgot I had them. Yesterday I read them through and was reminded of what a romantic he was. You and Minnette are very much like him, in your own ways. I'd give them to you to read for yourself, but they're of a rather personal nature. Perhaps once I'm gone from this world. Nothing will matter then.'

With that, Kamala left. Vernon stared at the spot she had vacated. An air of nostalgia about the past and resignation about the future hung behind in the room.

Chapter 21

Point

They were gathered together in the sitting room, Kamala and Minnette on one daybed and Saul and Vernon on the other. Gifts wrapped in colourful tissue paper and bound with ribbon lay on the floor. A tea service and a three-tiered tray—which contained cucumber sandwiches and sausage buns and little packets of Christmas cake wrapped in silver foil—stood on the carved-wood coffee table. It was four o'clock in the afternoon on Christmas Eve, and the house smelled of baked goods and spice.

Moments earlier, the mood in the room had gone from celebratory to sombre when Kamala pointed out that it was the Prins's first Christmas without Johannes. Her comment struck a chord even for Saul. He remained silent while Minnette and Vernon did their utmost to restore cheer to the occasion.

'Thathi adored Christmas,' Minnette said for Saul's benefit. 'On Eden Estate, when Vernon and I were little, he used to dress up like Father Christmas—somehow or other he got hold of a fake white beard and a red cape and bishop's hat. Every Christmas Eve, he'd show up in this silly costume with a bag full of gifts and say his name was *Sinterklaas*.'

Vernon's eyes shone at the memory. 'I asked him once why, if he really was Father Christmas, he wasn't a fat jolly old man. That was how he appeared in all the pictures I had ever seen, I said. *Nee, nee*, Thathi responded, that was just a myth, in the same way that the likenesses of Christ were ideal representations. The Dutch Father Christmas, the *real* Father Christmas, was young and tall and thin and muscular.'

Everyone laughed, including Saul.

Then Kamala said, wistfully and to no one in particular, 'So many things have changed.' She glanced at the wireless. 'There won't even be a king's message this year.'

Minnette set down her cup and clasped her hands together. 'Enough gloom and doom. It's high time we started traditions of our own, no? What do you say we play a game?'

'Such as?' Vernon asked, unenthused, helping himself to a sausage bun.

'We'll take turns saying at least one thing we're grateful for. I'll go first.' Minnette looked at Saul, then at Kamala. 'I'm grateful I've been afforded the leisure to write poetry. Most poets I know face constant struggle. But I don't, thanks to Thathi's hard work all those years ago on Eden Estate.'

Kamala smiled with her eyes. She appeared to have emerged from her despondency. 'Well said, dear.'

'Yes,' Saul concurred and took a congratulatory sip of his tea.

'Now it's your turn,' Minnette said to Vernon.

'Well, let's see.' Vernon pretended to think deeply. 'I'm grateful to be alive, I suppose.'

'You're such a spoilsport,' Minnette said, throwing her half-eaten sandwich at him. It hit him in the face and fell to his lap.

He picked it up with the intent of throwing it back when Kamala said, 'Children, please! Not in front of Mr Maccabee. I was going to say I'm grateful for my children, but now — well, I shall just have to think of something else.'

'Oh, all right,' Vernon said. 'If it's that important to you, I'll play along. I, too, am grateful for the opportunities Thathi's hard work has afforded me. I wouldn't have been able to attend university without it. And I'm grateful for my family and friends: you Amma and Saul and Zoe and even — dare I say it? — Minnette.' He gave her an impish smile.

'I love you too, Brother,' she said and stuck out her tongue at him.

Kamala folded her arms and sat up straight. 'I've just thought of something. I'm grateful for the Buddha and his teachings, which have helped me still my mind during trying times.' She eyed Minnette and Vernon. 'I'll have to think long and hard about whether I'm grateful for the pair of you.'

'And you, Saul?' Minnette prompted, giving him a warm smile.

He evaded her gaze and instead directed his response to Kamala. 'So as not to sound like a broken record,' he said, 'I'll take a different approach. I'm grateful for the generosity and hospitality of the Ceylonese — Romesh and you, the Prins family, principally, but also the little people, those who often go unnoticed.' He had in mind people like Prema and Rani as well as people back home in London. A few days ago, he had cabled his mother reminding her to give her parlourmaid, Jessie, a Christmas pudding and a ten-pound note. And he had sent a separate cable to Sidney and Mrs Grant wishing them a merry Christmas and urging them 'to spare no expense' in celebrating the holiday with their respective families.

Kamala seemed to appreciate Saul's sentiment. She smiled and said, 'That reminds me. Minnette, dear, won't you go to the kitchen and ask Rani to please join us.'

Minnette left the room and returned a minute later with Rani in tow.

'Ah, Rani, come,' Kamala said, scooting over to make room for her on the daybed. 'You must have a piece of cake with us and open your gifts.' Kamala repeated the last sentence in Tamil.

'Yes, miss,' Rani said, in a rare use of English, and then she and Minnette sat next to Kamala on the daybed.

Kamala passed everyone a piece of cake and a napkin.

'It's delicious,' Saul declared after taking a bite. He turned to Vernon. 'You really made this yourself?'

'Yes — well, with a little help from Rani, of course.'

Rani covered her mouth with a hand and giggled.

'He always was interested in cooking,' Kamala said. 'When he was a little boy, he used to get under foot in the kitchen, watching my every move and asking endless questions.'

Minnette clasped her hands together again. 'Shall we open the gifts now?'

'Oh, yes, let's,' Kamala said, daintily setting her unfinished piece of cake onto the coffee table. She picked up one of the gifts at random. It was wrapped in dark purple paper and black ribbon. 'Whose is this?'

'That's Saul's,' Minnette said. She took the gift from Kamala and handed it to him. 'Open it. It's from all of us.'

He opened it slowly, taking care not to tear the paper. Inside, stacked one on top of the other, were two pieces of clothing made of a finely woven white cotton. He unfolded and held them up, each in turn — first a sarong, then a kurta. 'Very nice.'

'For the next time you go to temple,' Vernon explained. 'I secretly took measurements of a pair of your trousers while you were out, so the sarong should fit much better than Mr Gunaratne's.'

Saul laughed. 'I dare say it will.' He re-folded the clothes and set them back onto the paper and said heartfully, 'Thank you. Thank you to all of you.'

The other gifts were distributed and opened, one at a time. Wrapping paper was torn or crumpled amid expressions of admiration and gratitude. There were gifts of all kinds: books, boxes of sweetmeats, handbags, lengths of chintz and silk to make dresses or sari blouses, rupees, stationery, and sundry off-the-peg articles of clothing. As the last of the wrapping paper was tossed to the floor, the excitement in the room waned.

Vernon noticed that Saul seemed perturbed. 'Is everything all right, Saul?'

'A gift appears to have gone missing. For Minnette.'

'Why didn't you say so before?' Kamala said. She got down onto her hands and knees and lifted one piece of paper after another until she found the missing gift, which fit snugly in the palm of her hand. She resumed her seat, gave the gift to Minnette, and smoothed out the pleats of her sari with an air of propriety.

Minnette beamed at Saul, then unwrapped the paper to reveal a velvet box. The box creaked as she opened it. Gingerly she drew out a Navaratna brooch and held it up for the others to see. The brooch's nine Ceylonese gemstones glistened brilliantly even in the faint light of the sitting room.

Vernon expected Kamala to react — to say something, good or bad, about the extravagance of the gift — but she simply smiled.

'It's lovely, Saul,' Minnette murmured as she pinned the brooch to the neckline of her blouse. 'Thank you ever so much.'

'I had Romesh take me to a jeweller's the other day,' Saul said, blushing. 'I'm glad you like it. It was the least I could do after you so kindly bought me the menorah candles.'

Vernon's bemused expression seemed to say, 'It wasn't exactly the least you could have done, Saul, now was it?'

//

There was a moment of confusion, after the seven of them came into Dr Fernando's sitting room, during which everyone spoke at once. Slurred apologies and laughter ensued. They were all rather giddy from the champagne they had been drinking to ring in the New Year.

'We seem to be tuned in to the same wavelength,' Romesh observed, his voice louder than usual.

'Or seven different wavelengths,' Dr Fernando said on a less sanguine note.

'I prefer Romesh's interpretation,' said Celine. She sipped from her champagne and glanced at the clock on the wall, which read ten minutes to midnight. 'Can you believe it? It's almost 1937.'

Kamala ran a finger along the rim of her glass. 'You should put on some music, Bernie, before the clock strikes twelve.'

'Yes, Bernie, do,' Celine agreed.

'What shall I play?'

'Anything will do,' Kamala said. 'Except "Auld Lang Syne". It's such a tiresome old song.'

'You only say that, Amma, because you can't sing it properly,' Minnette teased. On her blouse was the Navaratna brooch. Celine had enquired about it earlier, just when everyone was beginning to get tipsy, but Minnette pretended not to have heard and promptly the question was forgotten.

Saul cleared his throat. 'Would you mind terribly if I choose the song?' He was dying for good music.

'Help yourself,' Dr Fernando said.

The gramophone, an ancient-looking contraption with a tulip-shaped horn, stood on a console against the wall. In a pull-out drawer beneath the turntable was a stack of records. Saul searched through them, mostly Ceylonese and Indian indigenous music, until he came to one in a blank jacket. He pointed it out to Dr Fernando. 'What's this?'

Dr Fernando squinted from across the room. 'A Bach cantata, if I'm not mistaken. An Indian friend, at The Gramophone and Typewriter company in Calcutta, gave it to me. He worked on it with some German chaps in Hanover.'

'Anyone object to my playing it?' Saul enquired of everyone.

No one objected. The consensus, in fact, was that playing the record would be just the thing. Only Vernon refrained from chiming in, the alcohol having gone to his head. 'Shellac is a resin secreted by female lac bugs in the forests of India,' he said now rather discordantly.

'I'm sure no one cares, dear,' Kamala chided him.

With a flourish Saul removed the record from its sleeve.

'I should forewarn you,' Dr Fernando said, 'the quality isn't quite up to snuff.'

That was of no consequence to Saul. Bach was Bach. His hand trembled ever so slightly as he placed the record onto the turntable and lowered the needle.

The recording had the reverberant acoustics of a cathedral. An instrumental interlude of violins and horns, muted and in the metre signature of a waltz, opened the song. After a cadence, a chorus entered fughetta-like. For perhaps thirty seconds the voices continued, twice holding notes on the German partial-word 'lo-' together at the same pitch. Not since before the Great War had Saul heard such antiquated music.

He left the gramophone and re-joined the others to the sound of gently swaying violins. Two or three conversations were going on at once. He wished to say something himself — he found the cantata inspiring, even if it was from a bygone age — but he thought it would be impolite to interrupt. So he waited, listening to the music, listening to the others, between sips of champagne. At last his moment came. 'Orchestral music is the pinnacle of human achievement,' he pronounced with a hiccup.

But no one heard, for just at that moment the clock struck twelve. The others raised their glasses and shouted 'Happy New Year' in chorus. Saul raised his glass as well, but his reflexes were too slow. The others had already moved on, to hugs and kisses and handshakes and laughter. Amid the commotion, Saul's glass disappeared, and then Minnette took him by the hand and whisked him away.

'What the devil?' he said before he knew what was happening.

She led him down a dark hallway and into a room that smelled of talcum powder and a hotchpotch of fragrances. Next to an open window, she let go of his hand and spun round. She was laughing, girlishly. Half of her face was in shadow, the other half in moonlight. She whispered, 'Now that we're finally alone, we can have a proper talk.'

He knew, despite his inebriation, that her remark was only a pretence. He took her in his arms and closed his eyes and pressed his lips to hers. She tasted of champagne. Instantly he drew away. 'Forgive me. I seem to have forgotten myself.'

'Happy New Year,' she said, and flung her arms round his neck and kissed him back passionately.

//

During the weeks before the LSSP rally, Saul brushed up on his Ceylonese history, reading a couple of books and speaking at length to Vernon and Minnette. To his surprise, he learned that Sidney Webb, a former Colonial Secretary, had been instrumental in creating Ceylon's 1931 Donoughmore Constitution and its unicameral legislature. Webb was a member of the Fabian Society's Old Gang, as well as a founder of LSE. Georgina knew him intimately, and at some point prior to Christmas, Saul wrote to her with a list of questions for Webb and to propose an article for *The Masses*.

Her response came in early January, three days before the LSSP rally. The envelope, which had been spritzed with violet perfume, contained two pieces of paper. One gave succinct, type-written answers to the questions for Webb. The other simply read, in an old Victorian lady's scrawl: 'Dear, dear, Saul, I was afraid you had forgotten me and my humble magazine, hiding away as you are all the way out there in the colonies. Your idea for an article about imperialism in Ceylon sounds superb. You must write it at once.'

By the time he received Georgina's letter, he had already written his speech for the rally, but the answers from Webb allowed him to fine tune a few details about which he had been unclear. An important point of clarification was that the Donoughmore Constitution had been set up as a 'pilot project' with an eye toward eventual self-government. Somewhat oxymoronically Webb envisioned a socialist British Empire, and in his view the only way such a thing could come about would be for all Crown colonies, white and non-white alike, to hold general elections with universal suffrage. Under the Donoughmore Constitution, Ceylon was the first non-white Crown colony to be allowed to do so. It was a monumental achievement. Saul never really cared much for Webb—the man, with his Russian-looking pince-nez and goatee, had always seemed so uncouth and plebeian—but Ceylon's progressive constitutional arrangement cast the socialist reformer in a more positive light.

The LSSP rally was held on a maidan at the base of a hill between Kandy town and Peradeniya. The maidan doubled as an event space and a cricket ground, and for the rally, a stage was set up in the shade of a giant flame tree at the back of the ground. Minnette, who had organised the day's events, scheduled Saul to speak first. Over three hundred people of various races were in attendance: Sinhalese, Tamils, Mohammedans, Burghers, and even a few Europeans. Vernon and Kamala and Romesh also were there, to give Saul moral support.

After Minnette explained to the crowd the purpose of the rally and gave a short introduction, Saul took the stage. He looked almost Ceylonese. He wore a white linen suit that had been tailor-made for the occasion, and his hands and face and neck were two shades darker than when he first arrived in Ceylon. It was as though several years had been taken off his age. To a large extent Minnette could be thanked for that. She had made him feel alive again and had given him a sense of purpose. In the week since New Year's Eve, they had not spoken of what transpired that night, but an understanding developed between them. No one would have guessed, on the day of the rally, that that very morning Saul had lit a *yahrzeit* candle for Esther.

On the stage, he stepped up to what looked like a church pulpit. He set his notes onto the lectern and searched the faces in the crowd until he spotted Minnette. His hair fluttered in the wind, and dappled sunlight flitted about his head and shoulders. He cleared his throat and adjusted his spectacles with trembling fingers. There was only a single microphone and amplifier, so he had to project his voice. 'Today, all over the island, the colonial government are celebrating the retirement of Sir Herbert Dowbiggin, the Inspector General of Police. We — the defenders of liberty and equal rights — should celebrate this moment, too, not in honour of Dowbiggin's illustrious career but in recognition that Ceylon will at long last rid itself of a scourge of oppression.'

Applause and shouts of approval erupted from the crowd. The

sounds boosted Saul's confidence, and he realised he did not need his notes.

'We have all heard the stories,' he continued with greater animation, 'of Dowbiggin's bloodstained record, of the brutality and terrorism he perpetrated in the aftermath of the 1915 riots. He is no hero, my friends, to be thanked for his service. Like The Leader in Britain and his fascist counterparts on the Continent, Dowbiggin is merely a thug masquerading as a public servant. We can only hope that after his departure from the island, his successor, P. N. Banks, will be a significant improvement and will look to the Constitution for inspiration.

'I must digress for a moment and say that I am impressed with the Donoughmore Constitution. Under it, Ceylon is the only non-white dominion of the British Empire to have been granted universal suffrage. That is *something*. But more yet needs to be done to free the country and the rest of the world from bondage. Let me be clear, however. In advocating "freedom", I do not mean to suggest that it's a time for nationalistic fervour, one group pitting itself against another. No, indeed, it is not a time for *that*. Instead, it is a time to unite behind a common purpose, a purpose that will improve the lot of average men and women and of humankind as a whole. The world is at a crossroads. We can choose to move forward, or we can choose to move—'

A tussle broke out at the back of the crowd. Within seconds several LSSP stewards were on the stage forming a barrier round Saul. One of them said something in Sinhala that sounded like a command.

Saul watched apprehensively from the pulpit as Vernon, head and shoulders above everyone else, moved through the crowd to the location of the disturbance. When he reached the back of the crowd, there was a brief commotion, and several white men hurried off the maidan, with much yelling and raising of fists. Two minutes later Vernon and Minnette were up on the stage standing in front of the pulpit.

'Imperialist sympathisers,' Vernon said to Saul, a hand over the microphone. 'They didn't put up much of a fight because they were so outnumbered, but they let fly some rather unpleasant threats. They're accusing the LSSP of paying whites to do their dirty work. I recognised the ringleader. He's a creeper for a British planter, although for the life of me I can't remember his name. In any case, his presence here isn't good. I think you should call it a day, Saul, and wrap up your speech.'

Saul looked at Minnette.

'I agree with Vernon,' she said, sounding concerned. 'We've had threats before, but they've never been backed up with violence.'

'Very well.'

As Vernon and Minnette left the stage, Saul had an inspiration for a few impromptu concluding remarks. He took a deep breath. 'There are those,' he began again, 'who would have you believe that I am not here of my own freewill, that I have been induced to speak only for monetary gain. That is untrue. I am here because I cannot in good conscience stand by while the evils of imperialism persist. What's more, during my short time in Ceylon, I have grown to love the country and its people.' He stopped and again scanned the crowd for Minnette until he spotted her standing front and centre. He had not intended to make a withering attack on imperialism, but the planter hooligans had provoked him. Besides, with Minnette there looking up at him as though he were a sage, he could do no wrong. 'I would like to end by saying something, if I may, about tradition and societal change.' His voice had become still more animated. 'Certain traditions are worth cherishing because they bring us closer together, but others are simply remnants of the past that deserve to be discarded wholesale. Imperialism — albeit more of an ideology than a tradition — is doubtless one remnant that deserves to be discarded. It is no respecter of national sovereignty or land and labour rights for the indigenous people, and it is an impediment to progress. Those who would resist its overthrow do so out of greed or ignorance or a blind preference for the status quo. But make no mistake, the conservative defenders of imperialism are a dying breed. They, as an ever-dwindling minority, feel change in the winds, and it makes them bluster and shiver with fright.'

Saul's final words were like a shot across the enemy's bow, prompting someone in the crowd to yell 'Down with the blackguards!' that soon turned into a chant. When the noise eventually died away, Saul gathered up his notes, said 'Thank you, ladies and gentlemen,' and, with the stewards flanking him, scuttered off the stage.

Chapter 22

Counterpoint

Saul's anti-imperialist rhetoric created a stir all over the island. Several newspapers, including ones in Colombo and Galle and Jaffna, ran stories about it, with sensational headlines such as 'Briton Decries Imperialism' and 'LSSP Speaker Stirs Up Anti-British Feeling' and 'Sedition-monger Field Day in Kandy'. The public furore was worrying to Vernon because he thought it could easily spiral out of control. Ceylon was a small country, and although it had a relatively liberal constitution, the British and the moneyed elite were still more or less in charge. Vernon suggested to Saul that he lie low for a while, but instead, two days after the LSSP rally, Saul submitted to *Samasamajaya*, the LSSP's Sinhala-language weekly, a translation of an article he wrote for *The Masses*. Vernon did not directly criticise the move until a few days later, when the forthcoming article came up casually in conversation.

'You're fanning the flames, you know,' he said pointedly. It was late afternoon, and he and Saul and Minnette were sitting on the verandah drinking toddy. The irony of Vernon's remark was not lost on him—four months ago he was on the receiving end of a similar admonition—but his agitating against the Jackboots had been done under a cloak of secrecy, not publicised in newspapers for the world to see.

'Is it really as bad as that?' Saul replied. 'It's only an article, after all.'

'And *Mein Kampf* is only a book.'

'Touché. But if you recall, it wasn't so long ago that I was warning *you* about your involvement with the Jackboots, and while you didn't dismiss my concerns outright, you weren't, shall we say, "amenable" to my advice.'

'That's hardly a valid comparison,' was all Vernon could bring himself to say. He was in no mood to argue, in spite of his concern for Saul's wellbeing. Earlier that afternoon, he had received his fortnightly letter from Zoe, and the thoughts about her that had been swirling round in his head ever since acted like a tonic now against bloody-mindedness.

He and Saul drifted into silence and sipped from their drinks and stared out into the jungle. It was an enchanting day. Somewhere nearby a wood pigeon called, a deep hoo-hoo like that of an owl, the sound reminiscent of a wilder, a simpler time.

Minnette interrupted the stalemate between friends and said to Vernon, 'Are you ever going to tell me about your involvement with the Jackboots?'

He took a dim view of her question, as if it were a subtle indictment. She had been asking him for weeks to regale her with stories about the Jackboots, but at every turn he put her off. He still had no desire to explain why he had delayed in returning to Ceylon. 'I'm afraid I have even more reason not to now,' he said. 'I don't want you or Saul getting any ideas.' Vernon downed the rest of his toddy, got up, and withdrew to his room.

Zoe was still at the forefront of his mind, along with the vague feeling that the LSSP rally had set in motion a train of events that would lead to disaster. He sat down at his writing desk and took up a pen.

Dear Zoe,
So much has happened since last I wrote to you. I believe I
mentioned that Saul was scheduled to give a speech for the LSSP.

Well, it happened this past Sunday, and things didn't go quite as planned. First his speech was cut short because some planter thugs turned up and disrupted the rally. Then the press twisted what little Saul did say and portrayed him as a communist agitator. Why is it that every time someone challenges the powers that be, accusations of socialism or communism are shouted from the rooftops? It makes one wonder whether the accusers even know what such political and economic concepts mean. I assure you that Saul's a proponent of capitalism and that he would bristle at the thought of having a government control a country's means of production. I'm left to draw the conclusion that when used as invective, the words 'socialism' and 'communism' are simply bywords for anything that's not the status quo. But that's a stupid, reductive way of thinking. It's as if, in the minds of colonialists at least, free enterprise and social justice are mutually exclusive. What I think it comes down to is that colonialists, and their conservative supporters, don't want any encroachment on their wealth or their power or their privilege and that the political ideologies they espouse are merely a means to an end. In any case, the blowback from Saul's LSSP speech would have been bad enough, but now he's making his situation far worse by publishing a scathing exposé about imperialism in the LSSP weekly. And my attempts to persuade him against it have been in vain. It isn't helping, either, that Georgina and Minnette are encouraging him. His exposé was originally written for The Masses (whose readers, needless to say, are more receptive to political activism than are the Ceylonese and their colonial rulers), and so he had to get permission from Georgina to publish it elsewhere. She gave it to him readily, and then Minnette translated the article into Sinhala for him. Saul doesn't know this, but I cabled Georgina expressing my concern. Do you know what her response was? 'Saul's a big boy.' She's right, of course. But that does little to assuage my concern. You and I (and Georgina and Saul, for that matter) have seen up close what the fascists are capable of, and they differ from the colonialists only in degree. The fact is, these types of people will stop at nothing to protect their hegemony. I may be overreacting, but I fear Saul's in over his head. I could see him at the LSSP rally being swept up in the moment, and his love for Minnette no doubt is a powerful driving force. But Saul's no Gandhi. Sorry for going on and on like this. My letter has devolved into a political rant. What was it you said in your last letter, 'We each must choose our own path forward'? I know you made the statement in a different context, but it's in the same vein as Georgina's cablegram about Saul. I suppose I should be a better Buddhist and accept the things I can't control.

Amma has been asking about you a lot lately. She's constantly fishing for details, presumably to determine how you'll measure up as a daughter-in-law. Last week I remembered the photograph we asked Georgina to take of us for Minnette. It has been hidden away in Minnette's room all this time. When I showed Amma the photograph, her reaction was similar to the one I had when I first saw you at Action House. She said you're gorgeous. And you truly are, both inside and out.

Forever Yours,
Vernon

He set down the pen and sat back in his chair. The writing had alleviated his concerns to some extent, but he was still concerned about what might happen if events were left in the hands of fate. Perhaps it was time, he thought, to take up Geoff Overlund on his offer for a drink. If anyone would have an ear to the ground for anti-LSSP intrigue, Geoff would.

//

'I hope you didn't mind that I called you Nandhimitra the other day,' Geoff said, clapping Vernon on the back. 'Old habits are hard to break.'

They had just sat down on stools at the Queen's Hotel bar and ordered pints of bitter.

'Why would I?' Vernon asked.

'I don't know, it might bring back memories you'd just as soon forget.'

'But it was the "land of youth and dream". What's wrong with that?'

Geoff laughed. 'I see you haven't lost your sense of humour, *men*.'

'That's about all of the Trinity song I can remember. The end of it, I think, is equally rosy. How does it go?'

'"They were great days and jolly days" ...'

'Right.' Vernon pictured himself at assembly — his uniform-clad adolescent self — half-heartedly reciting the lyrics to 'The Best School of All'. Even then he had no interest in the song.

The barman came by with their bitters.

Vernon picked up his tankard and raised it. 'A toast,' he said. 'To the great and jolly days of our youth.'

'To the great and jolly days,' Geoff echoed, clinking his tankard against Vernon's. He took a drink, wiped his mouth, and then leaned back in his stool and scrutinised Vernon. 'I can see why we called you Nandhimitra. You're not quite the colossus your pater was, but you're close.'

'I'll take that as a compliment.'

'At school everybody was just a little bit afraid of you, weren't they? Even Rev. Fraser was, and he prided himself on putting the fear of God into Trinitians.'

It was true, Vernon thought. Others at Trinity *were* afraid of him, but not because of anything he had done. They simply found his size off-putting. During his thirteenth and fourteenth years, he grew at the extraordinary rate of half an inch a month, and by the end of his growth spurt, he was at least a head taller than all of his classmates and most of his teachers. The Reverend Father was as intimidated as everyone else, even though he was a stern disciplinarian. He seemed to view Vernon as a freak of nature. Vernon remembered one particular experience he had with Rev. Fraser and said to Geoff, 'He called me into his office once. I think he was intending to whip me with his riding crop. The entire time I was there, he kept slapping the bloody thing against the palm of his hand. But in the end, all he did was give me a bollocking.'

'It was a mistake on his part. He lost credibility after that.'

'And he held it against me till the day I graduated.' Vernon took a long draught of his bitter, more to signal that he was ready to change the subject than to quench his thirst. He laughed at himself inwardly. He was becoming like Saul: impatient with small talk.

'Do you remember Saul Maccabee, the friend of mine you met a couple of months ago?'

'The English chap?'

Vernon nodded.

'The one who gave the incendiary speech at the LSSP rally?'

'So you heard about that?'

'It was hard not to. The story made the headlines in all the papers.'

'Is there anything else you've heard? Through official or unofficial channels?'

'What do you mean?'

Vernon thought for a moment. He had to choose his words carefully. Despite what Geoff said about Mr Overlund's admiration for Johannes, that had not always been the case. In fact, Mr Overlund and Johannes had clashed at times over attempts to expand plantation labour rights, and now that Mr Overlund was the president of the Planters' Association, he might even be hostile to calls for reform of the Ceylonese colonial administration and its 'planter raj', the phrase Saul used to refer to the plantation system in *Samasamajaya*, the latest edition of which was published earlier that day. Vernon retrieved a packet of cigarettes from his pocket, tapped one out for Geoff and one for himself, and lit them both. After taking a quick draw, he said, 'I'm hoping to find out if any planters might be plotting retaliation against the LSSP.'

'You think Saul is in danger?'

'Perhaps. Perhaps not. All I know for sure is that he hasn't endeared himself to the planters.'

'I haven't heard anything one way or the other.' Geoff puffed on his cigarette. 'But I'll let you know if I do.'

'Thanks, Geoff. I owe you a debt of gratitude.' Vernon finished off his bitter, satisfied that he had enlisted another set of eyes and ears to help him keep Saul out of harm's way. Now all that was left to do was to remain vigilant. Instinctively he glanced round the room. No other customers were there, but a plaque on the wall caught his eye. It contained a quotation from Queen Victoria: 'Give my people plenty of beer, good beer, and cheap beer, and you will have no revolution among them.' Vernon had read the quotation somewhere before, perhaps at Trinity. His head was filled with no end of useless historical facts and aphorisms then. The school's motto — *respice finem*, Latin for 'look to the end' — was one of the few positive things that stuck with him all this time, no doubt because of its Buddhist connotations. It called on Trinitians to consider the consequences of their actions, both for this life and the next. Even during his most dangerous moments interacting with the Jackboots, Vernon had 'looked to the end', and the practice stood him in good stead.

//

Late one evening Romesh turned up at the Prins's bungalow, breathing laboriously and looking like he had seen a ghost. He came into the sitting room, where Saul and the Prins family were gathered, and explained in faltering words what happened. He had been on his verandah, he said, when several white men appeared outside his house. They were brandishing lathis and spewing obscenities.

'What did they want?' Vernon asked.

'I'm sure I don't know,' Romesh said. He fell into a chair and wiped his brow with a handkerchief. 'They had a grievance of some kind, but what it had to do with me, I couldn't tell. I thought for certain I was done for. But it was the strangest thing: I got up to lock myself in the house, and when the men saw me, one of them mumbled something I didn't catch, and the lot of them ran off.'

Saul removed his pipe from his mouth. 'Did you get a good look at any of them?'

'No,' Romesh replied, 'it was too dark. But their accents were definitely British.'

'I see,' Saul said, directing an apologetic smile at Vernon and then turning back to Romesh. 'You're in no danger, Romesh. The fools got the wrong house.'

'How so?'

Saul felt everyone's eyes on him. He should have been mortified — never before had he caused so much trouble — but instead, he was exhilarated at having created a stir. 'I'll wager my pipe and a hat full of sovereigns that the men outside your house meant to come *here*. If so, they're the planters who sabotaged my speech the other day, and their quarrel is with me, not you.'

'Oh dear,' Kamala said.

'Do you think that's true?' Minnette asked Vernon.

'In all likelihood. But whether it is or not, we mustn't take any chances. I'll phone Geoff to see what he advises.' Vernon went to the telephone and placed a call. After a brief conversation, he rang off, then turned back to the others. 'Geoff's sending a constable over to investigate. He thinks we should leave town till things blow over.' Vernon glanced at Minnette and added, 'We could make the most of it and go on one of those road trips we've been talking about.'

'We certainly could,' she seconded.

'Do you have any objections, Saul?' Vernon asked.

'No objections at all. I could use a change of scenery.'

Kamala held up a hand with the palm facing outward and waggled her head. 'Is leaving town really necessary?'

'I'm afraid so,' Vernon said. 'We'll leave first thing in the morning.'

Chapter 23

Interlude

The police investigation went nowhere. Enquiries were made, but other than Romesh, no one in the neighbourhood had seen anything, and since the men who had stormed Romesh's house disappeared without a trace, there was nothing more that could be done for the moment. It was decided, however, that Saul and the Prins family should leave town anyway, out of an abundance of caution. As it happened, a Scottish planter friend of the family from the Badulla District was away on business, and he offered up his bungalow as a place for them to stay.

So early the next morning they loaded up the Austin under cover of darkness and set off for the Badulla District. The drive took them over four hours, as the highway between Nuwara Eliya and Haputale was little more than a dirt track narrowly winding its way through grass-covered hills. Just past an old single-lane stone bridge, with the sun still low in the sky, they came to a signpost that read Galbraith Estate.

Vernon turned the car onto a cobblestone road and descended a steep hill lined with jacaranda. Either side of the trees, lush tea terraces covered the slopes. The road continued for a quarter-mile, at which point the roof of the estate bungalow came into view, and Vernon stopped the car on an upper lawn in front of an outbuilding.

Saul was taken aback when he got out of the car. The air temperature could not have been more than 60 degrees Fahrenheit, and he felt like a young man again on holiday with Esther somewhere in the Bavarian Alps. At any moment he expected to see a gang of pink-cheeked *Fräuleins* wearing dirndls and carrying baskets of wild strawberries. He breathed in a lungful of the cool sweet air and went to the edge of the lawn and stood there for a moment, taking in the view. Beyond the bungalow roof, velvety green hills stretched for miles down to Ceylon's southern plains. Featureless cloud wisps hung above the hills and in the canopies of the trees surrounding the bungalow. He turned back to the others. 'Ceylon never ceases to amaze.'

The words seemed to revive Kamala, who had been quiet the entire drive over. 'This was Johannes's second most favourite place on earth, after Eden Estate.'

'I can see why,' Saul replied.

A Tamil man, dressed in the mandarin-collar shirt and dhoti of a house servant, emerged from the outbuilding. 'Welcome, welcome. You have been expected.'

'Hello, Subramanyam,' Kamala said. 'How are you?'

'I am well, madam. It is good to see you again.' Subramanyam gathered up their bags. 'Come,' he said, waggling his head, and escorted them across the lawn and down some stone stairs to the bungalow. Inside, he set their bags onto the floor before a fireplace in the front room. Off the fireplace was a set of French doors that led onto a terrace. He opened the doors and stepped outside, and Saul and the others followed.

The area surrounding the terrace looked like a Scottish garden. A low hedge and various flowering plants—eupatorium, globe thistle, glowing asters, salvias—bordered a lawn. To the south, the lawn ended at a gentle embankment; Saul went to within a few feet of it and looked out over the hills. The view, which was completely unobstructed, was even more spectacular than that from the upper lawn. With the rising sun, the mist was dissipating, and reservoirs could now be seen on the plains in the far distance. Scattered along the immediate slopes, acacias and eucalyptus and silky oaks stood like watchtowers. In their branches, the silhouettes of roosting birds were visible, and what sounded like magpies and a hornbill could be heard. Saul was annoyed at himself for not having brought his binoculars.

Minnette came over and stood beside him. 'Isn't it blissful?'

Her presence was like an anodyne. He wanted to take her by the hand and kiss her on the cheek, but he did not dare in front of the others. 'Very much so,' he said, catching a surreptitious glimpse of her out of the corner of his eye.

They remained silent, meditative. To have spoken further would have broken the spell. It was enough, just now, that they were together, enough that they were seeing the same sights and breathing the same air.

'Whenever you two care to join us,' Vernon said, startling them out of their thoughts. They turned to see him and Kamala seated at a small wrought-iron table, which had a tea service and four place settings atop it. Subramanyam stood next to the table holding a salver. He lifted the cloche to reveal steaming bangers and scones and scrambled eggs. The view, the fresh air, the inviting food — it was a breakfast fit for royalty.

'You've given us a wonderful reception, Subramanyam,' Kamala said. 'Thank you.'

'My pleasure, madam.'

Saul and Minnette sat down at the table, and Subramanyam doled out the food.

'Where would we be without people like Subramanyam, eh, Saul?' Vernon asked.

'I shudder to think,' Saul said without a hint of irony.

//

An hour before sunset they played a friendly game of doubles badminton, Vernon and Kamala on one team and Minnette and Saul on the other. A net was already set up on the upper lawn, and

Subramanyam tracked down four racquets and a shuttlecock. It was all rather shabbily done: the net sagged several inches in the middle, one of the racquets had a cracked frame, and the shuttlecock was missing a couple of feathers. But since their only reason for playing was to pass the time, they made do with what equipment they had.

Right before the start of the game, Vernon inspected the middle of the net to see if he could fix it, and as he stood there, his head jutted nearly two feet above the cord.

Saul could not help laughing. Both the state of the net and the image Vernon presented towering above it, incongruously wearing a V-neck sweater like a Wimbledon tennis player, bordered on farcical.

'Glad to be a source of amusement,' Vernon said good-humouredly, resting his neck on the cord as if it were the lunette of a guillotine. 'But I assure you, you won't be laughing a few rallies from now.' He stepped back from the net and swung his right arm in a mock overhead that, if it had been real, would have resulted in a powerful kill.

Saul took up the gauntlet. 'As the saying goes, "The bigger they are" …'

'… "the harder they swing",' Vernon filled in the missing words with a laugh.

'Well, yes,' Saul replied, unable to think of a good rejoinder, 'I suppose that's true.'

'No net kills,' Minnette exhorted Vernon, 'or I refuse to play.'

'All right. To even the odds further, Amma and I could be on a team together. I could also use the broken racquet.'

'That won't be necessary, dear,' Kamala said. 'I'll sit out, and the three of you play. It's a lovely evening to spectate.'

Minnette pursed her lips. 'Nonsense, Amma. We agreed to play doubles, and play doubles we shall.'

'Doubles it is, then,' Vernon said. 'There aren't any markings of service and boundary lines, so it's on everyone's honour to call shots fairly.' He tossed the shuttlecock to determine who would serve first. It did a wobbly somersault in the air and landed with the cork facing Minnette.

'Right,' Saul said, picking up the shuttle and a racquet. He did a few practice strokes, as well as some light callisthenics, to stretch his muscles and get his heart pumping. 'Do you want to serve first,' he asked Minnette, 'or shall I?'

'You serve first.'

Saul went to the imaginary long-service line and sized up the competition. Kamala stood in the forecourt directly opposite, and Vernon stood in the backcourt, waiting to receive. Saul knew he would have to use a strategy of deception, since he was at a disadvantage in both speed and strength relative to Vernon. He switched his racquet grip to the backhand position, held the shuttle at a low angle away from his body, and then in a single motion dropped the shuttle and flicked his wrist. The shuttle floated over the net and, before Vernon could take two steps off the baseline, dropped just inside the receiver's service court.

Vernon looked incredulous.

'Nice one, Saul,' Kamala said.

Minnette giggled. 'I think we've a serious chance of winning.'

'Beginner's luck,' Saul said with false modesty.

'If you're a beginner,' said Vernon, moving up to the forecourt, 'then I'm the king of England.' He picked up the shuttle and tossed it back.

Saul positioned himself on the long-service line again. 'One-love,' he said and with a strong forehand drove the shuttle straight at Kamala.

She closed her eyes as it flew by and played an air shot.

'Amma!' Vernon exclaimed. 'At this rate, we'll be shut out.' He did not mind losing, but as a rule, he wanted to make a strong showing, at least.

'Sorry, dear. I've never been very good at sport.'

On Saul's next serve, Vernon rushed the net. With perfect form, he smashed a passing shot down the line, but the crack in his racquet altered the trajectory of the shuttle to such an extent, it landed wide. 'Bloody hell.' He threw up his hands in disgust.

Minnette walked over to where the shuttle lay in the grass and lined up her body with the net post. Clearly the shuttle was out of bounds. 'Fault,' she said, rubbing it in.

Saul continued his strategy of deception, mixing up his serves, and, in a series of one-sided rallies, he and Minnette scored nine more points. It helped that Vernon was unable to master his racquet; with each mishit, he grew increasingly frustrated. On the thirteenth serve, however, he lobbed his return over Minnette's head deep into the backcourt, and Saul failed to chase down the shuttle in time.

'Finally!' Vernon shouted, shaking his fist in victory.

'Very nicely done,' Kamala said.

Saul sighed as he picked up the shuttle.

'What to do?' Minnette said to him. 'We can't win every rally.'

True enough, he thought, but they needed as large a lead as possible before the service-over. Who knew how many points Vernon might score once he figured out his racquet and got into his stride? Saul blew on the shuttle and handed it to Minnette. 'For good luck,' he said.

She smiled perfunctorily and went to the long-service line and assessed her options. Vernon stood in the farthest corner of the court, seemingly daring her to hit a short serve.

'I can feel an air shot coming on,' he taunted.

'Don't listen to him,' Saul said.

'Yes,' Kamala added, 'don't listen to him. He's just a poor loser.'

Undaunted, Minnette served, using a forehand tapping motion. Saul could see from her agile movements that she had played a great deal before. That explained her perfunctory smile at his good-luck gesture earlier; she did not need luck when talent would suffice. Her serve stayed low over the net and landed midcourt right on the centre line.

'Bravo,' Saul said. 'An ace. That makes it thirteen-love.' Just two more points and the game would be won, though he knew it was premature to celebrate.

'I never doubted you, Sister,' Vernon said as Minnette prepared for her second serve.

'You can't rattle me, Brother, if that's what you're attempting to do.' She followed Saul's example and drove a forehand straight at Kamala.

But somehow Kamala returned it. The shuttle clanked on the throat of her racquet, tumbled through the air, clipped the net, and fell onto the other side of the court.

Vernon applauded. 'Brilliant, Amma.'

Minnette gave Saul a stupefied look.

'There's nothing you could have done about that,' he said.

'It's about bloody time we had a service-over,' said Vernon as he snatched up the shuttle from under the net and walked back to the long-service line. He turned and, without pausing, lifted his serve high into the air.

Saul, who was not adept at overheads, waited until the shuttle was almost at eye level and then flicked it defensively back over the net. At the same time, Vernon rushed forward. He misjudged slightly where the return would cross the net, but with a quick rotation of his body hit a perfect backhand block. The others watched in awe as he won the point.

'A sight to behold, old chap,' Saul said graciously, tossing the shuttle back over the net. As Vernon caught it, he had a fiery look in his eyes, and Saul again had the sinking feeling that Vernon was about to mount a comeback.

That was exactly what happened. For Saul it was like watching a rapid succession of images in a moving picture; he was a mere bystander in someone else's story. Over the course of a ten-minute period, Vernon singlehandedly scored eight straight points. He used every trick in the book he could: cross-court shots, clears, lobs, drop shots, and the occasional block. And everything that possibly could go wrong for Saul and Minnette went wrong. Twice when they were about to win a rally, a paradise flycatcher flitted across the other side of the court and forced a let.

Saul's hopes of winning the game, at a score of thirteen-nine, were fading fast. He realised he had to do something, and soon, to disrupt the rhythm of play, something unexpected and offbeat. For the first time in the game, he moved in to receive from the short-service line.

Upon seeing this, Vernon hesitated for a moment, then crushed his serve high into the air. The shuttle reached its peak directly above Saul and fell straight down.

Instinctively Saul raised his left arm to balance himself, waited until the shuttle was directly overhead, and swung a forehand smash. He could scarcely believe his eyes as Vernon dove for the shuttle at midcourt and missed it.

Minnette and Kamala clapped.

'Now *that*, I must admit,' said Saul, suppressing a laugh, 'was pure luck.'

'I don't believe that for a second,' Vernon said as he got up and brushed the grass and dirt from his clothes. 'But either way, it was well played.' He picked up the shuttle and handed it to Kamala, whose turn it was to serve. 'You're up, Amma.'

Her first serve cleared the net, and Saul returned it straight back to her. Then Kamala returned it to Minnette, and Minnette returned it back to Kamala. For several shots, this singles-like back and forth played out, the women hitting the shuttle to each other and avoiding the men, until finally Minnette tried a lob and sent it long.

'Out!' Vernon called. 'Ten-thirteen. Just five more points, Amma. You can do it.'

But her second serve went into the net. 'Fiddlesticks.' She stomped her foot in disappointment. 'You made me nervous, dear.'

'Sorry, Amma. I got a little overzealous.'

It was Saul's turn to serve again. He thought perhaps he should try another backhand. This time he disguised his intention with a forehand grip that he switched over at the last second. His movements were too spasmodic, however, and the shuttle sailed wide of the boundary line. A faint smile formed on Vernon's lips. Saul could have kicked himself. What had he been thinking? He seemed to be mentally, as well as physically, tired. He looked at

Minnette as if to say, 'It's up to you now.'

She had the same fire in her eyes that Vernon had earlier. At the long-service line, she stared her brother down before driving a forehand straight at him. He was thrown off guard but managed to return it. In the same instant she rushed the net and, jumping half a yard off the ground, smashed the shuttle for a decisive win.

'I say.' Saul had never seen anything like it before. The games of badminton he had played in England were always so mannerly and staid. He went up to Minnette with a look of admiration. 'You've been holding back.'

'It didn't seem fair,' she said, 'to do net kills if Vernon couldn't. But now that the game is on the line, the gloves are off.'

'Indeed.' Saul, too, had another trick up his sleeve: a shot he had saved for just the right moment. But given his last shot, he was not sure he should risk it.

Minnette went to the long-service line and hit a short serve. Kamala was able to return it, but Saul got to the net in time for a block. The moment his racquet connected with the shuttle, he sensed Vernon rushing forward. Quickly Saul dropped back. He was at midcourt by the time Vernon lunged and hit an underhand high into the air. As Saul watched the shuttle coming down, he visualised himself employing his trick shot and, without another thought, swung with a slicing motion. The shuttle slung off his racquet and spun over the net. Vernon was not expecting the return to come at such an odd angle, so he reacted too late. The shuttle ricocheted off the top of his racquet and hit him in the head. He fell to the ground, rolled onto his back, and just lay there, sprawled out.

'Are you all right, dear?' Kamala asked, at which Minnette burst into laughter.

'I can't say for sure,' Saul said, trying to defuse the situation, 'but I may have committed an illegal motion.' In executing his trick shot, he felt like he might have carried the shuttle. 'And far be it from me to claim a win I didn't rightfully earn. We could re-play the point if you'd like.'

'No no,' Vernon said, still lying on the ground and staring up at the sky with apparent embarrassment. 'You and Minnette won fair and square.'

'Very well,' Saul said. He walked round the net and helped Vernon to his feet. For all their bravado, Saul thought, it was a rather anticlimactic finish to the game.

//

Galbraith Estate, like Eden Estate formerly, was one of the few Ceylonese tea plantations that had its own dispensary as well as a school to educate the labourers' children. Vernon told Saul of this over tea the morning after their arrival on the estate. They were sitting on the sofa in the bungalow's front room. A fire burned in the fireplace, and they both wore woollen sweaters against the chill in the air.

The information about the progressive measures on the estate piqued Saul's interest. He asked if he could to take a tour of the place while they were there.

'A brilliant idea,' Vernon said. 'I was going to suggest something of the sort myself.'

Minnette entered the room. Her hair was dishevelled, and she had on her lace nightdress. 'What were you going to suggest?'

'Taking a tour of the estate. I have some research to do for my thesis, and Saul wants to see the dispensary and the school. Would you care to join us?'

'No, thanks.' She sat down in a wingback chair opposite the sofa, tucked her legs beneath her, and rubbed the chill from her arms. 'I've started a new poem, and I want to keep working while the iron's hot.'

'Where's Ammi? Perhaps she'd care to join us.'

'I doubt it. She stayed up all night reading that Christie book she brought. I don't know how Ammi can stand such drivel. Mrs Christie publishes novels like Victorian women birthed children: one comes out every nine months.'

Vernon and Saul laughed.

'Looks like it's just you and me, Saul,' Vernon said, referring to the tour.

They finished their tea, ate breakfast, and, after bathing and changing into walking attire, climbed the stairs to the upper lawn. It was an overcast day. Clouds obscured the mountain peaks to the west and north, and a thick veil of mist floated above the estate. Tamil women dotted the tea rows, plucking leaves and storing them in the wicker baskets strapped to their backs.

Vernon gestured to the women as he and Saul crossed the lawn. 'They'll have worked for four hours by now, including their morning chores at home.' It was close on 8.30. 'And except for a short tea break and a lunch break, they'll be harvesting until late afternoon: climbing these steep slopes, being exposed to sun and wind and possibly even rain, and carrying loads of up to twenty-five kilos in their baskets. Then they go home and the domestic chores start all over again and continue well into the night. They'll follow this schedule day in day out, except perhaps on Sundays and holidays. But even then, they might work to earn double the normal rate for what's called "over-kilo" plucking.'

Saul looked at the women with compassion in his eyes. 'That doesn't sound like much of a life.'

'No,' Vernon said, 'it doesn't. And Mr Galbraith's an enlightened planter. So you can imagine what it's like on other plantations.'

'I'd just as soon not.'

They reached the cobblestone road and turned right, into the heart of the estate. The cobblestones gave way to gravel, and after they passed a small stand of eucalyptus, a ramshackle shed appeared on the side of the road. Tea pluckers were going in and out of the shed with their baskets.

'This is the weighing station,' Vernon said. 'Each time one of the women fills her basket, she brings it here to be weighed, and she gets paid by the kilo. Later the picked tea is transported on bullock carts to the factory for processing.'

A Tamil man with a weather-beaten face stood outside the shed doors, directing the women.

'That looks like a foreman,' Vernon said to Saul. 'He might be able answer one of my questions. Do you mind if I talk to him?'

'Not at all.'

They made their way to the shed. The wilting tea leaves that lay in a heap just inside the doorway gave off the pleasant smell of freshly cut grass. Vernon conversed with the foreman in a mix of English and Sinhala and Tamil, interspersed with sign language, and slowly pieced together the information he needed for his thesis.

Five minutes later he and Saul were back on the gravel road.

'Did you get the answer to your question?' Saul asked.

'I did.' Vernon pointed to a small tree among the tea rows. 'Do you see that tree?'

Saul nodded.

'It's all over the plantation. According to the foreman, it's called calliandra. I was aware of its existence, but I couldn't remember its name. Thathi planted it on Eden Estate before I was born, before it was common practice to do so on Ceylonese plantations. He got seedlings from a Dutch friend who went to Guatemala. The tree serves a variety of purposes on the plantation: nitrogen fixation, soil stabilisation, wind protection, and, with frequent pruning, fertiliser and mulch. It's one of the reasons yields were always so high on Eden Estate.'

They rounded a bend and descended into a deep gully. Past the gully, the land opened out onto a flat situated along an escarpment. Enormous oak trees skirted the edge of the slope and provided shade for the labourers' dwellings, a long pastel-green building two cricket pitches in length. To the west, on the opposite side of the flat, were the school and the dispensary. On the façade of one building a sign read GALBRAITH ELEMENTARY in large block letters, and on the façade of the other was a blue circle three feet in diameter with the rod of Asclepius inside it.

Vernon stopped a hundred metres or so from the pastel-green building, and Saul drew up alongside him. 'We don't want to seem to be prying,' Vernon said. 'The long, barracks-like building is where the labourers live. They're called line rooms. Each family gets a single ten-foot-by-twelve-foot room with a verandah. The rooms have enough space for perhaps a single cot, which the man of the house sleeps on. Women and children sleep on gunny bags on the floor.'

Three young girls were gathered on the verandah of one of the rooms. They noticed Vernon and Saul and began to confer in whispers. One of them, who appeared to have been designated as their ambassador, walked over to Vernon and Saul. She wore a chintz dress, a shawl, and anklets. Her feet were bare, and her elbow-length hair hung loosely over her shawl. She could not have been more than ten years old. 'Hello,' she said in stilted English, putting her hands together and bowing.

Vernon and Saul repeated the greeting.

She giggled and looked over her shoulder at the other two girls, who also giggled and coaxed her to say more. 'How are you?' she continued shyly.

'We're well,' Vernon said. He turned to Saul. 'She seems to be practising her English.'

'Shouldn't she be in school?'

'No doubt she and her friends are skiving off,' Vernon said. 'Probably to help their mothers cook and clean.' He turned back to the girl and told her in broken Tamil that he and Saul were friends of Mr Galbraith's.

She waggled her head. Then she dropped her eyes, said something in Tamil of which Vernon caught only a part, and hurried back to her friends.

'What did she say?' Saul asked.

'I think she said I'm the first giant she has ever seen.'

The three girls waved, giggling again, and said 'Bye, bye' in their Dravidian accents.

Saul and Vernon waved back.

The sky to the east suddenly brightened. Vernon glanced up. The sun was emerging from behind a cloud. 'We had best be on our way,' he said. 'Neither of us thought to bring a hat.'

They turned round and headed back to Mr Galbraith's bungalow.

'I'm curious,' Saul said as they descended into the gully for a second time. 'Are there reasons other than cost why a plantation owner would deprive his labourers' children of an education?'

'For a ready supply of labour, mostly. I've heard a number of planters say they don't want to give estate Tamils ideas in life above their station. Such statements have racist overtones, but they're mainly rooted in economics. The fact of the matter is, tea pluckers and other estate labour are hard to come by. If you let your existing labourers create the next generation of labour for you, you solve your labour-supply problems at a single swoop.'

'I see.'

'Keeping the children illiterate keeps the tap running, so to speak. Of course, nothing is ever so simple. The issue is complicated by the rigidity of the Indian caste system. Nearly all of the estate Tamils belong to agricultural castes and are loath to seek opportunities in other occupations. That was why the planters brought them here from India in the first place. Tamils also start out at a disadvantage because they don't know Sinhala, the Ceylonese majority language, or English, the language of the colonial administration. Unless they learn one or both of these languages, they're unlikely to venture very far off an estate.'

'In providing a school, isn't Mr Galbraith shooting himself in the foot, then?'

'No. His kindness fosters goodwill, for one thing. But he also pays his labourers more than the market rate to entice them to stay, taking a hit to his short-run profits. At first blush this might seem purely altruistic, but it's more than that. Like Thathi used to do, Mr Galbraith takes the long view: by keeping his labourers relatively happy, he prevents many of them from leaving, raises productivity, and lowers his implicit costs, thereby increasing long-run profits.'

'Makes perfect sense.'

Vernon's heart thumped as he warmed to his subject. He enjoyed few things more than discussing the content of his thesis.

'There's an argument in conservative circles that the poor should just try harder and pull themselves up by their bootstraps. It's obvious from visiting almost any plantation in the Indian subcontinent that such an argument rings hollow and is an intellectual dodge. It implies equal opportunity for all as a starting point. But there can't be equal opportunity when planters and other owners of capital deliberately queer the pitch against their labourers.'

'Indeed.' Saul glanced at the women in the tea rows and grew pensive. Then he said, 'Perhaps a connection exists between the conservative mindset and myopia. After all, by definition conservatives look to the past and not to the future. The same may be true of capital owners generally. They tend to be conservative in outlook, particularly with regard to labour, and hence are more likely to seek short-term gain. Never mind that they and their labourers, as well as society, would be better off if everyone took the long view. At any rate, this queering of the pitch, as you call it— it makes one ashamed to be a part of the human race, doesn't it?'

'Yes,' Vernon said, 'it most certainly does.'

//

On their drive back to Kandy, they took a slight detour to Matale and stopped off at the Aluviharaya rock cave temple. The area, known as Wiltshire to the British, was located in the foothills of the Knuckles Mountain Range. Vernon and Minnette had been contemplating going there for months, and since they were driving from Haputale to Kandy anyway, now seemed like the perfect time to do so. Vernon also was keen to delay the return to Kandy as long as possible, to give the incident with the planters more time to blow over.

They arrived at the temple late in the morning. It was a grey, dreary day. Overhead, dark clouds threatened rain. Between the temple grounds and the car park, a blackish-grey formation of exfoliated granite, as tall as any of the surrounding trees and as wide as a dozen elephants, dominated the landscape. Vernon parked the car. As the others got out, he remained in his seat, staring at the granite formation through the windscreen. He felt out of sorts. Some childhood memory lay just beyond reach at the periphery of his consciousness.

Minnette rapped on the exterior of the driver's side window. 'Are you coming?' she said, then hurried after Kamala and Saul, who were already heading for the temple. They were all barefoot and dressed in white. Saul looked perfectly at ease in his new kurta and sarong.

The sight of them — like flashes of light amid the greyness — brought Vernon out of his abstraction. He removed his shoes and socks and got out of the car and caught the others up.

A frangipani tree along the path was in bloom. They each picked some of the flowers and then climbed a long set of stone stairs to an upper level of the grounds, where they tarried awhile to take in the views. A stupa, with its whitewashed spire and dome, towered up to their immediate right. Farther afield, past the temple entrance, the jungle extended for as far as the eye could see. Various colours and leaf patterns were on display, of both endemic and imported trees: breadfruit, flame, ironwood, mango, and palm, among others. Here and there mist clung to the treetops, and in the distance the Knuckles loomed.

Saul said, 'I understand why the monks chose this spot for a temple. It's an ideal place to meditate.'

Vernon nodded. 'It was also an ideal place to protect Buddhist scriptures from South Indian invaders. This is where the scriptures were transcribed onto palm leaves during the first century BC.' He turned and looked up at the hill they were about to scale. Dirt paths and stone stairs followed the contours of several heavily weathered granite formations. Palms and ferns and reed bamboo grew out of cracks in the rock face. As if taking a lesson from nature, the monks had built their temple structures half in, half out of the rocks' many recesses. 'Before that,' Vernon continued, 'the *dharma* was memorised and transmitted orally. Those two-thousand-year-old manuscripts used to be stored here in a library, but it was destroyed during the Matale Rebellion.'

'The Matale Rebellion?' Saul asked, turning and looking up at the temple grounds, as well.

'Don't encourage him, Saul,' Minnette said with a laugh. 'You'll get history lessons till the cows come home.'

Kamala came over and stood between Vernon and Minnette. 'Your *thathi* used to be like that, too. He was such a talker. He thought he knew something about everything, and even when he didn't know anything at all about a subject, he pretended he did.'

Saul laughed. 'I can't say I'd mind a history lesson. After all, what's the purpose of history — or scriptures and most other forms of writing — if not to impart lessons? Go ahead, old chap. Fire away about the rebellion.'

'I don't want to offend Minnette,' — Vernon gave her a lowering glance — 'so I'll keep it brief. In 1848, the British colonial government imposed an onerous tax on the Ceylonese peasantry that caused a rebellion. The British sent Malay soldiers to put it down. Rebels took refuge here, and the temple became a battleground. When the rebels lost the battle, the soldiers burnt the Buddhist manuscripts in retaliation.'

'What a shame,' Saul said.

Minnette had a meditative look on her face. 'Thathi once said that if you want to see the true colours of a nation, simply ask whether they've subjugated another people.' She sighed. 'He would have enjoyed this trip. That was why we wanted to come here, wasn't it, Vernon? As a tribute to Thathi.'

Vernon suddenly recalled the memory that had been hovering on the periphery of his consciousness. Looking up at the temple grounds again, he said with excitement in his voice, 'There's a rock tunnel near one of the caves. The last time we were here, Thathi took turns putting me and Minnette on his shoulders and pretending not to notice when our heads almost hit the roof of the tunnel. He thought it was so funny. Do you remember, Minnette?'

A glint of remembrance came into her eyes. 'It's near the top, I think. We should see if we can find it.'

They walked up a dirt path between two steep-sided granite formations. The first of the caves, at the back of a colonnaded verandah, was on the left. More than a dozen people were already inside.

'Perhaps we should go straight to the top,' Vernon suggested. 'I'd prefer to avoid crowds if we can.'

The others agreed, and so they continued to climb the hill, ascending a series of stairs and acclivities and passing other caves, until they reached the bodhi tree near the top of the grounds. Flickering lamps and smouldering incense covered the tree's altar. A strong odour of coconut oil and sandalwood filled the air.

The main cave was across from the bodhi tree. They entered the outer chamber. Only a few other people were inside. A mix of natural and artificial light—coming through the latticework of the exterior wall and from a couple of lanterns—gave the space a strange, unearthly quality. Frescoes of grotesque, frizzy-haired demons taking pleasure in torturing humans adorned the interior walls.

Vernon turned to Saul. 'The images are supposed to represent the hellish afterlife that awaits sinners.'

Saul stood in front of a fresco that depicted two men and a woman impaled on a thorny tree trunk. A demon held one of the men by the hair as it swung a club at his body. 'Remind me to repent of my sins before the day is through,' Saul said. He looked up. Above the frescoes was a frieze with a bird-like creature on it. 'What's that? It looks rather like a duck.'

'It's a *dandu-monara*,' Minnette said, standing next to Saul in the dim light. She laughed. 'Now you've got *me* playing the historian. The Sinhala translation of *dandu-monara* is "wooden peacock". In Sinhalese folklore, Ravana—who Sinhalese Buddhists believe to have been an actual human king, not a mythical one like in the *Ramayana*—is said to have used a wooden-peacock flying machine to kidnap Sita to convey her from India to Ceylon.' Minnette laughed again. 'Thus ends the lesson.'

'I couldn't have said it better myself,' Vernon said.

'No,' Minnette replied, 'you couldn't have.'

They all held back their laughter and did their best to remain serious as they stepped past the two protector statues and into the inner chamber. Inside, there was no light except for what came through the doorway. But the paint on the walls and statues was so colourful, the artwork was still visible. The frescoes depicted Jataka tales, lotus flowers, and the Hindu god Shiva. The centrepiece of the chamber was a large reclining Buddha statue. Frangipani and jasmine flowers lay scattered across its altar. Several smaller standing or sitting Buddha statues lined the walls. A dank, earthy smell pervaded the air.

They placed their flowers onto the altar, did a quick circuit round the chamber, and left the cave. Outside, it was mizzling.

'Oh drat,' Kamala said. 'I was hoping it wouldn't rain.'

'Let's find the tunnel,' said Vernon, 'and be on our way.'

As they hurried along in search of the tunnel, Minnette said, 'I've just had a thought.'

Vernon laughed. 'Imagine that.'

Minnette was undeterred. She had become meditative again. 'Suppose the inner and outer chambers of the cave are metaphors for nirvana and hell: the cessation of suffering for the enlightened and the continuation of suffering for the unenlightened. And suppose the bright colours in the inner chamber are a symbol of serenity.'

'An elegant idea,' Saul said. After a few more steps, he added, 'Very poetic, indeed.'

Vernon agreed that the idea was rather elegant, but he kept the thought to himself.

Presently they came to the tunnel, right before the final ascent to the second of the temple's stupas. Vernon stopped well short of it. 'It's much smaller than I remembered. I don't know how Thathi could have got through without crawling.'

'Children's perceptions of size are always so distorted,' Minnette observed and without further ado stooped down and made her way through the tunnel.

Saul followed closely behind, holding a hand above her crown and at the same time ducking. 'Mind your head, now.'

Kamala said, 'It's not *that* short' and walked through fully upright, giggling like a school girl as she went. 'I might just stay in here awhile, to escape the rain.'

Vernon was about to go through himself when he saw a flash of light come from the other side of the tunnel. Then he heard a shout and the sound of a scuffle. A young Sinhalese man with an Exakta camera round his neck suddenly darted out, straight toward Vernon. They collided, and for a split second the man stood stock-still, as if he had just collided with a stone wall, before limping off. 'Oi!' Vernon shouted after him.

The others re-emerged from the tunnel, visibly shaken.

'What the devil was he up to?' Saul said. 'He took our photograph and stole away like a common criminal.'

'And he nearly ran me over in the process,' Kamala added in complaint.

Vernon glanced over his shoulder through the mizzling rain. A thought struck him about the man's camera: the average Ceylonese was unlikely to have a sophisticated German contraption like that. 'You don't suppose he's a journalist, do you?'

'How could he have known we were here?' Saul said, sounding doubtful. But the instant the question escaped his lips, he blanched. 'You mean to say the bugger's been trailing us?'

'It's as likely as not, I should think.'

'The cheek!' Minnette exclaimed. She gave Vernon a vexed look. 'Whatever are we going to do?'

He shrugged. 'What *can* we do?'

'For a start,' Kamala said, 'we can get out of this rain.'

On that much, at least, they all agreed. In double-quick time, they retraced their steps back down the hill to the car park.

Chapter 24

Crescendo

The article appeared in *The Ceylon Herald* later that week. It was on page three of the main news section. Saul came across it by accident one morning while in bed perusing the paper. The headline read 'White Man Goes Native', and next to the article was a blurry photograph of him and Minnette at the Aluviharaya temple.

'What the devil?' he said and spilled his tea on his pyjamas. 'Oh for God's sake.' He set down his cup and the paper and got out of bed and frantically dabbed his pyjamas with a napkin. His hands were trembling, because of his carelessness as well as the article.

He dropped the napkin onto the floor and, after getting back into bed, picked up the paper and stared with mystification at the headline. A part of him refused to believe that anyone would resort to such measures to silence a perceived opponent, even after everything that had happened with the hooligan planters. He was inclined to assume the best in people until they proved him wrong. Besides, in his own estimation, he was no threat to anyone, least of all to the upper classes of Ceylon. His only offences — if they could even be called that — had been to give a speech and write an article condemning imperialism. And no one in their right mind would defend the evils of imperialism. So clearly whoever was behind the article in *The Ceylon Herald* had something to lose other than credibility. Plantation profits perhaps? A lot of profits indeed would be lost if the status quo went the way of the dodo and planters were forced to pay their labourers a living wage.

He snapped the paper taut and read the article's by-line. Edwin Jayawardena. The name meant nothing to him. But he supposed that if *The Ceylon Herald were* in the pocket of the planters, every journalist at the paper would be suspect.

The upshot of the article was what he expected: an unscrupulous character assassination: sentence after sentence of *argumentum ad hominem* with no substance whatever. One particular sentence stuck in his throat: 'That Mr Maccabee would go as far as to adopt the national dress puts him beyond the pale.' Beyond the pale? A kurta and a sarong? What utter nonsense. Adopting the 'national dress' of another culture was no more scandalous than drinking a cup of tea or eating mincemeat—which Britons did every day and in droves thanks to imports from other countries. *Beyond the pale*. The phrase implied artifice on Saul's part, a mere affectation. But for a person to wear the clothing of another culture, the opposite would have to be true. It would be a sign of respect, an endearing, not an alienating, gesture.

Surely the readers of *The Ceylon Herald* would see things for what they were? They could not be so biased as to accept distortions and blatant lies. But then Saul remembered the political stances of certain newspapers he subscribed to back in London. It went without saying what the stance of the *London Morning Post* was. Historically *The Times* was not overtly pro-Tory or pro-Labour, but its editors supported the British Empire unwaveringly and for years had close ties with Downing Street. As for the editorship of *The Observer*, at different points in time they were liberal or conservative and made publishing decisions accordingly. And so on and so forth. There was no escaping bias. Most people did not read newspapers to discover the truth but rather to validate their own political views and personal prejudices. Readers of *The Ceylon Herald* doubtless were no different, any more than readers of publications like *The Masses* and *Samasamajaya*, with liberalism as their watchword, were different. At any rate, in the case of 'White Man Goes Native', readers had no means with which to discriminate between truth and untruth when Mr Jayawardena employed rhetorical fallacy after rhetorical fallacy and painted Saul as a radical. Balanced opinion never entered into it. And application of the epithet 'communist agitator', near the end of the article, served as the *coup de grace* to discredit Saul in the readers' eyes.

He tossed the paper atop the dirty napkin on the floor. The article was libellous — a crude form of propaganda — and he had had enough. He doubted he would be able to read the rest of the paper, either. How could he trust a single writer in a publication that had sold its soul to the highest bidder? Saul could easily discern lies that pertained to his own life, but what about lies in matters on which he had no personal knowledge? To read *The Ceylon Herald* from cover to cover, day after day, would be to risk indoctrination into a way of thinking that ran counter to human progress, the very essence of which was not permanent stasis, as extreme right-wingers would have it, or permanent convulsion, as extreme left-wingers would have it, but continual adaptation and improvement.

Saul noticed his hands were trembling again. He must calm himself, he thought. The Jayawardena article was an attempt to defame him into silence, nothing more. He closed his eyes and concentrated for a moment on the unsyncopated rhythms of his breathing, and felt his anger slowly drain away. Then he lit his pipe and took a deep draw. In the past, some of his best thinking had been done while smoking.

He would have to tread carefully going forward, that much was certain. One wrong move could cause him to lose face entirely. Of course, he had no intention of taking the attack on his character lying down. But a direct response to the Jayawardena article would only lend it credence. Better to let it wither on the vine. There was, at any rate, no worse insult than to pretend an interlocutor did not exist.

Perhaps he could write another article for *Samasamajaya* — about something controversial that would go against the colonialist grain. A subject had already presented itself: the Matale Rebellion. After Vernon mentioned the rebellion at the Aluviharaya temple, Saul had determined to learn more. He remembered seeing a Ceylonese history book in Romesh's library and upon returning to Kandy borrowed it.

The book contained an entire chapter on the Torrington administration. Under the short, violent reign of Viscount Torrington, who was Governor of Ceylon from 1847 to 1850, the invidiousness of imperialism was never more apparent. But the stage for Torrington's tyranny had been set well before his arrival on the scene. In 1833, the Slavery Abolition Act outlawed slavery in most of the British Empire — save in Ceylon, Saint Helena, and the 'Territories in the Possession of the East India Company'. Without slavery in the West Indies, coffee production declined dramatically, and as such, British coffee planters sought a more lucrative outpost. To this end, in 1840, the colonial government in Ceylon passed the Crown Lands Ordinance to expropriate coffee-growing land from the local peasantry. The Sinhalese, however, refused to work in the nightmarish conditions prevailing on the new plantations, and so the British imported Tamils from India using a bonded-labour system in which the Tamils paid their own way to Ceylon. Tens of thousands of them died en route or on the plantations, and most of those who were lucky enough to survive remained indebted for life.

All this went against the spirit of the Slavery Abolition Act, as well as against common decency. So why were such abuses allowed? In the name of commerce? Certainly not. The so-called bonded labour was not free commerce at work; it was the result of political backscratching, business owners using their influence to queer the pitch and institute slavery by another name. Slavery was officially abolished in Ceylon in 1844, but by then, the practice of bonded labour was well established. Another seventy-eight years would pass before it, too, would be banned.

Complicating matters during the mid-1840s, Great Britain experienced an economic depression that severely affected the

Ceylonese coffee industry. Planters clamoured for, and received, an elimination of export duties. To make up for shortfalls in revenue, the British government proposed direct taxes on the Sinhalese peasantry.

Enter Torrington stage right. As the new Governor of Ceylon in 1847, he was tasked with overseeing tax reforms. A year into his term, he imposed license fees on carts, dogs, guns, and shops and made labour compulsory on plantation roads for six days a year if individuals did not pay a special road tax. Most Ceylonese peasants could not afford the taxes. Nor could they afford to stop working their subsistence holdings for the sake of building roads. Riots broke out.

Torrington suppressed the riots within four days. And in the weeks and months that followed, he continued his tyranny: he had a rebel leader flogged and deported to Malacca; he had nearly twenty rebels, as well as a Buddhist monk, executed; and he had approximately a hundred others sentenced to imprisonment or hard labour. It was not the British Empire's finest hour.

Saul got up from the bed. His thoughts about the Matale Rebellion had roused him to such a pitch, he wanted to start writing his article immediately, to shine a light on the sins of Britain's imperialist past so that progress might be effected in the future. But he would not rush forward in a blind rage. He would do what he always did in his writing: take the balanced approach. He had no illusions that an article would persuade his harshest critics, but he understood the art of rhetoric enough to know that a balanced argument would be more effective than one that obfuscated the truth or one that employed mindless *ad hominem*. If nothing else, a balanced argument would put his critics to shame. He sat down at the desk in the corner of the room and scribbled myriad notes. His ideas flowed with such rapidity, the article practically wrote itself.

//

Vernon had a change of heart, and *The Ceylon Herald* article about

Saul was the catalyst. He was less outraged by the article's content than by the lengths to which the editors had gone to acquire the photograph. They, and the planters supporting them, had the effrontery to track Saul, perhaps all the way to Haputale, for the sole purpose of smearing his name. Such behaviour crossed the line. It was worse, even, than physical intimidation. On principle, Vernon now favoured taking a stand. He read with avidity a draft of Saul's latest *Samasamajaya* article and even translated it into Sinhala himself.

When Saul's article came out, it created a sensation. Both political camps reacted vociferously. LSSP leaders called for Saul to give another speech. The next rally was scheduled for March on Galle Face Green in Colombo, with a general topic of 'How Can We Smash Imperialist Might'. It was expected to be the largest anti-imperialist protest ever held in Ceylon. The conservatives, for their part, had other plans for Saul. *The Ceylon Herald* published a response to his article entitled 'Arrest the Reds Who Flout the Law'. In it, the writer accused Saul of instigating riots akin to the Matale Rebellion and called for his arrest on charges of sedition. No riots actually materialised, but apparently that was neither here nor there to the scandalmongers.

As the dust from the mutual outrage swirled, Saul received a threat in the post. It was typewritten on greyish-white onionskin paper in uppercase letters: 'YOU'LL QUIT CEYLON IF YOU KNOW WHAT'S GOOD FOR YOU'. Saul found the note amusing at first, but when he showed it archly to Vernon and Minnette, neither of them laughed.

'It isn't funny, Saul,' Minnette reproached.

'Perhaps not, but you must admit, it's rather juvenile. I half-expected to see pastel drawings of Peter Rabbit accompanying the text.'

Vernon examined the paper the threat was on. It crinkled to the touch. In its centre was an Eaton's-Berkshire watermark. 'I can't imagine a creeper having a supply of this on hand. It seems more like the kind of thing an office would have.'

'You mean a newspaper, I presume,' Saul said, adjusting his spectacles. 'Would they really stoop so low?'

'If their articles about you are anything to go by, then yes, I think they would.'

Minnette made a face. 'Does it matter who wrote it? A threat's a threat. Given everything else that's happened, I suggest we contact Geoff Overlund.'

'It certainly wouldn't hurt,' Vernon agreed. He went to the telephone and placed a call. He was prepared to hand-deliver the note to the police station if necessary, but when he offered to do so, Geoff insisted on coming over to the house himself because he had something else he wanted to discuss, and, he said, it would be best to keep the matter on the strict QT.

Geoff arrived a couple of hours later, after dinner. The entire household sat at the dining table drinking Douro Port. Instead of coming to the front of the bungalow, Geoff sneaked round to the kitchen. Vernon could hear Rani letting him in through the back door.

Presently Geoff entered the dining room. He was dressed in plain clothes, and his hair, longer than when Vernon last saw him, was slicked back. He seemed embarrassed for having intruded on an intimate family gathering. 'Please,' he said, before Vernon could stand, 'don't get up.' He smiled at the others. 'Sorry for the interruption.'

'I didn't hear your car,' Vernon said, 'or I would have let you in myself.'

'I parked at Mr Gunaratne's and cut through the jungle.'

'Why all the secrecy, *machang*?'

'That's what I came to talk to you about.'

'Have a seat, darling,' Kamala said. There were two bottles of port on the table, one empty and one full. She tapped the full bottle. 'Could I interest you in a glass?'

'No, thank you, Mrs Prins. I'm not officially on duty, but I'd like to keep a clear head.' As Geoff sat down, Minnette excused herself from the room. She returned shortly with the onionskin paper and handed it to him. Recognition seemed to flicker across his face as he held the paper up to the light.

'Do you recognise it?' Minnette asked.

Without responding, Geoff set the paper aside and glanced round the table. 'Everything I'm about to tell you stays within these four walls.' He ran a finger along the paper's watermark. 'I've seen this before. At the Planters' Association. I worked there for a summer, in the old Victoria Commemoration Building, after I came down from Trinity. The paper they used for business correspondence looked exactly like this. That in itself doesn't prove anything, but it's highly suggestive. And then there was the conversation I overheard last night.' He looked away for a moment, as if he were ashamed of what he had to say. 'I was visiting my parents. Shortly before I left the house, Pater received a phone call. I was passing his study when I heard him speaking to someone about Governor Stubbs and a political favour. Mr Maccabee's name was mentioned — in the same breath as the words "deportation order".'

'You can't be serious!' Saul suddenly cried out. Until that moment, he had been silently drinking his port. Now his face was ashen and his hands were shaking.

Minnette clenched the stem of her glass. 'They wouldn't dare.'

'How could anyone do such a thing?' Kamala added. 'Saul's a British subject.'

'No one has done anything just yet, Amma,' Vernon pointed out. Even so, he was worried, too. Mr Overlund did not seem the type to go off at half-cock.

A bit of colour returned to Saul's face. 'I won't be strong-armed,' he said, his hands hidden beneath the table. 'Freedom of expression mustn't be subverted by threats or thuggery.'

'I'm not suggesting you bow to pressure, Mr Maccabee,' Geoff said, 'but as you may or may not know, the colonial administration have deported people before without reasonable grounds. And the inspector generals of police have a long history of responding aggressively to champions of what they consider to be subversive ideas. Look at D. M. Manilal. Dowbiggin deported him simply for having communist affiliations. As far as I can tell, Banks is taking up where Dowbiggin left off. You didn't hear this from me, but Banks's first action as inspector general was to intercept all foreign correspondence intended for Labour Party leaders. The rationale was that ideas coming from abroad pose a threat to national security. But that's a camel's nose, if you ask me. Censorship and the banning of ideas are what the Nazis do, not upholders of a liberal democracy. What's next, book burning? Anyway, I wasn't surprised at all to learn that the LSSP and Mr Maccabee are on Banks's blacklist.'

'Do you think it was Banks your pater spoke to last night?' Vernon asked.

'Probably so. Rumour is, Banks has the Governor's ear.'

Vernon sat back in his chair. 'There's one thing I still don't understand. Assuming for argument's sake that the planters who disrupted the LSSP rally—and the same ones, presumably, who stormed Mr Gunaratne's house—are also behind the note and the newspaper articles, why the sudden change of tack from physical intimidation to written threats and a smear campaign?'

'I don't know, *men*. Perhaps the investigation I initiated before your trip to Haputale scared them off. There's also the fact that sending anonymous notes and commissioning newspaper articles are less conspicuous ways of frightening someone.'

'So where does that leave us?' Minnette asked impatiently.

'There's the rub.' Geoff picked up the onionskin paper, folded it in four, and tucked it into his shirt pocket. 'If the culprit proves to be someone from the Planters' Association, I'm afraid I'll have to drop the investigation. My pater and the Superintendent ...' Geoff's voice tailed off. Then with a self-conscious laugh, he said, 'You understand. But you should know, I'll do whatever I can to help.'

It seemed to Vernon that whether he and the others understood or not, discretion in this case was the better part of valour. 'I agree it makes no sense for you to rock the boat. With you on the inside and free from suspicion, we'll all be better off.'

Geoff looked at Vernon apologetically. 'If my pater is to blame in any way, I can say this much: he's not half the man your pater was.'

'Thanks, *machang*.' Vernon took small comfort in the complement, but it was something, at least. He topped up his glass with port and said, 'Allow me one last question. If a deportation order *is* in the offing, what do you advise we do in the meantime?'

'The only thing we can do: wait and watch.'

Saul gave a nervous little laugh. 'Like a lamb to the slaughter.'

Chapter 25

Nocturne

After Geoff left the Prins's that night, a feeling of restlessness descended upon the household. Everyone lent a hand with the dinner clean-up. For the best part of half an hour, they banged round in the dining room and the kitchen and talked about everything except the problem in hand. Then, without another word, they all dispersed throughout the house.

Vernon went to his room. He decided to write to Zoe again, even though he had already responded to her most recent fortnightly letter, because he did not think he could wait another ten or twelve days before informing her of the latest turn of events. The ceiling light in his room was inadequate to write by, so he also switched on the bedside lamps and lit the candelabrum on his writing desk. The candles crackled as they burned. He sat down at the desk and took out a piece of stationary and unscrewed the celluloid cap from his pen. Then he leaned over the desk in the artificial light, like a Buddhist scribe, and put pen to paper.

Dear Zoe,
I know I last wrote to you only three days ago, but something has
happened that compels me to write again sooner rather than later.
The situation here has gone from bad to worse. Yesterday The
Ceylon Herald published another article about Saul, this time

making false accusations of sedition, and today he received a threatening note in the post. There's also a possibility – how likely of a possibility is unclear at this point – that Saul could be deported back to England. My friend Geoffrey Overlund came by earlier and said he overheard his pater talking to the Inspector General of Police about Saul and a deportation order. I put on a brave face upon hearing the news, but between you and me, I'm worried. As Geoff said, it wouldn't be the first time the Ceylon government have deported someone – and for offences far less egregious than those alleged against Saul. The first Herald article about him was nothing compared to these latest outrages.

I feel badly for the part I played in getting him into his current predicament. (I persuaded him to become politically active in London this past autumn, I dragged him to Ceylon, and I didn't stop Minnette from talking him into associating with the LSSP.) It took months for him to recover from his wife's death – and now this. Being treated like a pariah certainly wasn't what I had in mind for his stay in Ceylon. Needless to say, I'll miss him dearly if he's forced to leave. He has been a devoted friend to me. And his insights into plantation history and economics have been invaluable. I've made significant progress on my thesis during the past month, mainly because of the discussions he and I have had. I can say without exaggeration that he has been more helpful to me at times than my LSE supervisor. In any case, how can what Saul did – advocate for plantation labourers and for British subjects generally – possibly warrant deportation? I'm beginning to wonder what the point was of my fighting against fascism if British politicians and other government officials are as corrupt and blinkered as the fascists themselves.

Perhaps I should join the LSSP. They aren't as radical as the communists or even the Scipians, but if they were to get into power in Ceylon, they would be a vast improvement over the current lot. I wish Thathi were still alive. He would be proud to know that his children have been working toward a better future. But now that I think about it, I don't see the point in my joining the LSSP when I'll be returning to London in eight months and perhaps will remain there for good. Unless of course you'll come here with me after my doctoral work is done. I shan't pressurise you into doing anything against your will, but I hope you'll at least consider coming to Ceylon one day. You might actually like it here, even if there is a chance you could be deported simply for exercising your basic human rights.

Forever Yours,
Vernon

He put away his pen and blew out the candles, which sent tendrils of smoke up toward the ceiling. As he got up from the desk, he heard voices come from outside. He stepped to a window. Saul and Minnette stood in the garden, bathed in moonlight. Vernon could not make out what they were saying, but from their body language, they appeared to be having a heart-to-heart. No doubt they had a lot to talk about, Vernon thought. It was sad to think that their time together might soon come to an end. Is that what life was all about? Separation and loss and struggle and forever saying goodbye to the ones we love?

//

'Don't look now,' she said, 'but we're being watched.'

Startled, he removed his pipe from his mouth and looked toward the road. It was a little past nine o'clock. Even in the dark, with the moon and stars so bright, he could see that no one was there.

'I told you not to look.' She turned her head slightly and the jewels of the Navaratne brooch shone in the moonlight.

'Are you leading me up the garden path?' he asked humorously.

She giggled. 'You're a bundle of nerves.' She glanced at the bungalow. 'Vernon was standing at his bedroom window a moment ago, but he's gone now.'

Saul followed her eyes. All the bungalow lights were off, save the electric lanterns on the verandah. He *must be* a bundle of nerves, he thought; he had not even noticed the lights go out. The Overlund chap could be thanked for that. Ever since the news about the deportation order, Saul had had a foreboding that at any moment a Black Maria would turn up at the house and bundle him off to a high-security detention centre somewhere in the island. He turned back to Minnette and took a few deliberate puffs on his pipe. Then he said, 'I wish I had your devil-may-care attitude.'

'I'm only pretending to be brave.' She stared into his eyes. 'Like I was at Mr Arunasalem's that day.' She had discussed with Saul the 'incident' at the greengrocer's. 'I was afraid then, too. It wasn't so much what Mr Arunasalem said as how he said it. There was an intense hatred in his voice and eyes—the sound and image of which I'll never be able to erase from my mind. And people like him are the same kind of people who would have you deported. The difference is, most of the planters are British and white and in a position of power and so are that much more dangerous.' She looked away, toward the jungle. She seemed to be thinking of that day at Mr Arunasalem's. 'Thathi wasn't afraid of Mr Arunasalem,' she added thoughtfully. 'He knew when to pick his fights.'

Somehow her candidness settled Saul's nerves. It was all right to be afraid, he thought. But come what may with the planters, he had to stand his ground, for Minnette's and Vernon's sakes, if for no one else's. He was not by nature a truculent person, but there was a time and a place for everything, and now, in the face of adversity, was no time to be meek. He thought of the Fabian Society's original coat of arms—a wolf in sheep's clothing—before it was abandoned because of its negative connotations. That was what he needed to be now: a wolf in sheep's clothing. Be damned the Society's logotype of a tortoise, which was supposed to represent a slow, imperceptible transition to socialism. And socialism be damned, too. The important thing was what socialism strived for, not how it managed to get there. It represented equal rights and fairness and progress, not in some unattainable utopic future but now, in the living present. Revolution was not necessary to attain this; people just needed to do what was right. He looked at Minnette earnestly. 'What I said before about freedom of expression—it wasn't just empty rhetoric. Some things are worth fighting for.'

'Yes,' she said and kissed him on the cheek. She turned back toward the jungle, its mysteries seemingly reflecting in her eyes.

He watched her watch the jungle, in silent communion, and as he listened to the night's music with ever-growing appreciation, it occurred to him that *she* was worth fighting for. Indeed, he was less afraid of what the planters might do to him than he was of being deported and never seeing her again. He loved her with all his heart, and he did not care who knew it, not even Esther, if she did happen to be observing his love-sick behaviour from the heavens above. Surely Esther would not begrudge him happiness; she could not expect him to remain alone for the rest of his life. He wanted to say some of this to Minnette, to express his undying love for her, but from her demeanour just now, and from the look in her eyes, he knew he did not need to.

//

Days went by without further news from Geoff, and Vernon was beginning to think that Saul was out of the wood. As Saul himself repeatedly said about the matter, 'No news was good news.' But the uncertainty and feelings of helplessness were driving Vernon mad. And yet there was nothing he could do about it, really, so he busied himself with his thesis. Saul, meanwhile, continued to agitate. He began another *Samasamajaya* article and, after being pressurised by the LSSP leadership, agreed to deliver the keynote speech at the upcoming rally in Colombo.

Late one night, while Vernon was in his room reading, he heard what sounded like an affray outside the house. Then he heard Kamala and Minnette shouting on the verandah, saying alternately, 'Stop that! Get off our land! Or we'll call the police!' Vernon dropped his book, jumped out of bed, and stepped into his sandals. He reached the front door at the same time that Saul did.

Saul had a hangdog expression on his face. 'Look what I've brought on your family. Sorry, old chap.'

'Bollocks,' Vernon said, thrusting open the door. 'You've done nothing wrong.' He charged out onto the verandah with Saul behind him.

'There you are,' Kamala said. 'You must make them stop.'

In the front yard, two white men were hoisting up a scarecrow-like figure, and from a short distance away, Minnette was pelting them with rocks. 'Oi!' the men kept saying as they simultaneously attempted to finish their work and fend off the rocks.

Vernon bounded down the verandah stairs. One of the men saw him coming and fled. The other one stayed behind and turned to face him. It was the British creeper from the LSSP rally. He had a box of matches in his hand. He gave Vernon a baleful look and then lit a match and held it to the figure's head. Vernon came to within a few metres and stopped. In the dim lantern light, he could see that the figure was not a scarecrow at all but a crude effigy of Saul: it had black circles drawn round the eyes, vaguely resembling spectacles; its face was pink; and it was dressed in a white kurta and sarong. The creeper let go of the match, setting the effigy's head alight. It must have been stuffed with straw because it burned quickly. With an aura of flames atop it, the effigy looked for all the world like the Hindu god Agni.

Minnette threw another rock, and this time it hit the creeper in the face and drew blood.

'You fucking cockroach bitch!' he cursed. He started forward, but Vernon was there to block the way.

Vernon grabbed him by the shirt with such force, the creeper's feet lifted off the ground. 'Say that again,' Vernon dared.

The creeper flailed his arms and legs. 'Unhand me, you bastard!'

An errant boot struck Vernon in the shin. He grimaced and dropped the creeper, who got to his feet, gave Vernon another baleful look, and ran off.

'You'll quit Ceylon if you know what's good for you!' the creeper yelled as he hurried down the road.

The effigy was now fully ablaze. Vernon had to put out the fire. He picked up a large tree branch from the yard and was about to knock over the effigy when he inhaled a bit of smoke and hesitated. The scent reached his brain in a synapse or two. Suddenly he felt nauseous, as if he might retch. Tears came to his eyes. In a painful flash of memory, he saw Arthur Fitch lying next to him on the parade ground at Action House. It was unbearably hot, and ash was falling from the sky. Not far away on the verandah, Stewart Morley lay stone-dead.

Vernon came to himself and swung the tree branch at the base of the effigy until it teetered and crashed, sending sparks flying. Then he removed his shirt and used it to smother the flames.

'What's the world coming to?' Kamala said as she joined the others next to the charred remains of the effigy.

Minnette glanced at Saul. 'I think we know who sent you that threatening note.'

He did not respond. His mind seemed to be elsewhere. He just stood there watching the dying embers of the effigy glow and smoulder.

As the others looked on, the sounds of night coalesced into a tone cluster, and amid the dissonance an eagle owl screeched somewhere deep in the jungle.

Chapter 26

Exile

The dreaded news came the next day. It was Johannes's three-month death anniversary. A *dānē* ceremony had just been performed in the Prins's sitting room, and Romesh and the three monks had one foot out the door. The telephone rang as the door clanked shut. Vernon answered it. While he listened to the voice on the other end, blood drained from his face. He shot Saul an agonised glance and rang off.

'What is it?' Minnette asked.

Saul had already guessed at the thrust of the call. He girded himself for the news.

'A deportation order,' Vernon said in a defeated voice. 'One was issued. And the Kandy police have just received orders from the Governor's office to apprehend Saul.' As Vernon said this last bit, Kamala cried out 'Oh dear!' He paused for a moment before continuing. 'The police will be here within the hour. Geoff's going to stall as much as he can, but we've no time to lose. We must get Saul into hiding.'

'Into hiding, where?' Minnette asked. 'There's no place for him to hide.' Her stridency belied her distress.

'He'll take sanctuary at the temple,' Vernon suggested.

Saul maintained his composure. Now that the moment was

finally here, when it was time for him to do or die, he did not feel afraid in the least. 'I've a better idea. I'll hide in Udawattekele.'

'What do you mean?' Minnette scoffed. 'You wouldn't last a day there.'

'Thanks for the vote of confidence.'

'I only meant that you're not accustomed to roughing it in the jungle.'

'With the right provisions, I'll be fine. I know my way round the reserve, and when I was there with Romesh, he mentioned some caves. I could find one of those and stay there. I was also thinking I could disguise myself as an itinerant monk to avoid detection.'

'All right,' Vernon said without protest. 'It's the best plan we've got.' He glanced at the front door. 'You can have Mr Gunaratne take you there if he hasn't left yet. It's not far from the temple.'

Minnette went to the window. 'No, he's still here.'

Out on the road the engine of the Humber started up.

'For goodness' sake,' Kamala urged, 'go and stop him.'

Minnette rushed out the door, yelling for Romesh to wait. The Humber went down the road a short distance before stopping. Minnette caught it up and conferred with Romesh for a minute. When she returned to the house, she said, 'He'll do it. The monks want to help, too. They said they'll hide Saul in the back seat. And one of them gave me his new robes.' She held out a bundle of saffron cloth for Saul to take.

'Right,' Vernon said. 'Let's get to it, then.'

Kamala and Minnette shaved Saul's head, while Vernon and Rani gathered up provisions from the kitchen: some dried beef, a bunch of plantains, and two canteens of water. Twenty minutes later they all stood outside, saying their goodbyes. Saul's head was shaved to the scalp, and he was dressed in the monk's robes. His rucksack hung over one shoulder. He did indeed look like an itinerant monk.

Minnette stood apart from the others. Only half of her face was visible to Saul, but from what he could see of it, she appeared to be about to cry. He would have kissed her if no one else had been present.

'It's only a temporary farewell,' he said, continuing to maintain his composure. As she forced a smile, he averted his eyes. He did not want to make her cry. To Kamala he said divertingly, 'Thank you for your hospitality, Mrs Prins.'

'Goodbye, Mr Maccabee. Be safe. And as you said, it's only a temporary farewell.'

Vernon produced a double-barrel pistol from the back of his sarong and handed it to Saul.

'What's this?' Saul asked, staring at the weapon in astonishment.

'It's Thathi's old howdah pistol.'

'I hardly think a pistol will be necessary.'

'Perhaps not against the police or rogue planters, but you never know what you might encounter in the jungle. Leopards have been known to hunt in Udawattekele. Do you know how to load it?'

Saul nodded.

Romesh was drumming the steering wheel with his fingers and looking down the road. In a high-pitched voice, he said, 'Hurry up, will you!'

'Mr Gunaratne's right,' said Vernon. 'We've delayed long enough.' He shook Saul's hand. 'Cartridges for the pistol are in your rucksack should you need them. I'll find you in a day or two, when the coast is clear to do so, and bring you more provisions.'

Saul stuffed the pistol into his already overstuffed rucksack. 'A wolf in sheep's clothing,' he remarked, shouldering the rucksack again and wrapping his off arm in the loose folds of the robe.

'Pardon?' Vernon said.

'Nothing, old chap.' Saul turned to get into the Humber, but before he did so, his eyes met Minnette's and a tender look passed between them. In their subterranean relationship, it was the strongest possible public avowal of their devotion to each other.

The eldest monk moved to the front of the car, and the two monks in the back made room for Saul to sit between them. As Saul squeezed in, one of the monks said something pleasant-sounding in Sinhala.

Minnette's face suddenly appeared in the back-seat window, which was open. 'Take off your spectacles,' she told Saul, 'or you'll be spotted a mile away.' She reached through the window and brushed her fingers across his cheek, then stepped back.

He removed his spectacles and slid them into a pouch in the rucksack. He could still feel the warmth of Minnette's fingertips on his cheek. The expression on her face just now was not visible without his spectacles, but he could sense it, and it was almost enough to make him cry himself.

Romesh drove off. Through the rear window, Saul watched the blurry forms of the Prins family recede from view. They were waving at him and getting smaller by the second. He felt a twinge of remorse. He did not want to leave Minnette, and he had the overwhelming desire now to hold her in his arms and tell her how much he loved her. Perhaps he had made the wrong decision in going into hiding. What if his farewell turned out to be permanent?

'Police!' Romesh shouted suddenly.

Saul turned in his seat. The Humber was approaching Hewaheta Road. What appeared to be an open-top patrol car idled at the intersection. Saul felt exposed without his spectacles, as though his carapace had been torn away. His heart began to pound and his hands began to shake.

'Act natural,' Romesh said, glancing back at Saul. 'From a distance, you look just like a *bhikkhu*.' Then he said something in Sinhala to the monks, at which they nodded.

Act natural, Saul thought. That was easier said than done.

The police car accelerated at the same time that Romesh braked. As the two cars passed each other, moving at less than ten miles per hour, time itself seemed to slow. Squinting, Saul could just discern in rough detail the features of the policemen. A constable was driving. Geoffrey Overlund sat in the front passenger seat, gesticulating and talking spiritedly; he appeared to be deliberately distracting the constable. The last thing Saul saw, before the police car disappeared from view, was the triple chevron of Overlund's tunic rising and falling convulsively as though he had been seized by a fit of laughter.

'Thank the Buddha,' Romesh said as he brought the Humber to a stop at the intersection. 'I thought for sure we'd be nabbed.'

'We have more than the Buddha to thank for our escape.' Saul thought: the Buddha, Overlund, fate, karma, the stars, or what you will — individually or in concert, they all could be thanked. Perhaps even Providence deserved a little credit.

Romesh turned the Humber onto Hewaheta Road and drove a couple of miles to the reserve and parked in the grassy clearing. After Saul put his spectacles back on and swapped out his sandals for boots, he and Romesh and the eldest monk walked to the edge of the jungle. It was much cooler than the last time Saul was here. A bank of billowy clouds filled the sky, and a strong wind swept across the grass in waves. The birds, chattering raucously, and the trees, looking less wilted, seemed to rejoice in the reprieve from the tropical heat.

'I couldn't have asked for a better day to be tramping round in the jungle,' Saul said.

Romesh translated Saul's comment into Sinhala for the monk's benefit.

The monk pointed to the white thread on Saul's wrist and said something in Sinhala that Saul did not understand.

'What did he say?' Saul asked Romesh.

'He says the *pirit* thread from the *dānē* will also provide you with protection.'

Saul thanked the monk in Sinhala — one of the many phrases he had picked up during his time in Ceylon.

The monk smiled serenely and put his hands together and nodded.

After a while they reached the entrance to Byrde Lane. Saul and Romesh embraced and clapped each other on the back.

'Good luck,' Romesh said. As he stepped away, something in the sky caught his attention. 'I say.'

A shrill whistle-like call rang out over the clearing.

Saul looked up and recognised immediately the paddle-shaped

wings from the colour plate of his field guide: a pair of Jerdon's bazas. They soared and undulated high above the trees, on the verge, it seemed, of a sally. Their light-coloured banded underparts were scarcely visible against the brilliant white of the clouds.

'The white man's burden,' Romesh noted with a mix of gravity and mirth.

Saul laughed. The reference had become their own private joke.

Romesh waggled his head. 'Perhaps the sighting's a good omen.'

'Is it?' Saul said, raising his eyebrows. After a moment, he added, 'Yes, let's hope you're right' and, catching one last glimpse of the hawks' aerial acrobatics, turned and entered the jungle.

//

A police car pulled up in front of the Prins's house, and Geoff and a Sinhalese constable got out. They came up onto the verandah. Vernon, Minnette, and Kamala were there, pretending it was a day like any other.

'Detective Sergeant Overlund, how are you?' Vernon said. 'You should have told us you were coming. We'd have put the kettle on.'

'Mr Prins. I'm quite well. Thanks for asking. And no need for tea.' Geoff looked at Kamala and Minnette. 'Ladies.'

'What brings you here?' Minnette asked.

'Mr Maccabee, as it happens. Where might I find him?'

'Funny you should ask that,' Kamala said. 'We were just discussing him and wondering how he is. He left us a few days ago under rather mysterious circumstances.'

'Is that right?' the constable said in English. He looked at Geoff in disbelief.

'He has been nothing but trouble since he came here,' Minnette added, half-smiling. 'And we rowed about it no end. I think he left because he felt unwelcome, in all honesty.'

'Now look here—' the constable started to say.

'It's all right, Constable,' Geoff interrupted. 'They won't be so coy once they've read this.' He retrieved a folded piece of paper from his tunic pocket, unfolded it, and handed it to Vernon.

It was the deportation order, with official-looking letterhead from the office of Governor Sir Reginald Stubbs. Vernon read the document aloud: 'In pursuance of the powers in me vested by Clause 3 of Article III of the Order made by Her Late Majesty Victoria in Council on the 26th day of October 1896, I, the Governor of Ceylon, do hereby order you Saul Bartholomew Maccabee, of Kandy to quit the Island of Ceylon, on or before 6 p.m. on the 21st February, 1937.'

'So you see how it is,' Geoff said. 'I expect you won't mind, then, if we search the house.'

The constable smirked.

Vernon shrugged and handed the paper back to Geoff. 'By all means.'

Geoff motioned for the constable to conduct a search.

'Oh, please do watch your step,' Kamala said as the constable entered the sitting room. 'We had a *dānē* for my dear departed husband this morning, and the maidservant just cleaned.'

After the constable moved from the sitting room to the back of the house, Geoff winked at the others and said in a whisper, 'Mr Maccabee's somewhere safe?'

Vernon nodded, although, he thought, perhaps 'safe' was not the right word. He envisioned Saul trudging through Udawattekele in a monk's robes. It was an incongruous image, like Johannes in a Father Christmas costume. Minnette's point about Saul's not being accustomed to roughing it in the jungle had been putting it mildly. Birdwatching was hardly sufficient preparation for living in a cave. But however Saul happened to be faring at the moment, he definitely was *not* in police custody, and that was the important thing. In that sense, at least, he was 'safe'.

The constable re-appeared, shaking his head. 'He did a bunk.'

'We'll nab him before long,' Geoff said, like an actor in a talkie. He turned to Kamala. 'May I use your telephone, Mrs Prins? I have to put out an all-cars alert.'

//

In among the trees the wind was less intense. Similar to the last time he was here, birdcalls and flashes of colour overwhelmed his senses. He did not have his binoculars, but he did not need them. With the sun behind clouds, the ambient light was soft and even, and greater distances and the upper branches of trees were visible to the naked eye. Even more than usual the bold colours of the birds' feathers stood out starkly against the earth tones of the jungle.

A half-mile up the path he stopped and sat on a small boulder and drank some water to slake his thirst. There was no need for him to rush, he thought. It was scarcely noon — which meant he had six hours before sunset to find one of the caves. And what harm would it do in the meantime to enjoy a little scenery? At any rate, the police were unlikely to track him here, if they bothered to track him at all. He was only one insignificant man. But whether they tracked him or not, his having absconded doubtless would create at least temporary turmoil at the Kandy police station. He could see it now: constables scuttling about like cockroaches and patrol cars racing to and fro in the streets, and here he was meanwhile safely hidden in the jungle. The thought made him laugh.

He retrieved a piece of dried beef from his rucksack, sat back composedly, and, while eating, observed his surroundings. The path was lined with thin-trunked trees. Several of them were choked with devil's ivy, whose trailing stems and oversized, heart-shaped leaves ran the length of the trunks. In various places lianas and other vines hung from the uppermost branches like the rigging of a ship.

A parrot somewhere nearby emitted a harsh ak-ak-ak. The call was rather jarring. Saul looked up and scanned the tree canopy. Off to one side of the path was a small clearing. A fifty-foot *jambu* tree stood at its far edge. Myriad pink and red oblong-shaped berry clusters dangled from its branches like Christmas ornaments.

Something moved among the leaves—Saul glimpsed a flash of colour—and there the bird was, with its yellowish-green feathers, grey hood, and red beak. A Layard's parakeet. And not just one but an entire flock. Some of them preened themselves, while others fed on *jambu* fruit. Saul made a mental note of the tree; its fruit might come in handy if his provisions were to run out. Then something else caught his eye. One of the parakeets, using its beak as an aid, was crossing a vine that stretched like a tightrope from one end of the clearing to the other.

The birds' namesake came to mind. Edgar Leopold Layard, a diplomat and a naturalist. Still another Brit putting his nose where it did not belong. It went without saying that the name of the parakeets would be incomplete without that apostrophe-s. As surely as the parakeets lived and breathed, Layard possessed every inch of what he had 'discovered'.

Another, different birdcall sounded, and then another. The long, slurred notes of mynah birds. They, too, moved among the branches of the *jambu* tree, preening and feeding and intermingling with the parakeets. Saul remembered from his field guide that the more common name for the mynah bird was the brahminy starling. Its feathers were buff-coloured, and it had a black cap.

Something—a snake perhaps—startled the birds, for the *jambu* tree erupted into mayhem. Feathers fluttered, and raucous chatter echoed and re-echoed from branch to branch. It was like the staggered entrance of instruments in an orchestra. The mynah birds' more subdued calls perfectly counterpointed the harsher calls of the parakeets.

At length, as the bird chatter subsided, Saul set off on the path again. He had not gone far before the foul stench of rotting flesh assailed him. He covered his nose with a fold of his robe. The carcass of what looked like a decapitated wild-boar piglet lay in the middle of the path. By the looks of it, it had been there for only a few hours, carpeted as it was in ants and flies. Perhaps a leopard had killed it for sport or had been scared off in the midst of the kill. The flies, at any rate, were enough to make Saul's entrails contract.

With his free hand, he picked up a stick and poked the carcass. A cloud of blue bottles rose buzzing into the air. He dropped the stick and hurried past. Behind him for ten yards or more he could hear the collective beating of the flies' wings.

Shortly he came to the fork in the path near the royal pond. Before proceeding, he dallied beneath the bower to gawp at the troop of macaques.

'Hello, old chap,' he said to the monkey that bore an uncanny resemblance to Lloyd George. It was sitting by itself on a large branch, looking at Saul with apparent interest. 'I don't suppose you recognise me without my hair. *Your* hair is why I recognised you at once. I'm Saul Maccabee, thorn in the flesh of British imperialists.' Two other monkeys climbed down from higher branches and sat next to the Lloyd George lookalike. All three of them had expectant looks on their faces, as though they were waiting for Saul to deliver an erudite lesson on the ways of primates. 'You're surrounded by your Garden Suburb of illuminati, I see. All you need is a tea service, some Bakewell tarts, and an orchestra, and the cultivation of your mind will be complete.' Saul saluted. 'Until the next time.' Then he turned up the path in the direction of the caves.

The path meandered, veering north, then west, then east, then north again. As Saul trudged along, his upper robe kept shifting and sliding off his shoulder; he had to adjust it repeatedly. He was not used to walking so much, especially in boots. Eventually he became fatigued, and a painful blister formed on one of his feet. It occurred to him that perhaps Minnette's reservations about his hiding in the jungle had been justified, after all. He was considering turning back when a large granite outcrop, in the shade of an immense peepal tree, came into view through a thicket. It was just the sort of place a cave might be. A narrow breach in the thicket suggested the remnants of another path. As he pushed his way through the branches, rain began to fall, lightly at first, then heavily. Soon the ground became slick.

Saul slipped. His fall was broken with an outstretched hand but not before a stray branch caught him in the face and sent his spectacles flying. He dropped to his knees and rooted round in the muck. His robes, now sodden and muddy, kept getting in the way. Rain poured down his face, further obscuring his vision. At last he saw the outlines of metal frames sticking out of the mud. He pried his spectacles loose, let the rainwater rinse them off, and put them back on; at the same time, the rain let up. Suddenly he could see again, as though scales had fallen from his eyes.

He got to his feet. A few yards in front of him stood an eight-foot-high deposit of sedimentary rock. Beyond this was the granite outcrop he had seen from the main path. He went to the wall and attempted to climb it, but the rock was wet and he could not get purchase. He decided to go the long way round. Backtracking to a tangle of trees, he cut through the jungle for thirty or forty yards until he came to a gentle incline that led directly to the cave.

Vines hung before its mouth like a curtain. He drew them aside and entered. The cave was musty and smelled faintly of ammonia, but its floor was dry; before entering, he noticed above its mouth a man-made drip ledge that prevented rainwater from pouring in. Enough sunlight shone through the vines to make the cave's dimensions discernible: roughly twenty feet square. Someone, presumably a monk, had lived here before. Broken clay pots and other signs of human habitation lay strewn about. Living in the cave, Saul thought, would be worse than living at Romesh's, but as a temporary accommodation, and when the alternative was deportation, it would have to do.

He removed his rucksack and checked its contents. Everything at the top, including his clothes, was soaked through. He pulled out his tobacco pouch, and it, too, was sodden. His heart sank. So much for a smoke. He truly would be living the life of an ascetic, forced to abstain from his one remaining vice. He reached down into the bottom of the rucksack and retrieved a box of matches, a torch, and the pistol cartridges—and was relieved to find each of them bone dry.

He switched on the torch and looked for the cleanest spot on the floor next to the mouth of the cave and sat down. His foot with the blister on it was throbbing. He unlaced the boot and slid it off along with the sock and then shone the torch on the sole of his foot. The blister was the size of a florin. No wonder it ached so much.

He put the sock back on, and, as he did so, his hand rubbed against a lump of slime on his calf. In the half-light, the lump looked like a fleck of mud. But as he aimed the torch at it, his entrails contracted. The lump was a leech. He set down the torch and struck a match against the matchbox and held the flame to the fat end of the leech. It squirmed and detached its posterior sucker. Saul continued to apply the flame to the leech's anterior. A second before the flame extinguished, the leech finally let go and dropped to the floor. It writhed, raised up its anterior for a moment, and then crawled toward the mouth of the cave. Blood was running down Saul's leg. He tore off a clean segment of his robe and used it as a tourniquet round his calf. Then he picked up his boot, limped a few steps, and with a thud sent the parasitic worm to meet its maker. It was not a very Buddhist thing to do, the wanton taking of a life, but Saul could not stomach the thought of a leech crawling off into the jungle with a crop full of his blood.

Chapter 27

Tutti

At dusk, an hour or two after the rain had stopped, little flashes of bioluminescence sporadically lit up the jungle outside the cave. Cicadas and crickets and frogs added vocals to the visual display. Then Jerdon's nightjars joined in, with two different calls, one like the croak of a frog and the other like an underwater pulse. As night fell, more and more fireflies appeared, and before long their individual signals became perfectly synchronised bursts of light.

For some time, Saul had been standing at the mouth of the cave, watching and listening. He could not rest, not with the deafening sounds of the jungle surrounding him like an echo chamber. Besides, the air in the cave was close, and the floor was extremely uncomfortable. He had intended to use his robes as a mattress, but they, along with his other clothes, were still wet.

He heard a branch break in a nearby tree. Only a sliver of a moon hung in the eastern sky, so it was difficult to see beyond a few yards. He switched on the torch, stuck his hand through the vines, and fanned the torchlight into the tenebrous night. A yellow-amber eyeshine glowed for a second. Saul retraced the arc of the torch until the eyes shone again. The animal froze in the light. It appeared to be a civet of some kind, with its brown fur and long bushy tail. No more dangerous, Saul thought, than a mongoose.

Still, he felt it wise to be prepared should anything more menacing come creeping out of the night. He retrieved the pistol and cartridges from his rucksack and sat down. With the torch on the floor pointing toward him, he opened the breech and loaded each barrel and snapped the pistol shut. He hoped he would not have to use it, on man or beast, but desperate times …

He did not finish the thought, for another branch broke. This time the sound came from the ground. With the pistol in one hand and the torch in the other, he returned to the mouth of the cave and stuck his hand through the vines again, illuminating the jungle. There was no animal on the ground that he could see. But perhaps there was one he could not see. At the thought of something lurking in the darkness, his hands began to perspire. He clenched the pistol more tightly. He would fire it into the air if he had to, but he preferred not to waste any cartridges or alert anyone as to his whereabouts.

'Shoo!' he threatened, brandishing the torch.

A sudden hiss came from the tangle of trees. Then he heard a strange rattling noise and more branches breaking. He could make neither head nor tail of the sounds. Certainly they were not those of a leopard. Perhaps they had come from a porcupine. Porcupines were known to hiss like cats when alarmed, and it was not inconceivable that their quills could rattle. Saul kept telling himself this — that the unknown animal was a harmless porcupine — at the same time that he tried to block from his mind the image of the decapitated wild-boar piglet he saw on the path earlier.

He was on the verge of firing a warning shot when a lantern appeared in the direction of the main path. He quickly switched off the torch. His first thought was that it was the police. How could they have tracked him here with such dispatch?

The lantern light fragmented for a moment as it passed behind a clump of trees. Then it appeared whole again, and became immeasurably brighter, on the path that led to the cave. It was coming toward Saul. He backed into the depths of the cave and with trepidation waited for the light to draw nearer.

Suddenly the lantern was on the other side of the curtain of vines. In the briefest of moments Saul wrestled with what to do. He was not a violent man, but he had every right to stay in Ceylon. And then there was Minnette. A composite of memories flashed through his mind: the first time he saw her, in the sun hat and culottes, on Romesh's verandah; how lovely she was in her silver dress that night at Queen's Hotel; their intimate conversations at the Prins's bungalow; his schoolboy confusion in the garden at the Temple of the Tooth; how she wore the Navaratna brooch every chance she got; their unforgettable first kiss on New Year's Eve. He simply could not allow himself to be taken by the police. If he *were* taken, his memory-making with Minnette would become a thing of the past.

He fired. When the shot rang out, it was so deafening, it drowned out the sounds of the jungle. A split second later there was a loud thwack against the cave wall and then a sharp stinging pain in his left arm. He dropped the torch and the pistol and fell backward. The darkness became darker.

He opened his eyes to a blinding light. After a moment, the light moved and the shadowy features of a man's face appeared.

'You ought to be more careful with that thing,' the man said in a German accent. He wore saffron robes, and his head was shaven. A bundle hung over one shoulder.

Saul winced and reached for his arm. The shoulder wrap of his robe was torn, and beneath the tear, the flesh was singed.

'You were only grazed,' said the monk. 'I had a look at it while you were out.'

'Much obliged,' Saul said, holding his arm and sitting up with a groan.

The monk set the lantern onto the floor and sat down in the lotus position. He seemed to be considering Saul's robes. 'I am curious to know what a *bhikkhu* is doing with a gun.'

'I'm not a *bhikkhu*, if you must know.'

'What are you, then?'

'A fugitive.' It struck Saul, as he voiced the word 'fugitive', that he was in rather curious company: a member of a motley group of renegades: deserters, escaped criminals, exiles, refugees, runaway slaves, tramps. He added proudly, 'A wolf in sheep's clothing.'

The monk's expression did not change. 'We have something in common, there. I am a Jew in self-exile from Germany. I left Hanau in 1932 for Vienna, but even there, I did not feel safe. I could see the way the winds were blowing, so in 1934, I left the Continent altogether and came to Ceylon.'

'And you took robes.'

'And I took robes.'

One of the lucky ones, Saul thought. Ernst came to mind — and other non-Aryans and political rivals of the Nazis who had *not* been so lucky. Now the Nazi's poisonous intolerance of individuality and difference was spreading to Britain, the Mile End Road Pogrom the most outrageous in a series of antisemitic attacks. 'We've more in common than you know,' Saul said.

The monk smiled. 'Are you a fellow Jew?'

'I am.'

'*Shalom.*'

'*Shalom.*' Saul let go of his arm. The pain had eased. 'Why have you come to Udawattakele?' he asked. 'Aren't you afraid wandering round in the jungle at night?'

'It is not my habit to travel after nightfall, but I was delayed because of the rain. I often come to Kandy on pilgrimage from the Island Hermitage. One day I will start a forest hermitage here. I find the Kandy climate preferable to Dodanduwa.'

Saul was about to ask the monk why he had taken robes in the first place and if he enjoyed monastic life, but he thought better of it and instead told the monk his name.

'Maccabee,' the monk repeated. 'It is a warrior's name. In Aramaic it means "the hammer". Good to meet you, Saul.' The monk put his hands together and bowed. 'Upon ordination, I was given the name Nyanapatara.' Before Saul could respond, the monk lifted up the lantern and shone it round the cave. 'Nothing has changed, I see, since I last was here. I planned to stay the night, but perhaps two is a crowd?'

'Not at all. It would be rather discourteous of me to send you back out into the jungle in the dark.' Saul was heartened, at any rate, to know that someone else would be with him in the cave overnight.

'Thank you.' The monk unravelled his bundle and placed a reed mat onto the floor and lay down. Then he opened the lantern's glass case and turned the knob until the wick went out. *'Gute Nacht.'*

'Gute Nacht.' The words echoed in the cave. Curiously, Saul felt like he had just wished himself, and not the monk, a good night. In the pitch black he removed his boots and lay back down. Sleeping on the cave floor was like sleeping on a pile of bricks, but the presence of the monk made it bearable. And the ambient sounds of the jungle that earlier had grated on Saul's nerves now had a soporific effect. He fell asleep at once.

//

Vernon entered the jungle just as the sun was coming up over the trees on the eastern edge of the clearing. He had his pater's paradox gun slung over one shoulder and a pack of provisions over the other. He was fortunate to have evaded the police. A couple of constables had surveilled the house overnight. Before sunrise, he sneaked out the back door and met Mr Gunaratne a kilometre up the road, and in the Humber the two of them took a circuitous route to Udawattakele. They passed a patrol car on Hantana Road, but the police seemed not to have noticed them.

Vernon had not planned to come to Udawattakele so soon, but yesterday, after Saul went into hiding, some rather exciting events occurred. The police, far from giving up on their pursuit of Saul, initiated an island-wide manhunt. The Governor's office issued orders to every police station in the island to apprehend Saul at all costs. Word of the manhunt leaked out and spread like wildfire among the general public. By late afternoon spontaneous demonstrations broke out in the centre of Kandy town, the protestors chanting, 'We want Maccabee—deport Stubbs!' Not even the rain deterred them. Similar demonstrations ensued in other towns and cities. Meanwhile in Colombo, the LSSP were organising 'monster mass meetings' and the distribution of leaflets to agitate for the repeal of the 1896 Order-in-Council, or 'Slave Proclamation' as the LSSP referred to it, which empowered the colonial government to deport 'any person in Ceylon […] without trial, charge, or cause and without possibility of appeal to any authority'. Dr de Silva, the LSSP president, asked Minnette to organise similar 'meetings' in Kandy. Late into the night she and Kamala and a few local LSSP peons made placards that read 'Maccabee must stay!' or 'Down with the Slave Proclamation!' or 'Long live a free people in Ceylon!'

Minnette had another reason to be excited. Her poem 'Il Poya Day' had been published. While she was busy making placards, the post arrived with an acceptance letter from *New London Magazine*, one of the most prestigious poetry magazines in England. Submitting there had been Saul's idea, and she did so reluctantly because she considered it such a long shot. So when the acceptance came, she was bowled over. She wanted Saul to share in her success. She asked Vernon to give him a handwritten version of her poem in Udawattakele. Saul deserved as much credit as she did, she said. Also, having the poem might cheer him up. She imagined he desperately needed cheering up. She had had all sorts of premonitions of things going wrong for him in the jungle.

Vernon felt for the poem in his pocket now. It was there all right, like a missive—and he, like a herald delivering good tidings. It could not have been easy for Saul to spend the night in a cave, and to awaken to Vernon's gifts and news would be like going from darkness to light, from sackcloth and ashes to gladness and hope, from an upside-down world to one right side up. That was why Vernon came to Udawattakele so soon.

He turned right at the fork in the path like Mr Gunaratne told him to do. Sunlight was trickling down through the trees, and the jungle was coming to life with birdsong. The ground, still damp from yesterday's rain, smelled of plant oils and rotting vegetation.

It was good to be back in Ceylon, Vernon thought. He had forgotten how much he loved it here. The wild sounds, the heady smells, the vibrant colours. He wished Zoe could be here to share it all with him. Perhaps he could convince her to come for a short holiday some time, sell it as a languorous trip to the tropics, a respite from the cold weather and the hustle and bustle of London.

A little farther up the path, he encountered the remains of a small animal. He knelt down to have a look. A faint odour of putrescence hung in the air. He could not say for sure, but the remains appeared to belong to a wild boar. Much of the flesh had been picked clean. Ants were already at work in the early-morning light finishing the job; a trail of them extended several metres along the jungle floor. Vernon found it strangely comforting to observe nature leaving nothing to waste. In the jungle, with death and decay and rebirth constantly in flux, the wheel of life showed itself in stark relief.

He stood up and continued on. His pater would have been proud to see him reading the signs of nature, slogging through the jungle with the paradox gun slung over a shoulder.

An hour or so later he rounded a bend and saw a granite formation a short distance from the path. It was the landmark Mr Gunaratne told him to look out for. Vernon stopped to determine the best route there. A gap in the shrubs suggested another path. He snapped off some branches to widen the gap and squeezed through. A few metres in, he noticed boot indentations in the soft earth and smiled to himself. He was on the right track.

//

He awoke at daybreak to an aching body and a dry mouth. He sat up and, retrieving a canteen, slaked his thirst. Strands of sunlight filtered through the curtain of vines. He yawned and glanced round in the feeble light. He had a vague sense that something was wrong, that something was missing. Looking round the cave, he realised what it was: the monk was gone. No reed mat. No lantern. No bundle. Why had he left so early?

Then Saul had a disturbing thought. In a panic he got up and switched on the torch. The dirt where the mat had been was undisturbed, and there were no marks from the lantern that he could see. Had he imagined it all? Perhaps yesterday's events had caught up with him and allowed his anxiety and fatigue to play tricks on his mind. But that, as an explanation, was decidedly unsatisfying.

Unconsciously he reached for the tear in the shoulder wrap of his robe. It was there, as were the skin abrasion and the minute lacerations in the flesh. So he had not imagined the injury itself; the soreness in his arm was not an illusion. He switched off the torch and set it down and then picked up the pistol and opened the breech. It smelled pungently of sulphur. One of the cartridges had been fired. But what had prompted him to fire, then, if the monk was not real?

With his mind churning, he removed his socks, retrieved the leftover plantains from the rucksack, and limped barefoot through the vines out into the jungle. He thought perhaps a meal in the open air would help calm him and revive his spirits. The granite that formed the cave had a low ledge on one side. He sat down on the ledge. It felt good to be out of the cave. As he slowly peeled a plantain, he breathed in the earthy, greenhouse scent that infused the air. It was a glorious day. Dappled light spilled down through the trees, and, all round, birds sang their dawn chorus. Breakfast in the jungle, he thought, and laughed to himself. He was a regular naturalist.

He finished the last of the plantains, and while he sat there enjoying the scenery, the backs of his legs began to itch. Mechanically he pulled up his robe. 'What the devil?' he said aloud and slid off the ledge to examine himself. He looked like he had been in the wars. Unsightly red bumps and tiny pustules covered both legs. A streak of dried blood ran from his left calf to his ankle. His robes were torn and muddy. A pistol wound scored one arm like a stigma. Clearly he had not thought through very well the practical aspects of roughing it in the jungle. He did not even have enough water left in the canteens to bathe and clean his wounds.

And now, besides all that, mosquitoes were assailing him. He could hear them whining round his ears, could feel their proboscises piercing his ankles and feet. The day before, he put on citronella oil, but already it had worn off. What other afflictions would be visited upon him? he wondered as he swatted away the pests.

'What in God's name happened to you?' Vernon's voice came without warning from the trees.

At the sound—the familiar voice of a comrade and a kindred soul—Saul's heart filled with joy. He looked up from his accursed body. Vernon stood at the edge of a clump of trees in a stream of dappled light. Inkblot-shaped shadows played about his face. 'Aren't you a sight for sore eyes?' Saul said. 'You're not a figment of my imagination, too, I hope?'

Vernon gave him a puzzled look. 'Why would you say that? I'm as real as the ground beneath your feet.' He came forward, and the two of them embraced. Immediately Vernon felt a sense of relief. Only moments ago, he came across what looked like a struggle in the dried mud and was worried that Saul had come to a bad end. But Saul was alive and well, even if he did look the worse for wear. Lifting the pack off his shoulder, Vernon said, 'I've come bearing gifts and good tidings.' He noticed the discarded plantain peels on the ground. 'I see you've eaten already. Would you care for something more? I have a loaf of fresh bread and a flask of tea, among other things.'

'That would be splendid.' Saul paused. 'One moment.' He disappeared into the cave and returned shortly with a bottle of citronella oil. 'The mosquitoes are a curse.'

'Right,' Vernon said. He set down his pack and leaned the paradox gun against the exterior of the cave and, with a fallen palm frond, swept away a patch of leaf litter for him and Saul to sit. Then they both doused themselves in oil until the air smelled of lemongrass, rinsed off their hands with water from one of the canteens Vernon had brought, and sat down. 'It's not quite a Corner House,' Vernon said, laughing and looking round, 'but it'll do, no?'

'It'll more than do.' Saul smiled. He was feeling infinitely better since Vernon had arrived. And the curious episode with the monk the night before now seemed like a distant memory, or something that had happened to someone else. Saul added, 'Good food. Tea. Companionship. What more could we ask for?' He glanced up at the trees. 'We even have our own musical accompaniment.'

'Who would have thought before you came to Ceylon that this is how things would end, with you on the run and living in the jungle?'

'Yes,' Saul said with an ironic smile. 'Who would have thought?'

Vernon broke off a piece of bread and handed the remainder of the loaf to Saul.

Saul in turn broke off a piece and ate it greedily. The outside of the bread was crunchy and slightly sweet and the inside melted in his mouth. He broke off another piece and devoured it. With each bite, his mind became clearer and clearer, the bread like a tobacco pipe in its restorative power.

'The Dutch call it *tijgerbrood*,' Vernon said, seeing how much Saul enjoyed the bread. 'It's from an old Prins family recipe. Rani baked it yesterday. She sends you her regards, by the way. As do Ammi and Minnette.'

'You must give them my regards too.' As Saul said this, he thought of Minnette, pictured her in the modest white dress she wore at the *dānē* two days ago. Even a short time away from her had been too long. But the prospect of seeing her again soon, and of not being deported, was enticement enough for him to continue suffering the torments of the jungle.

For several minutes Vernon and Saul ate silently, contentedly, and took turns breaking bread and drinking tea.

'You never told me what happened,' Vernon said after a while, eyeing Saul's tattered robes.

'Just a few bumps and scrapes, is all, old chap.'

Vernon noticed the state of Saul's legs. It occurred to him that the night in the cave did not go well. Perhaps Minnette's premonitions had been warranted, after all. 'I should say it's more than that. You've developed a ghastly heat rash. I'll bring an Ayurvedic ointment the next time I come.'

Saul looked at his legs as though he were seeing them for the first time. 'Is that what that is?' He laughed. 'I was afraid Satan had smitten me with boils.'

Vernon was glad that Saul was maintaining a positive attitude, at least. The jungle was no place for the faint of heart. After taking another sip of tea, Vernon set down the flask. 'I have much to tell you. Where to begin?'

'At the beginning, of course.'

'All right.' Vernon crossed his legs. 'It's rather exciting what happened, actually.'

'The police called off their search?' Saul asked half-seriously.

'Not quite. The government are trying to silence you now more than ever. But there's even better news: I think you'll be free to leave the jungle soon.' Vernon described the recent outpouring of support for Saul, how spontaneous demonstrations had erupted all over the island, how the LSSP were organising mass rallies and planned to work tirelessly to repeal the Slave Proclamation.

Saul was touched. 'That's extraordinary.'

'It is, isn't it? The people of Ceylon aren't to be trifled with. They know the timing of the deportation order is no coincidence—just five weeks before you're due to speak at an LSSP rally in Colombo. It's an outrage against liberty. Everyone thinks so, except of course the colonialists and their toadies.' Vernon drew from his pocket Minnette's poem. 'This is the other good news. It's from Minnette. Her poem "Il Poya Day" was published.'

'I say. That's the best news yet.' Saul took the piece of paper from Vernon and crossed his legs and read keenly the writing that was in Minnette's own distinctive hand. As he sat there admiring the poem, his thoughts drifted to a conversation he had had with her at Galbraith Estate. He had just come back from his tour of the plantation when she appeared in his room with a leather-bound notebook in her hand. He was sitting on the bed, removing his boots. He still felt disheartened after learning more about plantation life, but when she entered, her smile instantly brightened up the room.

She came over and sat down next to him. She had had a productive morning, she said. All sorts of ideas had come to her. Would he care to hear them?

He said he would, but he had to forewarn her, he wasn't quite himself today.

That was all right, she said; she could be sweetness and light for them both. Her latest poem was about what it meant to be a Dutch Burgher in Ceylon. Vernon had suggested the poem to her months ago, as a possible submission to *The Masses*, but she hadn't come round to the idea till now. She held open her notebook for Saul to read. The handwriting was in flowing cursive. An initial draft of the poem's first three stanzas, in free verse, followed a page and a half of notes and diagramming. Even in its early stages, the poetry was powerful. Mixed-race people like the Burghers, Minnette's logic went, were the key to the future because of their dual perspectives: they could see the world through the eyes of both the colonisers and the colonised. In essence the poem conveyed a message of hope about race relations in the future.

Saul thought of the plight of plantation labourers and was not so sure.

'Things won't always be the way they are now,' Minnette said, intuiting his doubt.

'Won't they?'

'No, attitudes are changing. Among the young at least. And the attitudes of the young are changing not only toward imperialism but also toward colour and race. Things might get worse before they get better, but they *will* get better. I know it to be true. I can feel it.'

Saul did not respond. He thought again of his estate tour, of the three young Tamil girls who skived off school to help their mothers cook and clean, of the lives of drudgery they doubtless were destined to lead. He very much wanted to believe Minnette, but meaningful progress — the conscious evolution of man as it were — seemed such a will-o'-the-wisp.

Now, after hearing the latest news about anti-British agitation happening all over the island, Saul wondered if Minnette's words at Galbraith Estate had been the prophetic pronouncement of a sybil. Perhaps things *were* about to change for the better.

There was hope for humanity yet.

Acknowledgements

I am indebted, first and foremost, to my wife and son, who tolerated my delving into the world of *The Half-Caste* for the best part of two years. I could not have successfully completed the project without their direct and indirect cooperation. I am also indebted to my wife's family and friends, who over the course of twenty-some years humoured me when I asked to be taken to tea plantations and other places of interest in Sri Lanka.

I am particularly grateful to the Dutch Burgher Union and the organisation's president, David Colin-Thome, for granting me permission to use an article verbatim from the April 1936 issue of its *Journal*. Niemand, the author of the 'By the Way' article, was an actual person whose views were invaluable in capturing the nationalistic mood sweeping Ceylon during the 1930s. Certain excerpts in the novel, such as the language related to the Slave Proclamation, were taken directly from George Jan Lerski's book *Origins of Trotskyism in Ceylon* and are set off with quotation marks. The language for the deportation order used in the novel was taken from the deportation order for the Australian Mark Anthony Lyster Bracegirdle that the office of Governor Stubbs issued in April 1937. All other excerpts taken directly from sources are set off with quotation marks.

While *The Half-Caste* involves a great deal of actual history and frequently references real historical figures, the characters in the novel are wholly fictional. It should be noted, however, that the characters were not created in a vacuum. For example, Saul Maccabee and Georgina Wilson are loosely based on the lives of Leonard Woolf and Beatrice Webb, respectively. Also, the Jackboots are modelled after the Blackshirts, and The Leader is modelled after Sir Oswald Mosley. Portions of The Leader's opening speech in the great hall, in fact, come from one of Mosley's own speeches.

Besides the wealth of information that I found on the internet, including King Edward VIII's 1936 abdication speech, I relied heavily on the following sources in doing research for the novel.

1920s Britain by John Shepherd and Janet Shepherd, Shire Publications, 2010

1930s Britain by Robert Pearce, Shire Publications, 2010

Antiquities of the Jews by Josephus Flavius, Wilder Publications, 2018

Battle for the East End: Jewish Responses to Fascism in the 1930s by David Rosenberg, Five Leaves Publications, 2001

Beginning Again: An Autobiography of the Years 1904 to 1911 by Leonard Woolf, Houghton Mifflin, 2009

Blackshirts: Fascism in Britain by David S Shermer, Ballantine Books, 1971

'By the Way' notes by Niemand, *Journal of the Dutch Burgher Union of Ceylon*, April 1936

Downhill All the Way: An Autobiography of the Years 1919 to 1939 by Leonard Woolf, Mariner Books, 1989

Growing: An Autobiography of the Years 1904 to 1911 by Leonard Woolf, Mariner Books, 1989

Hurrah For The Blackshirts!: Fascists and Fascism in Britain Between the Wars by Martin Pugh, Pimlico, 2006

Leonard Woolf: A Biography by Victoria Glendinning, Counterpoint, 2008

Origins of Trotskyism in Ceylon by George Jan Lerski, Hoover Institution Publications, 1968

People Inbetween by Michael Roberts, Ismeth Raheem, and Percy Colin-Thomé, Sarvodaya Book Publishing Services, Volume 1, 1989

Sowing: An Autobiography of the Years 1880 to 1904 by Leonard Woolf, Mariner Books, 1989

The Journey not the Arrival Matters: An Autobiography of the Years 1939 to 1969 by Leonard Woolf, Mariner Books, 1989

The Apprenticeship of Beatrice Webb by Deborah Epstein Nord, University of Massachusetts Press, 1985

The Fabians by Jeanne MacKenzie and Norman MacKenzie, Simon & Schuster, 1977

The Jewish War by Josephus Flavius, Oxford University Press, 2017

Trials of the Diaspora: A History of Anti-Semitism in England by Anthony Julius, Oxford University Press, 2010

About the Author

Jason Zeitler is the author of the novella *Like Flesh to the Scalpel* (Running Wild Press, 2018), and his stories and essays have appeared in the *Journal of Experimental Fiction*, *Midwestern Gothic*, the British magazine *Spellbinder*, and elsewhere. He lives in Tucson, Arizona, with his wife and son. *The Half-Caste* is his debut novel.

If you enjoyed reading *The Half-Caste*, you might also enjoy the author's story collection *The Breatharian and Other Stories*, available at online retailers and local bookstores.